RETROSPECT

THE HIDDEN LIFE OF MAC SCOTT

Live for the Moments you Can't put
Into Words.

AJ

A novel by

A.J. Hutchinson-Forton

For everyone who wonders if I am writing about them,
I very well could be, you may never know.

David Ernest Forton
1950-2013
Who is, no doubt, smiling the crooked smile we miss so much.

Lisa Jane Forton
1976-2020
As brave as Mac Scott

An affectionate thank you from the author to…

Amie, who made my reality as magical as the worlds I scribble, by agreeing to be my wife.

My mum, whose belief in my ink slingings as with all I endeavour to achieve, far outweighs my own.

My family, you may want to skip past the sex scenes.

Evie, my loyal partner in crime.

Alisha, who I can always count on to bestow me with brutal honesty, with gentle kindness.

Alice, the second half of the creepy sisters, for keeping my wife (the other creepy sister) company in the countless hours I was lost in my laptop.

Google, my faithful and unjudgmental ally.

Every person who has inspired me throughout my life, both the heroes and the villains.

***

I would like to acknowledge my indebtedness to the various movie quotes that have enrichened Mac Scott's character, along with my firm favourite song, 'Sweet Home Alabama' which made its way into my prose, this novel wouldn't be the same without your inspiration.

CONTENTS

PROLOGUE

2 years and 3 months. 820 days. 19,680 hours. I fell away from the world, disappeared without a trace. Poof! My existence reduced to missing posters stuck to lamp posts and shared Facebook posts pleading for information. Absent, vanished, gone. I passed into oblivion. Until I didn't. Oblivion spat me back out, death rejected me. Materialise, appear, present and accounted for. I re-entered the world, my world, or at least it used to be.

I walked myself into a hospital, looking all sorts of corpse-like. My clearest memory – my only memory. I stumbled into the too-white waiting room of A&E, the world spinning at my feet, every eye was on me and I could see the horror of myself through their contorted expressions and shocked eyes. It felt like a marathon, a marathon wading through treacle before I made it to the reception desk. It took so long to get there, it cost me every inch of the will I had left to keep putting one foot in front of another, to keep my head above the treacle. It took all the energy I had to keep breathing – in and out.

"McKenna Scott," I croaked through dry cracked lips.

Then, the world went black.

820 days and that is my clearest memory, my only real and complete memory. The doctors say it's all still here, locked up inside my head. I envisage chains wrapped around my brain with many padlocks entwined. They say it will all come back, when I am ready. Maybe I don't want to be ready. The moment I start to remember a shard of a memory, I freeze up, as though someone pours liquid ice into my veins; invisible hands tighten around my throat; my mind goes blank and I am gripped by fear.

No, I'm not sure I want to remember, the scars that cover my body tell me all I need to know. For now, at least, I don't need to be joining the dots between scar and memory. For now, I need to remember how to be a person back in a world, I no longer recognise as my own. Over two years I was gone but my family and friends, my job, all still seem the same like they froze in time in my absence.

The part that has changed and no longer fits, is me. I am disconnected from them all. They all see me as the same Mac I was before I disappeared but the truth is, I am the ghost of her.

"My name is McKenna Scott, but most know me as Mac. I am 31 years old and I live in London. I was... am a photographer but I am many things, thanks to you. I was lost but now I am here. I am alive and I will find myself again and when I do – I am coming for you."

CHAPTER ONE

Return of the Mac

"Mum, you don't need to be calling me, I am fine – I'm good to go."

My mother the worrier, I guess I can't blame her but calling me every day is getting just a bit much. She means well, God does she mean well but if anything, she is actually persuading me I should be anxious. It's my first day back at work, maybe I should be nervous; truthfully, I don't really feel anything except relieved to have something to do. How much sitting at home 'resting' can a girl do before she goes batshit crazy?

"I never said that you're not fine, love, just that there is no shame in taking your time. You have been through a lot. What's the hurry? Have you eaten? I know you don't keep much food in that flat of yours. Maybe I should bring you—"

"Mum, seriously, stop," I interrupt, in an exasperated groan.

"Okay, okay, I get the message. I am shutting up. Have a good day, love you!"

"Ditto!"

I am as always, painfully early being ready for work. I look around my studio flat wondering how I can burn some time. I miss my old flat; my mum sold it a year after I disappeared. This flat is fine but it doesn't feel like home yet. Everything is military neat, just the way I like it but even for me this is minimalist.

When I got out of hospital I stayed with my mum until I could find a flat, I got the feeling she never wanted me to leave. She was always telling me that there was no rush but for me, there was. I needed quiet, I needed space to have a pissed off face without being asked if I am okay, I needed to be alone. Mostly I needed to wash my own underwear and not find my lady-boy boxers ironed and neatly folded into my drawers.

I look myself up and down, examining myself in new clothes, mine were given to good will apart from few select and favourite things. Thankfully Mum didn't give away my beloved combat boots and my favourite camera and messenger bag, these things alone make me feel a little more human. I wouldn't even have these work clothes if it wasn't for online shopping, I have only been out into town clothes shopping once since I returned and it is not something I am in any hurry to repeat. The onlookers' ogling eyes and not so subtle whispering about me, combined with my sudden short temper made for me telling them to do one.

It is a little harder for me to pick clothes I feel comfortable in now; for the most part I can hide a lot of my scars okay, but there are some that are impossible to hide. Like the one running jaggedly from behind my right ear and halfway across my throat, or the one that slits across my eyebrow interrupting the hair growth so that it never grows right. I have scars over sixty percent of my body and more broken bones than I can count, at least them – you cannot see. I guess I am not so bothered that people see them, it's more the staring that bothers me. Touching them on the other hand, is the biggest issue, it is an intimacy I can't stand anymore, that closeness provokes panic no matter whose touch it is.

I elect to walk to work, something my therapist Alisha has advised. The idea being that if I have a destination that isn't too far of a walk then I can practice being out in the world, walking from point A to point B, being around people in small manageable steps. I hate the need for therapy and the truth is, I haven't exactly applied myself; I don't enjoy my brain being prodded and my every word being analysed in ways I don't understand. The only upside is that Alisha is hot. At least I will be able to tell her at this afternoon's session that I actually did something she advised; she will probably get a kick out of that.

I don my headphones, turn the music on max volume, take a deep breath and set off. The walk is blissfully uneventful, it is nearing the end of summer so it is warm and breezy, I have to admit it's nice to feel the sun warm my skin. Walking feels good and I find myself standing outside of work far too quickly. The building is modern, lots of large glass sheet windows giving the photography studios inside an abundance of natural light. Now that I am standing here hesitating at the door, there are butterflies dancing furiously in my stomach, I am all too aware I look like a nut job standing here staring at the building and I am very visible from inside the giant fish bowl. I really don't need them thinking I am crazy on top of everything else.

With a deep steadying breath, I enter the building and climb the cold steel spiral staircase that leads to the main reception and when I reach the top, I see nothing has really changed much. The main studios to the left, the bosses' office to the right. Even the same receptionist, who I slept with once at an office Christmas party.

Aw crap.

"Can I help…? Mac! Ahh yes, they told me you would be in today, how are you?"

Jess speaks with a shrill tone and stares awkwardly; her eyes slide from mine down to my throat and back again. She attempts to hide her staring with the ever so annoying, sympathetic head tilt.

Jess is very tall and wiry with harsh bobbed blonde hair and a thin pointed face; she has full lips that are currently painted in shocking red lipstick, pretty sure she has some on her teeth. She wears a tight and short pencil skirt or maybe it just seems short because her legs are so bean pole long. She is a nice enough girl, but very intense and high maintenance.

"Hey girly, I am not too shabby, thanks, how have you been?" I ask with a wink.

That's right, just fake it till you make it, Mac.

Jess looks taken aback, as if the last thing she expected is for me to seem so – me. It's the last thing I expected too. Maybe I am still in here, somewhere.

"I am great, thanks; Emmitt is waiting for you in his office. You can go in."

I start to walk past her towards Emmitt's office on the right behind the reception desk, feeling glad to not have to go into the main studios yet.

"Oh, and Mac…" I turn on my heels, "it's really good to see you." Jess blushes.

"Thanks Jess, you too."

Inside Emmitt's office has certainly changed, for a start the last time I was here, Emmitt wasn't the boss but over two years have passed. I remember Emmitt, a slightly above average-looking guy who was a way above average douchebag.

"Hey Mac, take a seat. It is really good to see you," Emmitt says, smiling gently.

This time I am taken aback, he has a kind face and demeanour, I remember him just being a bit of a misogynistic prat, oozing with ego and I am not seeing that. Has he changed? Time will tell.

"Thank you, Emmitt, you look well. I appreciate you giving me the opportunity to come back."

Emmitt leans back on his large, fancy, leather executive chair with a creak, showing off a little, but that's okay, he has clearly earnt his spot. Paragon Images Co is just as successful now as it was when I worked here two years ago, he must be doing something right.

"It wasn't a hard decision, Mac, your work has always spoken for itself, which is obviously very lucrative for PIC, besides you are a member of the Paragon family. We take care of our own," Emmitt says, his voice smooth.

Hmm, I can't wrap my head around seeing Emmitt this way, really un-douchebag-like.

"Thank you, Emmitt. That, is… really generous of you to say. I wasn't sure what to expect coming here I—"

"Well you are welcome. Now, let's get down to business, shall we?" Emmitt interrupts. He leans forward on his chair, rests his elbows on his desk and his chin on his fists.

"I would like to offer you the same position you held before as freelance photographer but I would also like to offer you a promotion of sorts. Before you… left, you were working on editing your own shots and I wonder if you would be interested in making that a permanent thing in a more official capacity? You would be looking at spending more time in the studio, as well as freelancing on location, the work load will be heavier but it is a significant pay rise."

Emmitt reaches for his pen from his jacket breast pocket, scrawls on a Post-it note and then he hands me the small neon pink piece of paper. "I think this should be satisfactory." My mouth dries up like the Sahara Desert, I gulp dryly as I read the figures. That's significant.

"Of course, Mac, I need to know that you are ready for this and if this is even what you want? I wouldn't want to pressure…"

"When do I start?!" I blurt confidently.

It turns out that is right now, for a half day, just to warm me up and familiarise myself with the place and people again. Some faces I remember; some faces are new but all faces are scrutinising me with odd curiosity. I had to resist the urge to bitch slap Carl the coffee guy for singing 'Return of the Mac'. I guess it was only a matter of time before someone did it and he always was pretty cringy. I am shown through all the new editing software and the new updated Costa coffee machine in the canteen is a welcome sight; they even have caramel syrup, yum! A definite bonus.

Emmitt delights in showing off – ego still there but for the most part he is being surprisingly cool. The longer I am here the more grateful I am to him for leading me around; he would know that I know my way around, I worked here for three years before I was taken but he leads me around and acts like a buffer while introducing and re-introducing me to everyone. The longer I am here, the more the novelty of me being here seems to wear off of people, the stares my way are becoming less frequent and the whispers are quietening substantially, and I am starting to actually enjoy myself.

Just like that it is over and dare I say it, I am looking forward to going into work tomorrow. I ended up staying longer than I thought I would and looking at the time, it would make more sense to walk straight to my appointment with Alisha. It means walking across town, something I've been avoiding but I am feeling pretty good. I can do this, right? Let's do this.

Headphones back on and blasting in my ears, I keep my eyes down as much as possible until I've crossed town and hit the park. Caledonian Park, one of my favourite parks to hang out in. It feels good to be in the wide-open space, my boots crunching under the sun-scorched grass. I've missed this, walking freely and almost as if nothing ever happened. Children playing ball games, cyclists gliding around, couples sharing picnics. So normal, peaceful even.

I stop at a park bench and take a load off, my eyes gazing at the familiar clock tower. Everything seems so surreal, I used to play football here as a kid. I've always been a bit tomboyish, more in my interests than the way I look. I tend to wear a lot of black; I am not a 'goth', I just like the way I look in black, it makes my pale skin look even paler. I am usually found wearing ripped skinny jeans, band t-shirts, and my combat boots, or a pair of well-worn Converse high tops.

"McKenna?"

A hand touches my shoulder from behind me and I recoil. I jump up off the bench, spinning around, my heart beat pounding in my ears and my eyes flitting around rapidly in search of a threat. My gaze falls upon Nicole and my heart sinks, Nic is my best friend, although by the look on her face that is probably past tense.

"Sorry, didn't mean to make you jump," Nicole utters.

I try to catch my breath but my throat is so tight, I bend over, standing with my hands on my knees, not quite able to meet her gaze. I know she is going to be pissed at me, I know I deserve it. I also know I don't want to deal with her right now, no matter how unfair that may be to her.

"S'okay just, you shouldn't sneak up on a girl like that, give me a freakin' heart attack," I groan.

I begin to catch my breath and slowly straighten up and I look at her. She is definitely pissed; her eyes are full of hurt. She looks down, takes her phone out of her pocket and begins tapping the touch screen. Seconds later my inside pocket starts to ring.

Crap.

"Your phone works then! What the hell, Mac!? You have been home for 4 months and I haven't heard from you once. No texts, you ignore my calls and you never answer the door. Why are you avoiding me?" she rages.

"Nic, I can't give you a reason that is going to make you feel any better. I am a selfish dick; can we just leave it at that?" I look at the floor with too much interest, as if the way out of this confrontation is there hidden in the grass.

"How about the truth? I don't care if it doesn't make me feel better, I just want to know why. You know, everyone keeps asking me how you are because they assume I would know because I am your best friend and I know nothing! I have no answers because you shut me out."

I can feel the anxiety rising in my chest, it is beginning to make me shake from the inside out. I need to go, I want out, I can't deal with this, I start to walk away.

"You cannot be serious, Mac, don't walk away – answer me!?" she yells.

"I can't answer you; don't you get that?! I know you have questions; I was gone for over two years and I don't have the answers! Even if I did, I don't want to talk about it! It is too much, Nic, so, will you get the hell off my case!" I spit venomously.

I turn and walk away but not before seeing the pain in her eyes. I know I will regret that later, when the anger fizzles away. Right now, the overwhelming panic has me shaking, and my head is spinning out. I just need to keep walking, one foot in front of another, just like when... No! Don't think about that. The anxiety kicks up ten notches as the memory warps in my mind, my throat tightens and my ribs are in a vice, pain searing up my torso.

Alisha's house is a new build, it looks like something you would buy flat packed from Ikea, modern and shiny. The place is huge; I've never been inside her place, as such. It is a three-storey house and the whole bottom floor has been converted into her office and therapy space so I've never gone further than the ground floor. I walk straight in and enter the small hallway, making my way to the room our sessions are always in and knock the door, bracing myself on the frame. The floor is threatening to disappear beneath my feet as my head swims in dizzying waves. The door opens and she greets me with a smile that soon falls once she takes a look at me, seeing the terror in my eyes.

"Come and take a seat, Mac," Alisha says softly.

She leads me to the sofa, the same sofa I have sat on every week for almost three months now. I stumble onto the familiar squishy seat and lean forward, my head in my hands, my arms and legs shaking.

"I just need a minute, I'm fine," I grunt.

"Of course, you are. You are sunshine and daisies, you are so incredibly stubborn," she replies lightly. I can hear the smile in her voice as she speaks and I look up.

Alisha wears extremely well-fitted 'power women' suits. They are expensive looking and they hang off her curves so perfectly that it is as if all of her clothes were made for her. Her blouse is crisp and white, the buttons undone low enough to distract me. She is petite in stature but powerful in presence, fiery and blunt. Her face is obviously pretty and pixy-like which matches her short, dark and harshly angled haircut. Her dark eye makeup makes her eyes smoulder sexily.

"Well I wouldn't want to make your job too easy for you, Doc."

I sit up slowly and lean back into the sofa, the world no longer spinning. I am so annoyed at myself. Nic didn't deserve that, I am an arsehole. I close my eyes, breathe in deeply then let go of the breath, as I look up at Alisha. That is one of the reasons I chose to continue seeing her, right now there is no judgement on her face, she is just holding my gaze, unphased with those gorgeous hazel brown eyes. I look away. Those eyes are dangerous and powerful sometimes, I wonder if she realises that.

When I agreed to get therapy, it was mainly because it was the only way to stop my mum fretting. After a while though it became obvious, I could use the help. I went to Alisha because she was local to me, it is just that simple. The thing is, she turned out to be very good at ripping my pretences to shreds with no bullshit, which is both challenging and hot. I am that stubborn that it takes pushing me to get me to budge an inch and the girl can push.

"Are you going to tell me what happened?" she asks, playfully impatient.

I huff and then I explain a shortened and less detailed version of events.

"I can't believe you actually did some homework I set you, it only took you 3 months! Well done!" she teases, trying to cut the tension and I laugh.

"I thought you would like that; do I get a sticker or a lollipop or something?" I joke. I am starting to feel back to normal, whatever that is.

"Sorry, all out of lollipops but you are going to have to deal with me going all therapist on you. Why don't you want Nicole in your life?" Alisha probes.

"I never said I didn't, I am just trying to avoid her inevitable questions."

Alisha raises one eyebrow at me, sceptical. "Mac, if that is true then why didn't you tell her that? She was your best friend, right? You could have easily called her or even sent a text months ago saying that you want to hang out but you don't want questions about your disappearance. Instead you avoided her relentlessly until she finally caught up with you and you blew up at her, ensuring she isn't likely to call again anytime soon, if ever. Looks like self-sabotage if you ask me."

She has got me there.

"Fair point but not everything has a deeper meaning, Alisha. Sometimes I am just a world-class dick."

"I am the professional here, why not let me tell you if you are a dick?" She smiles and I struggle not to laugh. "You are not a dick, you just make avoiding anything emotional an Olympic sport. You acted like a dick to push her away, you are not a bad person, Mac, no matter how much you try to act like you are."

Ugh, she wasn't kidding about going all therapist on me.

"Now you can continue to pay good money to close yourself off from me all you want but don't insult my intelligence, McKenna." Alisha holds my gaze intensely, her eyes more serious than I have ever seen them.

"You full-named me, I must be in trouble," I banter playfully but this time she isn't smiling. The silence that follows is awkward and it feels like it is going on forever. I examine my hands; they are balled up in fists so tight that my fingernails are digging into my palms; it stings but it feels good to focus on that pain instead of the one building in my chest.

"How am I insulting your intelligence? That is not something I meant to do. I'm sorry," I offer without looking up, annoyed at myself.

"Don't be sorry."

For the first time ever, Alisha leans forward in her chair, closing the gap between us; she puts her hand on my shoulder and I tense up rigidly. I can't be sure – I probably imagined it but I thought I felt her fingertip stroke my collarbone and I stiffen, fighting the urge to flinch. She is usually so professionally distant and respectful of my intolerance to touch and this small action, has me frozen in place. I couldn't look up at her if I wanted to.

"Mac, I don't know if you ever plan on being honest with me. If you don't want to that is okay, maybe I am not the right person for you to open up to, but don't pretend there is nothing to open up about, that is all I ask," Alisha asserts gently but frankly.

I look up, she is closer than I thought, I can smell her perfume, it is floral and distracting. What she is saying is understandable, she isn't stupid enough to be fooled by my cool as a cucumber routine and that at this point, pretending is just insulting. Her closeness is getting harder to cope with every second, I want to look away but I can't, her eyes have me locked.

"You are the right person. I am just not sure how to let go, or where to even start," I admit and she leans back in her chair and there is a proud look in her eyes, smiling at me warmly and just a little smug.

"I think you just did, maybe I should buy some lollipops," she teases.

"Yes! You would have me babbling all of my deep and dirties in no time if there were lollipops," I joke. "I formally request sherbet lemons and Drumstick lollies."

The tension eases, we both laugh for a while and make small talk. I don't think she wanted to push me any further today and I am grateful for that but there is definitely something changed in the dynamics between us. We lightly chat about movies but I feel an intensity that wasn't there before. An urge to talk, it is painful not to, like I opened a floodgate that I can't seem to shut.

There are other urges too.

***

Wandering around my flat, I feel emotionally battered. The day started so well, work went better than I could have hoped, if only I hadn't decided to walk to my appointment. I am hit with a pang of guilt; it would have happened eventually anyway; I didn't want to hurt Nic but I am also relieved that in doing so, she can leave me be. We have been close for many years but, I am not sure how to be the person I was before I left. I used to be light, happy-go-lucky and comfortable with who I was. Now, I am bitter and angry and I have no idea who I am; the before me and the now me, may as well be two different people.

I decide to take a hot shower, followed by a cold whiskey; the hot water feels soothing but it makes the scars that cover my skin glow fiery red. I am like a road map, some scars are clear and easy to decipher, like the lashings across my back that could only have come from being whipped. Others are less obvious, most curious to me is the burn branded into my skin, like the marking of cattle. The branding is a simple triangle shape seared deeply into the skin under my right breast. Standing in front of the mirror, I analyse my own reflection, trying to accept myself with the scars and recognise the person underneath. I have always been quite skinny but more so now, I am still attempting to gain back the weight I lost while I was missing.

My eyes are big and blue, my lips are small, pink and doll-like. I have deep dimples in my cheeks that sometimes show even when I don't smile. My skin is ivory white and my long dark hair makes me look even whiter. It is tempting to cut it off, as I never do anything with it except tie it back messily in a surfer-like knot. The scar slit across my eyebrow at an attractive angle, coupled with the darkness of the circles around my eyes, gives me a cold and haunted look.

Someone did this to me, someone broke bones and tore skin, someone plucked me from my normal life and hid me from the world like some moving piece on a board game. How did I get away? And after so long too. Did I get away or did they let me go? My mind slips into a memory, the same memory of walking into the hospital. How can I remember walking into the hospital, but not remember where I walked from?

The doctors said I walked in barefoot but my feet only had old injuries and were too clean for me to have walked very far. The CCTV footage shows me walking into the hospital but there is no footage of me being dropped off by a car. My clothes were ragged, old and too big for me. I had 3 broken ribs, a dislocated shoulder, a concussion and I was pretty cut up and bruised all over, the worst being a deep wound to my forearm that had become infected. I was dehydrated, malnourished and had a substantial amount of benzodiazepine in my system that has obviously contributed to my memory loss.

I had to go into a drug rehab program for the addiction to benzos. I didn't crave it emotionally; I have no memory of ever taking it but that didn't change that my body was addicted to it from prolonged usage. It seems it was given to me regularly to mess with my memory, probably as a way of silencing me. Mission success, my memory is so bad, I am pretty sure I could arrange my own surprise party.

The bittersweet caramel whiskey warms my throat and slides down, spreading warmth through me. I want to remember; I want the pieces back of myself that were stolen from me. Alisha was right, I have been running from myself, running from everything and everyone that could open me up in any type of way. As long as I am running, I will never remember and I will never be able to connect who I am now with who I was, I will never be me again. Someone did this to me and that someone needs to pay, I want to make them pay.

I take out my mobile phone and unlock it; I have a grand total of 5 phone numbers programmed in. Mum, Emmitt, Alisha, Nic and Ryan – Ryan, being my landlord. I've never actually texted Alisha, in fact, I haven't texted anyone since I came back. I open up the message window and after spending far too long trying to figure out how to do it and I type:

Mac Mobile: 11.45pm
You awake?

I hit send without hesitation and stare at the screen. Funny, I thought I would feel more nervous or even apprehensive at texting her out of hours but I feel nothing but determined.

Alisha Mobile: 11.47pm
Yep. Everything okay?

Mac Mobile: 11.50pm
I want to remember.

Alisha Mobile: 11.55pm
About time! Come back tomorrow 5.30pm.
Get some rest, you are going to need it.

Mac Mobile: 11.56pm
Oh yeah? That sounds much more fun than I was expecting ;)

Alisha Mobile: 11.58pm
Behave, go to sleep!

***

I won't be walking to work today, my first photoshoot is halfway across town. An old regular client named Alfred, he is an eccentric artist around 55-60 years old and pure muscle. He builds tall scaffolding structures and uses them to create massive and bizarre sculptures out of the oddest things. Reclaimed wood and metal, things he finds from the local tip, a seemingly random mix of objects that somehow tells a story in the end. He is a genius, a lovely man with a creased face, sad eyes and a gruff voice. A nice easy client to start my day with.

I took shots of all of his work before I disappeared; he has a farm with an abundance of land and it is piled with heaps of junk that somehow, he makes beautiful. He is one of those people you don't have to try too hard with, he doesn't say much but what he does say is always to the point, no pretences, you never have to guess with Alfred. He would always greet me with a cup of tea and a plate of custard creams.

I pull up at his farm. My car is actually a pickup truck; it has the most obnoxious and loud engine with no subtlety to it and it announces my arrival long before I ever get the chance. The heaps of junk are still there, neat piles arranged in a huge semi-circle and at its opening, a large red barn on the left and a modest rickety house on the right, making it a complete circle. In the centre, standing proud is Alfred's latest piece.

It's beautiful of course and fascinating, it must be the height of a two-storey house. You could spend hours looking at it, trying to pick out all the different items. My eyes scan eagerly. A washing machine drum, barbed wire, unicycle, exhaust pipe, barbeque grills, warped sheets of metal, both rusted and chrome shaped like flames dancing together.

In the centre are the words "Blessed mess" made from hundreds of shaped coat hangers. When you stop scanning and look at the piece as a whole, it's a woman standing tall with her arms at her sides but lifted slightly, palms out. She looks like an angel; I am shocked when I feel a pinprick to my eyes and a lump rising in my throat. I am so transfixed, I don't even notice that Alfred has appeared, standing at my side staring up at the woman just like me. He has such a calming voice, gruff with a slight farmer twang.

"Alfred, this is… so captivating, she is mesmerising. I am in love with it," I gasp, and I really am. I tear my eyes away and turn to him. "It's good to see you, fella," I greet him and he smiles crookedly. He looks exactly the same as the last time I saw him, wearing an oil-stained plaid shirt and a pair of over-worn denim dungarees.

"I couldn't believe it when they offered me you, I called because the piece was finally finished and the last thing, I expected was… I am glad you are okay, kid," he grumbles.

It is always so easy to take photos of his work, the sunlight naturally making the shinier metal glitter and the rusted metal burn fiery orange. To have a camera back in my hands again after so long feels oddly alien but I am enjoying the moment. Unlike a lot of the 'firsts' I have had to endure since my return, this one is fun. When I am done, I turn around to find Alfred holding a tray with a plate of custard creams and a teapot and cups.

"You trying to fatten me up?" I ask, feeling touched that he remembered.

"You could use it, seen more fat on a turnip."

We sit together, enjoying tea and biscuits in the warmth of the morning sun. He fills me in on what he has been getting up to in my absence and shows me photos of the work I have missed. The photos were taken beautifully by someone at PIC named Savannah.

"She has done beautiful work; I don't think I've met Savannah yet. Did you make her tea and biscuits too?" I ask playfully and he chuckles, it is so easy with Alfred.

"Well yes, I am a gentleman but I was thinking about you the whole time," he grunts. I choke on a laugh and spill tea down myself. "No… No, Savannah is my granddaughter. She only does a little bit of work at PIC, more a hobby than anything."

I am trying to picture what the granddaughter of Alfred would look like but I fall short. Her work is beautiful, clearly an artistic eye runs in the family.

"Right, I best be off, don't want to be late back on my first day. Thank you, Alfred, it really is good to see you and congratulations on this piece, it is my favourite yet."

"Thanks, kid. Don't be a stranger, will you?"

***

It has been a good day at work, out and about shooting on location. Having a camera in my hands again has made me feel a sense of peaceful purpose that I have missed. Life always seems much simpler through a camera lens. You focus the lens on the here and the now and let the complications of everything else melt away into the background. Tomorrow will be harder, I am sure. I will be in the office all day editing all my shots, in the office, with… everyone. The thought makes me want a nervous pee.

As my appointment with Alisha grows ever closer, I am starting to feel anxious about what lays ahead. The whiskey I drank last night is long since out of my system, along with the false sense of courage it inspired. I need to know, that's what I keep telling myself and I really do want to remember. I just hate how scared I feel when a memory starts to come back, I hate feeling that weak. Surely though, to keep running from this is much weaker, cowardly even.

Suck it up – buttercup.

***

"How was your day, Doc?"

"It has been a long one, but good thank you, Mac. How was your first day back at work?" she asks lightly.

"If you want to reschedule its not a problem, I know you probably had to squeeze me in being short notice and—"

"Oh, nice try, Mac," she says, rolling her eyes with jovial banter. "No, you have had a breakthrough and, in my experience, it's best to strike while the iron is hot in those cases before you are able to talk yourself out of it."

"Pretty sure I started talking myself out of it as soon as I finished texting you and sorry by the way, for texting out of hours."

"I did tell you that you could text me if you needed me, so there is no need to apologise. Tell me… What made you suddenly decide you wanted to remember?"

"I don't think there was anything sudden about it, I think I have always wanted to remember. It's just…" I hesitate, already feeling embarrassed and inspecting my hands. I look up at Alisha, willing myself to man up. She is being patient, not pushing me. I know I just need to rip the plaster off, get it over with.

"I want to know but any time I start to remember anything I feel irrationally fucking scared and I hate…"

"You hate feeling weakness; you see emotion as weakness. It's not, it is the opposite, strength and bravery only exist if there is fear and pain. Where is the bravery in doing something you are not scared of? Isn't that just doing something, period? You start to remember and you panic, the best thing you can do is let the memory come and learn with repeated exposure that, you are safe and that the anxiety can't hurt you."

"I guess that makes sense. So, how do… Where do I start?"

"There are lots of things we can try but for a start, why not tell me what you do remember?"

And so, I do. I slowly explain my only clear memory of the hospital, everything the doctors said, the injuries, the scars. I speak slowly because at first it comes out in a struggle, like every word is hard work but the more I speak the faster it comes out. Alisha listens; she always has such a poker face; I keep waiting for her expression to change but it never does.

"…The scars probably tell some of the story but nowhere near enough for me to understand and if you could say something so I can stop talking, that would be great."

"I get paid to make you talk, not stop you," she replies with a coy smirk.

I laugh but it comes out a little strangled sounding as I feel my throat tighten and the shakes trembling through my limbs. I lean forward and press my palms hard into my temples, willing the dizziness to stop; my breath catches in my chest.

"It is just anxiety, it isn't the boss here, you are. Try to take control," Alisha encourages.

Fear. Irrational, crippling, dominating fear. It is like an invisible man is holding a gun to my head, threatening my life and no one can see him but me. A lonely and impossible feeling – I am fighting a ghost that is already dead. The shakes in my body jolt angrily as the panic takes hold.

"Mac, you are safe, centre yourself, look at the things around you. Look at me, if you weren't safe then I wouldn't be here. It is over, you are safe. Mac, look at me."

"No, no, no, no…" I mumble. I am losing control. My breathing becoming ragged till it is painful and hard to breathe. I can't catch my breath and that is escalating the panic inside of me.

"McKenna." I feel her move towards me and I flinch, covering my face with my hands in embarrassment. I just want to leave; I want the ground to swallow me up whole. Alisha kneels down in front of me and put her hands over the top of mine; they are icy cold.

"No, Mac, don't hide, okay – I can help you stop this but only if you look at me," she says firmly. She lets go of my hands and I uncover my face and look up at her, my jaw clenched tight.

"Good, now breathe, focus on the things around you, the feel of the chair you are sat on, the pattern of the wallpaper on the walls, the sound of cars driving past the window, everything that proves you are here now and not where ever you were. I am here, you are here and you are safe now. Say it, I am safe now," Alisha orders firmly but her tone is warm.

"I am… safe now," I choke.

"That's good, keep saying it to yourself and keep looking at me."

My breathing starts to ease; the waves of panic slows to trickles. As I calm down, I am aware how close she is and how embarrassed I am. What I would give to run from this room, I hate that she has seen me like this, I don't want anyone to see me like this.

"Ugh, God, do you have any idea how much I want to leave right now?" I groan, looking away from her at the door.

"Don't leave, it won't help. Instead tell me why you want to."

"Embarrassment, I guess. This is… so pitiful and pathetic, Alisha, I am…" The lump in my throat cuts me off.

I will not cry on top of everything else. Man, the fuck up.

Alisha hesitantly reaches out and puts her hand on my cheek and I flinch but she doesn't pull away, she pulls me back to her eyeline and I see a hint of sadness play in her eyes.

"McKenna, there is nothing pitiful or pathetic about you, certainly nothing weak. Don't be embarrassed; if the situation was reversed and I was in your shoes telling you I felt pathetic after those experiences, what would you say?" she asks, stroking my cheek with her thumb and it is terrifying. I am frozen, wanting to move but also, not wanting to.

Her eye contact is difficult to break, it has been so long since I have allowed anyone to touch me so intimately. Suddenly all pathetic thoughts evaporate and are replaced with… wanting, and I fear she can see it in my eyes because this time, she is the one to look away, she returns to her seat awkwardly.

Damn it. I clearly stepped over the line and she didn't like that. Say something, Mac, you complete idiot!

"Busting out the reverse psychology on me, Doc?"

"Well if it works," she says through a very weak smile.

Oh, for God's sake Mac, what have you done? You broke the fucking therapist, that's what.

"Umm… Yeah so… I don't think the key to remembering is in that memory, I asked you to tell me as I knew it would provoke a panic response and we first needed to show you that you can take control before we try to access more difficult memories. Plus, it helps me to understand a little better, if I at least know what you know. It helps me know what questions to ask to hopefully open your mind up to remembering."

"I hate you a little bit right now. You know that, right?" I tease, trying to keep it light.

"Hah! No, you don't." Alisha snorts and then she tosses something to me. It lands in my hands and I giggle with childlike happiness; a sherbet lemon lollipop.

"Okay, you are forgiven." I grin, unwrapping the lolly without delay.

We seem to have passed the awkwardness and it's a relief. I think I may just have to pretend that I didn't just almost lay one on her and choose to believe that she didn't notice.

"Oh good, I did wonder how I was ever going to be able to sleep tonight."

"You said that my memory at the hospital isn't the key to remembering. What is?" I ask, wondering what I am in for.

"The thing is in its simplest term; you have extreme retrograde amnesia which means you can't remember anything prior to injury. Except it is complicated because you can remember things from before you disappeared, clear as crystal. It's like someone deleted a block of memory but left everything before the block. I think given the high levels of benzos in your system when you came back, someone actually designed it this way or at least it became a happy accident. I think that, mixed with trauma means this is its very own original case of amnesia. Which means bringing your memory back will be all trial and error, not an exact science," Alisha elucidates and waits patiently for me to respond but I can't, my brain is ticking over, my stomach plummeting with a nauseating swoop.

"Mac – are you okay? Trust me, there are lots of things we can and will try to get your memories back."

"No, it's not that. Something has been bugging me since I got back and when you said all that, it just made it all the more obvious to me. Someone went to a lot of trouble to make me forget something, or a lot of somethings. Maybe they meant to make me forget or maybe they didn't but they used benzos, they must have known it would have some kind of effect. Think about it, why not just kill me? It would have been a whole lot easier, unless… They still need me for something."

I look up at Alisha. She frowns as her poker face slips a little, concern tugging at her eyes. "Which means, Mac, you are still not safe."

I nod, as the reality washes over me, waiting for some kind of fear to hit, but nothing does. I knew that all along, somewhere inside but something else hits me like a sucker punch to the chest. No one near me is safe; if I am not actually really free, then whoever is near me is in danger, especially Alisha.

"My life may depend upon remembering but that doesn't mean that you have to be the one to make me remember," I state flatly.

"Why do you say that?"

"Think about it, Alisha, whoever did this went to a shit ton of trouble to make me forget. You trying to make me remember is probably the last thing they want, it makes you a target, it puts you in danger and I don't want that." My words come out fiercely. The more I think about it, the more annoyed I am at myself for being too slow to work this out.

"How would they even know?" Alisha argues weakly.

"You think they did all this and they aren't watching me to make sure I don't remember? Oh my God, I have been putting you in danger this entire time!"

I stand up and pace, a fire igniting inside me, my every nerve alert and fizzing with tingles. What if I am too late? What if they already consider her a risk of exposing them? How could I have been so short sighted, so stupid!? I have to leave and never come back; it might be the only chance I have of keeping her safe.

"McKenna, calm down, it's okay. We don't even know if we are right about this, there is nothing to say you are being watched, let's take a breath and—"

"You really think I am willing to take that risk with you?! With anyone? You said it yourself, I am still not safe, I am okay with that, somewhere I already knew that. No, there is nothing to say for sure that I am right, but I have felt like I have been living on borrowed time ever since I got back because I never felt like it was over," I interrupt urgently.

Adrenalin pumps through my veins and throbs in my limbs. Fight or flight, that's what they call it. Right? Well I've spent too much time in flight, it is time to stand the hell up and fight and I have to fight alone, I can't risk anyone else being brought into this. I have already risked too much.

"I have to go. I can't risk you, Alisha, I can't risk anyone…"

"Mac, no! Listen, I shouldn't have said that, you are moving too fast and not thinking this through, at least stay and talk about this," Alisha rambles. Her poker face disintegrates and real concern, almost fear, is written all over her face and she grabs my wrists to stop me from leaving. I pull my wrists from her grasp, panic jolting through my chest.

"Don't!" I snap.

"I'm sorry, Mac, I shouldn't have grabbed you I just, I need you to slow down."

"It's okay, girl, I get it. Just, being restrained is top of the list of ways to wig me out. You have been there for me and put up with my shit and I appreciate that more than you know but if there is even a chance that I am right then you are not safe, no one near me is. Look – I am sorry, girl; but your services are no longer required," I assert plainly.

A low blow, I know, but if sacking her keeps her safe, it will be worth it. I watch the emotions play out on her face, hurt, anger, worry, fear and I cringe, looking away.

"Please Mac, don't do this, stay," she breathes.

"If anyone comes asking questions about me, you tell them that I just stopped coming. You alter my notes, make it sound like I refused treatment to try to regain my memories and burn anything that says otherwise. You feel like you are in danger at all, get the hell out of town. I am so sorry I put you in this position. Please, be safe, girl." I step around her, my hand on the door handle.

"Wait, Mac…"

She reaches out for my hand, slow and hesitant, uncertain how I might react but I let her, confused but I still let her.

"Please, don't leave. Let's get out of here, go somewhere and talk," she whispers.

I give her hand a little squeeze. "I can't, girl, if anything was to happen…" I say softly.

Alisha struggles with herself, like she is trying to work something out. It looks like her mind is going a million miles an hour, probably trying to figure out how to stop me. She tugs on my hand, pulling me a little closer. I go rigid, visibly so but she carries on moving. She runs her hands up my arms till her hands reach the back of my neck and her fingers interlace around it and then she steps into me.

I flinch, jumping to an embarrassing degree. Panic collides with excitement and I can't move, it is like my brain goes pop when it decides it can't decipher the equation between fear of, and wanting of, her touch. I let out a shaky breath.

"Sorry – I shouldn't have…" She struggles.

"Don't move," I say a little too harshly and I feel her flinch, "just give me a minute."

She stays statue still and I close my eyes. I try to quiet my mind of all the screaming doubt and anxiety, the words that make me feel not whole enough to be held, that make me feel too damaged to be touched and unworthy of being cared for or wanted. I lift my rigid arms up and put them on her back very lightly, almost not touching her at all and her body relaxes a little. It takes all I have not to push her away and she knows it. My breathing speeds up, the anxiety building momentum, smothering me.

"I have... to... go, s-sorry." I break away harshly and walk out without looking back, her calls for me to come back echoing behind me.

I've spent all this time trying to go back, back to my normal life and back to who I was but there is no going back. There is only going forward. I never came home, not really. There is no home until I find and destroy all the ties that bind me. There is no freedom till I expose the secrets entrapping me. There is no life for me or anyone I care for, while those out there are still threatening to extinguish it. It's time for the hunted, to become the huntress.

CHAPTER TWO

Genesis

"Aww, Mum, it's okay, I am going to have a blast! I need this, I need some fun. You understand that, don't you?" I whine.

"Not really, McKenna, no, I don't. I just got you back, you just got your job back and a new flat and now you've handed in your resignation and sold your flat to go off gallivanting around Europe, alone!" Mum snapped, her voice breaking painfully.

"Not gallivanting, Mum, backpacking, exploring and seeing the world. I need to get away, I know I can have my old life back, but I want a new one and I need time to figure out what that life is."

The lies are flowing out of my mouth so smoothly it is sickening. It rips my heart to shreds knowing I am breaking hers; I have to keep her safe and she will be safer not knowing where I am.

"I will send you lots of pictures, you will get phone calls and it will be like you are out travelling with me. I know it is hard, Mum, it is for me too but I won't be gone forever. Sooner or later I will run out of money and food and I will be home, expecting your most amazing Sunday roast," I reassure, hoping very much that isn't a lie too.

It has taken me over a week to tie up loose ends and put some plans in place but I still have things I need to do. I am mentally bushed; it doesn't matter how many spy-type movies you watch; it does not make you James Bond. Learning how to disappear or 'go dark' as they call it on the many websites I've been scouring, it is not as simple as it may seem. It is even less simple when you plan to disappear close to home, so you can operate under the radar to investigate your own disappearance. A steep learning curve for sure, I am so dog tired of my brain buzzing and this hasn't even truly begun yet.

I have, however, made some decent progress on mission – disappear. I bought a train ticket to Paris on the Eurostar that leaves tomorrow and paid by bank card to lay a false trail, just in case someone looks into my bank activity. I withdrew all my money from my account and closed it to end that trail as quickly as it begins. While trawling some of the less desirable streets of London I then managed to purchase a fake driver's licence. I turn the card over in my hands, the name reads Alexa Clarke. It is a fairly convincing fake as far as my unexperienced eyes can tell. I doubt it would stand up against police scrutiny but for what I need it for it is convincing enough.

Using my fake ID and fake name, I opened a new bank account and I sold my flat for a low-ball price just to get the money in the new bank as fast as possible. I sold my all too recognisable and much-loved truck and replaced it with a shiny Volkswagen Tiguan. I miss my truck already but I can't deny the power and speed the Tiguan has. The extra leg room has also been helpful, I've been sleeping in my car all week.

Tomorrow I get the keys to the warehouse I've rented; it is way too big for my needs but they take cash with no questions asked. There's an electronic loading door so I can drive straight in and keep my car out of view and there is only one personal door and it has video link intercom. The warehouse has a first-floor office space which I am going to use as a bedroom and a huge ground floor area big enough to house three lorries. It's a gated industrial development that you need a key card to enter and security guards roam at night making it harder to get to me. I am hoping it won't come to that and that no one would expect to find me at an industrial village. It's a 40-minute drive from there to the centre of London, easy access without being too far away. It will be, for the foreseeable – my hideout home.

Rooting through my rucksack I search for my meagre food supply. A couple of packets of crisps, some chocolate bars, a chocolate muffin and a warm bottle of Dr Pepper. I don't have many personal items with me. Clothes, toiletries, a pair of binoculars, some paracetamol, a pad of paper and pens, my camera and kit, headphones, a utility knife, and my mobile phone. My low-budget life on the run.

My phone is still an issue; I am certain it is traceable and I will be disposing of it tomorrow. I've had it turned off all week, I guess even though I haven't gone dark yet it's an isolating feeling knowing I soon will be and it's been a lonely week in my car. If I had my phone switched on, I may have been likely to lose my resolve. I bought a load of prepaid phones that I can use for a couple of days then throw away. I have bought a lot of tech that I don't really understand in the hopes I can figure out how to use it all.

Today was my last full day being Mac, tomorrow Mac goes to Paris and I become Alexa. Tomorrow or soon after, whoever took me will realise Mac has disappeared. Where will they look first? My work? My mum's place? I suppose if they want information, they will check out Alisha. I have been doing stakeouts at Alisha's place to see if anyone out of the ordinary comes knocking. I knew it was unlikely given that I haven't yet disappeared but needed somewhere to park up overnight and across the street from Alisha's office was as good a place as any. It is a very useful place to torture myself over our last encounter.

I have achieved a lot in a week but it feels like I have been hostage to this car far too long, only really leaving it to go shopping to buy everything I will need at the warehouse. The good news is, I have an agreement with the landlord to piggy back off the next warehouse down's Wi-Fi. I plan to create some fake online business accounts so that I can buy things to be delivered to the warehouse under a company name, not my fake new name Alexa. I figure that is harder to track and it means that whatever I haven't been able to buy, I will be able to order online easily.

My car is rammed, it is heavy to drive and there is stuff I bought for the warehouse crammed in every nook and cranny. Opposite Alisha's place there is a house for sale, I have parked on the driveway and taken my place in the back seat where I have a good view between the front seats and out of the windscreen. The back windows of the Tiguan are blacked out so I am mostly hidden from view but I still feel very exposed; I think that is situational though as I feel exposed no matter where I am. Like the Bogeyman is going to jump out at me at any moment, my muscles are aching from the constant tension of being on edge.

Staring out at Alisha's house, the memories are so vivid. Three months of sitting in that room together, emotionally charged for one reason or another. Whether it be that I was pissed at her for pushing my buttons, scared of the emotions she would force me to face or quite frankly aroused by her bossiness and mysterious unattainability. It has been awakening and confronting and I am uneasy about letting it all go; she has been my only constant since I returned, except my mum and I spend all my time trying not to be honest with her, she has been through enough. My mind travels back through time easily like a movie inside my brain.

"Oh, come on, girl. I am embarrassed for you! Pitiful, just pitiful!" I laugh ruefully.

"I am just not that into movies!" Alisha states innocently.

"That is not an excuse for never having seen Star Wars! It is genius! It is cinematic history. You haven't lived! Next you will tell me that you have never seen Harry potter or…"

Alisha raises her eyebrows and then looks away grinning.

"Oh, I think I just lost all my respect for you. I am shocked and appalled; I don't see how our relationship can ever continue under these troubling circumstances."

"I am more concerned with the extent of which you value a person over their like or dislike of movies. We can't all be gigantic nerds, Mac," she teases, her hazel brown eyes sparkling as she laughs.

"Name calling, that is very unprofessional of you, Alisha Cole," I flirt and she blushes, taking a little too long to respond.

"You have my sincerest apologies, Mac, what ever can I do to rebuild the bridges of trust in our working relationship?"

I bite my tongue and stop myself going too far.

A smile tugs at the corners of my mouth at the memory, but I shake it away. I need to focus so instead I dig around for my phone in my bag. I may as well make use of the phone for one more night and set up some fake accounts so I can do more shopping online. I turn it on and wait for the screen to come to life; it starts to vibrate immediately to notify me of text messages and my heart races a little as I see her name pop up on the screen.

Alisha Mobile: 20/07/22 - 9.00pm

I should have stopped you leaving,

this is all moving too fast Mac.

Alisha Mobile: 21/07/22 - 8.23am

Look, I know you sacked me but please let know what's going on,

as a concerned citizen – not your therapist.

Alisha Mobile: 25/07/22 - 1.15pm

Europe… Seriously Mac?!

My stomach clenches; how the hell does she know about Europe?! Damn it, what do I do? I could text her back but I don't want any record of what I might be up to on her phone. I suppose in that way it's good she has mentioned

Europe but how did she know? The only people I've told about it are my mum and Emmitt – someone spilled. I know who the more likely culprit is out of the two, pretty sure Emmitt has no idea who Alisha is or that I even see a therapist.

I shouldn't go over there, right? I hate the idea that after months of seeing her she is left with our last encounter to remember me by. The temptation to go over and knock on the door is very prominent, but the temptation with *her* is prominent – full stop. I don't really know when that started to change, I guess I try not to think too much into it.

She is my therapist, there is an automatic line there that you are not supposed to cross. I don't do well with lines, that used to get me in trouble a lot. I have tried very hard to respect this line but it blurs so easily when she looks at me all intense and bossy. Plus, it is hard to keep that distance when you are attracted to the person who is breaking down your barriers.

My fear of any form of touch, is at least useful in helping me keep a distance because sometimes, it can get really hard to bear and I almost feel like she feels it too. She will look at me in a way that makes my bones turn to pudding but then ten seconds later, she is in therapist mode again and I am left feeling like I imagined it. Maybe it is good that it is coming to an end, it is only heading to catastrophe… Namely mine.

No, I am not going over there, it is too complicated, I have a job to do and I don't need anyone trying to persuade me out of it and one thing is for sure, she would try and my resolve isn't at its strongest. It is hard to say no to her on a good day, let alone when I feel scared and alone in what I am facing. I could call her; it would probably be good to let her know I am not going to be able to get her messages anymore. I can't decide if it is better to warn her or just stop and make a clean break. I know if it was me, I would want the warning but then she is the professional here, my lines may be a bit blurry but I am pretty sure hers are not. Call her, not call her? Call her, not call her?

Ugh – screw it.

The dial tone sings in my ear and my stomach twists in uncomfortable knots.

"Hello," Alisha's voice answers, full of irritation.

"Hey, are you okay?" I ask, suddenly struggling with what to say. I hate talking on the phone. I come from a generation of text and Facebook messenger, this phone call business is alien to me.

"I'm fine, Mac."

"How did you know about Europe?"

"Your mum called me. She said you sold your car and flat, handed in your resignation and were off backpacking. She wanted to know if you had lost the plot, I told her that you had."

"Funny," I groan.

The silence is awkward, I have gone completely blank now and have no idea what to say. So, it was Mum, poor woman. I feel a pang of guilt, all I do is bring worry to her life.

"Why have you called? You ghosted me all week so you must want something, Mac?" she snipes cuttingly.

That stung.

"Sorry, that was harsh," she followed up.

"A bit," I chuckle. "I was calling because I won't be contactable as of tomorrow, I have had my phone off as I had a lot to organise this week, I wasn't ignoring you but tomorrow I have to chuck this phone and I don't want you to think I am ignoring you."

"Why tomorrow?"

I am not sure how honest to be with her. I can't help but feel the less she knows the safer she will be, she already kind of knows what I am up to so I can keep it clipped, no details.

"Because tomorrow I disappear and get to work finding answers, I can't tell you the details. You are safer not knowing."

"You are not going to Europe; I know that much."

"I don't know, I could use a holiday," I say with a haggard huff.

"How do I contact you if someone comes asking about you?"

I think about that. I do plan on staking her place out but how will I know if anyone who comes knocking is legitimate or a threat? It would be a lead I can't afford to miss.

"If someone comes asking questions, tell them I wigged out and didn't want to remember and that the last you heard I was on my way to Paris. Does your front porch light work? It's never on."

"Yes, it does. How do you know it's never on?"

Aw crap.

"Uh... Because I've been staking out your place, just in case," I admit reluctantly.

"Huh, I am not sure whether I am creeped out or impressed." Alisha laughs musically and I laugh with her. It's a relief, she doesn't sound so annoyed anymore.

"Be impressed, I've got this spy shit down but can't be here all the time obviously so if someone does come, I may not know. Leave the porch light on and I will know, then I'll call you on a prepaid phone," I instruct, feeling quite impressed with myself.

"You said, 'I can't be *here* all the time…' You are here right now, aren't you? If you weren't you would have said, I can't be *there* all the time."

Shit… I do not have this spy shit down. Being a cocky prat, that is what I have down! What a complete idiot, I've been made before I even disappear. Anxiety flares in my chest; she can't know this car; I can't afford for her or anyone else to know this car. My eyes flick over to her house just in time to see the curtains twitch and I slide further down in the back seat.

"Nah, girl, was a slip of the tongue; look, I've got to go. Things to do, people to see. Remember if anyone comes knocking, leave the light on and I will contact you. Keep your eyes open and be safe."

"Mac, why not—"

"I really have to go, Alisha," I snub bluntly.

"Be safe, Mac."

My thumb punches the red button and I end the call; I can't believe I was just caught out so easily, I am so annoyed at myself. In my defence Alisha has made a career out of being able to read people, she is not easy to lie to effectively and I have never been a good liar. Ugh… Well, it's done now, I am just going to have to be more careful from now on, this is all so new and exhausting.

I get to my online shopping. After making up some fake business accounts I order a mattress and some other luxuries to make my stay at the warehouse more comfortable. Just out of interest I end up on a spy equipment shop; I search through lots more tech, most of which I don't understand but some that may come in handy and I click buy without really knowing if I will be able to work out how to use it all.

Putting my phone away, I decide I will keep it on tonight in case I think of anything else I need to buy. I feel so alone without it in my hand, distracting me from the inevitable. Up until now this has all felt easier to cope with, like it was all theoretical, almost like a fun game. I was just going through the motions, role playing. The moment I put down my phone and lay across the back seats of my car, the fear engulfs me. Now I am on the precipice, I feel overwhelmed, it is all so uncertain, like a soldier on the eve of battle only I don't know who the enemy is or where.

I know they are out there though, ever since I got back, I've felt this itch, this… paranoia and an unease, a heightened sense of awareness like I could feel that I was being watched. I don't know if I am doing the right thing, I only know it feels like I am. I must find the people that took my life from me and bring them down. If I don't, they will take me again, or make me crazy with fear that they will. I must expose them, this is my crusade, mine and mine alone.

Fidgeting on the back seat trying to find a comfortable spot feels completely impossible. It is chilly tonight and I shudder under the blanket that, up until now has been enough to keep warm. I close my eyes and attempt to quieten my loud mind from all the thinking. The plans, contingencies and what ifs, echo round my mind with irritating perpetuality. I am in way over my head, I am so aware of that but what is the alternative? To continue life blindly, never knowing if or when someone will come for me, never remembering what I lost and letting the people that did this to me live, never see justice. No, that is no life. At least this way I have a chance of a normal life one day; if not, I will go down swinging.

When I finally succumb to sleep in the early hours of the morning, my dreams are fractured and chaotic. A tangled web of disorganised images, even in dreams I am aware enough to try to make sense of them through the fog and confusion. Faces I know, faces I don't but such fast glimpses they blur and pixelate like a badly recorded video. Then suddenly the jumping and glitching smooths out, stabilises and the memory swirls…

I am drowning, icy cold water fills my throat, freezing in my lungs and yet my body is dry. My eyes sting as they try to see through the flow of water, my ears strain to hear to the words around me.

"She's had enough, you will have to stop or you will kill her."

I strain, I struggle, I haul my weight up trying to draw air but I am tied down. Hands like long finger-nailed vices grip my chin still as I try to squirm away from the relentless flow. I choke but do not drown, I drown but do not die.

Choking… Convulsing… Gasping… On a moment, on a dream, on a memory.

Tapping, tapping. What is that fucking tapping?

I scream out, my eyes shoot open and I spring bolt upright in the car seat.

Tap, tap, tap. "Mac!"

The horror of the nightmare still etched behind my eyes, I jump at the sound of my name and follow the direction of noise to the front driver's side window where I find Alisha, tapping on the window.

Oh, for the love of all that's holy.

Leaning forward, I open the back passenger door in front of me, gasping for air. As I pull the handle all the doors unlock simultaneously with a clunk. Sliding across to the edge of the seat, I swing my feet out and lean forwards with my head bowed. I am desperate for air and soaked in a sheen of sweat, my body still jolting with shakes from the nightmare. The crisp, cool morning air freezes the sweat on my skin and it feels soothing. I gulp air so fast I wonder if I will ever catch my breath.

I see her feet step towards me hesitantly; she steps forward so my head is resting on her tummy and puts her hands around the back of my head, stroking my hair. My breathing is loud and laboured.

Not a nightmare, a reality... A memory.

"It's okay..." she coos softly.

I cringe away, I should be embarrassed; I have no doubt she heard me scream. All I feel though is fear... Fear and anger.

"You shouldn't have come here, Alisha. I think I made it clear for you to stay the hell away from me," I snap.

She takes a step back and I look up at her. On the floor next to her is a tray with two cups of coffee and some freshly buttered toast, she turns and walks away and guilt pangs in my chest.

Fuck.

"Alisha, wait... Wait!"

She stops walking away, but doesn't turn around.

"I'm sorry. That was awful, I am a dick. Please, come back," I grovel.

She hesitates and then slowly turns around, I get out of the car and run to the front passenger side, open the door for her and gesture for her to get inside. She obliges, I retrieve the tray and pass it to her from the driver's side. She takes it and I get in and sit down, she passes me a plate of toast and a steaming mug of coffee.

"Thank you for this. It is really awesome," I say politely.

"It's only coffee and toast."

"There is no such thing when you have been living in your car for a week," I explain gratefully as my stomach growls.

We eat together quietly, my mind racing to attempt to know what to say. She was trying to do a nice thing and I was a complete jerk; inexcusable, yes, but I need her to stay away. I can't keep saying goodbye to her and at this point I don't know why she is here. I finish my toast and take a good slurp of coffee; I look over at Alisha and she is finished too.

"I am sorry for how I snapped at you," I confess, rubbing my eyes. The caffeine hasn't quite hit me yet.

"No, I am sorry. You are right, I shouldn't have come, Mac."

"Why did you?"

She hesitates, tripping over herself. I don't think I've ever seen her struggle for words, she always knows what to say, she is the woman that has all of the words. Till now – that fact alone is making me nervous.

"I am having trouble letting go of you, I don't... know why." Her voice is as steady as always but a lot quieter, mouse-like.

"Well, you spent months being my therapist, seeing me every week and getting to know me. I am sure it's only natural to care for people and whether or not they are okay," I say, trying to reassure her.

"As a therapist we are trained to be detached, you care but with a wall between your patient and yourself. If you let emotions get in it can get complicated and painful. I don't know when that wall came down for me, but at some point, it did."

I look at her; her eyes are staring off somewhere distant. This is the last thing I expected to hear, I know we have always flirted a little but I never thought and still don't think there is anything in it. I don't feel that from her, I feel a sadness coming from her that I don't really understand.

"I think that my situation must be quite unique, it has been super intense and you know that what I am about to get into is going to be dangerous. I think maybe you just have a big heart; you took on a job to help people and you want to help me and it must suck that, you can't complete that process. You have helped me though; I hope you know that."

"Jesus, Mac!" Alisha snaps, her words coming out in a bitch slap.

Alisha gets up out of the car and slams the door, leaving me shocked and completely perplexed. I get out and walk round to her side of the car; she is leaned against the door, her eyes full and threatening to spill. What the hell did I say? I run the conversation over in my mind and it doesn't help, I am clueless.

"Hey, girl, please don't cry; I don't know what I said but I can promise I never meant it to hurt you."

I feel like such an arse and I don't even know what I have done. I go to comfort her; my hand goes to reach and then inevitably, drops back down to my sides. I just can't take that step forwards, instead I freeze in place feeling incompetent and awkward.

"You didn't say anything wrong, McKenna, you are just so incredibly blind sometimes."

"Blind to what? I don't understand," I ask impatiently.

"Can we just get away from here, go someplace and talk? I know you want to leave but let's talk about this first," she suggests, calmer now.

Tempting, but I really don't need this right now, if I don't move, I will never go through with this.

"I really should—"

"Mac, please."

I cave at the sadness of her voice. Her eyes are troubled and conflicted, it is impossible to say no to her right now and to be honest I really do want to understand what is going on. I can't leave this unresolved, not after how much she has tried to help me.

"Where do you want to go?" I ask softly.

"Anywhere but here."

***

Anywhere turns out to be the nearest pub, I am not really sure where else to take her, I wanted someplace close, hoping to move things along fast. We enter a dingy little music bar with floors that stick to your feet as you walk; I love bars like this, grungy and quiet even with the rock and heavy metal rumbling quietly in the background. It's the sort of place that has small dishes on the bar filled with peanuts to nibble on while you drink and the last place, I envisage that Alisha would ever want to go.

"Can I get you a drink?" I ask awkwardly, stifling a laugh. It is an odd feeling, being in a bar with her and I think she feels it too, she smiles at me sheepishly.

We order our drinks and find ourselves in a dimly lit, little den-like seating area and I watch her curiously, this definitely wasn't in the plan, I am confused as hell. She doesn't look at me at first, she busies herself with taking off her jacket and then starts sliding her fingertip around the rim of her glass.

Is she flustered?

"I am not used to seeing you this way," I say finally and she smirks.

"What way is that?"

"You seem nervous and fidgety; you always seem so infallible."

"Oh, believe me I am not and I have my reasons," she illudes.

"Well Doc, are you going to dance around those reasons or are you going to tell me what is wrong?"

"Probably both." She frowns.

She takes a deep breath and then looks up at me, her deep hazel brown eyes glittering and her expression tight with stress. Now I am the flustered one, I sip my Pepsi and try to maintain my nonchalant composure.

"Mac, I don't think you should do this. Even if you are right and these people are still watching you then disappearing is going to provoke them, you will be in danger and I don't want you getting hurt again... I can't..."

Alisha closes her eyes and sighs a pained huff; it is unnerving to see her this way. She is on the edge, only I am not sure what she is on the edge of – anger, worry, sadness? It is hard to tell but whatever it is, it hurts to watch and I feel useless and incapable. I have long since forgotten how to comfort someone; even if I hadn't, what am I comforting her for? I understand it is her job to care but her upset feels out of balance. I feel like I am missing something and it is both confusing and frustrating and because she is my therapist, I don't want to say something inappropriate and make the situation worse.

"What is going on, Alisha? I don't want to overstep the mark but you are confusing me, girl. I understand you don't think I should do this and that probably doesn't feel great or comfortable because you don't want to see anyone hurt. Who would? But your reaction, to me leaving, that is what I don't understand."

"I... Mac... I can't... This was a mistake, I am sorry," she stutters, standing up and putting her jacket on. I stand up too, clearing the cobwebs from my brain just quick enough to stand in her way. She bumps straight into me trying to leave and she stops, just inches away from me.

"Alisha, stop. The mistake is not being honest with me. Now please just tell me what is wrong."

She bows her head, rests it on my chest and lets out a shaky breath as her hands lay on my tense shoulders. I freeze; her breath is heavy and pained while I have forgotten how to breathe altogether. The battle rages inside me again between fear and want, this makes no sense in my head and yet my body understands, I am so completely divided.

"There is nothing I can say to stop you, is there?" she sighs.

"I don't think we have that much time."

Alisha lifts her head, her eyes intent on mine, her face so close I can feel her breath tickling my lips, my stomach erupts in tingles.

"Then let's make time," she whispers.

All thought and intention fly out of my brain, it is like someone else is driving now. No fear or doubt, I am nothing but a passenger watching my suddenly steady hands move with complete certainty around her waist. I lean in and watch as my lips draw closer to hers, her lips are cool and sweet from her drink and just as soft as I imagined they would be. My kiss is slow and deliberate and she gasps in my mouth; the sound of her excitement spurs me on. I walk her backwards, my arms keeping her stable till we hit the wall behind her and my hands slide firmly up her waist and into her hair. My brain is short circuiting so much so it almost feels like my body is acting without my permission. I press my hips into her as my kiss builds in speed, nibbling on her bottom lip and her reaction is intoxicating me, her hands pulling on my hips urging me closer as she gasps, "Fuck..." into my mouth. Pleasure explodes like ecstasy in my chest and radiates across every inch of me. God damn, this girl can kiss.

"...Mac," she utters breathlessly and I stop, my hands cupping her flushed cheeks, my forehead against hers.

"I'm sorry... I shouldn't have..." I stutter.

"No... No... God no. It's not that, you just... You can't kiss me like that if you're going to leave. Please, stay. We can work this out together, I know we can, just stay with me," she pleads.

Now more than ever I feel myself being sliced in two. I want nothing more than to surrender to her, I want the world to leave me alone so I can get lost in her. I don't want to do this alone; I want to drag the duvet over our heads and disappear into childlike safety but... as long as she is near me, she is in danger and as long as I am with her, I am not focusing on what I need to, to end this hell.

"You know I can't, girl, I have to do this alone, it's the only way I can keep you safe," I say, pained, and I lift my lips to her forehead and kiss it lightly. "I wish I had met you before all of this."

I pull away gently and see her eyes begin to fill with tears and my chest wrenches painfully. I watch the pain leak from them as it is quickly replaced with a cold deadness.

"Just go, Mac... Just go and be safe," she mutters hollowly.

"You don't want me to drive you back?" I ask and she shakes her head no. I hesitate, not sure what to do or say.

"Remember – the porch light."

I drive for ten minutes before I pull into a random car park because I begin to lose it; too much happened since my eyes opened and I haven't had time to process it. The memory, Alisha, the kiss. I rest my head on the steering wheel, my mind is dominated by Alisha, her touch, her taste, her words and then, I hurt her. My insides cringe at the images of the pain on her face.

Better hurt than dead.

I must put Alisha and the memory out of my mind, I need to focus; I need to swallow it all down and keep moving forward because this is crippling me and I am running out of time. McKenna Scott is due to be on a train to Paris 5pm today which means I have roughly eight and half hours before I go dark and moving around will become extremely difficult. I take out a prepaid mobile, breathe in a deep steadying breath and dial.

"Paragon Images, this is Jess speaking – how can I help you today?"

"Hey Jess, it's Mac."

"Mac? Aren't you supposed to be on your way to Paris?"

"Not till later, still have some bits to do before I leave."

"Right okay… Can I help with something?"

"That's what I am hoping, girl. I am looking to get hold of all my images since day dot at PIC, is that something you can help me with?"

"Well, there is a file on your system that has all your published work, surely you know…" Jess begins but I interrupt her.

"Yeah, I know about that. No, I am looking for all of my photos, all SD cards with every shot I've ever taken," I explain.

"That must be thousands upon thousands of shots, Mac, why could you possibly want those?"

"It is just a project I plan to work on while I am away," I lie and I am a crap liar so I am one hundred percent pinning my hopes on her still having little crush on me.

"It shouldn't be a problem; I will have to run it by Emmitt but I can't see why—"

"Could we possibly leave it between you and me and let's say, I will owe you massive when I come home? What do you say, girly?" I flirt.

There is a pause and it feels like it is going on too long, my leg twitches as it bounces nervously on the ball of my foot.

"Okay… Listen, you can't come in here to get them, you are more than a little obvious to spot and in about ten seconds I would be questioned as to why you came. I can send them with one of our photographers out on route to a client. Let's see…

"…Ah yes. Savannah has a client in an hour and a half. I could get her to meet you to pass them off. Say 10.30am? She has a shoot at The Shard for a new restaurant opening on the 72nd floor."

I internally groan; nothing about going inside that building appeals to me enough to actually go in, let alone to the 72nd floor outdoor viewing gallery, my knees are weak already.

"Jess, you are an absolute star, thank you. I owe you big time!"

"I will collect," she flirts. "Have a great time in Europe, Mac."

"Thanks, girl, take care."

I can't believe I just pulled that off.

The drive to The Shard is hectic, but then it is London. When I hit London Bridge, I lower my car window and toss my old phone out and into the River Thames. It actually feels pretty good, maybe a bit overdramatic but still, they do that stuff in the movies, right? It does mean of course, that now my mum can't call me and neither can Alisha. I can't help but feel a little relieved, as well as sad.

***

Standing outside The Shard I am still struck by the enormity of the monstrous building; I wonder how much glass it took to make this thing. Maybe I shouldn't think about it because when I do, I get visions of it sloping off like the Leaning Tower of Pisa. Best to go inside, keep moving and attempt to ignore the niggling nerves in my tummy. I enter the lift, the doors shut behind me and I immediately feel trapped. Anxiety building in my chest, I decide to watch the images playing on the video screens on the ceiling of the lift to distract myself. At level 33, I exit to transfer to the next lift going up to level 68; the whole thing is very fast but for me any time in a lift is too much time. I take a third and final lift up to level 72 and then I walk out onto the Skydeck.

It is breath-taking, a true spectacle. The Skydeck is partially open and even on a warm day you can feel the wind blowing harshly from the intimidating 244-metre height above the ground. My legs are shaky as I move across the floor, I feel like I want to hold on to something. The Skydeck has been booked out by PIC so the only people on this level are either involved with the photoshoot or are Shard workforce serving refreshments.

Suddenly I realise that I have no idea what Savannah looks like; her being

Alfred's granddaughter doesn't really help, all that really gives me is a plaid shirt, messy hair and a crooked grin. I settle for looking for someone who is carrying a camera, my eyes finally find a woman standing in the right corner, she is leaning against the glass fiddling with her zoom lens, that's brave. I know you won't fall through the glass but still, it isn't something I would casually do.

The woman I assume to be Savannah is very attractive, around my height and slim but still curvy somehow. She has loose curled strawberry-blonde hair and black chunky-framed glasses. Her skin is pale, her face slightly freckled and her eyes are vivid green and sparkling. As I walk closer, she looks up at me, at first confusion furrows her brow but then recognition hits and her face transforms with a radiant smile that stupefies me for just a second.

"You must be Mac." She smiles; her voice isn't what I expected, it's feminine but croaky in a sexy way.

"Guilty." I grin.

"Listen, I am in need of a break, do you fancy a coffee?" Savannah asks, taking off her glasses. I am taken aback, I really shouldn't, I have a lot to do but it may be my last time having coffee in a public place with company for a while.

"Um, where?"

Please God anywhere but here.

"There are some decent eateries down on the 31st floor if you are game?"

"Oh yeah as long as it's not here, I do not like this floor. Lower to the ground – good, up in the sky – bad," I ramble nervously and she laughs animatedly.

We waste no time getting down to level 31; the restaurant is quiet and the view awesome but I choose to sit with my back to it, pretending it doesn't exist. Savannah eyes me with a soft smirk and flicks her hair out of her eyes.

"Not a fan of heights then?" she asks, breaking the ice.

"I am learning, not. To be honest they don't usually bother me too much, it's more the building that wigs me out. I've had the opportunity to shoot here before but I avoided it."

"I have seen a lot of your work; you took all of my pa's work before…" Savannah trails off.

Ah, the inevitable pause when people don't know what word is polite and socially acceptable to use when mentioning that I disappeared. Taken, kidnapped, shanghaied, captured, snatched, plucked from the world, temporarily relocated against my will. It is all the same to me.

I smile and nod mockingly. "…Disappeared, it is okay, you can say it, girl. I did in fact go POOF." I gesture a motion with my hands to dramatize the poof and she laughs brightly.

"I guess that happens to you a lot."

I slurp my caramel Frappuccino and delight in its coolness on my dry, anxiety-ridden throat. I feel better lower down, I am a little calmer than I was but I still feel better holding on to the table subtly.

"Yeah but, I can't really blame people, it is awkward at times but I am getting used to it. I am hoping it will one day be old news."

"My pa was gutted when you were gone, you know. He has quite the soft spot for you."

That surprises me.

"Really? I thought he gave custard creams to all the girls," I joke and we both laugh easily.

Savannah has one of those smiles where it's like her whole face smiles, it's incredibly infectious and beautiful. I feel like I am staring so I make the conscious effort to look away. This random coffee is doing wonders for my mood, I feel lighter. Sure, the Alisha thing is weighing on me, I am not a robot but I know that for now I am doing the right thing. Savannah is light and fun and secretly, I am grateful for her making me laugh when I really needed it, even the height is starting to bother me less.

"Yes, really, he doesn't warm to people well, he can be pretty blunt and it puts people off," Savannah explains.

"Huh… That's actually one of the things I like about him. I always know where I stand with him, there are no hidden agendas he is just, Alfred. His latest piece was like a sucker punch to my soul, it really got me. He actually showed me the shots you took while I was away, beautiful work," I commend her and she blushes.

"Aw thank you, that is sweet of you to say. I only really do it part time; I am no McKenna Scott but I get by," she teases, casting a playful eye.

"Hah! I dunno about that. I am very much out of practice."

"Ah well, you had a two-year-long – POOF! I say being a little rusty is perfectly acceptable."

I can't help but laugh, I've never really had anyone talk about me disappearing so casually, people mostly avoid the subject. I think she has a bit of her grandad in her, she is blunt without being mean, it is refreshing to not have the subject be so taboo and for it to be treated lightly like afternoon tea. It is usually either hard questions to answer or avoiding the subject completely; this girl is a breath of fresh air and I am actually having fun but I am aware that time is ticking.

"Well lady, I have to get a wiggle on if I am going to get everything done today but this has been… Pretty awesome fun, even if inside a tower of terror," I say, flashing her a charming smile.

"It has been fun. It is a shame that you are off travelling but look, here are your SD cards and here…" she reaches into her pocket, takes out her purse and hands me a card from inside, "take my number, we could always catch up when you get back. No scary buildings – Scouts' honour."

"I would like that, thanks Savannah," I say with a wink and she smirks at me with a daring glint in her eyes, paralysing me for a second.

Damn – those eyes.

"Anytime, have fun in Europe and Mac… It's Anna."

"Anna, right. Take care of yourself, Anna."

***

As I arrive at the warehouse, I feel a little overwhelmed. This is really happening; this is not a game. I collect my keys, use the electronic fob to open the loading bay doors and drive into the eerie darkness. When I exit my car and begin searching for the light switch, it takes me a while because I am foolishly groping blindly for a normal light switch, when in fact the 'switch' is a lever handle that I have to push up. By the time I find it and flick it on with a clank – it has my eyes in a complete white out that takes a while to readjust to.

The echo in the vast empty space of the warehouse is deafening and jarring as I close the shutters down; maybe I will be using the personal door more than I thought. The moment the shutter closes I am hit with a tidal wave of loneliness. As I take in the enormity of the place, I suddenly feel so small and insignificant, my confidence shakes and crumbles into dust.

No, I will not allow this to overtake me. I will breathe, I will explore and I will centre myself just like Alisha taught me.

Alisha…

Nope, none of that! Okay, let's make a bat cave.

The walls are painted brilliant white but you can still see the outline of the breeze blocks that construct it, they are cold and smooth to the touch. It smells faintly of wet paint; the warehouse is like a gigantic garage, on the entrance wall there are the electronic shutters to the loading door on the left and a personal door on the right. The personal door has a small L-shaped corridor then two doors, the left door leading to the main warehouse and the right door to a very small but functional bathroom. I look at the door that leads outside, there is just a standard key lock but on the wall to the left of the door is a small screen and speaker, the video intercom. The glass is one-way mirror; I can see out but people can't see in… Awesome.

I walk down the length of the warehouse towards the steps that lead up to the second level. It is huge – everything I have brought with me would fit up there 10 times over but I want a separate area to sleep, away from everything. The platform is built on massive steel columns that have been painted glossy black, there is a guard rail that runs across the front edge of the top platform with smaller brace beams criss-crossing each rectangular section. The floor is just simple sheets of plywood a couple of inches thick.

The stairs are very wide metal industrial steps designed for two people to be able to walk up and down at a time; they are fixed to the left-hand wall with a long steel banister down the open side. There must be 20 feet worth of stairs that reach the 15-foot-high platform. I climb the many steps; the platform has almost as much floor space as my entire studio flat, the plywood floor makes a bouncy thud with every step I take. I requested some pallets be left up here and I am happy to find them leaned up against the far wall.

Back on the lower level I look up at the ceiling that seems so far away, there must be 20 tube lights brightening up the entire space and at least 10 more under the platform. On the back wall under the platform to the left is the fire exit and to the right is the most basic kitchen set-up you have ever seen.

Time to get to work.

The first thing I need to sort out is the lighting in this place, it is either startlingly bright or pitch black, there is no in between. I have fun stringing fairy lights around all the support beams, banisters and guard rails and strategically place tall lamps around the place. Then, I turn all the lamps and fairy lights on and switch the main lights off. The warehouse glows moodily like a romantically lit-up restaurant but on a huge scale and I grin, pleased with my effort and the sudden warmth that it brings to the place.

I do love me a shed ton of fairy lights.

Setting up the kitchen takes mere minutes and I wolf down a chocolate bar while I am at it; the hunger is real but so is my need to keep moving, because more moving means less thinking. It takes me a lot longer than I wanted to set up all the tech. I am still a beginner at this stuff but I am quite proud when I see the video coming through the monitor from CCTV cameras that I bluffed my way through installing, outside at the front and back doors. I install bolts on the front door as an extra safety measure, I am sure this is overkill but I feel more secure for it.

The moment that I am finally finished and fit to collapse, the intercom buzzes to life and I jump out of my skin. "Alexa Clarke, I have a delivery for you."

My brain takes far too long to register my new alias, making me slow to respond. I bring the shutter up and take possession of my mattress, punch bag and weights. The punch bag hooks on to the metal ceiling crossbeams with no drama. The mattress, however, takes me about half an hour to drag up the steps, nearly sending me toppling down twice in the process. I make my bed by laying the pallets down and placing the mattress on top. With a little bedding it actually looks quite inviting and homely, in a rustic type of way.

I walk to the edge of the platform and sit down, bum shuffling to the edge so that I am sat in the middle of one of the Xs of the crossbeams. I let my legs dangle off the edge and my chin rests on the centre of the cold metal X. The silence is so loud my ears are ringing. I look at my watch – 7.20pm, the train to Paris has well and truly departed – McKenna Scott is gone.

Panic.

Ten seconds, Mac, that is all you get. You can let the fear in for ten seconds and then you must dump it away and man the hell up.

One… Two… Three…

My heart aches with loneliness at the reality of my solitude. Can I really do this? The uncertainty makes my insides jitter and snag like a beaten-up rusted motor.

Four… Five…

Terror is so neat, so clean and pointed, sharp against the soft edges of your soul. My soul is scarred from the constant slicing, toughening with scars from every wound inflicted. How long before my soul is nothing more than cold and twisted remains?

Six… Seven… Eight…

Anger – the fire that drives me towards justice; if my soul gets lost in the pain, how long before anger becomes enmity and justice becomes revenge? Will I be lost forever? Will I ever be Mac again?

Nine…

What if I fail? Will everyone just assume I got lost backpacking, never to return? Will I ever get to go home again?

Ten.

"My name *was* McKenna Scott but it is now Alexa Clarke. I am 31 years old and I live in London. I was a photographer but I am many things, thanks to you. I was lost but now I am here. I am *alive* and I will find myself again and when I do – I am coming for you."

CHAPTER THREE

The Honest Liar

It's like that part in Harry Potter, where Harry sets off on his quest to find and destroy all of the horcruxes and once he leaves, he realises he really has no freaking idea where to start. Yeah, it is definitely like that; at least he had Ron and Hermione. All I need is one lead, one clue of where to start. I have considered that maybe, I should look at my medical records, it would mean breaking into the hospital somehow and I am not quite sure how to pull that off, not yet anyway.

I have been at the warehouse for 4 days now, there has been a lot of working out, I have a bit of a routine going now. I have been watching instructional videos on boxing and self-defence, the boxing mainly to build my stamina and strength. I've rigged a chunky climbing rope to the ceiling of the platform that surprisingly, I am able to climb up and slide down twice in quick succession before my arms give up the ghost and turn into noodles. I have also been running sprints up and down the warehouse, using the sheer size of the place to my advantage.

On top of that the warehouse has really taken shape; all the extra bits I ordered online have arrived and I have everything I need to keep me comfortable. So far, I haven't left the warehouse but I will have to soon to get food, plus I really need to do a drive by at Alisha's place to see if the porch light is on. I did plan on staking her place out but after what happened, I am hesitant. She now knows my car and would easily be able to spot me; if the idea of going back screws with my head then I am sure it would hers too.

I have thought about that day a lot, played it over and over in my mind. I can't deny it has been hard to wipe her from my thoughts. The intensity of that moment is hard to escape, so is the nagging feeling that it seemed so out of character for her. I don't know, maybe she is right, maybe I am blind. Maybe I am so wrapped up in my own crap I can't make sense of anything or maybe in the heat of the moment she confused her feelings, it has been very intense and now she maybe regrets it. No… There is no mistaking the way she kissed me. Unhelpful tingles flutter between my legs as the memory flashes.

Nope! Chill your bean, Mac.

Then there was the dream, the dream I am very sure was actually a memory. It prompted me to Google search water torture which led me to waterboarding, a technique used to make the victim feel like they are drowning. The subject is restrained while cloth is held over their face and water is poured over it intermittently. It gives the feeling of drowning and if done too continuously can cause dry asphyxiation… Horrific. I am certain that is what I was remembering but I feel numb to it, like I can't connect the memory as mine. I also remember a man's voice telling someone to stop before they kill me, the voice thick with an accent that I can't pinpoint.

I look over to the right-hand wall of the warehouse; it is like a mind exploding. I have been spider charting; the wall is covered in any evidence or ideas I have. I have managed to track down all the newspaper clippings from my disappearance online, plus the ones from my return. The headlines scream, 'Mac, the girl who came back.' Like I am a punchline to a bad joke.

I have a map of London, articles on retrieving lost memories and ideas for what to do next. The word hospital in capital letters with a question mark is glaring at me from the paper but for now, it's a possible plan for another day. My eyes fall on the photos of my scars and I cringe. I took them because there is a chance, they could jog a memory, so I will continue to cringe every time I see them, also hoping maybe it will even desensitise me to the ugliness they make me feel.

Today's plan is to start with what will no doubt be a long and laborious task; I have 15 SD cards full of photos from 40-odd photoshoots. I can't remember anything from a week or so before I disappeared but according to the work logs, I was working. I had 3 photoshoots the week I was taken. It may be a long shot but it is something to investigate, the trouble is there are thousands and thousands of shots, they are dated but it is going to take me some time to find those three photoshoots.

I am hoping maybe the photos may bring on more memories; it wasn't so long ago that I didn't want to remember, the thought of even trying scared me and it still does but ever since that memory of the waterboarding came back to me, I actually feel some relief. This really did happen to me, I know that I have scars and medical records and the fact that I was gone without a trace for over two years but until that memory, it all felt like it happened to a different person. It was easy to live in denial but that pretence is enough to drive you crazy.

I have a break sifting through photos and make some coffee, my eyelids are heavy and flicking through the photos on the brightly lit laptop screen isn't helping. I make my coffee tar dark to wake me up but also, because I am out of milk. I am so tired and burnt out, I feel safe here and yet my sleeping seems to be getting increasingly worse. Nightmares plague me every night but so far, they haven't led to anything clear, I just hope that it means that my memories are trying to break through, it would make the lack of sleep worth it if I learned something.

Temptation to go out and clear my head is building; there is no denying I need to buy food, there is only so long I can delay it. It is 7am, the earlier I go the less likely I am to bump into someone I know. Plus, I chose this place because it's far enough away that I am not likely to bump into anyone that I know.

Screw it.

I am prepared, it may seem a little overboard but I have bought some items to disguise myself a little. I don't know a lot of people but a lot of people seem to know my face. 'Mac, the girl who came back' was a newspaper sensation on my return, ensuring my face and scars make me easy to recognise. So, that being said I thought it a necessary precaution. I adjust and re-adjust the blonde wig – tucking in my long dark hair is the tricky part – then I put on some big-frame glasses and dress in a lady's business suit with a scarf to hide the angry scar across my throat.

Looking in the mirror I feel pretty secure I won't be discovered, uncomfortable as fuck and a bit ridiculous but secure. I am not the most feminine girl, not over the top tomboyish but certainly not feminine and this outfit is making me feel self-conscious. My stomach flutters with anticipation as I rev the car engine to life. I open the loading door, pull forward and close it behind me using the key fob. It's a chilly morning but I drive with the window open, the morning breeze blasting me awake and clearing all the cobwebs in my mind, it feels so good.

Freedom!

The plan is to bulk buy as much as I can, I don't want to be having to do this any more than necessary. As uncomfortable as I am, the prospect of having a decent coffee when I get back excites me. I don't think I've ever shopped so fast, I would totally rock Supermarket Sweep. I use the 'scan as I go' system so I can just pay at the end and not stand at the tills bagging up and feeling exposed by the eyes of passers-by, I keep my head down and manage to get in and out in record time.

After I load the car I get moving again; with Alisha on my mind I wonder if maybe I should run by her place and see if the porch light is on, but it's morning, I can't see her leaving it on in the daytime. So, I head back to the warehouse, the whole trip taking me 30 minutes and my mood has improved immensely. After I unload and pack away the food, I set myself up ready for more photo sifting. Now I have an icy cold bottle of Dr Pepper and some chocolate M&Ms, junk food is my brain food. I stick my headphones on, Black Stone Cherry blasting in my ears and I feel much more focused.

It is still laborious but my mood is so much better and my mind clearer. I flick through the dates, so many files that although are all date stamped it does little to speed up the task and it is still arduous and tiring. Every 15 minutes or so I have to close my eyes as it all becomes very difficult to read. Finally, I find the first of three albums I've been hunting for, I open it and start flicking through the photos.

I don't remember the photoshoot; it seems to be an outdoor public event. My eyes strain to inspect every photo carefully trying to place the event and location hoping that something may jog a memory. It is insane to think I took all of these photos; I was there and yet it seems so alien to me. I recognise the park, it's Hyde Park but that isn't hard to recognise to anyone who knows London. I click, click, and click though endless photos till I come across a photo of a banner that reads 'BBC Radio Live in Hyde Park'.

Now I have an event and date I jot it down, adding it to the timeline that I am attempting to establish. Every detail I can find could lead to a clue of when and where I was taken. I don't remember being taken or anything leading up to it, any missing piece of the puzzle is recorded and put on the timeline I have created on the wall and hopefully, something will eventually click. Maybe if I am able to find the exact time and place that I was taken it could be a good first step to figuring out where I was held.

Taking my time, I look at every face I can individually and analyse them carefully, I could have been watched even then, the face of the person who took me could be in this crowd. However, all I see are smiling faces and families of people enjoying the show. Then I see the face of someone I recognise, the person is standing alone, leaning against the tree. This person wasn't in the frame of intended shot but more in the background. I see the face of Alisha and my heart races a little.

Huh, small world. This isn't weird, I am sure plenty of people came to enjoy the show. Still, it feels a little weird, like when you are a kid and you see a teacher outside school and it's a shock, as if your young mind expects them always to be at school. To me, she is Alisha the therapist; even with what has happened between us it is odd to see her outside of that world in casual clothing enjoying a concert. I print the photo out; I am not really sure why; I hear the printer acknowledge the request while I stretch out my back dramatically, groaning like a porn star.

Taking a break, I decide to write an email to my mum, somehow, I have to pad out my alibi and keep her mind at rest. I come to the conclusion the best way would be to create a new email address and email her. I don't know a lot about tracking, I am sure it's a risk but so is her getting suspicious.

Dear Mum,

I am having an amazing time in Paris. The weather has been kind to me, there are so many amazing sights to see. I am emailing you from the balcony of my hotel room, while I munch on gorgeous pastries. Are you jealous? ;)

I know that it was tough to say goodbye and I miss you something rotten, but I am feeling much better. I will call you soon, Promise. Love you Mum and I hope you are well.

Speak soon,

Milky Bar Kid x

Milky Bar Kid; Mum's nickname for me, it could be worse. I earned it for my pale skin and apparently, I used to want to be a cowboy when I grew up. I attach some photos I stole from the internet and edit them, one of the Eiffel Tower and one of some beautifully delicious-looking French pastries. Satisfied that it is convincing enough for Mum, I hit send and the heavy guilt in my chest lifts a little knowing that she will feel better to have heard from me.

I do miss her terribly; it has only ever been Mum and I because I have no siblings and Mum raised me alone. I don't know anything about my father, only that Mum wouldn't talk about him, he walked out on us when I was barely born. From that information alone, I decided a long time ago that I don't need to know him. I hate that I am lying to her, the one person in my life that has loved and cared for me without condition. I hope one day I can tell her about all of this and I hope she will understand.

Rubbing the tiredness out of my eyes, I go back to the task at hand and after much tedious searching, I find the album from six days before I was last seen, which according to police records was at my local convenience store. I know the shop owners quite well and they reported my presence there buying a newspaper, a bottle of milk, bread, Haribo sweets and cheese. Sounds like me, all things that I practically live on owing to my inability to cook.

Opening the album, I see that the photos are of a corporate event, a black-tie gala of some sort. I don't recognise the venue but it is grand. The scene is set in a ballroom that looks like it has come straight out of a fairy tale, huge, white and magnificent. The floor white polished marble and the walls, ceiling and pillars are carved in beautiful detail. There are chandeliers glittering dramatically and in the centre of the ceiling lives a tremendous, domed, stained-glass window.

The attendants are all dressed to match the occasion, men sharply dressed in tuxedos and women glowing in elegant evening dresses. Round tables are dressed lavishly with white lily centrepieces, the tableware is polished and glinting in the light. The photos tell a story as I move further through the images and I watch the evening unfold; first a sit-down meal with champagne being served, then the dancing and mingling of people circulating the room, faces gleaming with warmth and satisfaction.

A woman in a red dress catches my eye; the red dress clings to her so perfectly, accenting her every curve. I cannot see her face; she has her back to me in the shot but I am drawn to her. A fractured image flashes in my field of vision, glasses clinking and smiles beaming. The sounds of laughing and the buzzing of conversation is alive in my ears. The room around me bright and warm, the smell of perfume, alcohol and cigarettes, thick in the air and is distinct and familiar as I breathe it in. My head begins to swim, feeling heavy and sloshy.

The memory swirls.

I am dancing slowly, swaying on the spot, her body held tight up against mine. One hand holding hers, the other on her waist. I feel the soft fabric of the dress against my fingertips, her skin frustratingly close beneath.

I feel her breath against my throat and I want so badly to kiss her, the desire, the want, the need is intoxicating. Her lips begin kissing their way up to my ear, making me tingle.

"I want you," she breathes tantalisingly.

I gasp on the memory, like I have forgotten how to breathe. My head spins as I try to make sense of what I saw, of what I felt. My breathing shallows, my body is excited and tingling, it felt so real. Who is she? The images invade, they swirl up in my conscious like a colourful tornado, blowing roughly into the forgotten crevices of my mind and uncovering misplaced memories. The dust starts to settle revealing buried emotions, then the tornado intensifies, blowing harder and uncovering more.

The memory swirls.

I am standing behind her leaning over her shoulder, her floral perfume alluring me as I kiss her collarbone tenderly. My hands holding her hips, my fingertip lightly tickling the crease of her groin through her dress, she squirms and it drives me wild. My kiss becomes rougher and moves up the side of her neck.

"Let's get out of here," I mutter breathlessly.

I snap back to reality so fast I am disorientated. My breathing heavy, my heart racing, my body still tingling as the memory of her lingers, awakening me. I scan the photos furiously, trying to find the woman in the red dress, I just need to see her face. How can I feel I know her so completely, yet not know who the hell she is?! Come on! You have to be here.

My vision blurs with another invasion, so vibrant that my surroundings completely disappear, I am there and not here, I am here but not there. I feel everything I see, the excitement, the touch of her skin beneath my fingers, somehow the line between the past and present is blurring.

The memory swirls.

Her teeth nip at my neck inspiring pleasurable pain and a moan rumbles in my throat, she giggles – her musical laugh echoes around my mind with familiarity, my heart thrumming with anticipation. Her hands wander up my shirt, burning in the path they leave behind, making my insides melt and quiver.

I grip hold of the desk for stability as reality jars me back to the present, the evidence of my excitement sliding in my pants. I breathe a shaky breath, close my eyes and I focus on the memory of her floral scent, the sound of her laugh, of her touch against my skin. My mind erupts with images, jumpy at first like a flick picture book and then the images smoothen out fluidly like video inside my head. I feel the desk grasped in my fists and it is as real as the sensation that her touch inspires. My head swims, the weight of it forcing my chin onto my chest as it bows.

The memory swirls.

A frenzy of hands grabbing, urgent kisses that weaken my knees. We stumble through the door of the hotel suite and I kick the door behind me, her laugh beautifully sexy and bright, her gorgeous hazel brown eyes alight with desire and mystery. I push her up against the wall, drag her dress up her thighs and lift her up till her legs straddle around my hips. I press into her and her mouth falls open, breath hissing from her. I kiss her feverishly, my tongue sliding against hers and I feel her body tremble in my arms as I carry her over towards the bed and slowly drop her to the ground. She rips my shirt open, buttons popping off revealing my unscarred torso. I turn her round, unzipping her dress, my face nuzzled into her hair. She turns back to face me as the silky red material dances off her body and pools onto the floor. She smiles at me with shamelessly wanting eyes.

"*I didn't catch your name?*" my voice repeats in present time, my eyes wide and unfocused.

"*Does it really matter?*" *she replies giggling playfully.*

I kiss her demandingly as I lay her down with gentle dominance, my hand sliding firmly up her thigh and she squirms beneath me.

"*Alisha… My name's Alisha,*" *she moans.*

The tornado comes to a stop, the dust settles and the landscape clears revealing every thought, every emotion, every touch and every word. They re-connect like a chain reaction, fusing my past with my present. The warehouse comes back into my vision and all I hear is my own heavy panting.

My heart pounds so hard inside my chest that it is booming in my ears, my eyes burn with angry tears threatening to spill out. The disbelief turns to understanding and the anger turns to pain; she has been lying to me all along. I stand up and pace with no real direction and I grab the chair and upturn it, screaming out in a strangled wail of grief. I scream and scream and scream, long after the noise stops coming out.

Alisha…

The one person I thought I could trust has been misleading me, why!?

It was all a lie…

The pain envelops me and my knees buckle, I sob violently, my body quaking in trembles. I cry out, a lonely, overwhelming cry. I am beside myself; I am ruined, I have been such a fool, so naïve and gullible.

All this time…

My head swims with her voice, her words ring in my ears from the hours in therapy and I ache with shame; it was all a game.

Alisha…

My heart shatters for the girl I once knew, the girl that got under my skin so deep, so quickly, the girl I fantasised over meeting again. My fists pound uselessly on the floor, I scream and I yell and I cry like the pathetic child that I am inside this moment. I am obliterated, laying crumpled on the floor but my sobs are slowing. I am not sure how long I stay like that, feeling completely naked and alone. Eventually I am able to calm myself enough to pull myself up off the floor, stand the chair back up and sit down.

With puffy eyes I peer at my laptop screen, flick through the last pictures and then I finally see her face, clear as day. We are in a lift that is walled with mirrors, she is standing in the corner with her hands resting on either rail, her smile alluring. In the mirror's reflection I can see myself wearing a ladies' cut tuxedo with shiny black lapels, a black shirt and skinny tie. The camera is at my face as I admire her through the lens.

Why has she hidden this from me? All this time. Why? Why even take me on as a patient if we have history? My mind is too slow to connect the dots, overwhelmed by the overload of information. She was at both photoshoots, that is no coincidence; she hid our history, she… was watching me. She was watching me before I was taken and she has been watching ever since I got back; she must know who took me. No, worse… She must work with whoever took me.

I print off the photo but I leave it in the printer, shutting the laptop. I don't need to see any more right now; the memory is enough. I feel violated and dirty, my skin crawls with disgust. I never planned on bringing Alisha in on this, it was always going to be me here alone, it is my mission but it was a comfort knowing that just one person knew what I was doing and now that comfort is gone and I am left with a cold feeling of loneliness and betrayal.

What do I do? Do I confront her? She knows my car, fuck… But not this place, a small victory. I am so angry, I can't think clearly so, I get up and stride towards the bathroom, ripping my clothes off as I go. I step into the shower with the water as hot as I can stand. My skin turning red with the heat, I stand allowing the water to trickle over me, burning the itchy revulsion off of my skin. Very quickly the tiny bathroom fills with steam, misting my vision and I close my eyes as I try to quieten down my manic mind.

There is no choice here, I have to confront her. I wanted a lead, well now I have one and I must follow it. How though? If she works for whoever took me then it is so risky to go back but I need answers, what choice do I really have? I need a plan, I need a way in. I get out of the shower with purpose and I feel clearer, the rush of adrenalin slowing in my veins and a calm washing over me.

She knows my car but she doesn't know that I suspect her at all, I could break in and have a look around her office. I know that she keeps a key in the crook of her porch roof, I saw her use it once. I highly doubt she would keep any sensitive information just lying around but I can't afford not to check. I need to go, late tonight, she will be up on the second level and the lower floor where her office is should be clear. I could sneak in, go through her desk and be out before she even notices.

My mind feels dismantled; I get dressed in a rush, anger and determination fuelling me as I tug on some black ripped skinny jeans, a white tank top and my black leather jacket with my military boots. I look in the mirror and tie my hair up in my usual loose messy knot; my skin is turning milky white again now the heat of the shower is wearing off. I look tired – dark rings encircle my eyes making my usual bright blue eyes seem darker and so does the anger, apparently. Now all I can do is wait for nightfall.

I aimlessly wander around the warehouse. What I wouldn't do for a Jack and Coke. I have some, how ironic that I bought some today. I can't though, I need my head clear for tonight. I walk over to the printer and hit the print button so it reprints the last image that I printed. Alisha's pictures are now on the wall. I take the duplicate printout of Alisha, fold it up and slide it in my inside jacket pocket. I will leave this there for her; when she awakes tomorrow morning, she will know that I know. That will be a subtle goodbye, as subtle as a jackhammer.

***

With shaken breath, I step out of my car, my mind firing on all cylinders. I am parked down the street a little from Alisha's house; the last thing I need is her spotting the car. I stalk towards her house, my heart hammering inside my chest so hard it feels like it may bust out of my ribcage. Pausing at the wall that borders her driveway, I peek around it; the second level boasts a large balcony double door that leads on to a small courtyard with an outside seating area. The balcony doors are shut but there is light glowing from them, the lower office level and very top level are dark, still and quiet.

She hasn't left the porch light on, I expected that it would be, maybe she is trying to leave it a believable amount of time before she lures me in. I slip around the wall and walk around the edge of the garden space, keeping to the shadows for cover and my feet out of the loud crunchy tread of the gravel driveway. Once I reach the front door, I reach for the crook of the porch roof with hope, my hand groping for the cold metal of the key and I grab for it. My trembling, clumsy fingers fumble the key and it drops to the ground with a loud ping.

Panic flushes through my chest and I freeze, I hold my breath as my ears strain for any sound of movement. After 30 seconds of silence I exhale in relief; there is no movement from inside. I pick up the key, push it into the lock carefully and turn it. Pushing the door open silently, I creep inside and shut the door behind me with a tiny click. My eyes scan the room and I am relieved to find I was right; it is all quiet. I tiptoe over to her desk, there is nothing on the top of it but that isn't unusual for Alisha, she like me, is obsessively neat. I open the top drawer gently and it's empty; I open the second, third – empty. I open the fourth and find a lone memory stick rattling around in the otherwise empty drawer. I pocket it and move over to the filing cabinet.

All the drawers are empty, not a single file. This filing cabinet has either been emptied or it was just for show and has always been empty. Is it all a show? Was I her only patient? Is she even a fucking therapist? Anger bubbles in my chest like a boiling pot about to simmer over, I hear movement upstairs and my face flushes with angry heat. I should leave now while I can still go undetected but I hesitate, taking the photo from inside my jacket pocket and flattening it out. My feet move lightly toward the stairs; the carpet is luxury thick and bouncing under my feet and it ensures my footsteps are completely silent.

I climb the stairs with a heavy, pounding heart and when I reach the top, I see the second floor for the first time. It is a big space, warmly lit with modern decoration in white and gloss red. Along the left wall a luxurious white queen-sized bed, to the right a red curved sofa. Straight ahead I see the doors that open on to the small courtyard and there she is standing, looking at me, dumbstruck, I close the gap between us, striding towards her.

"Mac…"

"You lied to me!" I yell, holding up the photo.

She runs towards me, her eyes wide with pure terror and it rocks the anger out of me. For a moment, my anger dissipates, the only thing I care about is why she looks so scared and how I can make it stop.

"Mac… You have to go; baby, you have to go right now! They are coming for you! Now! Go!" she shrieks.

I am confused, my brain still stuck on the image of her terror-filled eyes and I am too slow to comprehend the meaning of her words. I hear a loud bang and my insides turn to ice as I begin to understand.

They are coming.

"Mac, they are watching the office… Run! Run!" she screams.

I drop the photo as I hear footsteps pounding up the stairs. I launch into a run towards the double doors and I slide them open, bursting into the courtyard. I can hear them behind me, panic surging in my chest; there is nothing I can do but jump but my insides cringe, it is a fair drop down, and I falter. The hesitation cost me, fear of jumping had me pause for the briefest of seconds and I hear an ear-splitting crack, followed by a blood-curdling scream.

I feel the impact of a hard blow hit my shoulder, knocking the wind out of me and throwing my tumble down to the ground completely off course. I land badly and my knee twists at a painful angle, yet somehow, I push myself up. The pain is blinding and I stumble out of the garden as quickly as my leg will allow. Everything feels like it's moving around me in slow motion as I cry out, begging my body to move faster.

Adrenalin fuels me, I make it to the car and fall in. I lunge forwards to slot the key in the ignition and pain ignites in my shoulder. Looking down in horror, I gasp fearfully as I see a bullet wound flowing with warm, vivid crimson blood. I pull away, wheels spinning against the ground in reaction to me slamming on the accelerator pedal. I drive, twist and turn randomly, putting as much distance and direction confusion between me and any pursuers as possible. I drive and drive until I am forced to pull over, my head swimming as my body tries to black out.

What do I do?! Fuck! I don't know how to fix a bullet wound! Think Goddamn it, think! There is nowhere to turn. I can't go to the hospital, I would be discovered immediately. I can't go to the warehouse; I will just bleed to death. Think, Mac, think. Who can I trust? Where can I go? My mind races. I have to go somewhere to get help, somewhere no one would look for me.

My fingers jab the release button and the glove box opens. I pull out a box of tampons, the 'just in case' stash that I always hide there. My jaw clenches as I take one, unwrap it and then I scream as I ram it into the bullet wound. The pain is unbelievable, it darkens my vision, my head slumps forward and I hit it on the steering wheel jolting myself awake again. Tears blur my already warped vision and I wipe them away roughly. Now is not the time to lose it, I need to move before it becomes impossible to.

There is only one place I can go.

***

I skid to a screech, stopping practically metres outside his front door and I see it open, he peers out of it and in my direction; relief floods my chest. My body is shaking and I feel cold and hot all at once, I open the car door, car engine still running and fall out on the ground, pain searing in my shoulder.

I made it… Ouch, there's the floor.

I hear heavy footsteps coming towards me fast, Alfred skids to a stop at my side and kneels down beside me.

"Mac! What happened?" he asks urgently and then his eyes widen as they fall upon the bullet wound.

"Had nowhere else… to go. They are after me… Again. You need to hide the car, don't call the police, please – they will find me." I struggle, my mouth feels so dry and tired.

"It's okay, kid, I got you," he reassures me. "Savannah!!" he bellows. "Come quick!"

I feel the floor disappear beneath me as Alfred lifts me off the ground swiftly, the movement makes my head spin with nausea; he carries me towards the house, my head slopping as I slip in and out of darkness.

"Mac!? Oh my God what has…?" Savannah gasps.

"Savannah, drive her car into the barn out of sight, then fetch my bag and bring it to the house… Hurry," Alfred directs.

As my head swims in and out of consciousness, I lose all bearings on where I am. I hear a jarring crash of pots and pans hitting the floor and I am laid down gently on a hard wooden surface. Pain rouses me and I recoil; my eyes open and they squint to adjust to the strange surroundings, I am laying on a dining table in a country cottage type kitchen.

"Here's your bag. Has she been shot?!" Savannah's gravel voice screeching up in pitch. "We need to call for help, Pa, she could die."

"No, we can't. Whoever took her tried to give it a second go. We call for help, they will find her. I have dealt with enough bullet wounds in my time, I can sort this," Alfred assures.

That is confusing, my mind is too foggy to work out why that was a weird thing to say. I wince as feel my body lift and my jacket is peeled off. I shudder, I feel cold to the bone.

"The good news is, the bullet hasn't hit anything vital, the bad news it is still in there. I have to try get it out before I can stop the bleeding. Savannah you are going to have to hold her down, it is going to hurt like hell but if she moves it will hurt much more," Alfred orders grimly.

I feel a warm hand hold my uninjured shoulder and pressure across my gut as Savannah leans across me, holding me down with her weight; even in this much pain I cringe at the closeness of being touched.

"No, no, I can't…" I utter in a panic and Savannah pulls back, looking at me with concerned, soft eyes.

"Hey, it's just me. You are safe," Savannah coos.

I squint to clear the fuzz in my vision and my eyes find her powerfully emerald green eyes, glinting back at me.

"Anna?" I croak.

"Yeah, it's me. I am just going to hold you still, alright. The quicker you stop fighting and let me, the quicker Pa can help you."

My eyes flicker over Anna's shoulder, everything is fuzzy but I can just about make out Alfred's giant frame, his expression is calm and unphased.

"I am sorry, Alfred," I mumble.

"It is alright, kid. You are going to be okay but listen, I have to take the bullet out and it is going to hurt. You need to let Savannah hold you down, can you do that for me?"

I groan, taking some deep breaths and I nod. Savannah leans back over me, holding me in place. For a moment, I panic at her touch and then suddenly being touched is the last thing on my mind. Alfred doesn't hesitate, the pain comes quickly. I told myself I wouldn't scream but there is no way for me not to; I bolt and cringe away from him and hands push me down. The pain is all-consuming, like a red-hot poker being rammed into my open wound. I scream and scream then everything goes blissfully black.

***

Is this a painful dream, or an excruciating reality? I don't know anymore; I only know it hurts either way. My mind is a chaos of disturbed images, I see Alisha's face, fear in her wide eyes and her mouth shouting silent words. I run and I jump and the bullet hits but I never hit the ground, I just keep falling and falling deeper into darkness. A swooping sensation swirling in my stomach like I am on the world's largest swing.

The light is blinding, my eyes can't adjust. The outline of two dark figures looms over me; my arms ache, I try to move them but they are suspended up above my head by chains. I try to scream but I am gagged by wood, the taste of salty blood filling my mouth. Icy cold foul-smelling liquid is thrown at me from a bucket. My eyes finally focus in time to see the cattle prod drawing nearer to my naked chest. My muscles contort, my nerve endings scream and my jaw clamps down as the electricity pulses through me.

I am screaming… Screaming…

My eyes open, the scream still bursting shrilly from my mouth.

My mind splinters with disorientation and I feel like I have been hit by a truck. Slowly I sit up, the pain in my shoulder throbs but is bearable. I am covered in a sheen of sweat, the bedsheets are wet. There is a glass of water on the bedside table and some tablets that I swallow down without even caring what they are. My shoulder is bandaged up and the bandage is soaked in my sweat. When I peel the damp sheets off myself, I find that my jeans have gone, my knee is swollen and is forming colourful bruises and there are grazes down my other leg that have been cleaned and neatly dressed.

My eyes survey the unfamiliar scene that I've awoken to; I am in a bedroom that is dimly lit and musky smelling. It is decorated with dated wooden furniture, there is a dresser with old peeling stickers on the fronts of the drawers and some teddy bears sat on top along with my jeans that are folded tidily. On the wall, mounted in dusty sun-bleached frames are some very old photos of a young Alfred, dressed in military camouflage and holding a rifle. Next to that is a box frame proudly displaying medals with ribbons of different colours.

Well that is the first thing that has made sense to me all day.

Standing up gingerly, I wobble on the spot, I feel weak and I can't weight-bear on the swollen knee; there is no way I can get my jeans back on. Ah well, I think all my dignity has flown out the window at this point anyway, I am wearing women's boxers so I am pretty well covered. I hop and hobble my way to the door, there is no quiet way to do this and I cringe, it must be the middle of the night. I hear movement coming up the stairs, the door opens and Anna smiles at me with a yawn.

"Hey, let me give you a hand," she offers.

"It's okay, I can do it."

"You are going to hop all the way down the stairs, are you?" she asks with sarcasm and an arched eyebrow.

"Okay, you raise a good point."

Savannah hooks my good arm around her shoulder and holds on to my waist, my chest tightens fearfully at the contact but I really have no choice but to let her help me. It takes some time and some pain but I get down in one piece and I am soon sat at the kitchen table, feeling rather awkward and out of place.

"Where is Alfred?"

"He's asleep. We were going to take it in shifts watching over you but turns out, you woke up before my first shift ended. It's 3am, I am meant to wake him at 4am," she explains.

Guilt pangs at my chest; I feel so bad for getting them involved, I know I didn't really have anywhere else to go but now I have made them a target. If anyone finds out I am here, they will both be in danger. I lean my elbow on the table and rest my face in my palm and sigh.

"I am so sorry, Anna." I speak without looking up, rubbing my eyes to get the sleep out of them.

"I'm sorry I held you down while my pa ripped a bullet out your shoulder," she replies and I look up to see her face mock wincing.

"Ow, don't make me laugh, it hurts," I gripe, giggling.

"I have to say I know we had fun having coffee the other day but I didn't expect to see you so soon, is my company really that awesome?" Anna asks playfully.

She is probing. I mean, she is doing it carefully, but she is still probing. I am not sure how much I should tell her; trust isn't something I can afford anymore; I smile but I don't answer.

"Mac, what's going on?"

"You are safer not knowing."

"That's a cop out, you just don't want to tell me. Haven't I earnt just a little bit of your trust?" Anna presses.

She has got me there; they have taken care of me. They could have called the police or taken me to the hospital but they haven't because I asked them not to. They already know I am in trouble; I blow in with a gunshot wound, it's obvious someone is after me and yet they hid me anyway.

"The people that made me go poof, they never really let me go, they have been watching me the whole time," I croak.

"And Europe?"

"Cover story, I told everyone that to keep people safe. I laid a false trail to give myself time to establish my hideout."

"You have a secret hideout? Oh my God… Are you Batwoman?" Anna giggles.

I have to laugh; she makes talking easy. It's like she knows exactly when to tell a joke to relax me, before pressing a hard question, then she puts me at ease with another joke. It is effective and a little unnerving.

"If I was, I probably wouldn't have got shot."

"Eh, you would have; you just don't have a bulletproof bat suit to keep you safe," she muses.

"I will get right on that."

I smile and that is something that I didn't think would be possible right now. My heart hurts worst of all; so much has happened, I haven't had time to process it but now isn't the time. I feel at breaking point and I really don't want to break down, not here.

"So, what is your plan?"

"Do you mind if I go lay down? I am feeling a little woozy," I divert.

Okay so I lied, the truth is I don't feel like I want to divulge anymore and I don't have the energy or the brain power to think through what I should or shouldn't say. Anna leads me toward the stairs and my head swims.

"You got a sofa or anything?" I groan.

"Yeah in the living room right behind you, why?"

"I am guessing I was put in your bed, why don't you go and get some rest and I will crash here?"

"Mac, I am fine with the sofa, besides, Pa said to keep an eye on you."

"Seriously? What do you think I am going to do? Do a runner? Anyway, I don't think I have it in me to get back up those stairs right now."

"Yes, that is exactly what I think you would do, given the chance but you are right, I don't think you are going anywhere. I've got your jeans upstairs, what a spectacle you would make if you tried." She winks and then helps me to the sofa, before disappearing off to bed.

She is right, the thought had crossed my mind but I really have no chance of going anywhere till I can walk, or even limp. I lay back looking at the ceiling, my mind falling back to Alisha. She told me to run, she didn't turn the porch light on so she didn't set me up, as such. No matter how you spin it though, she betrayed me. She has done nothing but lie to me from the start.

Why would she do this? I don't know what is real anymore, I never really got the chance to know if we could be more, I never had a chance to process but I know I wanted to find out. Was it all an act? A way of manipulating me? If so, to what end? That is what hurts; I trusted her, I let her in, I let her know the parts of myself that I didn't even want to know myself. Tears well up in my eyes, the lump rises in my throat and I swallow it down, I refuse to cry over her anymore.

The conflict between being hurt and being thankful is painful. I have no doubt that without her shouting at me to run, without those few seconds she gave me, I would be dead or taken. Did she put herself at risk to save me? Is she in trouble now? No matter how hurt I am, I don't want any harm to come to her. I am not going to understand, even if she were to explain herself, how could I ever believe another word she says? No, I have to find a way to let it go. To swallow it down to some dark place where it will eventually stop tormenting me, only then can I hope to move forward with my plan.

My plan, what a joke. I look down at my shoulder and chuckle darkly to myself. At least I will remember how I got this scar. What am I going to do now? My car is a liability to me now, I can't walk, which means I am stuck here till I can and that puts Anna and Alfred at risk. I could recover at the warehouse; I would prefer it but that means telling them where it is so they can take me there and how the hell would I get up and down those steps on my own?

They have given me no reason to distrust them but after last night, I don't ever want to trust anyone again. They are going to want answers; I told Anna as little as I could get away with and to be honest, probably nothing much that she couldn't have surmised on her own given the circumstances. How long before they push me for more and what am I going to tell them when they do?

***

The salty aroma of bacon activates my stomach-growling hunger. I feel like I only closed my eyes for a second and when I opened them, Alfred was in the kitchen cooking. I hobble to my feet and I notice that a single crutch has been left leant against the wall. I take it and clamp it under my armpit and it definitely makes getting around easier. I hop with a wobble to the kitchen table and take a seat, the smell of bacon and coffee filling the air.

"Morning, kid, are you fit for some brecky?" Alfred grumbles lightly.

"Morning, yes please, it smells amazing."

Alfred serves up bacon sandwiches with coffee and takes a seat at the table with me; he has a calming and chilled out presence and yet I couldn't feel more awkward sat opposite him.

"Don't stand on ceremony here, kid, you must be hungry – dig in. There is more if you want it."

I laugh a slightly embarrassed chuckle. "Thank you, I am starved."

I don't need to be told twice and I do in fact have seconds. I feel so much better for it, the dizzy spin in my head subsides. Alfred's home has a warm feel to it; the inside of his home is in complete contrast to the outside piles of his scrap. He waits till I stop eating before he asks me any questions.

"Alright now, why don't you tell me what is going on?"

I decide to tell him exactly what I told Anna, nothing more, nothing less but I suspect that it won't be enough for him.

"I am guessing you never really expected them to think you were in Europe," he grunts.

"No, I just needed the time to set up my hideout."

Alfred nods thoughtfully, his brow furrowed. He really is a sweet man, the guilt I feel for exposing him and Anna to this hell is immeasurable.

"Alfred, I really don't know how I'll ever thank you for what you did for me, you saved me, there is no two ways about it." I look down, unable to meet his eyes. "I am sorry that I brought you into this. I need to go as soon as I can, the longer I am here the more danger I put you both in and I can't have that."

He is quiet for the longest time and eventually I can't help looking up to see his face, hoping that he isn't mad at me, it would be deserved.

"Firstly, I am not the only person that saved you, you did too. Tampon in the bullet wound – that was smart, I could have used that trick back in the day." He chuckles. "Secondly, you don't need to be sorry, kid, you will stay as long as you want or at least till you get your strength back."

"I appreciate everything you have done but I need to get away from here, fella. I am not putting you and Anna at any more risk than—"

"And what about the risk to you?" He cuts me off bluntly.

"There is risk to me whatever I do and I can handle it as long as I am not putting anyone else in the line of fire and right now, I am. I can't live with that."

I rub my temples; frustration is starting to build, not at Alfred but at myself. This sweet and caring man would do anything he could to help anyone, he is just that kind, a gentleman. I couldn't be more grateful to him, that doesn't mean I have to let him help me. That doesn't mean I have to let him get himself killed.

"You can't do this on your own, kid. I'm a soldier, well trained and well prepared and I didn't survive war alone," Alfred argues, his voice somehow gruff and soft at the same time.

That just fills me with confidence and sunshine, ugh.

He has a point, I know I am in way over my head, I don't need anyone to tell me that but there is no choice for me anymore. I chose to fight and clearly the people that hunt me are now all too aware I am fighting back. I've stirred the hornets' nest and they won't stop coming for me now, I just know it. This is a war but it is my war and I will not allow it to cause collateral damage.

"I don't have any choice, Alfred."

"Actually, you do."

I groan. I don't want to argue with him but I don't know how to make him see, instead I say nothing because my mind is too exhausted to fight back. I hear footsteps coming down the stairs and I am relieved as Anna walks in. Alfred sits back in his chair, stretching his back while I sit with my head in my hands.

"Oo, intense. What have I walked into?" Anna asks brightly.

"Not a lot, Mac here was just refusing my help," he jibes playfully.

"Of course, she is."

Relief dispelled.

"Oh, you two are just a family of funny, aren't you?" I joke and the kitchen erupts in laughter, melting away the tension and ending the debate. Something tells me though; this conversation is far from over.

I spend the day not doing a lot, I'm not really able to do much. My shoulder throbs hotly and my knee is still swollen stiff and growing more and more colourful. Anna gave me a pair of her PJ bottoms and a clean t-shirt so I feel a little bit more human. I am desperate for a shower but with my bandages covering a nasty wound in my shoulder, it is too soon to get it wet.

Alfred popped out with 'off to get supplies' and was out the door in a flash and Anna is busy preparing dinner. Outside, I am sitting on a stack of logs in front of a fire pit. The long fields of farmland that surround me are beautiful and make me feel like I am in the middle of nowhere; it is so peaceful here and it feels good to be outside. I really need to figure out what my next move is before I get too comfortable.

The truth is I like it here, it will be hard to leave the warmth, the safety and the laughs to return to the solitude of the cold warehouse. Hard but necessary, I will leave as soon as my injuries allow. First, I need another car, I've donated mine to Alfred, it is useless to me now and I know Alfred could use the parts for his sculptures; his eyes lit up like it was Christmas when I offered it to him. What couldn't be used has been burnt in the fire pit and quite frankly it's nice to see the thing burn. I cringed a little when he yanked the front seat out and I saw for myself how much blood I had lost. Yes… Burn. It felt a little like watching my mistakes turn to ash.

My eyes are hypnotised by the flames dancing with each other, like watching nature's TV. It is calming and the warmth is making my eyes droop with heavy tiredness. When Anna joins me by the fire, she comes and sits by me and I yawn out my greeting.

"How are you doing, Mac?"

"Me? I am fine. All cool in the ball pool. Why?"

"Because you got shot by some creepy psychopaths that are hunting you and you don't seem to have blinked since."

"Ah well, that happened yesterday, I've slept since then," I deflect.

"Not much by the look of it. Why don't you go for a lay down?"

"I don't want to move; I like it here – it's warm and the fire fascinates me," I say thoughtfully and she chuckles.

We both stare into the fire for a while with no words, the crackles and the fizzes of the fire are the only sounds. I used to be a Scout, I love the outdoors and I would spend countless hours by the fire, chatting with friends and singing campfire songs. I preferred to sleep without a tent under the canopy of stars, watching the orangey white embers float against the inky sky. I used to call them fireflies, that was always my happy place. I wonder if this is Anna's happy place too.

"Anna, why do you stay with Alfred? I mean, I know you don't live here full time. Where are your parents?"

"How do you know that?"

"Because I've slept in your bedroom, I get the feeling if you lived here then there would be more of… you, around the room. There is a dresser in there that has stickers on it, but they aren't old enough to be from either of your parents, I can only guess they are yours which means you probably stayed here a lot as a kid," I explain.

"You are very observant, I get the feeling you live inside your head a lot, most people wouldn't have noticed that."

I wait. I can tell that she isn't done talking and I am happy staying quiet, I am not one of those people that feels the need to talk to fill the dead air, I guess I do live in my head a lot but, doesn't everyone?

"My nan and granddad brought me up mostly. My mum and dad died in a car accident when I was 3, I've been with them ever since. I don't live here; I have my own place, I come and stay with him every so often, more so now Nan has gone. We lost her 2 years ago," Anna explains, her voice even. I look up at her and she smiles warmly and I am kind of amazed at her strength.

"Wow, that's… heavy. I'm sorry Anna, sounds really rough."

"It could have been but they made it easier, I was lucky to have them."

I look up at Alfred's sculpture. "Blessed Mess." The angel looking down us, glorious and beautiful and my heart aches for him a little.

"Mac, can I ask you a favour?"

"Sure."

"You don't have to tell us everything you have been through, you don't have to let us in but please, hear us out. If you still don't want our help afterwards then we will stop pushing, I promise. All I ask is you hear us out. You have nothing to lose by doing that and even better, it will shut me up."

"You should have led with that," I joke, throwing her an impish grin.

"Hey!" she pouts and she shoves me playfully, her laugh animated and bright.

"That sounds… fair. Just, don't get your hopes up, okay." I struggle and she laughs at my difficulty to admit defeat.

"Thank you, Mac, and don't worry – completely hopeless, pinkie swear!" Anna vows and she holds her little finger out to me expectantly.

"What is that?" I frown.

"Oh my God, where did you grow up? Under a rock?"

"I'm just playing with you, girl," I jibe, holding my little finger out.

"You are such a goof." She tugs my little finger in hers.

"I would be more concerned over the fact you still pinkie swear in your early thirties, than how goofy I am."

We laughed, I laughed… So hard it hurt. The farm, the fire, the laughs. It was almost enough to forget everything I still have to do.

Almost.

CHAPTER FOUR

Revelations

Oh my God, that feels good! My skin tingles in delight, my muscles loosen and I moan in pleasure. Hot shower... Water running over my bruised and bloodied skin. I have waited so long for this. I wash the crusty blood out of my hair and the water is rinsing out brown, yuck! Alfred returned from his supply run with the awesome gift of new bandages and duct tape. He covered my bandage in tape and sealed the edges to my skin as tight as a drum; the man's a freaking genius.

He also returned with some new clothes for me. I asked him how he knew my size as he handed me a pair of skinny jeans and his reply was simply, "I have lived with a wife, daughter and a granddaughter – it pays to learn this stuff, believe me, kid. Plus, it says right there on the label – skinny."

After the most blissful shower, I put on the new pair of skinny black jeans and a navy blue and black plaid shirt. Totally not my thing but I am so grateful for clothes that are clean and new. Anna and Alfred wear plaid shirts a lot, it's like a thing if you live on a farm, apparently. I feel more human than I could have hoped for, I am even able to put some weight on my leg. Progress that couldn't have come too soon.

When I get out of the shower and head downstairs (bum shuffling down the stairs is the new way to travel), I realise that there is no one in the house, then I look out the kitchen window and I feel my stomach tighten. They are both sat down by the fire pit, damn it. They want to talk; I just know it and I really couldn't want to less.

I have been here for five days now; I am so grateful to them both but it is time to get moving. My bullet wound is healing well and more importantly, there is a memory stick burning a hole in my pocket. I could have asked Anna if I could use her laptop to open it but I didn't want the questions and honestly, I am scared of what I will find. There is of course, a chance it's nothing at all but the fact that it might be something, is enough to drive me crazy. It weighs on me heavily, like a constant painful prod.

Ugh. A promise is a promise.

I hobble down toward the fire pit. It is getting a lot easier to move around now; with the aid of the crutch and being able to shift a little weight onto the bad knee, I am moving a lot faster. It's getting dark now and I am grateful for the fire light to guide me. My wet hair is making me shudder in the night chill. I spot Anna first, her gaze sweeping over me with a curious grin.

"What?"

"Suits you," she replies, blushing slightly. I am not sure if she is joking or not.

"I fit in with you farmer folk now," I reply, sticking my tongue out.

Anna and Alfred are sitting in camp chairs and they left me one; in the drink holder is an icy cold bottle of Budweiser. Hmm, Dutch courage? What am I in for?

"You have beer fairies, Alfred?" I ask, twisting off the cap.

"Who you calling a fairy?"

We sit in a sort of triangle facing each other around the fire; their faces are lit up in the dark by fire light. There is an intensity in the air, a tension. I drink my beer and brace myself in anticipation.

"I see you're walking better, kid; I am guessing you are going to want to be off soon," Alfred grumbles in his slightly farmer-accented twang.

"Yeah guys, look, um. I don't think either of you will ever understand how grateful I am to you both; you saved my arse, there is no denying that. More than that though, you welcomed me into your home and I will admit it will be hard for me to leave but, I have to."

"We know that, Mac. We were never going to try persuade you to stay, it is obvious that you have a job to do and no one and nothing is going to stop you and we don't think anyone should try," Anna states and my head shoots in her direction, I am momentarily surprised, but suspicion soon follows and I narrow my eyes.

"Okay, so where's the catch?"

"There is no catch, no one is stopping you from leaving. I do, however, think you should accept some help and before you protest, you promised that you would listen," Anna reminds me, her eyebrow raised. I mock locking my mouth and throwing away the key.

"Look, kid. I am not going to mince me words here, okay. I have too much respect for you to pussy foot around you," Alfred grunts.

"I didn't know that you knew how to pussy foot around, fella," I wink, "but go ahead, I can take it, I am not that delicate."

"Exactly. You are not that delicate, you are a tough cookie, you are smart and you have good instincts. I have no doubt you have what it takes to bring down the ghosts that are hunting you. What I doubt, is whether you know how."

I go to speak but he holds his hand up and I respectfully keep my mouth shut.

"What I am offering is to show you how. I could train you; I am not offering to protect you; I am offering to teach you how to protect yourself. I am not offering to fight this war for you, I am offering to give you the tools you need to win. I understand all too well the fire that burns in your belly, kid. I recognise the look in your eyes, I've seen it in the eyes of my brothers that fought next to me. The look of someone who is using their pain to drive them and that's okay, pain is a strong motivator but if you aren't taught how to drive it, you are going to get yourself killed and then who brings these fuckers down? You want them to pay, then make them pay, kid, but live – to enjoy the victory dance."

I am sure I look as gawped as I feel; my head is buzzing with an overwhelming clash of squabbling thoughts. I feel exposed, like a child who just had their blanket ripped off of them in the night. I feel so embarrassingly weak. I thought I was better at hiding my emotions than this, the dress-down rattles me and tells me that I am clearly not.

Plus… Is. He. Insane?

"Mac, are you okay?" Anna asks and I jump, my head snapping back to reality and I meet her questioning gaze.

"Yeah… Sorry. You're really okay with what he wants to do? You know I have a gigantic freaking target on my back, right? Either of you gets caught tied to me then you are a target too."

"You are kidding me; he lives for this stuff. There is no way I could stop him, as for me, isn't it my decision whether I get involved and therefore my responsibility if I get hurt? Plus, no offence but, I think you could really use my help with tech," Anna says proudly, showing off.

I look to Alfred for help. Surely, he will at least back me up about Anna.

"Give me more credit than that kid. I am an S.A.S. soldier, you think I don't know how to be covert; my whole damn life was covert, I was in the business of secrets. As for Savannah, she is right. She can do things with computers that blow an old man's mind. Plus, I can protect her and with my training, so can you, there is strength in numbers."

"You two are infuriating!" I blurt, annoyed but laughing incredulously. "Okay, so I will humour you for a while, let's just pretend I lost my mind and said yes. What exactly is it that you plan to do? Seeing as you seem to have all of this figured out."

Alfred leans forwards in his chair. Resting his elbows on his knees, his expression transforms from light amusement to intensely sober in the matter of a second and I tense up as I meet his no-nonsense, focused gaze.

"I plan to put you through the hardest training there is and believe me, kid, it is punishing. The failure rate of Special Forces training is sky high, it is the elite but if you can take it, you will be formidable. You will think differently, move differently, you will be able to assess every danger before it even happens and extinguish every danger as it happens. You will be able to squash fear and doubt. I will teach you everything I know about covert operations, hand-to-hand combat, weapons training, surveillance techniques, infiltration, evasion and survival. In short, I will make you a weapon and while I am kicking your butt into shape, Savannah will help you run down the leads and sift through all the information as we track the bastards down."

My jaw drops, my mind is blown. I was so sure, so utterly convinced that there was nothing that either of them could say that could even begin to sway me from my chosen course. I was so unbelievably wrong; I am tempted. Damn it! Can I really let this happen? No? I am annoyed at myself because there is no way I can say honestly, that I would ever have a better chance of ending this hell, without him. How irritating, he's like a modern-day Mr freakin' Miyagi.

"Why are you doing this, Alfred?"

"Because, kid, I believe you have got what it takes, because I never leave a man behind and because you remind me of someone I used to know." He pauses, looking up at his sculpture. "My sweet Victoria, my blessed mess," he says finally.

"My mum," Anna chimes, her voice small.

So, I was wrong, the sculpture isn't of his wife but his daughter. I shouldn't be surprised; I have been wrong about a lot lately.

"What do you say, kid?"

I look into both of their faces; faces I've come to know very well so quickly. Anna, holding my gaze with intense but kind eyes. Alfred, with handsome lined face and calm smile and I realise that in the short time I have been here, they have come to mean a lot to me. My friends, sincere and supportive friends who came out of nowhere and I feel blessed that they did.

"You mind if I take a minute?"

"Go for it, kid, take all the time you need," Alfred grumbles with a nod.

I saunter off into the darkness with a limp and a bowed head. Goosebumps pop on my skin as I leave the fire's warmth but I am enjoying the chill, I find it calming. I walk till I reach the barrier fence and I lean casually against it, staring into nothingness. It is so quiet, I can't even hear a single car, which is usually nice but the peace and quiet is making the hum of my thoughts even louder.

If this offer would have come from people I didn't really know or care for, I probably would have taken it by now but these farm folks have gotten under my skin and now I feel responsible for them. They could get hurt, they could get killed and it would be my fault and that is what is stopping me. How do I cope with that knowledge? Can I do this on my own? The gunshot wound has certainly shaken my confidence; being so wrong about Alisha has shook me to the core. I don't know who is a threat anymore and I don't trust my own judgement. In the silence I hear a tiny crack of a twig and I know that she is behind me, she comes over to the fence and leans on it in symmetry with me.

"What is holding you back, Mac? I could see it in your eyes back there, you were going to say yes but something is stopping you."

"Now who is the observant one?"

She doesn't answer me. That's one of the great things about Anna, she doesn't mind the quiet either and she doesn't push me when I retreat to it, she waits patiently for me to regroup and advance when I am ready.

"I can't bear it if anything happens to you guys," I admit, my voice strained and with my head hung down.

She turns to me and looks into my eyes with such fierce determination it is impossible for me to look away; she really does have the most incredible eyes I have ever seen, so powerfully green and expressive. I haven't known her very long but already feel I can read her emotions though her eyes, she displays them so honestly.

"You ever stop to think that maybe we feel the same about you?"

For that I have no answer, it is hard for me to view myself as anything other than an annoyance and a burden at the moment but I can see on her face, she means it and I smile warmly, before I have to look away.

"Let's head back," I manage eventually.

Back at the fire I walk straight over to the case of Budweiser, take a bottle, sit back down and chug it till the bottle runs empty and I hear Alfred chuckle.

"I am choosing to read that as a good sign," he grunts.

"Bring on the hurt, I am in."

"Good answer, kid, let's all have a beer. Tomorrow, we plan," Alfred announces.

***

My body jolts and judders in the aftermath of being rudely awaken by another nightmare and it is far too early. My eyes are heavy but fear is icily trickling down the back of my neck and I really don't want to close them again. I've had this nightmare twice already; I wish that once I got a memory that it would stop haunting my nightmares. If it is going to keep me up half the night then at least show me something new. I sit up on the sofa and rub the sleep out of my eyes.

The old grandfather clock clicks loudly from across the living room and I groan, just gone 5am. On the coffee table lays the memory stick that I stole from Alisha's desk. It is becoming a compulsion, I keep it in my pocket all day, feeling for the lump of it in the pocket in my jeans to make sure it is still there. Then at night, I put it on the coffee table till morning when I put it back in my pocket again. Ugh… It isn't healthy; the sooner I check out what is on there, the better.

Heading into the kitchen I start to make some coffee, even the smell makes me feel better about life. I can't help but wonder how today is going to go, at this point though, I figure there is no point trying to guess. I thought I knew how the conversation last night was going to go and I was well and truly wrong. Is there really any point in trying to predict anything anymore?

I take the memory stick out of my pocket and turn it over in my hands, it is the only real lead I have, what if it amounts to nothing? What else do I have to go on? Nightmares and scars, in other words, a whole lot of nothing. I can't help but wish I had gotten more time to question Alisha, she knew enough to warn me so she must know more and now the anger has calmed down I can't help but worry, is she in trouble for warning me?

No, that would be pointless, I am less angry, but not more stupid.

Questioning her would be meaningless because I could never know for sure that she was telling me the truth, she is a dead end, she is an unreliable source and… a traitor, but God – I hope that she is safe. I hear movement upstairs, what the hell? Then footsteps slowly trudging down the stairs, too light to be Alfred's.

"What are you doing up?" I ask Anna.

"You shouting in your sleep woke me up," she utters, yawning, and I cringe.

"Sorry, I guess that means I should make you coffee."

"Yes, you should, but not because you had a bad dream, that's hardly in your control. Make me coffee because I am considered possibly dangerous without it."

Chuckling, I get to work making her a coffee; when I turn to sit back down, she is holding the memory stick in her hands, frowning at it.

"What's this?" she asks and she sips her coffee, passes the memory stick back to me and I stow it straight back into my pocket.

"I don't know."

"You don't know what it is and yet I have seen it go in and out your pocket a million times," she points out, her expression sceptical.

I am not sure how to answer that, I don't know if I am ready to go into the whole Alisha thing, I haven't even got my head around it. I am not so angry anymore but it still hurts just as much when I think of her, the problem is we said we were going to plan today and it really is the only possible evidence I have.

"You don't have to tell me, Mac. It's okay."

"No, it's okay, if we are going to do this, I can't really not tell you, it's just still a bit… It sucks."

Anna waits while I try to find the words, I rub my thumb up and down the smooth arch of the mug handle, nerves tingling in my stomach. I don't like showing pain as it makes me feel weak, just like Alisha said and I cringe at my own thoughts. My eyes close as I attempt to clear the pain of the memory away, I feel Anna's hand gently take mine and I jump, whipping my hand away.

"Sorry, you just… You looked upset and I wasn't thinking and…"

"It's okay. Honestly, you did nothing wrong, girl; I am just not good at…" I falter, I am definitely not ready for that conversation, suddenly explaining the memory card seems a piece of cake in comparison.

"The memory card, I found out someone I trusted was actually working for whoever is after me. I guess I don't know that for sure, I suspect she was. I decided I would go to her office, break in and look for anything that might give me a lead. I found it, it's all I did find before I found out they were watching her office. That's when I got shot. I don't know what is on it, I haven't looked. It could be nothing, it could be something, I don't know," I explain robotically, shrugging my shoulders.

"Who was she?"

"My therapist but, it turns out she knew me before I was taken, but I forgot in the memory loss and she neglected to enlighten me," I say, my tone resentful.

"How did you find out, that you knew her before?"

I tell Anna her about the photos that came from the very SD cards that she passed off to me when we met at The Shard. About why I was sifting through them. Anna doesn't have a poker face at all, she wears emotion and I can't help but marvel at that a little. I spend so much time trying to hide mine, or trying to understand someone else's that to see her emotions play out on her face, so open and freely displayed is a little fascinating to me.

"I found her in the pictures and the pictures triggered memories of us," I conclude.

"What were the memories? Anything helpful?"

"Not really, we were in a hotel room… Together."

"Wow… That's… Oh. And she acted like she didn't know you this whole time?" Anna asks, her tone aghast.

I just nod, I actually feel okay, I thought it would be harder to talk about but then, I haven't really given her much detail. It feels more clinical, clip noted, like I have distance from the conversation.

"No wonder you have trust issues," she says, winking, and I laugh. It is good to joke about it and Anna has an easy way of making light at just the time when I need it.

"You still care about her a lot though," she points out.

"What makes you say that?"

"It is in your eyes, Mac. Sure, you don't want to, I can see that too but it is never that easy to let someone go that has meant something to you no matter how much they have broken you."

"Yeah… Um, breakfast?"

It is all getting a bit too close to the bone so I get up and fix us some French toast. When I was a Scout, we used to call it eggy bread. It is about the extent of my culinary expertise; I can, however, cook just about anything over an open fire. I miss those days, being outside so much and always with a fire nearby, I always felt most myself when everything was peeled back to its simplest and rawest form. No mobile phones or games consoles. Just the outdoors and playing games, hiking and abseiling and goofing around with friends.

Maybe that is part of the reason I like it here so much; it reminds me of those times. Only it's a farm and people are actually trying to kill me but hey, you have to take the good with the bad.

"This is yum, I've never had eggy bread before."

"It's good you are impressed; this is about as good as it gets with me in the kitchen. I pretty much survive on noodles and pizza at the hideout, it's a miracle I don't starve with how bad I am at cooking," I joke.

Soon everyone is up and ready and we all sit around the kitchen table; I am nervous but also a little excited because I am getting itchy feet and I need things to start moving again. I need to feel like I am moving forward, as much as I've enjoyed my time at the farm it feels like I am stuck in slow motion.

"So, what's first, boss?" Alfred asks.

"You are asking me?"

"Well I am in charge of your training, but I'm not in charge of this operation, you are. There is a lot you are not quite well enough for; I have other less physical things I want to run through with you but I want to know if there is anything you want to do before we get started."

I think about that, it is nice that he is handing over control to me, it makes me feel like I can push the momentum which as of yet has been at a standstill.

"I would like to go buy a new car, my knee should be okay to drive now and I will need it so I can come backwards and forwards between here and my hide out, but first I will need my wallet, it has my fake ID and bank card. So… I need to go to my hideout." I speak while winking at Anna.

"Oo! We are going to the bat cave!" she squeals, her excited reaction as I expected.

"Okay, kids. Saddle up!"

***

It feels so good to be out in the world, I was slowly becoming convinced it disappeared while I was away. Seeing it again makes me feel kind of more alive again, it reminds me what I am fighting for. A normal life, freedom, peace, a chance to be Mac again. When we pull up outside the warehouse and I click the key fob to open the loading door, Alfred drives the Land Rover into darkness. Everyone exits the car blindly and I go straight for the light lever; with a loud clank and a flicker, the warehouse lights up brightly.

"Wow! This is way cooler than a bat cave!" Anna exclaims in awe.

We all walk to the back end of the warehouse together, I let them explore and I go up to the second level to grab some clothes, my camera, laptop and my wallet. It takes me a while to get up there, my knee is much better but that is still a lot of stairs. Bum shuffling back down the stairs was much faster and less painful. When I get back downstairs, I can't see Alfred and Anna is standing analysing my spider chart wall.

As I move to join her, I cringe realising all the pictures of all my scars are up on the wall. The urge to rip them all off of the wall is powerful but I resist, it would only give me more to be embarrassed about. My heart sinks with a painful thud as I see the picture of Alisha and I in the lift; I take a step closer to it, calmly un-pin it from the wall and I look at it. It hurts, but it has served its purpose, it doesn't need to be up there anymore.

"Where is Alfred?"

Anna turns to me; she looks at me intently for too long and then blinks and smiles warmly. I can't really understand the look in her eyes and I look away because I don't want to. She has been looking at the horror that is evident all over the wall, a mirror into the ugliness of my true reflection, whatever she is thinking I am probably better off not knowing.

"He said he was checking out your CCTV, he said something about a blind spot."

Of course, he is. I've noticed a change in him, the moment I agreed to accept their help he has been more upbeat and playful. Anna was right, he really does live for this stuff.

"I brought something for you. Can I use your laptop?" Anna asks.

"Umm, sure."

Anna takes a seat at my desk and puts a blank CD into the disk drive, she moves through simultaneous screens and programs at speed and I can safely say even though I have no idea what she is doing, I am impressed.

"Whatcha' doing, girl?"

"And… I am done, I just installed cloaking software onto your laptop, it basically makes you as invisible as you can get. I also added a password, seriously Mac – no password?!" she groans, rolling her eyes. "Lastly, I added an auto wipe program. If someone enters the password wrong three times, your laptop will wipe everything from the hard drive."

"Okay, I see what Alfred was talking about. That is impressive, you're a super nerd, how do you know how to do this stuff?" I gawp.

"Well I could tell you, but then I would have to kill you."

"Ah well, you will have to get in line. So, what is the password?" I ask and she smirks, stifling her laughter.

"Anna is awesome, all one word and in lower-case letters. You know, in case you need reminding." She grins gleefully as her voice grows bubbly.

Alfred reappears looking very pleased with himself after lifting my CCTV cameras higher and angling the direction down, giving me a wider pan of shot both out the front and back.

"I have to admit, kid, I am impressed. I can add some more security for you but for the most part, the complex seems to have done that for you."

"That's why I picked it," I say quite proudly, puffing out my chest.

"Could use a woman's touch," Anna chimes in.

"There are fairy lights, what more do you want from me?"

***

The hunt for my new car has begun and it is unanimously decided that we drive out of town a bit further as an extra precaution and so that we can grab some lunch out on the way back somewhere I'm less likely to be recognised. This has me a little nervous, it wasn't so long ago I was chased and shot by baddies unknown. It feels odd to be out in the open but I need to push through that fear eventually, it may as well be now. At the used car garage there is lot of choice; I liked my Tiguan and I am still a bit sore about it, now I am here I really don't know what to get.

"What about this?" Alfred points to a Land Rover Discovery, his eyes lighting up.

"Farmer Giles wants me to get a Land Rover – that is not at all predictable."

I roam around the lot hoping something will call out to me. I miss my truck so bad; I like old cars, they have so much more character but they are not always so reliable. A sales woman approaches me and I stiffen a little; the last time I bought a car using my fake driving licence, the wait for the salesman to return after photocopying it almost had me hyperventilating. I really need to chill out, if anything, my constant nerves and the beads of sweat forming on my brow make me look more suspicious than anything.

"Hey there, can I help you at all?"

The sales woman was dressed in a starchy white blouse that was unbuttoned riskily and tight-fitting grey suit trousers, her name badge reads Sadie, she was one of those 'obviously pretty' girls that used to give me hell at school for being different.

"Hey Sadie, um… I'm not sure, can you?"

"I'm pretty sure I can." She smiles and twirls her hair round her fingers. I am pleasantly surprised at her obvious flirtation but then, isn't that a part of good salesmanship?

"Let me ask you, if you could have any car what would it be?" she asks, looking me up and down with leery eyes and zero subtlety.

"A 1965 Ford F100 pickup, hands down."

"Classic, I wish we had something that sexy here, we do have a Ford Ranger Pickup on the lot, if you fancy a look around? It is powerful, very reliable and…" Sadie leans into me, a little too close, making me tense a little, her eyes focused on my lips. "I am pretty sure I can offer you a great deal on it."

Someone is working off of commission.

"Let's do it."

After Sadie finishes showing me all the car's features, she offers me the time to think it over and respectfully walks off far enough to be out of earshot but close enough that she can still be seen.

"What do you guys think?"

"I think someone wants to take you for a test drive," Alfred says, his words oozing with innuendo.

"Yeah, she was really subtle," Anna snipes.

"Thanks, super helpful, guys."

I call Sadie over and she does in fact offer me a test drive, which I politely decline and decide just to buy it on the spot because I am a sucker for a truck.

"It was a pleasure doing business with you, Alexa. If you have any questions at all – please do call me, anytime," Sadie utters, handing over her card. The deliberate way in which she unnecessarily touches my hand while giving me the card makes me think, I may just call her.

Probably a bad idea.

The truck is indeed powerful and a joy to drive. I follow behind Alfred's Land Rover till we reach a little restaurant off the motorway. I was hoping it would be further away as I was really enjoying the drive, not only because of the new truck but also it feels superb to have the freedom of movement and independence back that having a car provides. I have to admit though, I am hungry.

The restaurant is styled like a 60s American diner, the walls are shamelessly brashly decorated in loud glossy red and turquoise with a black and white checked floor pattern. Everywhere I look there is something retro; there is a jukebox at the other end of the diner and pictures and vinyl records of rock and roll legends are littered over the walls. We find a little booth at the very back in the most discreet area, all take a seat and make our orders off the menu. The place has a nice atmosphere and my mouth is watering at the idea of a bacon cheeseburger and fries.

"So, what is the next move, kid?"

"Well, I am guessing that Anna told you about the memory stick?"

"Nope, what memory stick?"

"I don't tell him everything you know, Mac," Anna jabs with a little edge to her voice.

I explain to Alfred just as I did to Anna and as I look over to her, she doesn't really acknowledge me. I get the feeling I've done something wrong but this isn't the time to try to figure out what.

"So, I have been avoiding it, but when we get back, I will open it and if there is anything useful, we will go from there. There is a chance it's just some holiday photos or something and if that is the case, I don't have any other leads at the moment."

"It sounds like it could be promising and you must think so too or you would have looked at it by now," Alfred points out.

"True."

We eat in silence; the burger is amazing. I try very hard not to wolf it down too enthusiastically, but I fail miserably. We leave the diner and I make my way towards the truck, all too eager to take her for another drive.

"Savannah, would you mind if you caught a ride home with Mac? I need to see a man about a dog," Alfred asks.

In the truck we buckle up and get moving; there was an awkward atmosphere and my sense that I have done something wrong is strongly amplified.

"Is everything okay, girl?" I ask hesitantly.

"Yeah, sorry, I don't mean to be snappy, I am just tired."

"I know what you mean."

Somehow, I get the feeling that she isn't telling me the truth but I am not going to push it. It is not like I am the patron saint of honesty when it comes to talking about things that are eating at me. Plus, I did wake her at an ungodly hour with my bad dreams, she has earnt the right to be pissy at me today. We drive in quiet but the bad atmosphere is gone; it seems like we both have a lot on our minds. When we pull up at the farm, I suddenly wish the drive had been longer. I feel for the hard plastic bulge of the memory stick in my pocket, my mouth dries and my tummy flutters with anticipation.

Upon entering the house, I make my way to the living room and fire up my laptop. It prompts for a password and I can't help but giggle a little as I type 'Anna is awesome'. I take out the memory stick and put it on the coffee table next to the laptop, Anna walks in with a cup of coffee and places it next to the laptop.

"I will give you some privacy," she says, respectfully walking out of the room.

I click the memory stick into the USB slot and wait for it to open. When the window appears it shows twelve video files. My stomach lurches as I see the date stamps for each file, all recorded during the second year that I was missing. My instincts scream at me not to open them, my hand shakes as I move the cursor over one of the videos, hovering.

Don't be a coward.

With a double click, I watch as the screen fills with the backdrop of a dimly lit room. The walls are dirty and wooden, red rusting metal bars support the structure of the wood panelling. The room is sloping and curved; ropes are hung up in large bounds on the walls. There are a few small round windows giving off very little light and a lightbulb hanging from wire that is rocking from side to side softly.

In the centre of the room, strung up with hands bound by chains to the metal of the ceiling cross-braced bar is a woman with her head hung down, hair dirty and thick sways from beneath a black hood that covers her head and face. The rings around her wrists are bloody and raw, the woman is wearing a t-shirt and shorts so ripped and soiled it looks like the clothes will fall off her bony body at any moment.

I tense up, not sure if I can go through seeing anymore. I have an urge to high tail and run but I grit my teeth, steel myself and grip the seat of the sofa, white knuckled. A man comes into the frame, he is heavy set, very tan skin, wearing dark jeans, boots, a black t-shirt and a brown leather jacket. His loud footfall on a wooden floor echoes and the woman in the hood begins to stir and cringe. The man laughs deeply in reaction and pulls off her hood. Her head still hung down, he grabs her by the hair and yanks her head upwards revealing her gaunt and bruised face.

Revealing my face…

My insides revolt and turn to ice, my skin burns with a painful prickly heat as though someone poured hot water down my back and instantly panic grips me with an iron claw. My head begins to swim and the colours in my vision to blur as the living room melts away.

The memory swirls.

"Rise and shine, mala suka!" the man spits while holding me by the throat. He lets me go and slaps me across the face with the back of his hand and I yelp at the shocking sting of it. Then I feel the spray of his spit on my face, my nose fills with the loathsome scent of stale alcohol and sweat, my mouth salty and metallic with blood.

I close my eyes but the image won't go away.

The screen, the memory.

Her blood, my blood.

Her pain, my pain. It's not a video anymore.

The man reaches for a small wooden boat paddle and swings it down hard against my ribcage.

She cries out, I cry out.

Thwack, thwack, thwack.

Her pain is my pain.

"What is your name?"

Thwack.

"What is your name, mala suka!?"

"Mac! My name is Mac!" I gasp, my voice in the present in sync with the video.

The man growls in frustration and throws a bucket of water over me. The ammonia burns my nose and it is suffocating. Not water – my own piss and it is burning every open wound, I'm choking, gasping, my eyes streaming with the tears of pain.

"Mac? Mac are you… Mac!" *Anna calls but she must be miles away, everyone is miles away, I am alone, I have been alone for so long.*

He rips open my shirt and holds the cattle prod against my abdomen, ramming the point deep in and almost drawing blood. White hot pain courses through my body, my body jolts in bursts of violent tremors and I scream; the pain is so acute, so horribly real.

Jab, jab, jab.

Her screams are my screams. Her agony is my agony.

"Mac!" Anna yells, grabbing my tear-streaked face and then… I see her.

How is she here? I am hallucinating again. Why does she look so scared?

"What is your full name?!" the man spits.

"McKenna Scott," I *choke.*

I scream as my body turns rigid, electricity invading my system once again, my body convulsing violently. Every muscle taught and at breaking point, I scream but nothing comes out.

She can't breathe, I can't breathe.

"*Maaac!*" Anna screams, grabbing my hands and holding them on her face. "It's okay, you're here, your safe, it's over. You're here, it's Anna, look at me!" Anna shouts.

This is not a hallucination; I can feel her face, I can feel her smooth cheeks under my fingertips. My wrists, they are not chained, they were chained, I am sure of it. They're holding her face so they can't be chained? Am I here? Or am I there? He is here and so is she.

"Are you real?" I gasp through strangled breath.

"I am real, Mac, look at me – see… I am here, you are here, this is real, you are home," she soothes and my breathing begins to slow.

"Don't let me go, I am not all the way back. Ugh, God please make it stop," I plead.

I am more scared than I have ever been in my life or maybe, just more scared than I can remember being; holding onto her face feels like the only thing keeping me in the present.

"I've got you, just keep focusing on me. It will stop, it will stop," she reassures but the concern on her face tells me she's trying to reassure herself as well as me.

We don't move, we sit on the sofa facing each other, my hands gently holding Anna's face and her hands laid on top of mine. I am scared that if I let go of her face, I will fall back into that room. It feels like an eternity, but soon the realisation that is not going to happen again starts to hit. I realise that it was some of my memory returning and that it is past and not present and my hands slowly drop from her face. I feel so completely dismantled, my chest aching with a heavy sadness and then shame and embarrassment start to take me over.

"I'm sorry," I mumble and stand up but Anna grabs at my wrist and pulls me back down to the sofa.

"Where the hell do you think you are going?!"

"I… I have to go, I have to leave, I will come back but I have to go, I will drive and I will come back but I need you to let me go, please," I stammer, tripping over myself.

"No! For heaven's sake, do you really think you are safe to drive right now?"

"I will walk, okay. Please, I have to go," I choke robotically.

I try to walk away but Anna stops me again and I am losing patience. I just need some time alone and then I will be okay, why doesn't she understand? The panic is rising and I feel trapped.

"Mac, look at me."

"I can't. Please let me go, I am freaking out, if you just let me…"

"No… Stop running away, stop pushing me away, let it go. Stop ramming it all back in and let it out," Anna demands.

Memories of Alisha spark across my vision and the pain rocks me, taking hold of me. Her hand on my face, calming me. *"Mac, you are safe… Say it."* Alisha's voice vibrates in my mind with painful clarity, the lump in my throat rises and my vision blurs from the tears. Anna grabs me putting her arms around me and I fight, trying to pull away, I don't like this, I feel trapped.

"Let me go! Anna! Let…" I shout.

"No… I have got you, Mac, don't run anymore. Don't let it hold you hostage anymore, it is all inside you right now, tearing you up. Let it go, don't swallow it down. The longer you do, the more of your life they are stealing from you. Don't let them win, Mac, take your life back right now, let it all go."

"I… can't…" I whimper.

The lump in my throat screams for relief, Anna pulls me tighter and forces herself within my eyeline, her eyes lock on mine, powerful, warm and pained.

"You can, because you are safe with me. I have got you; I promise," she coos sadly.

My body loses its fight before my mind does; first my arms that were up at her chest pushing her away, fall down into my lap. Then my face finds its way to the crook of her neck and I hide there as grief washes over me. Shame pulverises my heart and I break; the sobs begin to drown me and I am powerless to stop them, she pulls me into her and holds me tighter and it is jarring how easily I break now that I am finally being held, after all this time.

I cry so much more than I ever thought it was possible to cry, my mind a blur of painful memories. The disappearance, returning, people staring, the hospital, seeing my scars for the first time, the memory loss, rehab, recovery, Nicole, saying goodbye to Mum, the isolation, first night alone at the warehouse, the bad dreams, the memories coming back, Alisha's betrayal, getting shot, Alfred ripping the bullet out of me, the memory stick. Pound, pound, pound on my useless, hollow heart. Each blow more painful than the next.

***

At some point it must have stopped because the next thing I know I am slowly becoming aware that I've been asleep. I can feel fingertips gently running through my hair and as good as it feels, I also feel panic and I can't quite make sense of where I am. I hear hushed voices and keep my eyes closed; I don't want to face reality yet.

"How long has she been asleep?" Alfred whispers.

"I don't know, a few hours."

"I can probably carry her upstairs without waking her, if you want to move."

So, I am still on the sofa, by the feel of it my head is in Anna's lap, half on her legs half on her tummy with her arm cradled around my head, her free hand playing with my hair. From this angle she can probably see right up my nose but that is lowest on my list of reasons why I am embarrassed right now.

"No, I'm alright here," Anna declines.

"Thought you might say that."

"If you would have seen…" Anna hesitates and I internally cringe. "She can sleep on me as long as she needs."

"She finally broke, I was starting to think she never would. Tough kid, that. Don't worry, Savannah, she's going to be okay; I can help her now."

"Where have you been? You've been gone ages, Pa."

"I've been getting all the gear I need to train her. I'm ready and now soon, she will be too," Alfred grumbles, then I hear his heavy footfall stomp further away as he leaves the room and I open my eyes.

"Hey…" My voice is hoarse and gravelly.

"Hey, you. Are you awake?" Anna asks softly.

"I think so, have there been false alarms?"

"Kind of, you were talking in your sleep and I kept thinking you were awake."

"I will add that the list of things to be mortified about. Ouch… I will try move in a minute, just my arms are dead and I need them to help me up," I explain groggily and she giggles.

My arms are somehow wrapped around her hips and my hands wedged between the small of her back and the sofa. How does that happen? I don't even remember how I got here.

"Here. Let me help," Anna offers, helping me into an upright position and I sway a little, woozy and light headed.

"Wow. Here, drink this, it will help."

I take Anna's coffee with shaky hands and drink it and it does help, almost instantly. I am so horribly embarrassed that I don't even want to look at her. I go to speak but she literally blurts, "Nope!" interrupting me and I look at her with a confused frown.

"No, I will not accept any word, relating to or directly speaking of, the word sorry," she teases and I snort.

"How did you guess?"

"You have a bad habit of apologising for things that don't need apologies."

I have nothing to say to that, my brain still not with the land of the living. I look away, staring into the coffee cup. I am as embarrassed as I am grateful.

"Thank you, for trusting me, Mac."

"Oh, like you gave me any choice, girl," I tease. "No, seriously, I must have been scary – thank you for not running away, for being there and for not letting me run away either. I am more than a little bit embarrassed but I guess it was bound to happen, eventually," I admit.

"You are not as scary as you think," Anna says softly.

"I don't know about that but I do know that things are probably going to be different from now on."

"Why is that?" Anna asks.

"Because… I think I know why I was taken."

CHAPTER FIVE

Faster, Harder, Stronger

"I… hate… you…" I gasp.

"That all you got, kid?! Come on. Move your arse!"

I've been running these drills with Alfred twice a day, once in the day time and once at night. The quickest I've been able to complete the circuit is 22 minutes flat, 25 in the dark. Alfred wants that time cut in half; there isn't an inch of me that doesn't ache. Alfred constructed an assault course designed to increase my fitness and enable me to move across any terrain with speed and accuracy by increasing my balance, strength and coordination and I have affectionately named it 'the doom dash'.

The doom dash starts with a huge tractor tyre that I have to flip over and over for about 15 metres until I hit the obstacle walls. First a six-foot rope-climb wall, followed by a ten-foot cargo net wall. The next section is a set of 3 balance beams, all different heights with different thickness of bar tread. Then a 15-metre crawl under cargo net, followed by a heavy log run through a course of tyres. Then a tug of war using a rope attached to more logs that I have to pull towards me, hand over hand. A long slog through hip-deep dirty brook water follows and that leads on to some makeshift beams that I have to traverse under and over. Lastly, a series of platforms made from scaffolding; the first has a ladder up to 20 feet, then I have to jump across to the next three from 15 foot to 10 foot to 5 foot and then jump and land on the finish line and if I miss the finish line, I land in a child's paddling pool full of icy water.

In the four weeks since this training started, I have rammed so much information into my brain that I feel like an overloaded laptop about to fizzle out and crash. Alfred was right though, I am starting to think differently; the man is a wealth of knowledge and I am keen to soak up anything he can teach me. He pushes me hard and there are moments I want to scream at him but so far, I have managed to supress that particular urge.

My favourite thing by far has been weapons training and it turns out that I am actually quite good at it. Alfred has been training me using the C8 carbine assault rifle and Browning pistol, both are standard SAS weapons. I started out practicing shooting at some stationary targets but very quickly moved on to moving targets. Alfred hung some sand bags from the ceiling of the barn and sent them swinging and it didn't take me long to master it. Alfred is now working on a course for me to attempt with moving targets to hit while I am on the run.

Today after the 6am start of my regular morning run at the doom dash, I have a meeting planned with a Staff Sergeant that Alfred trained. I was apprehensive about it; I can't help but think the less people that know about me the better. Alfred assured me that he doesn't know details and he is just going to train me in hand-to-hand combat, as per his request, and he will keep his mouth shut. I trust Alfred but I don't trust people I don't know; hell, I don't even trust half the people that I do know.

The first meet with him today is just after lunch but training will be at the warehouse after that too, I've been spending a lot more time there and now sleep there almost every night. It was a little weird at first but I am so used to having my own space that it soon became a good feeling. Plus, it has given me the time alone to try to process the memories that I got back after watching the video. I know now that although it felt like a lot, there are still massive gaping holes in my memory and so far, those pieces are eluding me.

I walk over to the fire pit, it is a good place to dry off after being soaked and beaten up by the doom dash, I think Alfred must know it is my favourite place to be as he keeps the fire burning 24/7 now. I take a seat in my usual camp chair and assess the damage, the assault course comes with its injuries, usually just cuts and bruises to my shins and elbows. It is a process, the faster I go the clumsier I am. I get used to the speed and become more accurate as I cross the course, so I speed up and make mistakes again and mistakes mean injuries.

"You shaved 3 minutes off your personal best, kid," slapping me on my back.

"Yeah... Feels like I did, I am knackered."

"Bah... Good meal and a rest and you will be right as rain. You are going to need to keep your strength up, can't see Billy going easy on you."

It didn't take me long to realise that wearing as little clothes as possible on the doom dash is the best thing. It's cold and my lips are usually purple by the end but as I get soaked and muddy, my clothes just become a dead weight slowing me down. So, when I finish the warmth of the fire is always welcome. Today though, it is just a little bit cosy and is making me sleepy. I yawn and stretch out, loosening all my tight muscles.

"Think I may need a pound of coffee before he arrives. Prepare myself for the ass whooping," I mumble sleepily.

"You'll do fine, kid. Just rest up for now."

Alfred leaves and I stay at the fire; that man has pushed me hard. I still remember vividly the first time he *really* shouted at me. He is always so gentle and calm, it was a shock to the system to see him switch into action man Alf so easily. We were at the first week of training, my knee was still a bit dodgy and my shoulder was still very raw and he had me chopping wood. Seemed simple enough at first but I tired quickly, if anything I think he was more trying to ease me into the reality of him being my trainer, than actually training me. He pushed and pushed and eventually I dropped the axe, pain burning in my shoulder.

"I… can't," I panted, out of breath and wincing in pain.

"Pick up the axe, kid, I know you have ten more reps in you."

"Seriously? I just did like 30, fella," I whined.

"Carry on and I will make it 20," Alfred barked.

I picked up the axe, swung it and brought it down onto the log. The axe felt so heavy and I know it shouldn't have, I was just still weak from the injuries I had. I lifted it and swung it back again and brought it back down on the log but this time upon hitting it, I dropped it, weakness over taking me.

"I can't, I am beat."

"Yes, you can, pick it up! Now! Stop thinking about all the reasons why you can't do it and think of the one reason you can. *Move!*" he hollered.

In that moment I have to admit I wanted punch him a little, I am sure my face said it all, every fibre of my being wanted to walk off right there and then, but I didn't. No one wants to be defeated by an axe and a lump of wood and I do hate looking weak.

"I wouldn't push if I didn't know you could do it, now come on; you can do this. Ten…!" Alfred encouraged.

He screamed the count down from ten reps and when I hit zero, I fell to the floor and laughed so hard. I realised, that I had convinced myself that I couldn't do that simple task, it was my self-doubt holding me back like a debilitating invisible hand tugging on my t-shirt. The more that Alfred pushes me, the more I realise how much more I am capable of taking.

The sound of a car engine catches my attention and I look over. Anna is back, pulling in and parking next to my truck. I haven't seen as much of her since I got some of my memories back, I have been busy training and staying back at the warehouse and she has been back at work. To be honest I've been kind of glad; she broke down barriers that day that I never intended to be broken. I don't know how I would have gotten through that without her, but it is hard to let someone that close. I close my eyes, heavy under exhaustion and my mind wanders back to that day.

***

"…You know why you were taken…?" Anna asks.

"I mean, it is hazy. There are still gaping holes, the memories don't join up smoothly or completely connect. When I remembered Alisha, it all kind of connected together and the memory felt like mine, like it had always been there. This hasn't done that, it is still only pieces, mixed up, but yeah, I think I do."

"I… Wow, Mac. Are you okay?" Anna asks, shock evident on her face.

"I don't have time not to be, we are in more trouble than I thought. Will you grab Alfred?" I ask, rubbing my temples. "I don't think I have it in me to explain this twice," I admit, my voice still hoarse from sleep.

"You don't have to do this now; you have been through hell today and—"

"I'm okay, Anna, I will grab a coffee though."

I look at their faces sitting across from me from the dining room table, patient but expectant enough that I feel pressure. I stand up and pace slowly as I speak; it is easier to talk this way, not looking at them, not really looking at anything. My eyes wide as I watch it all unfold in my mind, the words coming out quickly.

"I was taken from home, after that photoshoot where I met Alisha, we spent those five days together at the hotel and we never left. On the sixth day I walked home, I stepped into my flat and someone put something on my face, over my mouth and nose and everything went black. When I came to, I was in the dark in that room on the video. I think, I was always in that room. I must have tried to escape a thousand times in that first year and I nearly managed it once but then I learned it was pointless, I am not a strong swimmer," I ramble and then I see Alfred and Anna wearing matching faces of confusion.

"They kept me on a boat, below deck. I am guessing it was a large fishing trawler. It always stank of fish and I could feel the constant sway of the current and hear the water swell pounding across the boat. I think I was wrong; I don't think they intended the memory loss at all. They would inject me with some stuff and everything would go all bent out of shape and slow and then they would ask me questions and I would struggle to think, let alone answer questions."

"Sounds like truth serum," Alfred announces.

"Sorry, what?"

"Sodium pentothal. It is a drug that people used for interrogation back in the day, it doesn't actually make you tell the truth. It slows down the messages going to your brain making it harder to perform tasks, even moving your arms or walking is hard because it slows the ability to think. There is no real proof it will prevent you lying, just that it is harder to lie if you can't think," Alfred illuminates.

"Yeah, that sounds familiar."

"What kind of questions did they ask you, kid?"

I close my eyes trying to focus, everything still feels so messy in my head. The memory jumps like trying to watch a scratched DVD. It isn't a consistent thing; I am sure there is more that I am missing, a lot more. It is frustrating, like that feeling you get when you are trying to remember the name of the song stuck in your head – only much worse and it never goes away.

"They asked me about my movements, places I would go day to day. They would want details, stupid tiny little details, it all seemed so random at first. Then they started showing me pictures of men, mostly one man. He looked vaguely familiar at the time but I thought that could just be that they showed me his picture so much that he *became* familiar. Then, I came to realise all the questioning – it was all about finding that man. They thought I knew him and soon they realised I didn't."

"Do you know the man now?" Anna asks softly.

"To be honest, I can't remember the picture, I just remember that I didn't know his face at the time. The trouble is they would withhold sleep and food, they would drug me, put the hood on me for days at a time and I would get disorientated and messed up and I wasn't sure what was real anymore. I am not sure what to believe of my own garbled thoughts, I mean – I would be relieved by hallucinations that sometimes came because I at least had escape for a while then. My thoughts can't really be trusted, I don't know how reliable any of this is."

I am trying to ignore Anna's face, the wincing and sadness. I pace – trying to make sense of the mashup of images rotating too fast around my disordered head; there is too much missing, I know there is and it is enough to drive me insane.

"At some point the questions stopped because they weren't getting anything out of me. The beatings got more… intense, as they grew more frustrated with me. I was sure they were going to kill me; I was a loose end that could potentially expose them. They left me for days without out coming in, that part is definitely hazy. When they came back instead of killing me, they set up a video camera.

"The films were made for someone, that I am sure of. In the one I watched they kept asking me what my name was but they knew my name, they wanted me to say it for whoever the videos were made for. I don't know what use videos of me being tortured would be, except to hurt someone close to me or use as leverage for ransom but no one ever made contact, there was no ransom demand."

My insides clench at the knowledge that Alisha had these videos all along, she saw everything. Am I just hoping they weren't made for her because the very thought of that is more torture than I endured over that two-year period?

Probably.

"Alisha was supposed to be trying to help me remember and she was trying but she had these videos all along. Why? If she works for these people, does that mean they want me to remember?" I speak, more to myself than Alfred and Anna.

"There are only twelve videos, kid. You were gone for over two years, this is good progress but there are bound to be holes, it is starting to come back to you, I am sure it all will in the end," Alfred soothes.

"I think I was taken because they thought I knew the man in the picture. Whoever he is, he is the key to everything. So then that means I must be connected to him in some way. Otherwise – why me? They let me go, why? Killing me would have been a lot safer. Unless they hoped it would draw him out or that I would go looking for him in search of answers and lead them to him."

"There is something in that," Anna interjects. "Do you remember them letting you go?"

"Not clearly. I just remember being told to get out of the van. I don't know, maybe I am wrong, like I said, my thoughts can't be altogether trusted. There is still so much missing. Whoever that man is, he must have done something pretty bad to spur these people on to take such measures to find him and I am stuck between the two – somehow. Whatever this all is, I have a feeling it is much bigger than just me. I can't explain it, I just know. Something bad is coming."

"Well, boss, I will bet on your instincts. So that being said, what do you want to do about it?" Alfred asks.

"I want you to train the hell out of me, I want to be ready. Then I want to find this man and the people on the boat that took me and I want to end this. I think the first move has to be the videos; I need them analysing frame by frame. They may have made a mistake, left some kind of clue. If there was a way to find out what boat I was kept on it would be a good lead but I don't think I can watch them," I admit.

I look to Anna; she is the tech girl after all – she holds my gaze then looks away. That stung a bit, I am not even sure why so I shake it off.

"I can look through them. Watching videos isn't past my technical ability, besides, I know what to look for."

"Thanks, Alfred."

***

I hear the crunch of footfall on breaking twigs coming up behind me and I jump back to the present. I must have dozed off in front of the fire.

"Sorry, didn't mean to wake you," Anna apologises as she takes her usual seat.

"Nah, you didn't, girl. I was just inspecting my eyelids for holes. You know, just in case," I reply with a wink and she giggles.

"You are such a goof."

"It's one of my more endearing qualities, I am glad you noticed," I tease and she gets up and grabs me, taking me by surprise and poking me in the ribs with her fingertips.

"I-have-noticed-nothing-of-the-sort!" she emphasises with her jabs.

I am so ticklish that my legs start flailing around and I try to grab her hands to stop her and she straddles me, pinning my hands under her knees and then tickles me more for good measure.

"Stop, stop! Do you want me to wet myself or what?" I manage between the laughing and then she stops; we are howling so much that she accidentally headbutts me.

"Oww," I whine and she rubs my forehead, laughing.

All of a sudden, I am all too aware that she is sat on top of me, her hand still rubbing my head and her face so close that I get a little lost looking into her eyes for just the quickest moment. A feeling flows through me as she looks back at me, a feeling I am not used to.

"Kids! Lunch time!!" Alfred bellows, his voice somehow carrying across the farm.

"We should…"

"Yeah, before we get grounded," Anna chuckles.

I feel a little shaken. Anna is aware that I can't cope with being touched and she is usually careful to respect that. As we walk back towards the house I realise, for the first time, I didn't completely freak out at being touched. For some reason, the fact that it didn't completely wig me out has me feeling off balance. Alfred has made a good spread; he is a feeder at the best of times but this is something else. Bacon, eggs, freshly baked bread, hash browns, baked beans, chopped tomatoes and black pudding. My mouth is watering.

"Wow, that was some spread, fella. Thank you."

"Ah well, I figured you have earned a good meal. Besides, you are going to need your strength, kid."

I am not sure if he is trying to make me nervous or what. I guess I am a little bit, more of the unknown than anything but to be honest I am keener than anything to get started. From what Alfred has told me Billy is a good fighter. Alfred did a spell working as an instructor and trained Billy for two years; I am not sure what I was expecting when he arrived but it wasn't this. Billy has typical boyish good looks, his dirty blond hair is styled in a purposeful mess, he is muscular but not over the top and he has a posh, boarding school type English accent.

"Billy! It's great to see you. How is life treating you?" Alfred extends his hand and they shake enthusiastically.

"Alf, old boy! I can't complain. How about yourself?" Billy asks, his tone polite; he is one of those people that oozes confidence.

"Aye, less of the old, you! I am good thanks, son. This is my granddaughter, Savannah, and this here is Mac."

Billy shakes my hand politely and then Anna's. He seems a nice enough guy and I am ready to get to work. Anna and Alfred sit by the fire pretending not to watch, they are not so subtle. Billy starts off with some simple sparring to get me warmed up, I put on boxing gloves and get started.

"This is not your first time," he grunts through gritted teeth, while blocking my hits with the sparring pads.

"I don't really know much; I watched some online videos to use with a punch bag just to build up my strength," I explain while feeling a little foolish.

"Ah well, it seems to be working, you have some power behind that right hook especially but I can give you more."

Billy demonstrates how I can gain power from pivoting on my hips and I am pleased when it works; the next thing he teaches me are some blocks. He shows me first while going to hit me in slow motion while I practice three simple blocks over and over and gaining speed each time.

"I have to say, Mac, you pick up things very quickly, carry on like this and you will make my job a lot easier," he compliments.

I am actually feeling pretty awesome, we run through some disarming techniques using his unloaded hand gun, then once I get the hang of that he shows me a move to put him on the floor while disarming him. I am finding this more difficult because it means being touched. The anxiety is provoking me to move to hesitantly, making it impossible to use the momentum to throw him over my shoulder.

"Don't worry about hurting me, I am a fairly big guy – you aren't going to put me on the floor if you are tentative about it," he encourages.

"Right."

"Now, give it some welly, girl!" Billy mocks.

He points the gun at me but this time I move fast. I side step, grab his wrist and twist his arm round hard while I turn my back and bend forward. Billy goes flying over my shoulder and hits the floor hard with a grunt. I grab the gun and point it at him with a grin. Cheers erupt from the fire pit and I blush. I hold my hand out and pull Billy back up to his feet.

"Well alright then. Now we can really get down to business!" he commends.

I am having fun, my body hurts but I don't want to stop, I am laughing and learning and I just want to soak up more and more. Billy is a good teacher; we run though some defence moves with Billy attacking me from both in front and behind. Poor guy must be more tired than me the amount he ended up on the floor. Tomorrow we will be stick fighting, covering a few different styles of martial arts and going hand to hand using a blunt stick in each hand, it takes focus and good coordination.

"Thanks, so much, Billy. I really appreciate the help and that was actually really fun."

"No worries, you are a pleasure to teach. You are able to mimic and memorise movements fast and that makes it much easier on me."

Billy and I go back over to the fire pit; it is getting cold and yet I am covered in a sheen of sweat and only wearing shorts and a tank top, the wind chill is making me shiver. Alfred is grinning and Anna is looking me up and down oddly. I probably look as gross as I feel.

"How did she go?" Alfred asks.

"Well, you were right, she's got some fight, that one, and she picks up technique very quickly."

We all sit and have a beer, laughing and joking, making small talk and I am feeling more positive than I have in what feels like forever. I get up to go and grab my hoody as the sweat is starting freeze icy cold to my skin.

"Back in a minute."

"I am going to be leaving shortly, Mac, but I will see you tomorrow for training at yours. Say 10am?"

"That works well for me, mate, look forward to it. Thanks again, Billy."

I head inside to grab my hoody and my rucksack while I am at it. I should probably be off soon too and it will save me going back for it. I see Anna's laptop on the dining table and I smile mischievously as I go over to the fridge, tear a piece of paper off the 'to do' list pad and grab the magnet marker pen. I scrawl 'Goof' with a smiley face and slip the paper inside Anna's laptop. I walk away smiling, satisfied with my efforts.

Strolling back down towards the fire and I notice that Alfred is off collecting firewood and Billy and Anna are standing talking. Anna is laughing, a hand on his forearm and then something twists in my gut uncomfortably. I quickly veer away from the fire pit and off towards Alfred.

"Hey fella, I am beat. Think I am just going to head home, call it a night," I lie.

"Can't say I blame you, kid. Will see you in the morning then." He claps me on the shoulder. "Oh, and well done for today, Mac."

Driving away in my truck, an ugly green monster is attempting to ruin my buzz. I am on the road before I know it, telling myself I am just looking forward to the hot shower and failing to lie to myself. That was a stupid overreaction, probably just the adrenalin. Yes, that's it, adrenalin can be responsible for a lot of unpleasant… overreactions.

Today was a good day, my aches and pains actually make me feel good, like I am accomplishing something. I crawl into bed, turn on my laptop and enter the password 'Anna is awesome' with a groan. I really should change that. I search through my media library trying to find a movie to put on; upon scrolling through my collection I eventually land on Face Off. Oh yes, definitely! Just what I need. I click it while I wait for it to load but I am asleep before the first scene plays.

***

It's still dark when I get back to the farm; I fell asleep too early therefore I am awake too early. My clothes are ruined from the constant mud and I am running out of anything clean to wear. I don't have a washing machine and rather than handwash them, I made an online order of new clothes and they can't arrive too soon. All I have left is a tiny pair of shorts and a sports bra type top, my scars are exposed and glowing purple in the night's chill making me thankful that it is too early for anyone to see me.

It's so quiet and peaceful, I stoke up the fire and throw some new logs on, the embers crackle and fizz, a sound I've come to love. I set off to work on the assault course, moving quicker and more efficiently on my feet. I manage the course three times before I stop for a break. It is perfect timing, as I take a seat at the fire and chug the water from my water bottle, I see the sun's orangey beams start to rise up in the darkness. It is really beautiful, the sky glows glittery blue and pearlescent purple, my mind wanders back to a time when the only sky I saw was a tiny strip in the very top of a small round window.

Back then I would have given anything to see the sky again, to feel the wind on my face. Over two years without the sky. My instinct, my gut, my something – deep inside says that Alisha isn't responsible for this. Incomprehensible really, I have no reason to trust her but she warned me, her scared face is etched in my mind but so is the fact she had these videos. The to and fro is screwing with my rational thinking and making me feel lonelier than I ever have, no matter how many people I surround myself with.

I feel so angry, at her, at whoever took me, at whoever the man in the photograph is and even at myself for being so Goddamn weak. There is no real direction for my anger to point to, no certain culprit of blame, no true north to direct my rage at so, I just feel… rage. That rage forces me back up and onto to the assault course again, anger fuelling me like heated rocket fuel. I run just that little bit faster, I flip the tractor tyres harder, I am stronger. I end the course and

I turn on my heels and do it again, and again, taking out all my anger and frustration until eventually I jump one last time onto the finish line and drop to my knees, my legs exhausted.

"Looks like I am going to have to make this harder on you, kid."

I look up and Alfred is standing with a cup of coffee and some custard creams and I laugh, it seems so long since he greeted me this way, another lifetime ago. Now I know him better and I know the tougher side of him, this seems like such an odd gesture to me. I half expect him to bark at me, "Eat the biscuits now! Go, go, go!"

"You have incredible timing, fella," I say through panting breath, getting to my feet. "I didn't wake you, did I?"

"No, I am an early bird, you know that. Not as early as you though, apparently. Couldn't sleep?"

I sit by Alfred next to the fire; sipping on the dark, rich coffee is making me shiver. Morning has arrived and with it a misty dampness that clings to the air. I can't help but feel a little exposed, my scars out on display in the clear morning light but I am surprised that the urge to hide isn't dominating me quite as much as I expected.

"Nope, I figured I would make the most of being awake. I got itchy feet so I came here, thought I would run the circuit a few times."

"That was more than a few times, kid, I could see you out the window. You sure picked up some speed, almost like you were running from something," Alfred grunted, his tone softly accusatory.

"I guess I have a lot on my mind."

Alfred is quiet for a while; he seems a little awkward, which isn't like him. He is always so blunt and says exactly what's on his mind. He gets up and throws more logs on the fire but doesn't sit back down, instead he looks up at the statue, his dedication to his daughter.

"She was impulsive and headstrong, stubborn as they come. She had this way of embracing life, even the bad. She would jump straight in and ask questions later; she was my best friend and I see her in Savannah more every day," Alfred rambles thoughtfully in a way that makes me unsure if he is talking to me or himself.

"She sounds like an awesome person. Fearless."

"She sounds like you; she wasn't fearless, she just had a way of using fear, instead of letting it slow her down, it spurred her on."

"I think that is probably way too generous." I blush.

"Well you don't have to agree with me, kid," he grunts, sitting down again, "but I do have something for you."

Alfred reaches down the side of his chair and grabs for something, then he passes me that something wrapped in newspaper. I immediately feel a little uncomfortable, I never have been any good at receiving gifts. As the paper falls away it reveals a small metal figure; my breath catches in my chest as I see a replica of the blessed mess statue. So close to being identical, a lump rises in my throat, it is so perfect.

"Oh my God, I can't believe you did this. I don't know what to say." My voice cracking from the lump in my throat.

"You don't have to say anything, kid."

I lean back in my chair and then go to rest my head against Alfred's shoulder but stop at the last second. It is infuriating, the inability to show how you feel. I wish I could stop being like this, now more than ever.

"Thank you, Alfred. I know she was your best friend, but I think you might be mine."

I stare into the flames and I feel truly touched. Right in a moment when I felt alone, he made me realise that I am not, I haven't been for a while now. As I have already ran the circuit enough this morning Alfred runs through some evasion techniques with me. He teaches me some useful tricks like picking locks and laying a false trail on the run. Lots of things that I couldn't help but wonder, if they were ever going to be relevant but I soak it all up anyway, as always. I am blown away by his knowledge and I can't help but feel a little proud when I finally manage to pop open a lock with a pin.

Once I master a simple lock, Alfred handcuffs my hands behind my back and drops a hair pin in the palm of my hand. I drop the pin before I even get it anywhere near the lock but Alfred persists, picking it up and giving it back to me every time I drop it.

"You never run scared, kid, that is the important thing. If you face a danger that you know you cannot beat you don't run scared, you run smart. It is a deliberate thing; evasion is about avoiding detection. To be able to evade sticky situations successfully, it isn't about who can run faster or fight harder. It is about pre-planning for every possible outcome and that can be applied in both military and civilian life. If you already have a plan for when you are detected, then you know what to do when you are. It is about planning for every possible contingency, if there is a possibility that you may have to run, then have a plan for that eventuality and you are more likely to be able to successfully evade in any given situation."

I nod, listening intently while still picking away at the lock. I have very little confidence in being able to free myself but I keep trying regardless. Especially as he informs me that he is going to make some coffee and leaves me there. I wiggle the clip, trying to envisage the lock in my mind. When your hands are behind your back it's very easy to mix up which way you are supposed to be attempting to turn the lock.

"Oh, this is just too good to be true," Anna's voice calls from behind me. She comes into my view looking like the cat that got the cream and I raise an eyebrow.

"Whatever you are planning, girl – don't. It really wouldn't be fair to take advantage of me in such a compromising position," I warn playfully.

"Aw, but it would just be so easy, you really expect me to resist such a tempting opportunity?" she goads, laughing deviously. She's clearly enjoying messing with me, but I call her bluff.

"You know what, go for it, girl. What's the worst you can do? Torture me with tickles? Hah! I am shaking in my combat boots," I taunt her, confident that I will win.

"I would, but I don't want to be late for work," Anna said, forfeiting her position.

"A likely story," I tease smugly, very satisfied with the win.

"You disappeared in a hurry last light."

"Yeah… I was beat, decided to get an early night."

"A likely story." Anna repeats my own words against me, her face smug.

"And I thought you were going to be late for work."

"You'll keep," she says as she walks off. "You will probably still be stuck locked there when I get back."

"Ha-ha!" I bark sarcastically but I am starting to think she is probably right. I am clearly no Harry Houdini. I did eventually manage to get myself free, but I think it was more luck than anything. Alfred gave me the handcuffs to take back with me to practice while not wearing them. I decide to head back to the warehouse to shower the mud off me before my next training session with Billy.

***

I am not sure what made me do it, I was driving home and somehow, I ended up outside Alisha's house. Maybe I just want to see that she is okay, which annoys the crap out of me. Why should I care after everything? But I do, I can't shake the feeling that she might be in trouble for warning me. If she is not okay, then it's my fault. Isn't it?

I see a spot on the wall, more like a brown smudge really, I can't be sure from this distance hidden in my car, but I think it is my blood. My mind whirls with the memories of that night and the ache of betrayal twists deep in my chest again. I hate that she lied to me, I hate that I don't know why, I hate that I don't know if she is okay, but mostly, I hate that I can't stop caring if she is. My eyes fall on the for-sale sign post that is tacked to the wall and I can't help but feel a little lost. I remember what I was like at the start, when my sessions with her first began. I was a mess; I was hard work to get anything out of and in some cases, I was a bit of a dick.

The memory swirls.

"McKenna, I get that you don't want to talk about what happened to you. I understand how—"

"You know nothing about me. Don't pretend that you do," I snap, cutting her off.

"I am not pretending. By saying I understand, I mean that I can empathise with how hard it must be to talk about," Alisha replies patiently.

"Yeah well, I can't really talk about what I can't remember so, you may as well ask me about the weather."

"I am more interested in how life is for you now and how I can make it easier for you. You don't need to remember for that… Mac."

I look up at her, she never calls me Mac. The informality of it relaxes me for some reason and my hardened resolve melts a little.

"You are persistent aren't you, girl," I say with a cheeky smirk and she blushes.

"Extremely." She winks.

I take a deep breath, what have I got to lose at this point?

"I guess, I feel angry but there is no one to be angry at. People are staring and it is just easier to avoid people altogether at this point. I returned but I don't feel like I came back at all, most of me is still there. It's like my blood has gone cold, my humanity got stolen and with it, any ability to be warm or close to anyone."

"The fact that you can say all of that shows me that you are still in there somewhere, Mac, you haven't lost the ability to be warm or affectionate to people or you wouldn't be able to express that, or even be able to want that. You are not that far gone and we can get you back again. I can help you come you back, if you just put a little bit of trust in me."

"Trust is not an easy thing for me to give and that was before I was kidnapped and tortured for two years," I say harshly and I notice she flinches a little. "Sorry... I..."

"No, don't be, that was honesty, don't be sorry for that ever. I am only human; it is painful to think of you... of anyone, going through what you have. I guess my poker face game isn't always strong."

"I will work on it, girl. I can't promise but I will try, it could take some time," I admit.

Alisha looks at me intensely. "I can wait, Mac."

I squeeze my eyes shut trying to kill the pain that the images provoke. Even now I have no idea what was real and what was manipulation; did she ever want to help me or was it all part of the game? Was everything at the hotel a lie? Clearly, her poker face was stronger than she ever gave herself credit for.

When I get back home to the warehouse, I have a great lesson with Billy. The stick fighting isn't my thing but that just means Billy is determined to make it my thing, to not let me avoid the things I am uncomfortable with. The sticks are just wooden batons really, the one thing I enjoy is the satisfaction I get when they collide with a clank. It's like sword fighting with two hands at high speed. The more hits we block the more clanks the battens make and the faster it gets, the, more musical it sounds. Of course, the objective is to hit the other person, not make stick music, which stings a little but is good motivation to keep learning.

It is difficult to keep my focus and there really is no time not to be focused when stick fighting, which I notice when I miss a block and Billy's hit clips my eyebrow. Blood trickles and I feel its warmth spread down my face as I wince.

"McKenna, oh my God, I am so sorry, are you okay?" Billy asks, his face mortified. "Here, let me see?"

He steps towards me and I step back a little too abruptly and he freezes. I guess I am still not used to people getting close, I am getting better but only really with Anna and Alfred, I don't flinch so much with them anymore but there is still always a clear barrier I keep. I start to panic when anyone tries to cross it, especially if I don't know them very well.

"Hey, hey! Billy, chill, I am fine." I wipe my eyebrow with the back of my hand and he still looks concerned.

"Seriously, brother, look at me – I've had worse." I gesture down my body with my hands. I am wearing shorts and a sports crop top so my scars are very much obvious; I am getting a little better at being open about them.

"Fair comment, McKenna, but I should slow down. Go a little easier on—"

"No Billy, I need you to push me, okay? Please," I ask, holding his gaze. For some reason it works and he nods.

"Sorry, it's just, I don't enjoy hitting girls."

"Hah! I will have to just hit you; you will soon have to hit me back."

We continue stick fighting for a while and I am really started to get into it, I even manage to knock a stick out of Billy's hand twice. Okay, Billy may have disarmed me six times but I am still going to take it as a win.

"You are doing great, Mac. Next thing you need to do is work on your sequences of moves, mix it up a little so I can't predict how you are going to attack. Let's take a break, could I trouble you for a glass of water?"

"Oh man, of course. I am sorry, I am a terrible host," I apologise, grabbing him a glass of water. "From now on help yourself. I'm sorry, I am not used to having guests."

"It's no bother, don't worry."

We take a seat at the bean bags, I think I am really going to have to invest in a sofa, there just isn't enough seating now people are coming over. It still feels very odd to me, exposing, but Billy seems like a great guy and if Alfred trusts him, that is good enough for me.

"Not to tempt fate, because I really do appreciate you training me but... why are you doing this? You are giving up your time, getting your ass whooped by a girl you don't even know. Why?" I ask, winking.

"The simple answer is because Alfred asked me to. The not so simple answer is, I owe him a lot. My life, in fact, and he has never asked me for anything till now. So, I know it must be important or he never would have."

"Well, for what it is worth, it is important to me too. I can't thank you enough and I am really enjoying it. If I could monopolise your time more, I would."

"Actually, are you at the farm this evening at all?" he asks.

"Yes, I am there every morning and evening running the doom dash," I reply, then he looks at me, gone out, and I explain.

"Oh, okay hah! The doom dash, I like that." He laughs; even his laugh is posh. "Well I am going up this evening if you want to do some more stick work. It might seem annoying but it is actually teaching you a lot more than you realise. When it comes to hand to hand, after enough stick fighting you find it easier to predict attacks and use both hands in a fight more naturally."

"Really? Oh, that would be awesome, are you sure you don't mind?" My enthusiasm obvious.

"Not at all, like I said I am going to be there anyway so why not?"

After Billy leaves, I feel pumped and buzzed to do more work. I do some workouts on the punch bag and climbing rope then get myself showered. I am running out of clean clothes; my online order hasn't yet arrived so the next job is trying to find something clean to wear, I have nothing suitable left for the doom dash. In the end I settle on my oldest pair of ripped jeans, they are the only pair I own that aren't black. They are ripped to the point of almost being indecent to wear but I love them, I made them from a pair of very light blue Levi's. I couple the jeans with a white tank top and a pair of Converse high tops.

Standing at the mirror, I fix my hair into a messy ponytail and then I scrutinise my reflection. My body is starting to change; I have always been quite skinny but I am noticing muscle tone starting to develop, the cut on my eye from earlier is still a bit weepy and slightly bluing from bruising. The black circles from lack of sleep are fading, making my eyes look bluer. My skin is snowy white and I look healthier than I have in a long time.

All the working out is exhausting me into sleep and the nightmares have been becoming less regular, I eat better at the farm than here and altogether I am feeling pretty good. I never thought I would feel good looking in the mirror again, even my scars are bothering me less. I am not self-conscious about them and while I still find them ugly, I am finding more of an acceptance of them, they are a part of me now and I am starting to be okay with that. That doesn't mean, however, that I would cope with someone touching them but still, it's progress.

Motivated by feeling a bit better about myself I decide to put a little bit more effort in. I put on a necklace made from wooden beads and a matching bracelet – very surfer of me. Then I add a chunky silver thumb ring on my left hand and my black onyx crystal ring on my right wedding band finger. Next, I apply a little bit of concealer to completely hide what's left of the dark circles around my eyes and a little mascara and pink-tinted lip balm. I can't do anything to cover my cut to the eyebrow so I don't even bother trying. I spray some Diesel aftershave and I am good to go, I have always preferred men's scent on me.

Maybe Mac isn't dead after all; I feel more like myself than I have in a long time, I can't help but smile at myself a little. I never thought I would feel this way again, I am not all the way there by any stretch, but – I am starting to feel comfortable in my own skin again and it feels freakin' awesome. With pep in my step I leave for the farm early and decide to swing by Starbucks on the way and treat everyone to coffee and cakes. I grab my keys, wallet and phone and throw on my sandy brown cord blazer and set off.

***

When I arrive at the farm, I see Alfred is adding things to the assault course, it looks considerably more complicated and difficult but my mood must be good because I am looking forward to tackling it.

"Hey Alfred, I brought snacks! Come on in," I yell.

"Nice one, kid! Be there in five."

I head inside the house feeling light and giddy; it feels good to do something nice for them, it is the sort of thing the old Mac would have done, it was a risk going out in public but totally worth it. I bought an array of cakes, iced buns, doughnuts, cinnamon whirls and mini Victoria sponges along with some caramel lattes. I arrange them on the table feeling quite pleased with myself, then I walk over to the kitchen cupboards in search of plates and I hear Anna come down the stairs.

"Oo, you bought coffee and cake, woman after my own heart. Thanks, Mac. What are you looking for?"

"Little plates, I know they are around…"

"Top right cupboard."

"Ah, right, thank you."

I grab for the plates and turn back to the table and I see Anna; she is wearing a green summer dress and red Dr Marten boots. The green dress makes her eyes glow even more richly somehow, her rusty red hair hanging in loose curls around her pale face. Her lips are shimmering pale pink and I am floored by her. She turns to look at me and I correct my face from staring at her just in time.

"You look stunning," I blurt, the words coming out before I can stop them and she blushes. I turn away, busying myself with taking off my blazer and hanging it off the back of my chair.

"Thank you, I was about to say the same to you, I've never seen you…" She takes a step towards me, frowning. "What happened to your eye?" She reaches out to put her hand to my face and I jerk away. I see the shock in her eyes for just a second and then she smiles at me warmly.

"Sorry… I…" I stutter awkwardly.

"Don't be, I should be more careful. What happened? Will you let me fix it please?" Anna asks softly and I clumsily take a step back, looking away.

"Oh, it's nothing, training accident."

"It is still bleeding, here – take a seat."

"It's really noth—"

"Mac, sit down," she orders.

"Bossy," I mumble quietly.

I quite enjoy bossiness in a woman and right now it is helping distract me from the anxiety tingling in my chest. Anna fetches the first aid kit, kneels down in front of me and starts dabbing the cut with cotton wool buds without hesitation. I brace myself for the panic but it doesn't come.

"I heard that."

"You were meant to," I smirk.

She picks up some Steri-strips from the first aid kit and then she leans in closer to apply them to the wound, closing it. She is very careful to touch me as little as possible and I appreciate it. When she is done, she drops her hands and I realise how close she actually is.

"You are all set," she breathes softly.

I am paralysed, she isn't moving away, her eyes are slowly dancing around, surveying my face. I have no idea what she is looking for, she has a curious look in her eyes, a frowning, thoughtful look. Then my eyes wander, following every line and curve. I pause on her full pink lips and without thinking, I make the tiniest movement forward before stopping myself and I swear I hear her breath shake and my stomach flutters. My eyes find hers and she is looking right back at me, sending tingles up my spine.

"Did someone say snacks?"

Alfred bursts through the door and snaps me back to earth, Anna picks up the first aid box, straightening up, and walks off to go put it away.

"Uh… yeah, that would be me," I answer.

"Oh lovely! Thanks, kid. Oh, and you bought enough for Billy, he's just arrived. Isn't he here a bit early? I thought your dinner date wasn't till 8.00pm, it's only 4?" Alfred booms jollily and I feel a pulling sensation in my gut.

"Uh, no, he mentioned he was popping round and offered me a bit more training today as I was already going to be coming here," I explain, trying to keep my voice upbeat. Somehow, I think I managed it.

"Ah, he's a good man."

I turn to look at Anna and smile a little. "Yeah… he is a great guy." Then look away. "You will have to save us some cake, I better go out to him."

"Mind if I watch, kid? I love a good scrap," Alfred growls with excitement.

"Of course, fella."

I duck out of the kitchen and head outside to meet Billy. I can feel Alfred and Anna hot on my heels as I walk over to him, I swallow down hard.

Time to put on your happy face.

"Hey, brother," I say, my voice upbeat.

"Hey. Here, grab these, I will be back in one sec." Billy hands me the batons and walks over to Alfred; he shakes his hand and then he turns towards Anna and I turn away.

"You look absolutely breath-taking, Anna."

CHAPTER SIX

Many Happy Returns

Clank, clank, clank. Clank-clank.

I am trying with all I have to focus on the batons, the swinging and blocking, my eyes flitting from Billy's eyes to his hands, trying to predict his moves whilst simultaneously trying to mix up my own.

Clank-clank-clank-clank-clank-clank.

He is starting to push me now, I can tell. His speed is increasing and his weight behind the hits is increasing with much more force, sending vibrations down the batons into my palms. I push back, matching his speed, our footsteps moving us around in small circles and back and forth like a dance. He is so fast and it is like he is three moves ahead of me.

Somewhere in my head I make the conscious decision to repeat my moves three consecutive times so that on the fourth sequence, Billy is expecting me to repeat again. My arms are fatiguing, I count in my head, gritting my teeth. So focused that everything else disappears. Tunnel vision, it's like everything slows down. That, or I've sped up.

The fourth move comes and I side step to the left as Billy swings his right arm down, hitting nothing but air. The force of his missed swing throws him off balance a little, he loses his footing just an inch and as he does, I bring my baton down hard on his and rotate it fast. I watch in triumph as Billy's left baton slides out of his hand and up into the air. Billy's face drops, his expression stunned and Alfred roars and I turn, I completely forgot they were there. Alfred is Whooping and yelling, Anna is quiet but smirking.

"Oh my God, Billy, she got you! Aha! Nicely done, kid!"

I turn back to Billy and he is smiling proudly. "You were feigning, weren't you? You totally tricked me; I am impressed, Mac, well done!" Billy claps me on the back and I grin at him.

"It was the only way I stood a chance; you are so damn fast, brother."

We join Alfred and Anna over at the fire pit; Alfred is still whooping and cheering. My arms feel like rock and I am shiny with sweat, that was some upper body workout. Everyone sits down but me; I offer Billy my chair and knock back my drink quenching the burn in my throat, then I bend over and squeeze my sports bottle, pouring water down the back of my neck. The cool water feels awesome, I pass the bottle to Billy who takes it gladly.

"Thanks, McKenna. Seriously, well done back there, I am super proud. That was smart fighting." Billy commends me politely and I blush and nod in thanks.

Everyone starts making small talk and I really don't want to be here for it, making small talk would really make it difficult to avoid Anna. My head feels messed up and I haven't had time to process… whatever the hell that was.

"Alfred, you mind if we skip the doom dash today? I have a lead I want to follow up," I lie. I can feel Anna's eyes burning into the back of my head as I speak although why, I have no idea. I am no doubt imagining it.

"You were doing the dash from 5 to 7am this morning, I think you have earned the break, you want company?" Alfred asks, concern tugging at his eyes.

"No, I am good, fella, it's nothing to worry about but thank you. I will see you in the morning." I turn to Billy and Anna. "Have a great night, guys, and thanks Billy," I say, smiling.

"Anytime, McKenna, same time and place tomorrow?"

"Absolutely, see you tomorrow."

***

When I get home, I turn on all the fairy lights and lamps and turn off the main lights. Everything glows romantically; there are no windows to the warehouse so even though it isn't that late, the darkness gives the illusion that it could be. I walk over to the bean bag chair and crash onto it. I am so annoyed with myself, the absolute last thing I need is to have feelings… Nope. No, I will not think about it.

Standing up I stride over to my desk, I will do some online shopping. Yes, retail therapy, that will help. I fire up my laptop and then it asks for my password. Goddamn it! I type 'Anna is awesome' and hit the enter key rather hard. Ugh, chill out, it's not the laptop's fault. I buy a lot of stuff, some useful and some not and neither are helping to elevate my mood.

I go upstairs and bring my laptop with me, I figure maybe putting a movie on might help, watching movies has always been my go-to escape from life. I consider myself a bit of a film nerd. When I was taken, I would close my eyes and try to re-enact my favourites, picturing every detail I could and trying to remember the lines and voices of the characters. They always had to be favourites, ones I have seen many times or I would lose the fantasy trying too hard to remember, it was my only escape.

Flicking through the media library, I scroll till I find Con Air; I am not sure what it is but whenever I watch Face Off, I always want to watch Con Air afterwards and vice versa, it's like a thing. I hit play and lay back on my bed waiting for it to load, my eyes trace the panels on the ceiling and then I look at my watch – 8.30pm. I am annoyed at myself for looking, there is only one reason to look and that is to torture myself in the knowledge that Anna is on her date.

Ugh, this isn't working, I can't avoid this, it's happening and avoiding it really isn't going to magically make it go away. What is happening though? Confusion rattles in my stupid, horny, emotionally burnt out brain.

Alisha… Anna… Alisha… Anna.

Oh, for fuck's sake. I slam my fist down on the floor, anger at myself burning in my gut. This is ridiculous! I don't need this right now, it doesn't matter what I feel, it doesn't matter who I feel it for, I just have to swallow it down. No feelings – feelings kindly do one. I am no good for anyone, not right now, maybe not ever. Alisha is – a fabrication. Anna is – not interested. So, my tale in the quest of unattainable women continues. Ugh! Yes, crushing on an elusive ghost and a straight girl, I've upped my game in unattainability.

Nice job, douche bag.

Anna… Billy is a good man, a good person. He isn't broken or damaged, he isn't a target, he is a whole person and she already likes him. All I have to do is try to put some boundaries in place. She is dating Billy, that will make it even easier to keep my distance. She is my friend; I will squash these more-than-friend type feelings before they even begin. Yes, ladies and gentlemen, welcome to flight 445-idiot, we do hope you enjoy your journey to the friend-zone.

Boundaries, walls, bring them back up and fortify the hell out of them.

Alisha… I wanted her to unlock my secrets, but she became the biggest one instead. How ludicrous that the girl still eats at me, when the girl I knew – clearly doesn't exist. My heart still aches for her, my brain tires from trying not to think of her, my body wants her, my gut despises her.

Focus on the job, keep your distance, nice and clean. This is just an unwelcome distraction; one I can put to the back of my mind. I hear Nicolas Cage ask why he couldn't just put the bunny back in the box and I realise it must be getting late enough to sleep. The early start, the physically demanding day and emotionally charged evening, have me wiped out. I roll over and close my eyes.

I am just an anchor, fit to drag anyone too close to me down.

Anna...

Alisha...

I fall asleep almost instantly.

***

For once, the last thing I want to do is go to the farm. I make the decision to go up early again, I can slip out before Anna gets up, go back home and wait for my sofa to arrive. I think Alfred had a suspicion I would be here early because when I arrive the fire is still burning. Looks like he added some really chunky hardwood logs so it would burn through till morning.

The distances between sections have been stretched out which means more running, pushing the tractor tyres further, longer distance trudging through the brook water and a longer crawl under the cargo net. The six-foot climbing rope wall no longer has a rope to help me climb over. They are the only changes to the original parts of the course; thankfully it doesn't look like too many complicated things have been added.

For the most part I get on okay, I am sure my time is a lot slower but I am not surprised. The hardest bit is scaling the six-foot wall with no rope or footholds; I complete the course three times and then I decide just to focus on scaling the wall as it is slowing me down the most. I try lots of different ways to conquer it, sometimes falling straight on my butt. Eventually I find my groove and discover that the easiest way over is also the most precarious, I run and jump and use my trainers' tread to step up the vertical face, all I need is one good step up in height. With enough momentum, one step up gives me enough height that I can grab the top of the wall and haul myself up and over. However, if I don't gain enough speed and height on that one step, my hands don't hit the top of the wall and I slide down it, grazing my knees as I go.

After two hours I decide enough is enough and I go sit by the fire again, I don't plan on staying long, I would go now if I could but if I don't at least see Alfred before I go, he will suspect something is wrong, I don't really need him questioning me right now. The sun is almost up in the sky by the time Alfred comes down to join me. He is carrying a small wooden box wedged under his arm and two cups of coffee.

"Aw thank you, Alfred." I take the coffee from him and breathe in its bitter sweet scent.

"Anytime, kid. How are you doing? Did that lead pan out at all?"

"Ugh no, it was a dead end," I lie and the guilt pangs. "What's in the box?"

"A gift actually, don't fuss. I didn't spend much, I have my connections and I use them wisely," he boasts.

He reads my face in an instant, he knows I am not great at receiving gifts, I am not really sure why because I love giving them.

"It is for your birthday, you really have no place to strop, I know it is early but I didn't want to wait," he says, grinning, clearly excited.

I groan internally; I was really hoping that I could keep that quiet. I am living in a world where it feels like I am stuck in limbo, I'm not really living, it's more, just existing. Mac has to stay hidden; it doesn't exactly make me feel like celebrating.

"I guess I shouldn't be surprised that you know that, I was planning on skipping it this year."

"You should always celebrate being alive, kid, no matter what."

Suddenly I feel a little selfish, I am alive and it feels like I am alive against all odds. Considering the circumstances, I should be more grateful for that. How does he do that? It is like he jumps in my messy head and tidies up the chaos. He is also good at throwing the parental look that inspires guilt.

"Aww okay, hit me with it, you old softy!"

Alfred grins brightly, excited by my change in enthusiasm. He passes me the box, it is a warm amber-brown wood, polished to perfection. The weight has me intrigued; it is heavier than it looks. I lift the brass-coloured catch with a flick then slowly lift the lid. I am not sure what I was expecting, but it certainly wasn't this. Inside is a hand gun presented against a black velvet-like material. It looks much more modern than the hand gun I've been training with.

"It is a Glock 19. The new SAS model, it is lighter, has less recoil and a shorter barrel and pistol grip making it easy to conceal and also it should fit in your hand more naturally. The magazines carry 15 rounds. Also, there is a holster, this issue was designed for plain clothes operations, you could wear it all day long and no one would know," he gloats, very pleased with himself.

My jaw drops. I take the gun out of the box and marvel; it is much more lightweight and fits in my hand like it was made for me.

"I… Wow…" I struggle.

"McKenna…"

I look up at Alfred meeting his solemn gaze and put the gun back in the box.

"I bought you this because you have shown weaponry respect. Yes, it has been fun to shoot at targets but you haven't gone gung ho, you kept a cool head every time. I have almost finished watching all of the videos you found. Was harder than expected but worth it, I have some leads for us to follow." He pauses, looking at me to see if I am okay; once he is satisfied that I am, he continues.

"This is yours and I hope you never have to use it but there is no denying, with what leads I've come up with, this isn't going to be a cake walk. There is a chance you may have to use it and shooting at people is much different to shooting at targets, especially if they are shooting at you. If you actually have to pull that trigger knowing it's a kill shot, it will take pieces of you, every single time."

There is no doubt in my mind that he is talking from personal experience. The slight sadness in his eyes screams volumes; he is warning me and I hear him loud and clear.

"Your trust in me helped me keep a cool head. I respect you more than I can explain, Alfred, and I respect this. I won't be using it unless there is no other choice."

"Well actually, kid, that isn't true. Surely you want to take the girl for a spin!?" Alfred grins excitedly and I grin right back.

"Oh, hell yes I do!"

This gun was made for me. Shooting it felt much more natural than the Browning pistol, as easy as pointing my index finger, like it was an extension of my hand. It felt significantly lighter and the recoil much easier to subdue; it made shooting practice even more fun. I laughed and Alfred laughed along with me and I can see how happy it is making him, to have this moment with me. It hasn't escaped my thoughts though, that if Anna wasn't awake before she probably is now. I feel guilty after he has done this for me but I need to cut out on Alfred.

"Alfred. This. Is. Amazing! Thank you so much! Best birthday present ever." I whoop.

"Anytime, kid. It seems to be working for you, very accurate shooting."

"It is so much easier to use. Listen, fella, I hate to cut and run, but I've got some deliveries coming to the warehouse."

"Ah, that's alright. Will you come back this evening?"

"Um… I will see what I can do. I do have some errands to run. If I can't, I will see you in the morning if that's okay?" I lie, my chest tightening with guilt.

"No problem, kid, just give me a shout if you need anything, you don't need to be out in the open any more than needs be and I am happy to run any errands if you need anything."

"Nah, I am okay, thank you. It is mostly deliveries and the rest I don't have to leave my truck for. I will see you later, fella, and thank you, again."

I lie, I lie through my teeth. I really have no intention of going back today or running any errands. God, I feel crap about that. I am lying more and more; I just feel like I need the day. A day to try get my head together. I decide to send Billy a text and move him to tomorrow too. He was okay with it but requested we meet at the farm again, not so happy about that but what can I do when he is doing me a favour? I hold no bad feelings towards him, he really is a great guy. I just need a day, tomorrow I will get my head straight.

***

I spend the day watching movies. I lounge around in my girl boxers and a baggy t-shirt, lay on my newly delivered sofa and just… be. Sometimes you just need an ugly day, a day to allow yourself to look as hideous as you want, a day where you look so crap you scare the post man. Yeah… today is that day.

I overindulge in Jack Daniels and ready salted crisps, while listening to heavy metal and head banging like an angry bearded man in a mosh pit. I think that whiskey is the angry girl's Ben and Jerry's. I am angry, today I get to be angry, I get to be pissy at life. Today, I don't have to pretend to be strong and that I am okay, I can lay back and stare at the ceiling for two hours if I want. I don't have to put a happy-freaking-go-lucky face on because no one is here to ask if I am okay. I am riding the crest of a slump and I am okay with that.

The day moves fast, too fast. Probably because I had a four-hour afternoon nap, I don't even like naps but I like that I had the time to have one. I am bored and loving that I am staying still long enough to be bored. I even got to spend some 'quality time' with myself for an overdue release of… tension. That is probably what prompted the nap.

At some point in the late evening the alcohol haze starts to lift and being in a crappy mood no longer appeals, neither does boredom. I take out my camera from its case, remove the memory card and place it in my laptop. The photos load and I start to flick through the images, there aren't many of them, I took some shots of the farm, of the doom dash and of Alfred doing his farm chores. There are some of Alfred and Anna together by the fire, then randomly a picture of Anna pulling a face in selfie mode and I laugh, she really is a goof.

I print some of the photographs off to put on my wall, away from the spider chart. I choose a picture of Alfred and myself, one of the farm's fields at sunrise, one of Alfred and Anna and one of Anna's selfie and pin them on the wall. I also print off a picture of my mum, I guess I am feeling sentimental. I love photographs, frozen moments in time that have the capacity to hold memories for a lifetime. I needed this day, I felt like an over-compressed spring that was overdue to snap, I can't say I magically feel perfect but I do feel better. More equipped to deal with... everything.

***

I am slow on the doom dash; the whiskey hangover is heavy in my limbs. Alfred doesn't push me too hard; he is probably going easy on me today because it's my birthday and I am not going to complain at that. I was forward thinking enough this time to bring spare clothes to change into and Alfred graciously lets me use the shower. I am frozen, mud is caked to my legs, right up to my hips and I smell like a swamp monster.

My online order arrived and I dress in some of my new clothes. Some dark blue baggy dungarees with the bib and straps hanging down and a semi-see-through fitted black t-shirt. This was a bold buy; it is the sort of top I never used to think twice about wearing but that was before my body was scarred up; I am trying hard not to focus on that too much. I finish the look with my black and perfectly worn combat boots. When I walk the kitchen, Alfred is at the stove and Anna is sitting at the table.

"Take a seat, kid, I have lunch on the go."

"Smells awesome," I say, pulling out a chair. "Hey girl. How's tricks?" I ask politely and she looks at me shrewdly.

"What?"

"Are you really going to pretend today is just a normal day?"

"What? It is just a..." I mutter, staring at her blankly, then understanding hits.

"Dude! What did you tell her for?" I whine.

"It's a birthday. Not typically top-secret information, kid," he mumbles and I groan, very audibly and Anna giggles.

"Happy birthday, Mac," she beams.

"Thanks, now can we move on?"

"For now," Anna taunts, her face awash with mischief.

"I don't like that look, you are up to something and I don't like whatever something is. Can we please have none of the somethings? I want a something-less day," I protest. "Stop laughing, it is not funny!"

Alfred brings plates overloaded with a full English breakfast and sits down, chuckling. "Stop torturing the poor girl."

"Look, we are just going to have some music and drinks and cake, no big thing. Don't get your slacks in a swivel," Anna jibes sarcastically, her eyes sparkling at me as she smirks; her looking at me like that really isn't helpful.

"Okay, but if I so much as hear a word of Happy Birthday being sung – I'm out."

Billy arrives and wishes me Happy Birthday and I shoot a dark look at Anna. Training went okay but I was struggling to focus, mainly because I realised that Billy was actually invited to this little birthday bash. Soon, all four of us are sat around the fire drinking and laughing. It was hard at first having Billy here but I am doing a good job of shoving it down, I want to be okay with it, I will be. I try to take my mind off of it by listening to Alfred's old war stories. He is such a good story teller and he has no shortage of material.

"Mac, if you could have anything for your birthday what would it be?" Billy asks.

"You mean besides a Glock?" Everyone laughs and the sound booms in the night's silence. "I don't know, I am not one for wanting things. At least, not things people can buy. I mean sure, there are things I want but I much prefer good and unforgettable moments, memories. They never break or go out of fashion. They are a forever gift and if all else fails, I really like Haribo eggs."

"I will drink to that," Alfred toasts, slightly merry now.

"I would but I am out of drink, back in a minute."

I head inside for a top-up, I have been careful not to drink too much. Loose lips sink ships, the last thing I need is to get tipsy and say something I shouldn't. I decide to have a glass of water, then I will have another whiskey and keep myself on an even keel.

"What, no whiskey?" Anna asks, frowning.

"Maybe in a bit."

"You don't like losing control much, do you?"

"I like it just fine, depending on the circumstances but sometimes losing control isn't a smart plan," I point out.

"I know what you mean," Anna says thoughtfully.

I am pretty sure she has no idea what I mean, thankfully.

"We should probably head back," I suggest.

"I want to give you your present first," she says, reaching for a box from the kitchen counter. She takes my hand and places a small black box into it, it is tied up in a bow with silky black ribbon.

"You really shouldn't…" I begin to protest and she puts her index finger on her lips and gives me a playful 'don't argue' look and I stifle a giggle.

Anna pulls the tie of the ribbon and opens the box. Inside lays a chunky silver bangle, it is plain but striking. I run my finger across the smooth, cool metal curve – it is stunning. Anna takes the bracelet out and shows me the inside. Inscribed is the word 'goof' in tiny swirled script followed by a series of numbers.

"They are the coordinates of the farm, so no matter what happens, you can always find your way back," Anna says softly, her endearing smile playing on her full lips is *doing things* to me.

Damn…

"It's kind of perfect," I say, holding out my wrist.

Anna smiles and slides the bangle onto my wrist and I feel blown away by her thoughtfulness. I am touched and slightly frustrated, she isn't making behaving myself any easier. Again, my inability to show how I feel frustrates me, normal people would give her a hug and I can't seem to make that step forward no matter how hard I try.

"Thank you, Anna," I say, smiling warmly at her hoping that she knows it means a lot to me.

Laying on the sofa, it feels just like old times. I may not be drunk but I still can't drive; I suppose at least I don't have far to go to get in my morning doom dash. Tomorrow evening Alfred and Anna are coming to the warehouse to discuss what Alfred found in the videos. I can't imagine what he has come up with and I am not even going to try, I just hope it is a solid lead to work from.

The silver bracelet on my wrist catches my eye as it glints in the light and I smile to myself. She doesn't make it easy for me to keep her in the friend zone. Unknowingly, I am sure, but every time I push her back into the box marked 'friends', she does something that completely bursts the box open at its seams and then I have to build a newer, stronger box to contain her again.

***

Panic startles me awake, the disorientation as I open my eyes to find myself at the farm and not at my mum's place is like a thick fog that I struggle to clear at first. Dreams plaguing me, screwing with my befuddled conscious mind. I am used to it at this point, but this is different. Dreams of my mum screaming in pain, dreams of a once orderly and loving home in haunted disarray have me on my feet and hauling arse to my truck.

Driving a little too fast I am speeding towards my mum's house; my heart is in my throat. I am overreacting, I am sure, but I can't not check. I need to know she is safe; I know this is impulsive and quite possibly reckless. I hear Alfred's voice bouncing around in my head but I have an escape plan if I need it, I know this house and this area well, I can do this, I just need to see that she is safe.

I spend half an hour just scanning the street, looking at every tiny movement. Her car is gone, this is okay, she is meant to be at work now. Everything looks quiet, so with a stomach full of nerves I walk over to the house, keeping my head down, moving as fast as I can, my senses alert with awareness. Using my own key, I get inside and out of sight as quickly as possible, my chest heaving in breathless anxiety. My eyes and ears scan for anything that is out of place, but everything is quiet. Relief splashes and extinguishes the fearful fire in my chest.

I slowly creep through the living room; the place is alive with memories. I miss her, I miss this place, the familiar smells evoking loneliness, reminding me that, I don't really belong anywhere anymore. I creep up the stairs, it is unnecessary, it is all quiet and everything seems to be in its place but the sadness hits me and the thought of seeing my old room, a reminder that Mac still exists somewhere keeps my feet moving. It is like I have no control; I am moved slowly along like a marionette driven by the ghost of myself. I reach my bedroom door, wooden letters spread in an oval shape spelling 'McKenna' are still proudly displayed from when I was a kid. I open the door and enter the room.

It looks exactly the same as the day I moved out and that makes me miss my mum even more; she kept everything in its place all this time. Film posters still litter the walls along with old and poorly taken photographs taken from my practice days. My eyes scan the room, my heart feeling bittersweet. I am still here, so maybe one day I will be back again. At least some things don't change, it is kind of comforting, everything is familiar and in its place.

Almost everything.

My eyes fall upon a crisp white envelope propped up against the window on the ledge, on the front in writing that I don't recognise is my name. It is not my mum's handwriting and I can't imagine why she would put anything there that came for me. I walk over and pick up the letter, fear tingles from every nerve ending and fears start to erupt in my gut as I wonder if someone put it here for me to find. Suddenly, I don't feel so safe.

I make a quick exit, lock up and make my way back to the car, my breath held and walking quickly, looking around me as I go. I drive off as quickly as possible to get clear of the house. The further away I get, the easier it is to breathe. I drive back to the warehouse taking random turnings to double back, in case I am being followed; it feels like the longest drive ever with the envelope taunting me on the passenger seat.

When I finally get home, I go take a seat on the sofa and examine the envelope. I definitely don't recognise the writing, there is no address, the envelope just says 'Mac'. Now I am holding it, I am nervous about opening it. I can't see it being anything good, who would go to the trouble of putting it in my childhood bedroom? No one I know would by my estimation. I slide my finger across the back opening the seal, I pull out a crisp and stark white piece of thick paper and I read:

Dear Mac,

I am so sorry. I never meant for any of this to happen. I know you will probably never believe me, but I swear to you it is the whole & horrible truth. What we had was real, that night at the hotel, I had no idea who you were, it was all real Mac. Those days together, I fell hard for you, then just like that, you were gone. I was heartbroken.

Two years passed and the last thing I expected was to see you again. I was drinking my morning coffee and there was your face on the front page of the newspaper. In an instant everything stirred inside me.

A man came to my office. He said he had a new client for me, a client looking to regain their memories. He said that it was in my best interests to make sure you remembered and that if I did, then he would give me the one thing no one else could.

He offered me my father. He has been in prison since I was 15 years old for a crime he didn't commit and I was told if I did this, then he had someone on the inside that could confess to the crime he is charged with, that he had the resources to make sure new evidence popped up in his favour and that he would be released.

I accepted his offer, I persuaded myself that you wanted to remember anyway, where was the harm? But the longer time went on the more they wanted from me. They pushed me to get closer to you and use your attraction for me, to get you to trust me quicker.

I knew the person you were before they took you, I saw what they had done to you and my heart ached to make it better, to hold you and all I was doing was making things worse. I knew one day you would find out and never look at me the same again but I was trapped.

I signed a deal with the devil. They are everywhere Mac, I tried to pull out and they made it clear that there was no going back and if I didn't hold up my end of the bargain, they would kill me. They watched my every move; they saw every session we had through hidden cameras.

The night you came over it became obvious that you were starting to remember and that was the only thing that saved my life. I warned you and they punished me for it but they got what they wanted in the end. They said that was why they were letting me go.

I had to leave. I'm not convinced that they aren't still watching me, hoping you will come to me but I know you won't. I saw the look in your eyes, I know you never want to see me again and I can't blame you but Mac, I do have information that could help you. If you want to talk - call me, if not I understand.

I am so sorry Mac, please be safe.

Love Always,

Alisha

At the bottom of the letter is a phone number, a new one by the looks of it. I fold the letter back up, put it back in the envelope and place it on the desk. My heart is racing, I feel so many things I don't know what the hell I am feeling anymore. My instinct is to rip up the letter, burn it, destroy its very existence but my head says otherwise. My head says I cannot act on emotion with this, I need to be smart.

I go for a hot shower and just let my mind adjust. The hot water trickles down my skin, I turn up the heat, I feel dirty. Every word I ever spoke to her, every moment of pain I expressed, every fear I entrusted to her – was heard by someone else, by the very people that broke me in the first place. Every longing look she gave me, every flirtation – was motivated by someone else, it was all fake. I guess I already knew all that but to read it in black and white, rips open old feelings that I have tried very hard to turn my back on. I know that she was in over her head, I can believe that. I can even have empathy but it doesn't change anything.

"Wow, you have a sofa. Nice!" Alfred cheers. "I thought I was going to have to sit on one of them bean things again, they are not fun to try get back off of."

Anna and Alfred sit on the sofa, I make them a coffee and sit down, my head buzzing and my heart heavy. I know what I have to do, there is no choice here, but I really don't want to.

"Are you okay, Mac? You look kind of green," Anna asks, her expression wary.

I slowly get to my feet and walk over to the desk, then I pick up the letter and give it to Anna. "Read it," I request to them both. I watch their facial expressions warp and twist as they read the letter from Alisha. Alfred looks impassive; Anna, however, as always wears her emotions on her face clearly. Anger, disgust, anger again, and then disbelief.

"She can't possibly think you would contact her?!" Anna spits, livid.

"No but she is clearly hoping so," Alfred states calmly and he looks at me, examining my face, "and you are going to do it, aren't you?" he predicts and Anna's head snaps up.

"You can't be serious, Mac? The last time you saw her you ended up getting shot!"

"I am aware of that, but I am planning on being smarter about it this time. Look, it isn't like the thought of seeing her is filling me with the warm and fuzzies but she has information that could help. I figure if I call her, arrange a public meet-up somewhere there are a lot of people. If anything happens it will be easier for me to escape."

Anna is seething; I am not sure who she is madder at, Alisha or me for considering meeting her so I look to Alfred, hoping he can be a voice of reason. He rubs the palm of his hand against his whiskery cheek and sighs.

"If you are doing this, kid, you are doing this with backup. I can be there; I know of an outdoor restaurant we could use. I can get a good vantage point on the indoor upper level; she won't know who I am, I can listen in via earpiece, I can watch your six and I'll be able to tell you if trouble is coming. Any dodgy business and we can bug out."

"I am totally fine with backup. Thank you, Alfred." I nod, and then I look back over to Anna. She is annoyed, she is up on her feet with her hands on her hips, her feet shifting aimlessly.

"Well, you two aren't going off on a mission without me but for the record, I think this is a stupid idea. You two both drank from a stupid fountain this morning and I have to be there to make sure this doesn't turn into a tidal wave of stupid."

"Noted," I reply, supressing the powerful urge to laugh. "Alfred, what is the name of that restaurant?"

"The Waterway. I will book a table for 11am tomorrow, tell her to come for then, we will get there a bit early to check the coast is clear. The water is helpful, it takes away a whole side that no one can approach from. I will be roaming,

Anna if you are coming then I want you sat a distance back from behind Alisha. Mac, wear a blazer, you are taking your side arm and the blazer will hide it easily. I will go make the arrangements at the restaurant, book a table with the best exit strategy and I'll see what comms (surveillance communications) I can get my hands on."

My mouth loses all moisture, preventing me from gulping but I nod.

"Savannah, you coming with or staying with Mac?"

"I will stay," she says firmly and I cringe, I am totally in trouble.

Alfred leaves in a shot and I am left with Anna; we sit on the L-shaped sofa and I brace myself as I watch her. Her eyes are staring off distantly, her hands clasped together.

"How mad at me are you?"

"I am not mad, just worried, Mac."

"I get that."

"I don't think you do."

That annoys me. How can she think that?

"I don't want anything to happen to either of you! I never did, I tried to stop you both being in this position but you both pushed me to let you help. It doesn't mean I stop worrying about either of you, I never stop and it sucks you don't believe that," I snap.

I get up and walk away from her, anger bubbling in my chest. I never wanted either of them in danger, I never wanted this. Anna walks over to me but she keeps her distance, making me wonder if I have scared her and that sucks most of all.

"Mac, that isn't what I meant. We both know what we are signing on for, I meant I am worried about you, I am sorry if it came off otherwise."

"I'm sorry. I misunderstood. I thought..."

"I know what you thought. People caring about you always seems to be the last thing you assume; I don't know when you are going to see that we do actually give a crap," Anna says plainly but her voice is calm.

I relax a little. I am a jerk; I turn round but stay a good distance away. I hate the idea that I might have scared her.

"I am sorry, I didn't mean to snap. If I scared you... I..."

Anna frowns and takes another step towards me; all anger has melted from her expression, instead her eyes are warm and contemplative.

"You don't scare me, Mac. Don't think that," she says softly and I sigh as the relief eases the tightness in my chest.

"Maybe not, but I'm still sorry. Honestly, I just assumed because I still feel guilty and worried about accepting your help. It hit a nerve when my nerves are already strung out but you don't need to worry about me. I am working my butt off to be ready for what is coming. I'm not the same person who got shot, I am stronger now, more aware and more careful," I reassure.

"I am not worried you can't handle yourself; you do nothing but train, you are like a machine. I am worried she is going to get in your head, lately you have been… lighter. We are really starting to see who Mac is and I don't want her making you disappear again, I like…" She pauses and lets out a frustrated sigh. "I like that you finally trust us enough to let us see who you are. I don't want her pushing you back into darkness." Anna's voice begins to crack and she looks away; the sound of her sadness rocks me.

I walk over to her hesitantly, moving very slowly and robotic. I am scared to do the wrong thing and of making a fool of myself, scared because I can't remember the last time I went to someone to hold them. After everything, I have lost that part of myself that knows how to approach someone to comfort them. It is as hard and as alien as accepting the same comfort when it is offered to me.

I take her wrist gently in my hand, my jaw clenched with anxiety, self-doubt screaming in my mind. I feel her watching me but she stays incredibly still and relaxed, she lets me move at my own speed, just as she always has. I turn her towards me and she lets me but then I pause, losing my nerve, my hand trembles and I squeeze my eyes shut trying to steady myself.

"Don't stop… It's okay," she whispers.

When I open my eyes, I focus on my hand holding her wrist, unable to look up. I move my free hand, slowly put it on her hip, I pull her wrist and wrap it around my back and she holds it there. She doesn't as much as move a fingertip; I step into her and slide my spare arm around the top of her shoulders. My body trembles as I hold her awkwardly, my arms brittle and lost. I command my muscles to relax and after what seems like too long, they obey. She notices the surrender as my arms relax a little and she pulls me closer. Her breathing is so fast, she must have been holding her breath the entire time.

"I won't slip back into the darkness," I mumble.

"How do you know?"

"Because… you and Alfred, are the light."

CHAPTER SEVEN

Waterside

Anna melts into my chest, my arms tremble around her, my breathing is shaky but I am actually hugging her. I can't believe it and I don't think she can either, her breath is heavy and it is tickling my neck, sending tingles through me that force me to step away. I let her go and finally am able to look at her; she beams radiantly at me, her eyes luminous with pride. I feel more human, this isn't impossible for me, it is hard and scary but not impossible. I can have my humanity back, I can be… warm to people. I have affection inside of me, it is buried deep but it is there.

I feel joy, pure joy to have broken down that wall down, even just a little. I run over to my laptop, open the iTunes page and hit play. Music floods the warehouse and I turn back to Anna, grinning, clicking my fingers in time with the music. She laughs a loud animated cackle.

"What are you doing?!" she yells over the music.

The chorus hits and I walk over, swinging my hips as I go and I sing:

"Sweet home Alabama, Where the skies are so blue.

"Sweet home Alabama, Lord I'm coming home to you."

I walk towards Anna; actually, it is more like I 'dad dance' towards her.

"Oh no… Mac… Don't even think about it," she gasps.

I grab Anna by the hand and waist and start dancing terribly with her, spinning her round. My jubilant singing is utterly horrifying but we laugh, I laugh so much my ribs hurt. I sing loud and proud with my terrible voice and flat tone and I marvel in the moment. Anna relents and soon she is dancing too, her eyes sparkling with childlike glee. The song ends and we both collapse on the sofa, our bodies quaking in exuberant laughter.

"Just when I think you can't get goofier!" Anna cackles, out of breath.

"Oh, you love it. My moves are smooth as fuck."

We both regain some composure and realise, it is time to call Alisha. Apprehension hits, my stomach twisting in knots and tangles. I have no idea how I am going to do this; I need to stay cool, but I feel anything but that. That feeling when you are about to fall over, the whoosh of dread that hits you. That is how I feel only it isn't stopping, there is no floor to hit. Memories sweep across my mind transforming my field of vision, the warehouse disappears.

The memory swirls.

The landscape of a garden patio opens up in front of me. The sky is darkening, the stars are trying to poke through. I feel icy whiskey warm the back of my throat as I knock the glass back. When I bring it back down onto the glass of the table's surface, my eyes fall on her sitting opposite me – smiling at me shyly.

"So, tell me about Alisha," I ask coolly.

"Doesn't the Q&A typically come before entering the bedroom?" Alisha says coyly, her grin painfully sexy.

"Something tells me there is nothing typical about you, girl. Regardless of the timing, that doesn't mean I don't want to know. I can always take you back to the bedroom afterwards – for good measure." I flirt, looking at her daringly and she holds my gaze, turning my insides to play dough.

"You got that right," Alisha says as she sips her cocktail, blushing. She puts down her glass and begins tickling the back of my hand with her fingertips.

"What would you like to know, Mac?"

"How about... everything?"

"I don't think we have that much time."

I take her hand and look up at her intensely. "Then let's make time."

I blink my eyes and shake away the memory; my head swims as my vision slips back to the present and I jump to find Anna kneeled down in front of me, her eyes locked onto mine and tight with concern.

"Are you okay? You just completely zoned out."

"Uh... Yeah, just a memory coming back, that's all. It's nothing." I shrug and she looks at me thoughtfully. Her nose crinkling a little between her eyes.

"You seem to be... gone, when they come back. Like you have left the room but you are still here. I called your name twice and you didn't answer me."

"I didn't hear you. It's... I..." I sigh and look away. I don't want to have this conversation; it is going to make me sound fit for the loony bin.

"Tell me, please…" Anna says softly.

I look back at her; her expression is calm and encouraging and it is hard to say no to her when she looks at me that way. Her face is always so honest, I see no judgement there but I can't tell what she is thinking.

"Everything disappears, not every time but more and more. The first time it happened, I was sat at my desk and I was holding on to it and the warehouse just… disappeared, but I could still feel the desk in my hand, as… truly, as I could feel everything in the memory," I confide.

I am not even sure why I am telling her. I wait for her expression to change, to see something that means I should be embarrassed but nothing happens, she just continues to hold my gaze intently, with kind eyes.

"That sounds… terrifying," she breathes.

"It's not so bad, it's more that I never know when it is going to happen that is hard and that what I remember, isn't fun. I keep hoping I am going to remember a day that my kidnappers took me to Disney Land, but no luck so far," I joke darkly, smiling a little and she chuckles.

"You are the master of deflection, Mac Scott," she says, playfully scowling.

"Who's deflecting? I am deadly serious. I have always wanted to meet Woody, maybe Buzz Lightyear too, I guess but, I always found him a bit arrogant to be honest."

"Oh, Jesus, just when I think you couldn't be a bigger nerd." She giggles and then her face grows serious. "You want me to leave you alone to do this?" Anna asks respectfully, handing me a disposable phone.

"Nope, you can stay, I am good," I say and she smiles, looking slightly taken aback.

Anna takes a seat on the sofa next to me. I punch the numbers and hit dial and my chest becomes tight the moment it starts to ring.

"Hello?" Alisha answers and I close my eyes. Pain burning in my chest, pain and relief. I hate myself for being happy to hear her voice.

"Alisha," I breathe.

"Mac…?"

"Yeah, it's me."

"Oh my God. Mac. I… Sorry, I didn't think you would call, now you have I don't know what to say," she rambles.

"I very nearly didn't to be honest."

"I am so glad you are okay; I need to see you; I need to explain. Can we please meet?"

I hesitate, am I really going to do this? What if Anna is right? Can I take this? She hurt me; the woman gets under my skin. She has a way of wrapping me around her finger. If I didn't care for her at all then this wouldn't be so hard. She could destroy me. I look at Anna, she looks right back at me, with a tight jaw. I am more prepared this time and really, what choice do I have?

"Waterside, 11am, tomorrow. I will book a table, meet me there," I say, formally.

"I will be there. Thank you, Mac."

"Alisha, if this is a trap..." I say coldly.

"It's not, Mac, I swear to you."

"That really doesn't mean much to me, girl."

I cringe as the word 'girl' accidently comes out my mouth.

"I know," she says, her voice sad and small.

"See you tomorrow."

I feel so many things, all at once. The emotions collide like a hammer hitting nails; I feel like an arsehole for being cold to her, I feel stupid for feeling like an arsehole because she screwed me over and yet I feel relief that she is okay. I feel longing, to hold her and thank her for risking herself to save me, I feel anger for her betrayal, I feel hurt for her lies, her manipulation, I feel distrust, I feel excitement to see her face. I feel dread to see it too. I feel fear of what she is capable of doing to me.

Kryptonite.

"Mac... Are you okay?"

"Yeah... Sorry. I am fine. I just, I'm trying to keep my head straight."

"I will be in your ear the whole time; I will try to keep your head straight," Anna reassures.

I nod but really what I am thinking is... Anna... Alisha... In my ears at the same time. Does it get more complicated than that? The irony isn't lost on me. I chuckle. I'm doomed, what a cluster-fuck. Alfred returns carrying a bunch of bags and the smell of cheeseburgers hits me. God, I love this man. After food, Alfred begins the run through of the game plan; he draws a rough plan of the waterside restaurant and I feel nerves swirl in my stomach.

"There are 3 sets of double doors that lead in and out to the outside eating areas, you will walk out of the restaurant and there is seating to the left and right in two sections. I've booked your table on the right, it is set higher giving you a better line of sight around you. From there you have two possible exits. Either back through the restaurant which I'd avoid, it is too easy to get jammed up, or behind you there is a six-foot boundary wall separating the restaurant from the car park," he says, grinning. "You have become pretty good at scaling the one at the farm. If you need to escape you can jump the wall, it is the only thing that separates you from your truck, it's an easy out."

"Sounds doable. What about you and Anna? She absolutely cannot connect us at all, she has been in direct contact with these people. I say we take two cars; I'll drive down in my truck and you and Anna take your Land Rover. That way if I have to hop a wall, you can act like some random onlookers amused by my avoidance of paying the cheque. You wait five minutes, go back to your Land Rover and I will meet you at the farm when I am sure I'm not being tailed," I suggest.

I see Alfred's mind ticking over, analysing it, picking the plan apart like a jigsaw. Running over every contingency, he nods absentmindedly. What it must be like to have a brain that works like his.

"I like it, mostly. It works logically; if the objective was to keep us safe it would be perfect but it leaves you very exposed. I won't be able to cover you, kid. If anything happens, the moment you hop the wall you are on your own," Alfred concludes, his face grim and a mirror of Anna's.

"Don't worry, I will always find my way back to the farm." I wink at Anna and she smiles brightly, blushing a little.

"You have coordinates and everything," she beams.

"What are you two talking about? I feel like I missed the joke."

"Nothing. Look, the deal was to let you help me, it was never to expose you and Anna or the farm. You get discovered; you wouldn't even be safe there. This is the right play, fella. I've got this," I say much more confidently than I feel.

"I know you do, kid. It is smart, it just goes against the grain. Right, you are the boss. This is your play; we work it your way. I've booked the table under Mac Scott. I figure Alisha wouldn't know your alias. Anna, your table is two tables in front of Mac's, under the name Bella White. Make sure you sit behind Alisha's chair; you don't want her seeing you watching. Also bring a magazine or something, makes it less obvious that you are watching. I will be roaming the perimeter."

Alfred talks me through the communications. He gives me an earpiece that picks up my audio and also allows me to hear Alfred and Anna. It is tiny; it is hard to imagine something so small being able to do all that. We test them; it feels massive in my ear but it works perfectly.

"These earpieces pick up everything, it will pick up you and Alisha easy as pie, so don't shout because it's unnecessary and it will make you look weird. Don't fiddle with it either because that also looks dodgy. Right, remember, bring your gun tomorrow. Holster it under your blazer and hope that you don't need it. We meet there at 10.30 in the car park," Alfred concludes. Alfred and Anna leave just as Billy arrives for training; this day already feels so long but this is not the time to cut out on training.

"Hey Billy, no sticks today?" I ask.

"Not today no, I actually want to show you how much it improves all of your defence and attack moves across all martial arts. So, we are going to be boxing today and instead of you just hitting me, today I will be fighting back. Don't worry, we will be going slow at first."

"Sounds good to me."

I am excited. He will no doubt kick my arse, but I am eager to learn, now more than ever but I can't help but notice that he seems a bit off.

"Are you okay, Billy?"

"Yes… Yes, sorry McKenna. I'm a little distracted, I do apologise, I am okay," he rambles, giving me a rigid smile.

He is clearly holding something back but I don't press him; I don't really know him well enough for that. Besides, it would be my luck that it's about Anna and I am probably the last person he should turn to about that. We do some slow-motion fighting and he is right; I am finding it easier to block his punches than I was and I am finding that my left hand which is my weakest is hitting more effectively too.

I ask Billy if we could work on some hits that are likely to put someone down fast. I am not the best fighter yet and I want to know that I can bring someone down if I need to. He shows me a short quick jab to the throat that can make it hard to breathe, giving me time to get away, it also hurts like hell. Also, a hard kick down on the kneecap of a straightened leg, making it hard to walk after, let alone chase and in some cases can even break the knee. The palm to the nose is another but Billy warns me that it can be a kill shot.

"If all else fails, Mac, if you are being attacked by a man, you can always hit them in the crown jewels, never fails to floor a guy," he chuckles.

The training is over quickly and I am glad for that; I lock the door behind

Billy. I set to work preparing for tomorrow, I look at the doodle Alfred drew of the restaurant and flick through some photos he sent me that he took of the restaurant while he was booking the table but I really have nothing else I can do. Nerves are starting to hit me now and it is making time move with unnerving speed. Self-doubt is creeping in, clawing at the edges of me.

I am getting those same feelings I had the night I went to confront Alisha; it is all a bit too much déjà vu for me. There are new fears too, I see the wooden box on the desk, inside is my gun. Do I really have what it takes to use it? Can I aim it at another human being and pull the trigger? Even if it is to save my own life, I am not too sure. That fact alone scares me — what chance do I have if I can't even save my own life?

Do I really believe Alisha will set me up? No, she could have done that a thousand times over by now if she wanted to. I am just being cautious because above all else the only thing I know for sure is, I can't trust her and I won't go into anything unprepared again, that is what got me shot. It is hard though, the thought of facing her, I want to be able to keep my game face on but she has always seen through my pretences and I can't let her do that; somehow, I have to keep control.

I have another workout, nervous energy is tingling in my chest and arms so I punch the crap out of the punch bag and use the climbing rope; it does actually help, for a while anyway. I shower and I go to bed, knowing it is too early. There is nothing else I can do to prepare. I pour myself a whiskey and put a movie on that I have no intention of watching. I just want some noise to drown out the loudness of my thoughts. I get that feeling again, like a soldier who has been drafted to a war he didn't sign up for. I don't think there will be danger tomorrow but I know danger is coming.

My mind flicks to the various war films I've seen, when a solder has fallen and is dying, there is always a scene where the dying solder takes a bloodied letter out from inside their jacket and hands the letter to a comrade. The letter they pre-wrote to their loved ones in the event of their death.

Nope, this is not the time for morbid thinking, Mac.

Goonies never say die.

Memories flood my mind with a sunshine glow, melting away the ceiling of the warehouse, a warm sun-bathed quality playing with the essence of the images. My eyes widen, unfocused and glassy.

The memory swirls.

Alisha sitting on a grand ornate chair, the sun shining on her from the open balcony. I open my eyes and find her sitting there eating strawberries wearing nothing but my shirt, staring out into the brand-new sunny morning. I lay naked on my chest; the soft sheets cool on my skin. She hasn't yet seen me watching her, I could watch her for hours.

"You know it is entirely unfair that you wake up looking that beautiful. How the hell am I ever going to leave this room?" I mutter, slightly groggy.

"All part of my master plan, to keep you here," she says playfully as I get up and walk over to her. The sunshine warms the pale skin on my back as I stand over her.

"It's working," I whisper.

I brace myself on the chair arms and lower myself down to her, kissing her gently. My tongue tracing her bottom lip and tasting the strawberry juice that lingers there. Her hands reach around the back of my neck, pulling me closer to her. I put my hands on her waist and lift her till she stands. My kisses travel down her neck as I unbutton and take my own shirt off of her. With a flirtatious giggle she pushes me down on the chair roughly and straddles me. I nibble and I kiss her breasts, my tongue tracing the perfect round of her hard, excited nipples.

"I think I might be becoming addicted to you," she moans in my ear.

I shake the memory away but I am unable to shake the feelings they inspire; this conflict is a new kind of torture, as the memories come back the feelings attached become more real, both in body and in my heart. I am so gut-wrenchingly torn. I fall asleep with the ghost of her smile etched in my mind.

***

I stand in front of the mirror and scrutinise myself. Alfred told me to wear a blazer, I couldn't resist the overdramatic but also the quite fitting choice to wear an almost identical tuxedo that I wore the night I met Alisha at the hotel. Black blazer with black shiny lapels, black shirt and skinny tie. The original is lost somewhere with all my memories, but this is practically a duplicate.

I make some effort to cover my lack of sleep with some make-up, the bangle Anna bought me just sticking out under my sleeve. The cut I earned from training above my eye has just about closed up but still sits proud and angry across my eyebrow, giving me a slightly menacing look. My eyes follow down and find the scar that crosses jaggedly from the back of my ear to halfway across my throat. I now know from regaining some of my memories, how I got it. My mind recalls the images easily now, my body remembers the pain; it always struck me as odd, if someone wanted to slit my throat, they did a poor-ass job of it. I never could get anything right back then.

My reflection in the mirror washes away and is replaced with the memory, a

129

crystal-clear vision invades my mind's eye with a display of horror.

The memory swirls.

The video camera stood on the tripod; its lens set upon me – violating.

"You will slit your throat," a voice commanded, a thick accent I cannot pinpoint.

I shake my head; I did not survive all this time to kill myself. If they want me dead, they can do it themselves. It will even be a relief but I don't want to die, not like this, any way but this.

"Fuck you," I spit.

Pain erupts across my ribs, the impact sucking the air from my lungs. The exhaustion so dulling I barely grunt. My head slops around with each blow, the sound of air being forced out of my mouth with every impact.

"You slit your throat or I slit your mother's, you choose," the man spits, holding out a knife.

My hand grips the rubber handle, I take it and all I want in that moment is to ram it into his throat; cold blinding hate radiates from my core. I am chained to the ceiling and how many would I manage to kill before they kill me anyway? I am so crippled with exhaustion; I can barely lift my head let alone achieve a successful killing spree.

Futile.

I hold the knife to my throat and my knees shake violently, if it hadn't been so long since I was given water, I am sure I would have pissed myself. Thank heavens for small mercies, I guess. I apply pressure with a shaky hand; there is so much hate in my heart and that is all I have to cling on to, hate. My vision blurring with tears, the face of my mum scorching my eyes – I scream.

I feel the knife point begin to penetrate my skin; I just want it to be over. I push hard, dragging, digging and I push again, till I don't even feel the pain anymore. It will be a relief, I tell myself; I will dance my way to my own demise, I will happily shake hands with the Grim Reaper. I will expire, take an exit and become forever silent. I will do it and I will come quietly, just please don't hurt my mum.

It was all a game of course, a new and inventive way to screw with my head. The disappointment when my eyes opened again was more painful than a knife to the throat, I guess that is what they wanted. How much has Alisha seen? She had the videos, she has probably seen it all. I feel the anger bubble, I will focus on that; I need my blood to run cold. I need to keep her at arm's length and keep control. I need to remember her betrayal, her lies and her games.

My eyes harden in the mirror's reflection. I unbutton the very top button, loosen my tie slightly and take a breath. "It was all a lie," I breathe.

I am ready.

***

The truck comes to a stop outside the restaurant and I turn off the ignition. Alfred and Anna are already here, I do a double take when I see Alfred dressed in a suit.

"You scrub up well, fella."

"Monkey suit. My own fault for picking such a fancy spot for a meet," Alfred grumbles uncomfortably and I laugh, my eyes falling on Anna who is looking me up and down with an odd squint.

"What?" I ask, suddenly feeling uncomfortable.

"Nothing," she replies, looking away.

We all put in and test the earpieces and Alfred disappears to start circling the perimeter and I am left standing with Anna.

"Are you ready for this?" she asks.

"Do I look ready?" I ask, hoping my nerves are not obviously written all over my face and she looks at me.

"You look… quite hot actually…" She pauses, looking me in the eye with a daring, provocative look that sends shivers up my spine and then she looks away. "Alisha won't know what's hit her," she adds, smirking.

My stomach erupts with a different type of butterflies, she really shouldn't do that, that really isn't helpful right now. Does she realise what she is doing? I turn to her and move in right close to her ear, the ear that hasn't got an earpiece. I move close enough that only she can hear my barely audible whisper, so close that I can smell her perfume, it is sweet like candy.

"Careful, girl. This is not a game, there are consequences to fuelling the fire and I am very sure… you don't want them." My voice a playful whisper but the warning, clear.

"Okay kids, the coast is clear for now. Mac, you are clear to go in. Savannah, you wait for my go." Alfred's voice sounds loud and clear in my ear.

I pull back from Anna's ear and turn away. "I am on the move," I report.

Striding with purpose towards the entrance of the restaurant, I try to convey much more confidence than I feel as I cross the threshold and take the place in. Everything is wooden, the walls covered in weathered and aged reclaimed wood that has been transformed into cladding; some has been left natural and some has been painted in a dark nautical blue. The furniture gives the place a vibe of an old smoking room, dated but luxurious, it sets the scene perfectly.

The bar is grand, the wood polished smooth. Behind it is a backdrop of wooden structure holding wine bottles from floor to ceiling. It is dimly lit and quiet, not many people are inside. I cross the restaurant and move over towards the sets of doors that lead to the river-facing terrace. Just before I get there, I see a small desk with a man standing behind it, he is dressed to impress and greeting guests.

"Good morning, welcome to Waterside. Do you have a reservation with us today?"

"Yes, the name is Mac Scott, party of two," I confirm and the gentleman scans his book and finds the name quickly.

"Ah yes, Miss Scott, there you are. May I show you to your table? If you will follow me."

I follow, walking through the double doors and I take a seat where I am directed. It is a little busier outside and I can see why, the view is wonderful.

"Your server will be with you as soon as the rest of your party arrives, Miss Scott."

"Thank you, sir."

The outside is in complete contrast to the inside, everything is bright, modern and minimalist. Overhead is a huge white canopy that creates shade, it is laced with thousands of fairy lights creating a magical feel. The tables and chairs are completely transparent and deceptively heavy. They look like they will be incredibly uncomfortable to sit on but they actually mould to your body perfectly. To my right the River Thames is glittering in the mid-morning sun.

"Anna, you are a go," Alfred directs in my ear.

My stomach swoops and my jaw clenches, the time must be getting close, I need to focus. I need to keep my head in the game and my emotions in check. Anna walks out of the double doors and my eyes follow her to her seat, she smiles radiantly and thanks the greeter. Her eyes fall upon me as she speaks.

"I am in position," she confirms, then throws me a wink and I smirk.

My palms are sweating, I rub them against my thighs to dry them and take a deep breath. I can't help it, I hate myself for it, but I am excited to see her, God damn it. I close my eyes and my fist clenches on the table. Why can't I just hate her? Why? It would be so much easier if I could, I am sure it would hurt a lot less.

"It was all a lie," I whisper to myself.

"Mac…?" My eyes open at the sound of Anna's voice but I do not look at her.

"I'm fine."

I look at my fist on the table and make a point of releasing the clench of it, aware that I am being watched by both Alfred and Anna. I need to show more control than this. My eyes daze as I look out onto the water, my heart thudding in an uneven and slow rhythm and I calm myself.

"Mac… There is a woman approaching and the way she is strutting in that dress, she means business. Black dress approaching your position, two-minute warning," Alfred announces.

Not sure I find his commentary helpful but I appreciate the warning. I take a deep breath and tear my eyes away from the water, I sit up straight in my chair and keep my eyes forward in the direction of the door. Time seems to slow right down; this might just be the longest two minutes of my life. I keep my expression passive but inside my heart flies, inside the anticipation is mind blowing.

"Any other movement, fella?" I ask, my voice just about steady.

"She is alone, Mac, all quiet for now."

Then she appears and Alfred was right, that dress is by design. Worn with the specific motive to intoxicate me. It hangs off of her suggestively, the neckline plunges dramatically down to her navel. I am only human, there is no way for me not to be allured by that.

For fuck sakes.

She walks through the doors, walking by the side of the greeter, her eyes scanning for me. I set my jaw and then I stand, walk round to her side of the table and pull out her chair. When she arrives, I slide the chair back in as she sits down.

"Smooth, kid, very smooth," Alfred chuckles.

"She may as well not be wearing a dress," Anna spits and I smirk just a little before I walk back round to my side of the table. I undo the button of my blazer as I sit down slowly.

"If I saw the gun, Alisha saw the gun," Anna states.

"She was meant to; Mac is making a very clear point," Alfred explains chuckling throatily.

"Okay, that is sexy," Anna growls and it takes a lot of restraint not laugh and to keep my expression blank.

Their light frivolity warms the iciness in my veins, a calm steadiness washes over me and finally, I look up at her. Her eyes gaze at me with fierce ardency, we don't say a word at first, I think she is waiting for me to make the first move, trouble is I have no idea what that first move is. Thankfully the server comes over, giving me extra time to think.

"Miss Scott, Miss Cole. My name is Graham and I will be your server today. Can I get you any drinks at all?" Graham asks, his voice full of pep and my eyes don't leave Alisha's as I speak.

"Hi Graham, could I get a double shot caramel latte, please. Alisha?"

"The same please," she peeps, her voice small.

"Coming right up."

I stare at her; she is beautiful of course and so damn sexy it should be a crime. I keep my expression blank but inside the pain is palpable. The force of the desire I feel for her is impossible to quash; the anger and hurt that she inspires is sharp edged and needle pointed. The yearning blazing in my heart is threatening to char it into ash, the mania inside me is all consuming, a frenzy of emotions that takes every bit of self-control I have to prevent it from all spilling over. I take a deep breath and steel myself.

"I am relieved to see that you are okay, Alisha," I speak, my voice cool and even.

"Mac, I don't have the words to tell you how good it is to see you, looking so strong and so beautiful. You look so much like the girl I used to know."

"Except, I am not."

"No, you are stronger and somehow, you got even sexier," she states, her eyes alight with desire that dazzles me for a second, just a second.

"It is just that easy for you, isn't it? Don't try to handle me, Alisha, I am not as naïve as I used to be, it won't be as easy to manipulate me again," I snarl. Hurt sweeps across her face and my chest pangs with guilt.

"It is that easy because how I felt for you was never a manipulation, Mac, it was real, more real than anything I've ever felt. It wasn't a game."

"Is this a game?"

"How much do you remember of the hotel?" Alisha asks.

"Enough…"

"Then, how could you possibly think, that it was a game… Mac the knife?"

My eyes close reactively to the pain that punches hard in my chest at the use of her affectionate name for me. I feel her shaky and hesitant hand cup my cheek, a touch so familiar to me, my head begins to swim.

The memory swirls.

Alisha is standing leant against the hotel room door, her hair wet and smelling like flowers, her body wrapped in a silky night gown, her skin is still warm from the heat of the shower. I walk over to her, camera bag heavy in my hand I place it on the floor and go to her, I pull her to me and hold her. A movement so natural it is as if I have been doing it for years; she fits me, she melts into me and I don't want to let her go but, I do.

"I guess it is time for me to go," I groan playfully and she smiles.

Alisha lifts her hands and places them on my face, she draws me in and she kisses me. This kiss is different, it is a kiss that forces my heart to surrender, still passionate, still enticing, but it is eclipsed with emotion as if she is trying to tell me everything that she holds inside herself for me, with no words. The lust is enriched by something more, something altogether more and it ambushes me.

She breaks away.

"You better call me. It is completely unacceptable for you to mean this much to me so quickly, Mac the knife," Alisha says playfully, but there is vulnerability in her voice for the first time.

"I will call and I will call again and again because, you have got me, girl. You had me from the start," I reassure her with intensity.

I wrap my arms around her one last time, hold her tight and let her go; she steps away from the door to let me pass her.

"See you later, beautiful," I say.

I snap back to reality with a painful jolt and I gasp, my head dizzying with pain at the ghost of my former self. At her joy, her complete ignorance as to what she was walking home to.

"Mac…"

"Mac…"

Alisha and Anna's concerned voices vibrate in my ears like cinema surround sound; I am losing control, I take her hand away from my face and lean back in my chair.

"I am fine," I lie but the pain in my voice is obvious.

"I am so sorry. So, so, sorry. I know you are hurt and I don't blame you but you don't know everything. I will tell you everything, I promise I will but one thing you have to know, is that it was all real. Baby, please know that," Alisha pleads.

I slam my fist down on the table and she jumps, my eyes cold with fury, my words coming out of me in a feverish rant.

"I do know that now! It was real for you and it was real for me but that is what makes what you did to me so messed up! Alisha, I didn't come here to talk about that, so why don't you stop trying to screw with my head and tell me what you know!" I spit furiously and Alisha holds my gaze. I watch as a haunted look takes over her eyes.

"What do you want to know?" Alisha asks.

"Let's start with the videos."

"I can't tell you much about them because I didn't watch them, they were given to me about halfway through our sessions, they weren't happy with my progress with you. So, they gave me the videos, they thought they would help me understand how to trigger your memories. I was also told it should be a good incentive, seeing what they were willing to do to me if I didn't do what they asked."

The guilt pangs with a heavy thud. She must have been scared. I was like a living, scarred, messed up reminder of what they were threatening to do to her.

"You didn't watch them? Why?" I ask, confused.

"Why does that matter?"

"Why don't you want to answer?" I press.

"Because it is not relevant, you can't have it both ways, Mac. Either you want to hear how I feel, or you want to hear what happened." She looks up at me, anger and hurt so raw it paralyses me for a second.

"Okay, that is fair. What happened after I got shot?"

"They roughed me a bit, for warning you. Then one of them got a phone call and they just stopped. I heard them say, 'Yes, Mr Kaminski.' Then they told me that I have done my job and left. It happened quickly; they were clearly told to stop. I don't think they are done with me, I have seen people watching me. I move from hotel to hotel; I took three different taxis to get here."

More guilt, I wasn't prepared for all this guilt. She hasn't had it easy and she has been alone in this. I abandoned her right after she saved my life and left her to face the music alone, I left her exposed. I fume at the idea that someone hurt her, I fume at myself for letting it happen.

"Do you know who Mr Kaminski is?"

"I think so. The man that came to my office and asked me to help you regain your memory – his name was Mr Kaminski, or at least he told me it was."

The server comes back with our drinks and I politely nod at him.

"If they were watching my sessions with you, they must have known I was planning on disappearing. Why didn't they stop me?"

"I was told that I should try to stop you leaving by any means necessary but that if I couldn't, then find a way to keep the lines of communication open,"

Alisha spoke with her eyes distant and looking away from me.

"That is why you came out to the car that day, that's what made you drop the patient-doctor boundaries. You were trying to stop me leaving," I accuse but I keep my voice level. Alisha snaps out of her trance and looks at me.

"Yes, but not for the reasons you think. Mac, they didn't stop you disappearing because they want you to look for them and I had to try to stop you because if that is what they want – it is the last thing you should do. I kissed you because I wanted to, you don't have to believe me but I also hoped it would mean you would stay with me and not leave and go on a suicide mission. I hoped it would mean you would ask me to come with you so I could tell you everything safely away from the cameras, but you didn't, you were intent on leaving me behind."

I can't deny that, I had no attention of bringing her with me. I thought I was protecting her plus I had no reason to believe she would come with me. I sip my coffee; it quenches the burn of the anxious scorch in my throat, my head rattling with overactive thoughts and questions.

"Why would they want me to look for them? Why would they want me to remember? And what changed? One minute they want me to remember, the next they are shooting me," I speak flippantly and Alisha flinches.

"I don't have all the answers, Mac." Her voice warmer.

"Tell me what you do know. Please."

"I know pieces of it but I was never in on their plan, I never wanted this. I know why they took you – they think you know a man named Barrett?"

"I don't know any Barrett; it must be the guy they questioned me about but I don't know who he is," I groan, rubbing my temples, my head starting to throb with stress.

"There is something else, I know the name of the boat they kept you on. At least I think I do. I can't be sure but the night you came and they shot you, when they were on the phone and beating me up, they mentioned 'The Seabird'. I already knew they kept you on a boat, so when I heard them say it – I don't know, Mac, I just felt like it was relevant."

I rub my eyes. I had hoped for more, I can't deny it, but she is obviously risking herself coming to me and telling me and they are leads, however small. The biggest thing is it confirms what I thought, they want me to remember. More than that they want me to come for them. Why? I look at Alisha and I can't help but feel empathy for what she has been through; it is grinding on me uncomfortably.

"I left you alone in this, I'm sorry for that," I say, looking at her earnestly.

"I brought it on myself, Mac. You have nothing to be sorry for, I never thought any of this could happen. I thought they just wanted me to help you get your memory back and that it was something that you wanted anyway. It isn't an excuse; it is just the truth. The longer time went on, the more I tried to get out, the harder they pushed me. I can't tell you how much I wanted to tell you but I also knew that when I did, you would look at me exactly how you are now." Alisha's voice got smaller and smaller the more she spoke like shame and pain were suffocating her.

It hurts, it hurts bad. I just want to comfort her but I can't escape the lies she has told. I look at her, the pain in her eyes is making my resolve shake.

"You are not alone in this anymore. I am going to end it, Alisha, and if you need anything before I can, you have my number. Don't misunderstand me caring for your wellbeing as anything more than that," I say bluntly.

"I understand. Thank you, Mac."

Alisha gets to her feet and I do too, looking down at the floor. I am so pissed at myself, after everything she has done, a part of me still longs to be near her. A longing for her I have felt before, a longing that is so clear in my present that it stirs up the last moment of our past.

The memory swirls.

"I wish we could stay here a little longer," Alisha whines, her face resting on my chest and her fingertips tracing around in circles on my ribs, giving me goosebumps. I hold her a little tighter, my hand running up and down the attractive dip in her spine.

I lay in bed with her, my eyes flitting around the hotel room that we seem to have destroyed in our days here. In the time we have spent here alone and uninterrupted – I have gotten lost in knowing her, her mind, her body. I too would give a lot to stay in our bubble just a little while longer.

"You know, you could always do something that by today's standards is considered outlandish and vaguely old fashioned. You could give me your number, I could call you, take you out for dinner," I mutter.

"Careful Mac, you almost sounded like you wanted to go steady with me."

"Hey, easy, girl, I am just talking about McDonalds. You like happy meals, right?" I chortle, teasing and she rolls on top of me.

"You cheeky little…" She wrestles with me and I let her win as she pins my arms down to the bed, her smile enticing. "You are crazy for me, Mac the knife, just admit it!"

I roll back on top of her fast and playful and she giggles musically in my ear. I stare at her seriously for a moment and she stops, her eyes intense on mine.

"Yeah… crazy for you is right."

I shake my head back to reality. She has split me in two, there is a part of me that still cares for her and a part of me that can't stand her. I both want to pull her to me and push her away all at once, the most precarious balancing act and I have no idea which way the scales will tip or what will happen when they do. I button up my blazer and wait for her to leave.

"Mac…" Alisha calls for my attention. I look up from the floor and she walks right up to me; she grabs the tip of my neck tie and looks at me intently.

"The last time you kissed me, you told me that you wish we had met before all of this. At the time, you had no idea how fateful that sounded to me. How much it rocked me to the core. Something inside you kissed me and held me, just like you used to. You didn't remember me but your heart and body did. I am not giving up on that girl and if I know her, she hasn't given up on me either."

Alisha tugs on my tie and steps into me with dominance and passion, her lips are on mine quicker than I could stop them and then I didn't want to stop them. She pulls back and walks away leaving me breathless and dumbstruck.

CHAPTER EIGHT

The Calm Before The Storm

"Mac she is gone, you are both clear," Alfred's voice grumbles.

"Thank you, Alfred," I reply taking the earpiece out of my ear.

I finally look at Anna to meet the eyes that I have felt boring into me since Alisha walked away. Her expression is completely blank, unreadable and she looks away. I walk away, through the restaurant and back to my truck, leaving them both behind. Autopilot, isn't that what they call it when you drive home and you don't even remember doing it? I am running away and I don't even know what I am running from. At the warehouse I turn all the lights off, lay on the sofa and stare at the fairy lights. I lay here and let the pain ebb and flow, ebb and flow. I am not running away, I will go back, I just need time to be allowed to hurt in private.

I spend the day in darkness letting everything wash over me. I am so dog tired of all of the damn… everything. The sadness, the fear, the running, the hiding. It feels like the new normal, it feels like such hard work just trying to remember who I am, or was. My identity is overshadowed by the constant fight for life. I jump out of my skin when the intercom buzzes, it is so loud in the silence. I see a 2-inch version of Anna standing at the door and I groan. I open the door and she is stood there with her hand held out to me.

"Come with me," she says softly.

"I really don't—"

"Don't argue," she says firmly but her eyes are playful.

I take her hand; she leads me to her car and I keep quiet because I really do not have any words left to give. She drives and I let my eyes daze out the window, watching the world go by, a world I miss living in. We pull up to the farm and I get out of the car.

"Anna, I really can't take a pep talk right now, in fact, I can't take any talk at all."

"That's okay, there will be no talking, only watching."

She starts walking but I just stand there and she turns around once she realises I haven't moved and rolls her eyes.

"Seriously?" She giggles.

She comes back, grabs my hand and drags me towards the barn. This has confused me; the barn is full of junk. Why would we ever go in there? Plus, it is dark, what exactly am I supposed to see? We reach the massive red barn; it is aged and weathered and quite creepy at night. Anna unbolts the doors and opens them with a loud creak.

There are lanterns set up throwing some dim light; all of the junk and scrap metal has been pushed way back to the sides of the barn leaving the centre completely open. On the floor are some stacks of hay and blankets neatly arranged with a bowl of popcorn, a hoard of sweets and some bottles of Dr Pepper. On the second level, hanging off of the guard rail is a massive white screen. Anna walks over to the projector and suddenly my heart flies with excitement as the barn is filled with the wonderous sound of the Harry Potter theme tune and the opening credits start rolling on the big white screen.

"Oh my God, Anna! Ha-ha! This is amazing! How did you...?"

"I have been working on it for a while, I figured that you could use some normal, some fun. With what happened today, me and Pa kind of jump started the idea. Thought maybe, you could use it."

I am blown away; I look at her completely bewildered and she smiles quite proudly at herself, her expression warm and excited and I can't help but melt a little.

"Well? What are you waiting for? We are going to miss it!" she squeals gleefully and I giggle.

We both run over to the haystacks, tuck in under blankets and get stuck into some popcorn. I feel like a child on Christmas morning, giddy and high on too much sugar. I watch the film and stuff my face with far too much junk and for a while I don't think at all.

"I am going to bed before either of you think up another plan to get me killed, or worse, expelled!" I recite the words from the film without thinking.

"Oh my God – you are such a nerd, Mac Scott!" she jibes, howling with laugher.

"Yes, yes I am. I am totally okay with that. Nerds are in right now! This is my time!" I cheer.

I feel the weight of the day start to lift off of me a little, I look over at Anna and I can't help but be a little amazed by her.

"How do you do it?" I ask thoughtfully.

Anna looks at me confused. "Do what?"

"You have this magic about you. It's like, you see the world through a colourful filter lens. It is almost childlike, I've never known anything like it, even when things get bad, you have optimism. I must really drag on that; I am as far from optimistic as you can get and yet, when I need it most you always…" I trail off, embarrassed, I said more than I meant to.

"Is that what you think? That you drag us down?" She frowns and I hesitate, I never meant to get so deep and now I wish I hadn't said anything, I don't even know why I did.

"How could I not? Considering everything."

Anna is quiet, she doesn't speak for so long that I tear my eyes away from the screen to look over to her and she is staring right at me. She is looking at me curiously again, like the other day her eyes search my face for something beyond my understanding. This time though, she is not as close and that helps me keep a cool head.

"What is it that you are looking for?" I ask.

"You are not a drag on us, Mac. That man in there, he absolutely adores you. The change in him since you came along, you wouldn't understand but he was so quiet. He would just move through every day, just kind of… idling. Now he laughs and jokes, he is always moving, thinking, experiencing. He is happy."

My heart swells a little; the gentle giant, my unlikely best friend. I have so much adoration and respect for him, I can't help but smile a little. It doesn't escape my notice that she has avoided my question and that she mentioned me not dragging Alfred down, and not herself and it frustrates the hell out of me but I am not going to push anything. Quite frankly, I don't have the brain power to interpret the inner workings of her mind right now.

"Thank you for doing this. I needed it and I really appreciate that you would go to the trouble."

"Was no trouble, Mac, it's nice to see you happy," she says, smiling. "What is it that you love about these movies so much? You are full on geek-gasming right now," she teases and I laugh because I totally am.

"I don't know, I've always loved films that I can truly escape into and what better place to escape to than a secret magical world!" I pause, grinning like a child. "When I was gone, at some of the hardest moments when I was scared, lonely or hurt – I would play my favourites over in my head. It is my escape; it always has been but I think back then, it was the only thing that saved my sanity."

Anna looks at me intently, her eyes thoughtful and soft. "I've never heard you talk about it before."

"Sure, you have. I have talked about some of the memories a bit with you and Alfred, trying to find leads."

"No, we have heard the logistics, headlines. But how you felt, what it was like for you, what you went through, I have never heard you talk about once."

I look away from her, feeling like I've accidently caught myself in a trap. What the hell is wrong with me today? Why can't I seem to keep my mouth shut?

"Why would I? I have seen the look on people's faces when I am too honest about it, I don't enjoy being the reason people cringe and feel grossed out. So, I censor myself, I don't want to dim people's light, with my darkness," I admit.

"You are so blind sometimes, Mac."

My eyes close in reaction to the pain, the memory of Alisha using those exact words scraping against unhealed wounds like a cheese grater.

"What's wrong?"

"Sorry, its just – Alisha said the same thing to me not so long ago. It reminded me of it, I'm fine, it's nothing."

"I am reminding you of your ex, just what any girl wants to hear." She cringes comically, her nose crinkling.

"You don't, just the women in my life keep calling me blind, it is giving me a complex," I joke, trying to lighten the moment and it works, she laughs freely and easily and the tension lifts.

I find myself back on the sofa, again. I can't help but feel I am going round in circles; Anna drove me here so it would be a long walk back to the warehouse. My mind wanders, examining every facet of the day. Whoever took me, wants me to come and find them? Does that mean I shouldn't even try? It's not really an option now, for whatever reason they are not interested in watching me anymore, now they just want to kill me. What changed? I was the bait but now I am the prey. Even if it was an option to stop searching for answers, I wouldn't take it. I can never live peacefully while I know that these people, these monsters, are still out there.

Barrett… I say the name out loud, I say it over and over again but nothing connects. No memory, no recognition, just a whole lot of nothing. Is he the familiar man in the photograph? If they took me to draw him out, then who is he to me? What did he do to motivate these people to go to such lengths of depravity? How am I tangled up between the two? I strain, I concentrate and I fixate, trawling the very depths of my disordered brain but I fall short every time. I envisage a fishing net being dragged across the deep cold sea and re-emerging completely empty. The answers are there, like the fish in dark watery depths they are very good at hiding. Like my garbled memory, the sea holds its secrets. What is it going to take to uncover them? I am not a strong swimmer; I chuckle at the dark irony of my own analogy.

The Seabird? Could that really be the place that I was hidden? I remember clearly the constant sway of the boat, the sound of the water lapping across the wood, the nauseating stench of rotting fish. There has to be a thousand boats with that name, it is hardly original. I have no memory of actually seeing the boat even after getting some memories back. I can't shake the feeling that something is coming and every day as it grows ever closer, this constant fear is building, fear of who could get hurt when it arrives. Faces flash across my mind, magnifying my anxiety and solidifying my fears.

My mum – Plump, innocent and lovable, smiling with adoration and pride.

Alfred – Strong, wise and handsome, his crooked grin and deeply lined face.

Anna – Beautiful, elegant and captivating, the calm in the eye of a storm.

Alisha – Sexy, fierce and full of adventure and bewitching power.

How do I protect them all?

Alisha… What we had was real, I know that, I feel that, I ache for that, for her, but the pain of betrayal is always hot on my tail. It whips at me from around corners when I am least expecting it. A quick lash to remind me, she hurt me. She isn't evil, she has a purity hidden beneath all the layers of sexiness that she likes to hide behind and my God, is she ever but I don't know if I will ever be able to forgive her, only time will tell. I am still balanced precariously on the tip of the knife, waiting for the scales to tip one way or another.

I am three people; I have three parts. The Mac before, Mac during, and Mac after I was taken. There are gaps between my separate selves, dark voids making it impossible to pull myself together into one complete person. I feel everything from all of the Macs' perspectives. Mac before was infatuated with Alisha and excited for a possible future with her. Mac during hoped and fantasised over the chance I could meet her again. Mac now is still all of these things but can't stand her for the hurt and betrayal she has inflicted.

No wonder I am so messed up.

I don't think I will ever understand any of it till all three Macs collide. Who knows what will happen when they do?

***

"Games night? Seriously? And you call me a nerd!" I tease, unable to hide my lack of enthusiasm for the idea.

Anna and Alfred spent the day running the leads Alisha gave us, while I have been training all day with Billy on the farm. The trouble is, the names Barrett and Kaminski are not a lot to go on. Barrett could be a first or second name and there are way too many to choose from. Kaminski is a Polish surname, which makes sense because in some of my memories one of the men torturing me called me 'mala suka', which translates to 'little bitch', in Polish. Still though, it's a common Polish surname and not much to go on.

The boat is coming up blank at the moment too; there are many boats by the name *Seabird* as I suspected there would be and it could be any of them. Alisha wasn't sure they were even talking about the boat I was on; it isn't a dead end, more like a needle in a haystack. Alfred said he had a significant lead from the memory stick before I found the letter from Alisha and I am anxious to get on to it but Anna has decided she wants a games night.

"Oh, come on, Mac, it will be fun!" Anna whines.

"Billy has been kicking my arse all day, I probably smell as offensive as I feel. Why don't you three play and I will go back to the warehouse and come back tomorrow."

"Shower here, I have clothes you can wear! Yes! Let's go, come on!" Anna squeals excitedly.

"Fine, but I swear if you even attempt to make me wear pink so help me..."

Anna's face lights up and I can't help but laugh, although that doesn't diminish my annoyance any. She drags me upstairs by the wrist and I groan and strop all the way up, stomping my feet as I go but this just makes her laugh at me more.

"Get in the shower, I will find you some clothes – no pink, I swear."

It is good to be clean, it really has been one very long day fighting with Billy. I am gaining in confidence and everything he has taught me is starting to feel more natural but there is no denying how much my body aches. I am stretched and bruised and my muscles feel hard and knotted. The hot water feels amazing on the aches but getting out of the shower, I quickly begin to seize up. I wrap myself in a towel and make my way to Anna's room.

The memories of waking up in here after I got shot are so clear in my mind but it feels like so long ago now. I find the clothes on Anna's bed and quickly slip on some jeans when the sight of my own handwriting catches my eye. Taped to the side of her bedside table, the word 'Goof' scrawled on the note I left inside her laptop. I had forgotten I even did that; a warm feeling radiates though me and I smile. Does she have to be so damn cute?

Today has actually been good for me, I have spent most of it with Billy and the progress has been great but it also means I have seen him with Anna a lot. It is a relief that as hard as it started out to be, as the day went on it got easier and easier to see them together. I am happy to see her happy, I am happy that I finally found a friend box strong enough to keep her in. I feel quite proud of my growth as a human being, I've got this.

"Pa, that cannot be a real word. It looks totally made up! Are you cheating?"

I sip my whiskey and supress the laugh threatening to burst from me; it turns out Anna is super competitive and a poor loser to boot, her tantrums on the matter are incredibly entertaining.

"I don't cheat, Savannah, don't get stroppy just because my brain is bigger than yours," he teases.

"Okay, Google will settle this," I suggest, grabbing my phone. With a few taps of the screen I can't help but smirk. "Swarf: Fine chips or filings of stone, metal or material produced in machining operation," I conclude and Alfred laughs with gloating and Billy puts his arm around Anna.

"Darling, you can't win them all," Billy soothes.

"Sounds like a made-up word," Anna pouts. "Okay, okay, it is my turn. I am coming for you, Pa."

The whiskey is making me feel merry and warm and I am having fun; we are sat at the dining room table playing Scrabble. The idea filled me with dread and boredom but after a couple of drinks, it is not so terrible. Everyone is laughing and merry with alcohol and after all my protesting, I am actually glad I stayed. I put my Scrabble pieces on the board and I am quite happy with myself as I run over the triple-word score.

Poontang.

"Ha-ha, I love that word!" Alfred bellows happily. Billy looks embarrassed and Anna is scowling at me dramatically.

"Oh, don't get butt hurt, girl," I tease.

"Poontang? What is a poontang?"

"You are such a Disney princess; I am not really surprised you don't know," I snigger. Anna picks up my phone and then I laugh when it becomes obvious, she has found the word's meaning.

"Why am I not surprised, Mac-attack? I am the furthest thing from a Disney princess, thank you very much. Oh oops, your phone is vibrating. You have a… message." Her smile slips a little. I take the phone back from Anna and the screen is lit up with a message bubble reading, 'I miss you.' And my stomach falls into my gut.

Alisha.

My eyes flick to Anna who has moved away, avoiding my gaze and sat back on Billy's lap. I continue the game to the end without a single second passing without wondering what I am supposed to do about it. Do I text her back? Do I ignore her? The irritating table tennis is batting back and forth, bouncing in my brain so when Anna starts to pack up the game, I pick up my whiskey and make my way to the fire pit. As soon as the outside air hits me, I realise I am a little tipsier than I thought.

Oops…

My alcohol-fuelled judgement isn't very sound at the moment, I could reply but God knows what I would say. I see Anna standing with Billy at his car and I can't help but be a little jealous. Not at seeing Billy with her, although… Okay, maybe a tiny bit but mainly over the companionship they have.

I have never felt the need to be with someone, I am okay with my own company but now I know that I can't be with anyone at all, it is a lonely thing. The very idea of someone touching my scars scares me, yet I crave to be touched. The classic case of wanting what you can't have, the grass is always greener. It is safer for everyone; I am still an anchor, nothing has changed but that doesn't stop the loneliness that zero contact and affection inspires.

The chill of the night starts to set in and I fetch some firewood and stoke the fire; this was more challenging in the dark with alcohol sending me a little skewwhiff. I enjoy the sound of the crackle and fizzes as the trapped steam escapes the wood in little pop explosions. The darkened sky is cloudless tonight, the moon's beam is brilliant and mysterious. I take out my phone and type 'I need time', and put the phone away. I could write a lot worse. I hear the familiar light footfall of Anna's feet cracking on twigs.

"Hey, are you okay?" she asks and I smirk.

"Subtle," I reply, chuckling and she laughs. "I am fine, girl. You don't need to check on me, you know."

"Busted." She blushes.

"Are you okay?" I ask.

"Why wouldn't I be?"

"Just checking." I grin cheekily.

"McKenna Scott, are you a little tipsy?"

"Almost definitely, probably certainly. It is not my fault; I was going to go home like a good girl, I was corrupted."

"Oh, I see it is my fault is it?"

"Yes ma'am… Oo sorry, it's princess isn't it?" I tease.

"Careful Mac, you don't want to test me in your condition. You will lose."

"Oh my God I've got it, weren't you in Frozen? There is an Anna in that, right?" I say, goading her.

"You. Are. In. Trouble!"

Anna launches herself out of her chair and I bolt; she comes right after me and I run, terribly. It is taking too much focus not to trip so I stop and turn around to see where she is and she runs straight into me, knocking me flying and landing on top of me.

"Oww!" I whine with a chuckle. "As if I haven't been thrown on the floor enough today, woman!"

"Oh, as if you didn't deserve it and more!"

"That… is true, but I probably wouldn't lay on top of me," I say seriously, wincing and Anna stops laughing immediately.

"I'm sor—"

I roll her over fast so that I am sat top of her and pin both her hands with one of mine, while I use the other to tickle her senseless.

"Payback! Bahahaha!" I squeal gleefully.

"Oh… No… Mac! Stop… Stop. Not fair! You tricked…" Anna manages between the laughing as she attempts to pull her wrists free.

"Oh yeah, not fair? Why is that? Come on, Princess Anna, spit it out!"

"Oh you… Are… Dead… Macker Packer!"

I stop tickling her, the use of an old and very much hated nickname stopping me in my tracks.

"You did not just call me that! Take it back! Take it back right now!" I complain, dramatically aghast and I am momentarily distracted. I let go of her hands and she takes full advantage of having them free by pushing herself upright and then... She is right there, her face mere inches from mine.

"I take it back," she whispers.

Tingles enrapture me with dizzying power. Again, she stares intently at my face but this time with her so close, close enough to feel her breath tickle my lips, I am held hostage by her. She has bewitched me and I cannot move and... I don't think I want to.

"Are you ever going to tell me why you do that?" I whisper.

"You are not ready for the answer," she breathes and I see sadness highlight her deep green eyes and I frown; what I would give to read her mind just for a moment.

"Try me," I encourage.

"Close your eyes."

"Why?" I ask anxiously.

"Do you trust me, Mac?"

I hold her gaze and see the encouragement in her eyes, soft and warm. I don't want to trust her, I don't want to trust anyone ever again and yet, over time, somehow – she has made it impossible for me not to. I take a deep breath and I close my eyes. I feel the back of her hand stroke my cheek with feather-light touch and I flinch.

"Don't be afraid. You are sat on my lap, remember? You can move whenever you want," she says and I smile, despite the anxiety twisting in my chest.

Her fingertips trace the arch of my eyebrows and then down my nose, stroking the bridge between my eyes and my forehead. I feel her run her fingers through my hair, sweeping it out of my face and then she traces the hollow of my eyes with her thumbs, her palm resting across my cheek. My heart begins to burst with pleasure and pain, accelerating the beats and quickening my breath; the lump in my throat rises painfully against my will. I am being touched and it melts the icy loneliness that occupies me, it breaks away the walls encasing my heart, breathing life into it. I begin to gasp, my body trembling as I try to keep control of myself.

Anna holds my face in both hands, her hands completely still, sensing my fear and feeling my pain. I feel tears escape my closed eyes, they run down my cheeks hotly in the chill of the outside air, she wipes them away with her thumbs until I calm myself. One of her hands drops into my lap and she takes a hold of my hand. The other slides down my face, her fingertips resting on my jawline while her thumb slowly traces my lips. Through the pain my chest prickles with an excited thrill so potent it rocks me.

Anna's hand leaves my face, it slides slowly over my ear, then I feel her fingertips trace the jagged scar across my throat and I choke on a sob. She holds the sides of my neck in her warm, soft hands and her lips find my forehead; she kisses it and then her lips move their way down the side of my face to my ear.

"There is nothing cringe about you, McKenna Scott. I stare because you are beautiful, I stare because I want you to see yourself through my eyes and not this broken vision you have of yourself. You see us as the light because you think that you are the darkness, but you are wrong, you are the fire that keeps us alight. You don't drag me down, Mac… You wake me up," Anna hisses passionately.

My eyes open, my breath comes out in strangled gasps of exhilaration and grief and she holds me steady; her arms wrap around me as the pain of a thousand hurts expel from me. She holds me tight to her and I no longer flinch at her touch, I pull her close, my face buried in her shoulder, my hand knotted in her hair. I breathe her in, making no attempt to hide my sobs; she smells incredibly sweet, like candy.

As her hand holds the back of my neck her fingers lightly caress it; flurries of tingles shiver down my spine. My face is buried in her shoulder, my breath is ragged as the tears flow and I turn my head, bringing my lips to her neck and I kiss it, just once and she shudders in my arms. Desire, the need to kiss her is burning inside me like hell fire but… I resist. It is only then I realise, while I have to stop myself from kissing her, that I am no longer scared to touch her, nor am I flinching away at her touch. The revelation hits me hard in the chest. I am dumbfounded by the sudden change and the bombardment of emotions that it brings.

My hands are steady, they are sure. I hold her tight while my hand slides down her neck and onto her chest and I hold it curiously over her heart. I feel the beats against my palm, thunderous and booming, her chest heaving in and out breathlessly. I pull back from her, I can feel her watching me now as I run my fingertips up her forearms. How strange it is to be able to touch, strange and wonderfully astonishing.

I slide my hands back down her arms and watch my own hands hold hers, my fingertips tracing hers and then I pull her hand up to my lips, kiss her fingertips and I laugh through the tears. I marvel at the ease in which I can touch her fearlessly; I relish in the emotion. Anna interlaces her fingers with mine and I smile as finally, I look up and I meet her gaze. Her eyes are blazing emerald green and glittering with tears; she smiles at me radiantly with pride, affection and wonder.

"Thank you," I choke.

"Don't thank me, it means so much to me that you trusted me and that… was, so beautiful to watch, to be a part of."

Damn… I am going to need a bigger box.

***

I hear movement and I open my eyes; the whiskey is thick in my head; my neck is stiff and painful. I am slumped over at the kitchen table, my face stuck to the smooth wooden surface. The vague memory of not being able to sleep hits me; I went for a glass of water and sat down at the kitchen table, Anna went to bed and I was sitting here trying to process everything and I must have fallen asleep.

"Ugh, ouch."

"I was wondering when you were going to wake up, kid," Alfred chuckled.

"Oh… Ugh… Yeah… I need…" I struggled through the fog.

"Coffee, yeah I guessed as much," Alfred says, amused, putting a coffee down in front of me.

"Oh, you are a beautiful human being."

The coffee helps almost immediately. Alfred comes and joins me at the dining table, bringing with him the most welcome bacon sandwiches. I devour them quickly and I feel much more human by the end of it. The more awake I feel, the more I notice the troubled expression that Alfred has.

"How are you doing, kid?"

"I feel much better now, thank you Alfred. Are you okay?"

"Yeah, I'm alright. It's just, that lead I told you about – from the memory stick. I know you are anxious to get on it and now I have seen it, I am too but from what I have seen, kid, there is a shit storm coming our way and I need you to be ready. There are some things that can only be learnt in a storm and I would rather you learn them before this particular shit storm arrives. So, that being said – I do have a suggestion that I hope you will trust me on."

The concern on Alfred's face has me rattled, he looks weary and that is something I have never seen on his usually unshakable face. My stomach is in knots. What could be so bad? I clench my jaw, fear gnawing at me. I wish he would just tell me but I also trust his judgement.

"Speak your mind, fella," I encourage and he smiles, relaxing a bit.

"Your training is going well but a massive chunk of it is missing. This was intentional, I don't know, kid, maybe I hoped we wouldn't have to go there but now I am thinking avoiding it is doing you a disservice. In the SAS there is a stage of training we call 'survive, evade, resist and extract'. This test stage is designed to break you; the first phase requires you be dropped to an unknown location and the objective is to escape capture from a hunter force and reach a chosen rendezvous.

"However, whether or not a recruit escapes them and makes it to the rendezvous or not doesn't matter because that is only the escape and evade portion of the exercise. The next phase, resist and extract, is designed to simulate being captured by the enemy. Cadets are required to undergo 36 hours of resistance to interrogation, they are put through the ringer with physically and mentally uncomfortable situations and must keep hold of any sensitive information. They blab, and they are done.

"This portion teaches you a strength that I already know exists in you. The trouble is I don't think you know that it does. To be able to face what is coming, you will need to face the fear and pain of what they did to you and you will need to believe you have the strength to get through it. This part of the training – it is about facing fears and breaking your weaknesses and being able to think under stress.

"With everything you have been through, kid, you can see why I don't want to put you through this. The last thing I want is to cause you more pain, or traumatise you further. The thing is, I know that if you do get through it, it will help you break free of what they have done to you and when you do face them, they won't be able to hold your fear over you and that could save your life."

I can definitely see why he has avoided this and my initial reaction is to do the same. What kind of coward does that make me though? These people broke me and if I ever want to end them and the threat they pose, then I have to face the pain they have inflicted, I have to conquer the fears they have given me. Can I withstand that kind of pain again? Can I survive that amount of fear?

"Do you know what is coming?"

"No, not for certain, but I can read between the lines of what is on the memory stick. I know enough to be considering putting you through this." Alfred sighs, his face grim.

Yep – I'm scared.

"If we do this, how and when? Do you have a plan?"

Why would I even ask that? He always has a plan for everything. He is Stan, the man, who always has a plan.

"I do have a plan; if you accept it means we leave for Wales tonight. If you want to do this then I will run through it with you later today. I have some buddies willing to help. I can't be the one to do this, it will feel very real for you and for whoever puts you through it and I haven't got it in me to detach myself from you in that way but I will be around. When it is all over, we go through the lead on the memory stick."

This is the worst hangover in history.

"Let's do it," I say eventually and Alfred claps me on the back, reassuringly.

"You will be alright, kid; I would be more scared of Savannah than my buddies – I mentioned the possibility of doing this a few weeks ago and let's just say she wasn't happy about me doing this to you. So, I would expect her to be in a pissy mood, when she finds out," Alfred says, wincing, and I chuckle. That really doesn't surprise me.

"Alfred, you are not doing this to me, you are doing it *for* me and I can see why. Try not to feel crap about it. You gave me a choice, I made it, not you."

Alfred smiles at me. "Thanks, kid. Rest up today, eat as much as you can and I have all the gear you need here. Just take the day to get your head straight."

That sounds ominous. I shudder. I take my coffee to go sit by the fire, but my mind is too busy so I walk. It is misty out; it gives the huge open fields a mystical and eerie feel. As I walk through the grass the morning dew clings to my trouser legs, soaking them. I stop by the back fence and I lean against it, taking in the distant view of the farm. It was stood by this fence that Anna persuaded me to accept their help so long ago; I remember how anxious I was to leave this place, to leave them. The fear of getting close to anyone, the fear of them getting hurt weighed on me. Now, all this time later, Alfred is my best friend and Anna is… Well, she is whatever Anna is but they have become my family and in the end that is why I know I have to do this. The stronger I am, the better I can protect them.

My eyes follow to the middle of the main field where I was sat in the grass with Anna last night and my stomach fills with butterflies. Did she know about this then? Was she anticipating that Alfred would pitch this to me soon? Probably. Is that why she did what she did? I don't know why but the idea that of that hurts a little. She doesn't want me to do this so it was probably out of worry which should be okay – except, I can't escape that, I want her to have done it because she wanted to, not out of worry or obligation.

That really isn't the priority right now, preparing for what is coming is. How do I prepare for this? There will be pain, that I am sure of. Physical pain I can deal with, but mental… What if it triggers memories and I lose it? How long will it go on for? There is no way of knowing. The unknown has always scared me a little and it doesn't get much more unknown than this for me.

"Accept the things you cannot control," I mutter.

I keep walking, but I am slowly making my way back towards the farm. I can smell the smoke of the fire and I am getting cold from having wet legs. Anna is probably up by now and I am bracing myself because of Alfred's warning. Anna doesn't seem to get annoyed easily, she is patient and compassionate but when she is pissed, she doesn't hide it. Like all of her emotions she wears them outwardly; for the most part I love that because it means I don't have to guess with her. Lately though, I feel like I have to guess more and more.

Back at the house Alfred has coffee and custard creams waiting. I am not exactly hungry but his warning to eat as much as possible is still ringing in my ear. I see a lot of hunger coming my way, that's okay – hunger I've been through before. It sucks but of all the things that could happen it is the least of my worries. Alfred is running round getting things organised, he keeps disappearing and reappearing. Watching him is making me nervous so I am just about to take my coffee down to the fire when Anna comes down the stairs, groggy in her PJs, my fresh coffee is out of my hands in a flash.

"Thief," I jibe, trying to gauge her mood while I make myself another.

"You make good coffee, my eyes are inside out, I am not safe to operate the kettle right now," she mumbles groggily. She seems okay and the more coffee she sips the more approachable she becomes, this much I have learned.

"Pa, why are you running round like a blue-arsed fly?" Anna yawns and Alfred looks at me with a wince.

"Well err… I am getting mine and Mac's kit ready, we are leaving tonight, for Wales," Alfred mumbles carefully. Huh, he almost seems scared of her. I chance a look at Anna and her expression is blank; I've seen that expression before and I didn't understand it then either. She gets up from her chair and walks outside without another word, it is like she stormed out, without the storming part.

"Well, I knew that was coming," Alfred groans.

"I will talk to her, don't worry."

I walk out to look for her but she is exactly where we all seem to go for some quiet time, the fire pit. I don't really want to intrude on her but it is not like I have time to waste. I walk down and take my usual chair. Anna doesn't look up at me when I arrive, her eyes are dazed and staring into the fire.

"How much trouble am I in?" I ask, wincing playfully.

"Heaps," she says, not looking up.

"And Alfred?"

"Even bigger heaps."

I get up and walk around the fire and I kneel down in front of her so she can't avoid my eye line; her eyes are sad and the stress on her face is evident.

"Talk to me please, girl. I can't leave with you mad at me," I say softly.

"That doesn't really motivate me to talk to you."

I smirk and then she struggles not to too; I reach out and take her hand without thinking and realise that I feel no anxiety at all. For a moment I am shocked by it, I look up at her and she is looking at my hand holding hers, her eyes unblinking and quickly I let go.

"Sorry… I did it without thinking, shocked me as much as—"

"You goof, don't apologise, I was just surprised but that doesn't mean it's a bad surprise. Now give me it back," she says playfully, pouting, and I chuckle and I take her hand again. How odd that it feels so natural now.

"Why are you mad at Alfred? You know he is just trying to help me; I know you know that so, why?"

"Because he told me the things they do and it is going to hurt you, it is going to scare you and I… I don't want you going backwards when you have been through hell to get to where you are now. You holding my hand right now is just proof of that, Mac."

"Is that why you did that last night? Because you knew what was coming?"

I had to ask, it was eating at me but I look away when I do, worried the answer is going to hurt me and I don't want her to see it in my eyes when it does. Then I feel her hand on my face; she gently pulls me back into her eyeline.

"I did what I did because I wanted to, I wanted to long before Pa mentioned this," she says softly. Relief washes over me, relief and then tingles.

"Thank you… for wanting to."

"Thank you… for wanting me to want to," she says playfully and I blush.

"I will be okay, you know, if there is a chance that this is going to help me end this and help me protect you both, as well as myself then I have to do it. Pain and fear, it isn't something new to me, I can handle it. I will be back before you know it and you can rag on me all you like but don't be mad at the old man, he is dreading it as much as I am, I can tell."

"Oh no, I won't be waiting till you get home."

"What are you talking about?"

"Come with me," Anna requests and she gets up and starts walking back to the house. I feel like I missed something but I follow her anyway. When we enter the kitchen, Alfred is sat at the dining table writing a list of some sort. Anna sits down and I follow suit. Alfred looks up, his eyes wary.

"Savannah, I know you are not crazy about this but I have my reasons, surely you know I wouldn't do this if I felt there was any other choice. I will take care of Mac." Alfred speaks clearly and calmly, but I can tell by his face he is bracing himself for whatever he expects Anna is going to unload.

"I know that, Pa. I may not like it but I know you must have your reasons." Alfred looks up, surprised.

"Right, well. I am glad that we are on the same page."

"Oh, I never said that. We will only be on the same page when you accept the fact that if this is going to happen, then I am coming too."

How did I not see that coming?

"Savannah, that is not a good idea. I know you are worried but if you come you are going to have to sit by and watch all this happen to Mac and you just won't be able to do that, you will want to stop it and once it all starts that wouldn't be good for her. I understand why you want to…"

"Pa, I am going," Anna states so fiercely that I am taken aback. Alfred's jaw clenches, the tension in the room is uncomfortable and I rub my suddenly throbbing temples.

"Before this conversation continues, can you tell me what I am in for? Maybe we can find a compromise we can agree to, if I know what is going on," I suggest, trying to mediate.

"That sounds… fair," Anna agrees begrudgingly.

"Alright, kid." Alfred pauses and clears his throat. I can see that he is trying to get his nerve up, I have never seen Anna and Alfred at odds and I am not enjoying it.

"We will be traveling to Sennybridge Training Camp in Wales. This area is closed to civilians and is used by the military to train in everything from field exercise to artillery practice. The majority of the training area is on the Mynydd Epynt, a wild plateau covered by bog and grass. There are stream valleys that contain woodland and meadows, the area is remote and the terrain will be tough."

I listen intently, nervous butterflies flutter in my stomach. This whole thing has me nervous but surprisingly I am excited too, to test myself.

Masochistic much.

"You will be dropped in an area approximately 10 miles from your rendezvous with basic rations and kit and you will be hunted by a force attempting to stop you being able to reach the rendezvous. Their job is to capture you, your job is to evade them. When you reach the rendezvous the phase changes to the resist portion of the training."

"Who is the force that will be hunting me?"

"Billy and some of his squadron but don't let that fool you, they won't be going easy on you, kid. The sooner you see them as the enemy, the better off you will be because that is exactly how they will treat you. However, if you feel you need to stop just use the phrase 'all quiet on the western front' and the simulation will stop immediately.

"They will either capture you at the rendezvous or en route to it and when they do, they will begin the interrogations. Your job is to resist and keep your mouth shut; they will push you, kid, there will be physical and mental stress inflicted on you, it will feel very real. I will be watching through video link in the same complex that they will take you to. I will be there, but I won't be in the room with you, you won't see me till it is over.

"This phase has only a 10% pass rate in the SAS. I cannot stress how hard it is; they will humiliate you, hurt you and intimidate you but if you can withstand them long enough, the phase will end and you will have completed it and you will have gained in the strength and understanding you will need going forward. You will prove to yourself, that the people out there hunting you right now, no longer have a hold over you."

I don't know what to say for a while, what do you say to something like that? My head pounds and I have the urge to sleep. I rub the palms of my hands into my eyes.

"Ah, sounds a piece of cake," I say eventually, joking, and he laughs. Anna, does not.

"Are you still up for this, kid? I can abort this any time…"

"No, I am good, fella. I mean, I can't pretend I am looking forward to it but if there is a chance that this will help me then I have to do it. Besides, I have always wanted to go to Wales," I add, chuckling.

My eyes fall to Anna who has that blank look on her face again. Whatever that look is, I don't like seeing it. She is a person whose expressions are so animated that it is hard not to be infected by it. When she laughs, she laughs with her whole face and you want to laugh too. When she is sad, it really hits you in the gut and you can't help but feel sad too but this blankness, it is haunting and cold and so alien on her.

"Savannah, are you really telling me that you want to be in that room with me watching, as your boyfriend and his brothers interrogate McKenna? Are you telling me you would be able to just sit by and let it happen? Would you be able to look at your boyfriend the same, after seeing this?" Alfred asks.

I look at her, waiting to understand what is going on in her head and she looks back at me, giving nothing away. I can see why Alfred doesn't want her to come and to be honest I don't want her to come either. The idea of her watching as they try to break me, I don't want anyone seeing me that weak – her especially – and why she is so insistent on it is beyond me.

"I am coming. So, you two may as well just build a bridge and get the hell over it."

CHAPTER NINE

False Prophet

It has been a long and awkward drive to Wales; there has been small talk, there has been sniping and there has been silence. Alfred and Anna are still at odds and I have to say, I am with Alfred on this one. I am a little annoyed that he caved and I just don't see why Anna needed to come. I am sure she has her reasons but she has been extremely quiet about whatever they are, just like I have my reasons for not wanting her to come but I can't actually tell her what they are without making a complete chump of myself.

Whatever I am about to go through won't be fun and I just don't want to show that kind of weakness. She has seen me at some very weak points already but not since what happened in the field. Her touching me, breaking those barriers down and helping me break through the fear of touching and being touched has shifted something between us – for me. She is still my friend; I still want that but now there is a… wanting, much stronger than it was before and I haven't had the time to shut it down. It isn't as easy to shut that down without the wall separating us that my fears of affection had created.

She burst open the fortified friend box I put her in. To her, she probably thinks she is being a good friend right now. To me, I am still in the middle of the field trying not to kiss her and the last thing I want to feel when I go through this is watched or judged when I am weak, by someone I am attracted to. Of course, there is no way I can tell her that, so I am stuck keeping quiet and trying to mediate Anna and Alfred. Inside, I am pissed.

Smile and nod, Mac, smile and nod.

I am sat up front of the Land Rover with Billy and Anna sat in the back trying to prepare mentally for what is about to come. Alfred isn't able to give me any details, only that nothing is going to happen till tomorrow evening, which isn't a lot to go on but at least I know when we finally do get there, I have some time to get some rest and try to brace myself for the experience.

The whole evading capture phase, I am looking forward to, it is like a large-scale game of hide and seek and I am keen to see how I will fare. Nervous, yes – but keen. However, the weather has turned and I am concerned that it is going to continue to be cold and stormy while I am on the run. The interrogation part, I have no shame in admitting, I am scared of. I am trying to remind myself that I can stop this at any time and this isn't actually real but I know that it will feel real, that is the point. I am not scared of the pain, more what they can do to me mentally.

My only consolation is there is no way they can cause the kind of pain I have already experienced at the hands of men that have captured me. I can take pain but mentally, am I weaker after everything that happened to me? I have a feeling my buttons will be easy to push and that means I could easily fail and the only thing I know for sure, is that I don't want to fail.

"We are roughly thirty minutes out," Alfred announces.

I was looking forward to seeing Wales but it is pitch-black and pouring with rain; so far there hasn't really been anything much to look at. The sound of the rain pounding down would be soothing if it wasn't for the screech of the window wiper blade that clearly needs changing. I am cold, but enjoying the feeling, it is staving off the feverish panic that is burning on my skin.

"How are you doing, McKenna, nervous?" Billy asks.

"Yeah a bit. I am good, Billy, thanks."

I don't look round; my eyes have been firmly forward for most of the drive. I opted for the front seat to allow Billy and Anna to sit together, but I feel like I can sense her eyes burning into the back of my head every so often, I am probably just being paranoid. The truth is I was getting better at seeing them together, but since our encounter in the field, a green-eyed monster has reappeared, rearing its stupid, ugly head and I am having trouble stamping on it.

"Ah, that is completely natural, no shame in that," he says cheerfully.

The car begins to slow down as we reach the entrance to Sennybridge Training Camp. The headlights illuminate the entrance and my eyes squint through the rain-battered windscreen to get a view of what is ahead.

The site is closed off with a metal chain-link fence with barbed wire lace-looped around the top; my eyes fall onto two metal signs fixed to the fence.

First a large red sign that reads 'camp entrance only, all personnel' and the only other sign I can squint enough to say reads 'switch off headlights'. Alfred follows that instruction before I can read any more and Billy leaves the car to go get the gates open. There are a lot of small buildings all knotted close together in clumps and in the background behind everything, a huge green hill with clusters of trees. It looks more like a green mountain; I am reminded of the Teletubbies.

The car moves forward slowly creeping in the dark, we drive in and the gate is locked behind us and the moment I hear them clinking and clanking shut my nerves redouble. There is only one car to be seen of so far, all the lights are off in all the buildings except one, it is like a ghost town. Some of the buildings are really squat with oval roofs; there is a large main building that looks like a manor house, the kind of house someone important would live in.

Alfred finally stops the car and I jump straight out; being hit with the outside air, even if it is pouring with rain out, is pure bliss. I take in the place; it is huge and that is just what I can see. We have driven into a parking area that is surrounded by lots of long buildings but the road seems to go on and on as far as the eye can see.

"This place is huge," I say to no one in particular.

"It is 31,000 acres give or take but don't worry, there are only a few buildings you need to remember. This building here is headquarters," Billy explains. I note that is the building I thought looked like a manor. "You won't need to go in there but it is good to know. All of these small buildings here on the left are administration facilities. The ones on the right look the same but are all different, in those are research facilities, recreational, intelligence and commissary facilities. The big building in the middle there you want to remember because that is your mess hall, stocking all your food and drink needs. If you will follow me, I will show you more."

I follow suit with heavy legs; we walk past the small long buildings and make our way towards the mess hall. As we pass the mess hall the camp opens up wider and there are even more buildings, I begin to worry I am going to get lost.

"This large building here is the hospital wing and the building next to that is ammunition storage, followed by another recreation room. That is the one that gets used the most because that one has a couple of pool tables and we call it, rec 2. All down the opposite side is housing and the toilet and showering facilities and I think for now, that is all that you need to know."

I start to calm down a little, I can remember where I eat, sleep and poop – I am all good in the hood. We make our way back to the Land Rover to unload our gear and Billy shows me to my barracks, which is just a bare room with a bunk bed, some drawers, a sink and a kettle. We decide to go to the mess hall for some food before we settle in for the night. The mess hall reminds me of a school canteen only bigger and more modern. Sets of seating are uniformly lined up and towards the back of the hall is a huge catering area where the food is served in big steel trays. Right now, it is empty and cold.

"Take a seat, I had them make up some sandwiches and snacks for when we arrived, I will just put the kettle on and go get them," Billy offers.

"I will give you a hand," Alfred says as he dashes off. I get the feeling he doesn't want to be left alone with Anna at the moment, quite funny really, big giant of a man is scared of his granddaughter. I take a seat on a bench opposite Anna and give her a formal smile.

"Oh ouch, you are not happy with me at all, are you, Mac-Attack?" Anna says, cringing comically and I smile but say nothing, I don't want to have this conversation because there is no way for me to be honest.

"Question is, why?" she pushes.

"It really doesn't matter, girl. I am good." I shrug.

"I thought we were past the lying portion of this relationship."

I raise my eyebrow and her cheeks blush a little. "You haven't told me why it is so important for you to be here," I argue.

"You are deflecting."

"Maybe, but it is true. You have your reasons why you feel you need to be here; I have my reasons why you being here is going to be hard for me, so maybe we just leave it at that?" I suggest, a little bit firmer than I mean to.

I am relieved when the guys come back with food to put an end to the conversation. We all tuck into an array of sandwiches, crisps and biscuits and wash it down with the worst tasting tea I've ever had. Soon, everyone is making small talk and I just want some peace; so much has happened in the past 24 hours, I feel like I am verging on a meltdown. Whether it be panic, or anger or what, I am not sure. I go back to my barracks and decide now is a good time to see what Alfred has packed for me.

Inside my barracks it is nice and quiet and I feel better for it. I am not sure how long Alfred plans on us being here but the huge army rucksack he has packed for me has me nervous. I am hoping very much that he is just over planning, that man does like his plans. Yes, I am sure that's it. I heave the rucksack onto the bed and start unpacking.

The first thing I find is a couple of pairs of camouflage cargo trousers, some khaki t-shirts and some camouflage button-down shirts. I am amazed that he managed to get some that look like they will fit me. Underneath them are some real combat boots and I smile; I do like combat boots. The next thing I pull out is a camouflage helmet and a matching utility vest that weighs a ton. That makes me a little nervous; I am guessing the weight is because it's bulletproof. The helmet has a torch attached along with a little camera.

The utility belt has two water bottles attached and a hunting knife; I check the pockets and find a flint and steel fire lighter, a long coil of wire and a map of the whole training area, it is wrapped in plastic with a compass. I am not convinced I was meant to find this yet but I decide that I will definitely spend the evening studying it. I also find some food ration packs, night vision goggles, a small first aid kit and a smaller, empty backpack. I fold up all the clothes and pack the equipment in the small backpack so that I am ready to go at a moment's notice. As always, now I have nothing to do the anxiety is hitting. I have itchy feet from being sat in a car too long so I decide to go for an explore. I take a mental picture as I leave, hoping I can remember which barracks is mine when I return and then set off into the drizzly night.

Sennybridge is impressive, there is no doubt about it, I walk past all of the barracks and move past the point that Billy showed us. It is like a town, there is even a small museum of sorts. Alfred told me that there is a small German housing village here that was purpose built in the eighties for training in 'Fighting in built-up areas'. It has enough room to house two thousand people but from what I have been told it is just used for training. In my mind's eye I see these little white houses covered in bullet holes. This place seems to be shrouded in history, there are plaques and memorial statues dotted around the place. I come to a large square green with grass so well kempt that I feel guilty standing on it; to the back centre of the green are a series of flags representing Wales and the United Kingdom and behind those are some bleachers, I make my way there and take a seat.

The anxiety is making my body feel heavy and my stomach is a constant butterfly party. Alfred told me to eat as much as I can and I can't think of anything I want to do less. The wooden bench of the bleacher is soaked with small puddles of rain water and it makes me shiver but I don't care, I lay back on it anyway and look at the stars. The fear is definitely peaking, it feels like the world is closing in on me. Why the hell did I agree to this? I am in way over my head. What makes me think I have any right to be here, pretending to be all action girl!? I have no idea what I am doing, I am going to make a complete fool of myself and with everyone watching too. I can't do this, I can't, but there is no going back now, I can't just wimp out, oh God what am I doing?

I try to focus on the stars, on the cold wet shiver tingling up my spine, on the cool breeze but nothing is stopping this suffocating feeling like the sky is falling down on me. My mouth is dry and my head begins to spin making the stars move like a warp speed scene in Star Trek and suddenly, laying down is the last position I want to be in. I push myself upright and bend forward putting my head between my knees; it helps the spinning but not the breathing. The effort to breathe is becoming too much and my breath comes out in short sharp wheezes, making a horrible whistling sound. I panic from the lack of oxygen and fall forwards to my knees, clawing at my shirt to try to free my throat from the invisible hands that choke me.

"Mac. Is that you?"

"Mac? Mac!?"

"Alfred! Come quick!!" Billy yells.

He is grabbing at me, making the panic accelerate but I can't breathe to talk so I can't tell him to stop. I see two figures running towards me in the distance but everything is darkening. Is this what it feels like to die? I feel my body make impact with concrete with a painful thud and then… nothing.

***

"She passed out, must have been some kind of panic attack," Alfred grunts grimly.

"This is exactly why I didn't want either of you putting her through this! I swear if this messes her up, I will never forgive either of you!" Anna scolds.

"Ouch," I groan and my eyes flutter open to find Alfred sat over me, my head resting on his hand.

"She's awake. Hey kid, bumped your head so don't move yet, okay?"

"I noticed, that sucked."

Concern flashes across Alfred's face; his eyes are tight with stress and suddenly the thought of not being able to get through this, scares me more than the idea of actually doing it.

"Alfred, don't pull me out, okay. Please, I know I freaked out but I need to do this, it was just a freak-out; I am fine, okay?"

"McKenna, I don't—"

"Better a freak out now than when people are actually trying to kill me. This is why you brought me here, please Alfred, don't give up on me," I plead and Alfred looks into my eyes; I am not sure what he found but eventually he nods.

"Never ever, kid," he vows.

"Good, now can you help me up and give me a minute to talk some sense into your granddaughter?" I grunt and he smiles, pulls me upwards and drags me backwards so I can lean against the bleachers. My head throbs and I feel off balance but my vision is sharpening up.

"Anna, she wants to talk to you, alone," Alfred informs but Anna doesn't look at him. Billy offers her something and she takes it and comes over without another word.

"Hey goof," she says, smiling weakly.

"Hey princess," I reply and she scowls.

"Billy grabbed you an ice pack for your head."

I take it with thanks as she takes a seat on the ground in front of me, cross-legged and with that blank expression I am coming to dread.

"Anna, why are you so mad at them? I know you don't like this; I get that, but it was me who agreed to do it. Why aren't you mad at me instead? I could have said no."

"You wouldn't have had to say no if they hadn't offered it. Of course, you said yes and I understand why you did, I can't be mad at you for that," Anna says flatly. Her voice is dead in a way I've never heard before.

"That still doesn't explain where this is coming from, girl. I have never seen you go off like this before. Where is it coming from? I don't want to be the reason you are at odds with them both."

"You're not. I just…" Anna struggles.

I wait because she always waits when I need her to, I have no idea what is eating at her but I know I have to try help her fix this with Billy and Alfred. Whatever is going on with her can't be worth losing them over especially if it has anything to do with me.

"I don't… I am scared I am going to lose what little part I have of you. I don't know why it scares me but it does. I never thought I would get as much of you as I have, you have always kept yourself so closed away, but now I have got it…"

My insides melt and a warm feeling spreads through me, right from my heart to the very tips of my toes. That is the last thing I expected to hear. I crawl my way over to her so I am sat next to her.

"You could have asked me to come to you, you know."

"Where's the fun in that?" I grunt. "You are wrong, you know, and you will have to excuse me if I just marvel in the moment a little because you are usually so annoyingly right." I chance a look at her and she smiles. "You don't just have a little part of me, I am just not so good at showing you that yet and you are not going to lose me."

"How do you know?"

"Because… I am just as scared of losing you," I admit. I wrap my arm around her back and pull her to me, holding her and she wraps her arms around my waist, her head on my chest and giggles sweetly.

"Check you out, Mac Scott," she jibes playfully squeezing me tighter.

"I know, right, I am growing as a human," I joke. "Now, make up with Alfred and Billy, please… For me?" I request.

"You want me to make up with my boyfriend – for you?"

"Oww gross… Yeah, that sounded way less messed up in my head," I cringe and we both laugh easily. It is good to laugh, the anxiety is subsiding, I guess I just have to hope that is the last of it.

"Okay I will, but will you tell me why you don't want me here?"

There was me thinking I had gotten away with it, no such luck. I don't want to lie to her, nor do I want to tell her the truth, so I tell her a half truth, it is all I have right now.

"You are not ready for the answer." I repeat her words against her.

"How do you know that?"

"Because you tell me every day, in your own way," I say thoughtfully.

"Do you think I will be ready, one day?"

"Honestly, no but I have been wrong about a lot of things, you never know."

"I hope I am," Anna says dreamily and I chuckle at the irony; she really has no idea and that is probably for the best.

***

I wake a lot later than I usually would and I am grateful for it; the throbbing headache made studying the map painful but I persisted and I feel a bit better prepared for that phase at least. I look for some clothes and all I have are army combat trousers and a khaki t-shirt. I feel a bit self-conscious about the idea of wearing them but really, I have no other clothes. The boots feel amazing, a definite upside. I make my way to the mess hall hoping for coffee and I find Anna, Billy and Alfred already there chatting amongst themselves. I am happy to see that it looks like Anna has made up with them both.

"Hey kid, how's the head?"

"Will be fine soon, as long as I have coffee," I grumble.

"Army greens suit you, Mac," Anna says with a smirk and I blush.

"That explains a lot," I say, winking and smiling at Billy, but the smile isn't returned.

There are a few more people in the mess hall now; the strong smell of bacon is making my stomach growl and I don't wait long to go serve myself some food. Still, it feels oddly empty for such a huge place.

"I thought it would be busier," I say to Billy, trying to make conversation.

"Yeah well, the offices are full. There are a lot of people in the field both here and on assignment. So that explains that," Billy says, his voice polite but icy somehow.

I get the feeling he is a bit annoyed at me, I guess I can't blame him. Anna did have a go at him because of me but I never wanted her to do that. Ugh, that is not my problem right now, I need to put it out of my mind. Today is the day and I need to get a grip on my nerves and get through this. I am as prepared as I can be, Alfred thinks I can do this, I trust Alfred. If he says I can do this, then I can… I think.

The day passes quickly, like someone hit the fast forward button on my life. I am starting to be glad for that; the anticipation and the wait for all hell to break loose messes with my head and I know I will feel better when I am in the situation and forced to act. I am always more comfortable in the chaos, rather than waiting for it to find me. It has to be getting close now; Billy pulls me aside and informs me that I am expected at a briefing. I follow him inside the administration block. There, I enter an office at the end of a series of hallways and find a uniformed man waiting ready to greet me. He has dark hollow eyes that appear to have sunken into his head, a strong jawline and bushy peppered grey eyebrows that match his hair and moustache.

"You must be McKenna Scott, I am Commander Harold Wood, please take a seat. This won't take long," Harold drawls in a slightly pompous but raspy voice. He leans over his desk to shake my hand and I take it politely; this is an intimidating man. He is polite but he has a powerful presence; I feel a little shrunken just looking at him, like I have been sent to the head teacher's office.

"I just have some points to run through with you before you go out this evening, first things first, the terrain. Now, you have unfortunate timing, with the downpour that we have been experiencing the blanket bogs are going to be even more of a threat to you than usual. I would advise you tread carefully; the bogs are not always easy to see under the blanket of grass. If you fall in do not panic and flail, that will only pull you in further. I will be giving you a radio, if you find yourself a diffy, give us a mayday then we can come find you.

"Alfred will be watching your movements via your helmet camera, he will be monitoring your progress closely and the route you take so if you do call for help, we will have some idea of your location."

I nod but inside I'm squirming. The phrase 'I am not a strong swimmer' sings in my mind over and over again.

"Now, I have been informed that you are completely aware of the risks of this operation and the... difficulty, of the second phase but I have to cover my six and ask if you are certain that you want to go ahead. If you are, I will need you to sign this waiver. You are after all, a civilian and I can't have any blowback falling on the military if you are injured or traumatised. By signing this document, you are waiving your rights to take legal action against us in the future and there is also a gag clause. You cannot under any circumstances divulge any details of what happens during your operation, the techniques used must be kept surreptitious. So, take a minute to think about that, before you sign the dotted line."

I hold the commander's gaze unblinking with all the firmness I can muster and then I pick up the pen and sign the paper.

"Excellent. Thank you McKenna, I wish you luck in this endeavour. Grab some chow and get yourself ready, you leave at 2100 hours. Do you have any questions at all?"

"Not really, sir. Unless you want to offer me any advice," I reply and he smiles at me darkly.

"Embrace the suck."

My stomach churns as I try to eat as much as I can, but my appetite is missing in action. I have to believe that I am doing the right thing, I am scared but what if that meltdown had happened to me somewhere where I wasn't safe? What if it happens to me while the people that hunt me are on my tail and I can't think fast enough to save my own life? While I am full of self-doubt, my stubbornness seems to be kicking in just when I need it to.

Back at my barracks I gear up with the vest, utility belt, helmet and rucksack. It all feels a bit weighty but surprisingly less cumbersome than I thought it would be. I take a deep and steadying breath, tuck my helmet under my arm and walk out with my jaw set and when I do, I find Alfred is waiting for me.

"Come take a seat, kid."

I follow him over to the low wall that surrounds the manor and take a seat on it with him. The weather has turned, the rain has finally stopped, making way for clear, darkening skies and a bitter night's chill.

"How are you feeling?"

This is not the time for a front; it is hard for me to admit the weakness I feel but if there is anyone that will understand it, I have a feeling Alfred will.

"Honestly, pretty scared. I keep trying to persuade myself that I can do this but I come up short every time," I confess, looking down at my sweaty palms.

"That is why you are here; you have no belief in yourself. For now, try to remember that I believe in you, use that until you prove it to yourself. You have no idea how much you have learnt, kid; this is the chance for you to see that. It will be hard, but I know you have got this."

"Thank you, Alfred. I needed to hear that," I say gratefully.

"Anytime, now I do have some advice for you about the second phase so listen up. These guys are trained to extract information from people, your job is not to let them and it isn't as simple as keeping your mouth shut. You squeal, you lose. They can read body language and even read the tells of your eyes. So, always try to keep your eyes fixed straight ahead and become the grey man. Not too aggressive, not too submissive. Let them think they have some control over you but in your mind, you have to stay focused because that is what they are trying to break, your mind, not your body. They will do all they can to manipulate you, so you make sure you play a clever game back."

I look at him intensely; I am so grateful to him and he really has no idea and I have no idea how to show him so I just lean my head on his shoulder, wrap my arms around his arm and sit with him as time runs down. He doesn't move, he doesn't say anything, he just sits with me, strong and calm, letting me feel safe for just a while longer. No matter how scared I am, I also feel happy to have this moment with him. Soon, I see Anna approach and she smiles at the sight of Alfred and I huddled together. Billy is close behind carrying two C8 carbine rifles; my stomach does a backflip as he hands one to me.

"I hear you know how to use one of these, it is loaded with rubber bullets but they can still cause serious injury so if you have to use it, aim for the legs only," Billy instructs.

Well, this shit just got real.

My eyes fall on Anna who isn't smiling anymore, she steps up to me and wraps her arms around me and I hold her close.

"Kick some arse, Mac-Attack," she whispers and then kisses me on the cheek and steps back, looking away and I blink as I try not to react as my cheek burns from the contact. I look at Anna and Alfred, standing side by side, both trying very hard to smile encouragingly.

"See you on the flipside," I say with a wink. I turn and walk away from them, without looking back.

After I enter the back of the Jeep with Billy it moves off quickly; I am being driven to places unknown by a person who is keeping very quiet. The atmosphere inside is tense, I look over to Billy and his eyes have grown hard and distant. Apparently when soldiers are about to go off to war, they switch off, run cold and distant to the people around them in order to face the inevitable brutality they are about to face. Maybe that is what Billy is doing?

I don't take much notice of where we are going because I know from studying the map where the drop-off is and that my rendezvous is in the opposite direction to base camp. I will just be going further away, not trying to get back.

"Mac, we are two minutes out, when we stop – helmet on, jump and run. You have a 15-minute head start, use it wisely," Billy says coolly.

"Are you okay, Billy?"

"Yes, I am fine, Mac." He smiles robotically.

It is a bumpy ride off road, my eyes overwhelmed by the vast emptiness. It all looks so similar and that is going to be harder for my novice map-reading abilities to follow. The mountains are beautiful, but thankfully I shouldn't be having to go anywhere near the larger and more unforgiving peaks. There is a lot of open land, with some bush and rock formations for cover. Over to the far right I see the treeline to the woods I saw on the map and I realise, we are nearly at the blue cross marked on the map. The Jeep skids to a harsh stop.

"Go, go, go Mac!" Billy yells and I haul arse, I don't need to be told twice.

My boots hit the ground and I run, hard and fast towards the treeline. The chilly damp air licking at my face, the long grass dragging on my boots, the resistance burning on my calves. I hit the treeline and take cover behind some trees and take out my map. I had a route in mind, it was the most direct route to the rendezvous but now I think about it, that is exactly what they will expect from me. I examine the map, trying to think fast; there really is only one other route that I can take, it is longer and there is more chance to get caught in a bog, but that chance is out there in the dark, waiting for me whichever way I go, it is pointless factoring that in. I fold up the map, put it back inside my jacket and start a fast jog through the forest.

I am going the long way; I don't think they would expect that. It also means at some point I have to cross water, but this route has more cover to hide me and lessens my chances of being sighted. According to the map the forest I am running through is one of three and en route to the rendezvous, they are perfectly rectangular on the map and when we drove towards the first one, I was surprised to see they are like that in real life too. It seems such an odd thing, unnatural and alien, it gave me the creeps looking at it.

Night is falling fast; the darkness is sapping the clarity out of my view making the run through the first forest more and more challenging. I think I am keeping a decent pace but I am very aware that Billy and his hunter force know this place very well, I cannot afford to be complacent for a single second.

A calm begins to sweep over me, a peaceful focus that tunes me into everything around me. My feet stop pounding and start to bounce against the floor like springs, my body moves fluidly, my eyes adjust to the darkness and my mind begins to adapt to my surroundings. It is as if everything has slowed down, I analyse many steps ahead of myself and my body reacts to each danger with certainty and confidence. I register the fallen tree that blocks my path and my hands sweep around to the side of my hip; they push off against the log as I use them to vault over it. I fly over with ease and my feet connect with the ground beyond, sure footed and back into a run.

My insides tingle, I am enjoying the peace and ease of my movement, Alfred was right, I have learnt a lot from the doom dash. The path ahead darkens as the density of the trees increases; they are closer together, forcing me to weave in and out of them and the more I weave the more aware I am that I could lose my direction. It is easy in this kind of terrain to veer off course and get lost because everything looks the same, there are no features to run towards, just tree after tree after tree.

My eyes start searching forwards as I run, lining up three trees at a time, I run to those three trees and as I reach them, I scan for the next three trees that are lined up, methodically keeping my line of direction as straight as possible. I have a compass but foolishly, I didn't check the direction of run before I entered the forest and now, I am forced to wing it, causing an unease in my gut but I have lucked out, the trees begin thin and relief sweeps over me.

I find the end of the forest and stop to catch my breath and my ears prick as I try to hear over my panting. I hear running water which means I must be on course. I scan the open fields to look for the stream, keep myself crouched low and checking over my shoulder as I run, I race in the direction of the sound of the water. I feel a lot more exposed in the open and my senses are firing on all cylinders, making me feel jumpy.

The stream is quite large and the water is flowing much faster than I was expecting; I am sure it is icy cold, the last thing I need is to fall in it because then I have to choose between hypothermia and lighting a fire that will give away my position. I need something to help me cross it, my brain is working fast and I enjoy the problem solving, the buzz of it, my days in Scouting finally have a reason to pay off. I turn on my heels and run back to the edge of the forest, my eyes scanning the forest floor. I find a good and sturdy stick about three inches thick and roughly my height, pick it up and dash back towards the stream.

I keep a steady jog as I move along the bank, searching for the narrowest point to cross but the further upstream I go, the more off course I become. I can't afford to waste time so I grind to a halt, glancing warily over my shoulder and then I ram the stick into the water's flow as hard as I can. The stick bites securely into the sodden ground below and I grit my teeth, cringing as I step into the icy depths.

"Oh, holy guacamole." I shiver.

The water comes to just above my knees and it is just as cold as I expected. The flow of the water is powerful, in some places it is white and frothing and the rocks beneath are slick and slippery. I feel precarious, my heart is in my mouth with every step, my arms and legs so tense the muscles begin to burn in the effort. I carefully side step, keeping my knees slightly bent and I use the stick to keep my balance while I lean into the power of the stream's current. I repeat my movements, my breath held and my legs beginning to wobble from the cold and exertion of keeping myself upright.

It takes longer than I wanted it to but when I finally reach the bank on the other side, my heart soars and I grin with excitement and gratification. Hopefully it will be worth the time it took, if it slows Billy down then it will be worth it. I survey my surroundings with wary eyes, now would probably be a good time to see if I can spot him and his men, I see high ground in my direction of travel and my feet blast back into a run in an instant. I can no longer feel my toes and my feet squelch inside my boots with every pounding footstep.

My heart is pumping hard as I race uphill to reach high ground; it is fairly steep and progress is hard going, my body is starting to tire but the run is also warming me back up. When I reach the summit, I run and skid into cover behind a bush. I take out my night vision goggles and scan the ground below, everything through the sights glows different shades of green and I can see the landscape crystal clear, there is no movement. I am not surprised; something tells me that I won't see Billy unless he is close enough to attempt to capture me.

The way down the other side of the hill is much steeper, leaving me two choices for the route down. The slow, careful, plodding way or the fast, slightly risky but much more fun way. My gut clenches a little and I smirk, I take a few steps backwards, psyching myself up. My legs begin to fizz as the adrenalin floods my veins, I take my rifle off of my shoulder, wrap the strap tightly around my hand and grip the muzzle.

With my heart in my throat I burst into a thunderous run and I jump off the edge into a high-speed half run, half skid down the surface of the hill. I lean back slightly, digging the butt end of the rifle into the ground behind me to keep balance and I drag my heels to control my speed. Powering down the hill at high speed is exhilarating, I want to whoop at the top of my lungs and the fear of giving away my position is the only thing stopping me. I am loving every second of this, the problem solving, the thrill, testing myself. I move fluidly and lightly on my feet; I scramble down the hill with a huge grin on my face and then skid to a stop at the bottom.

My heart races and I laugh at the excitement I feel, I want to savour it, marvel in it a little but I know I have no time to mess around. To my left there is a bumpy-looking field of long amber-coloured grass as far as the eye can see, it is eerie looking and my instincts tell me that the grass is no doubt hiding the bogs I have been warned about. To my right, I see the second forest; from looking at the map, this forest is much smaller than the first. I launch into another run towards it but I am starting to feel fatigued, my chest is tight and my legs are cramping. I was hoping I would get a bit further than this without needing to stop. I can't stop out in the open like this, that is asking to be caught.

I will stop in the second forest and take a breather; it is annoying but I can't risk burning out too fast either. If Billy's squad catch up to me, I need some fuel left in the tank to power my escape. I run, substantially slower now but it is faster than walking. It feels so far away, my chest feels fit to burst as my stamina starts to gives up on me, I resent the long grass for existing and making every step harder work.

Breaking through the treeline I slow to a walk, trying to catch my breath. I walk a couple of feet in and find a good cluster of trees to hide in. My heart races, I gasp as I gulp water between laboured breaths and try to quiet my obnoxiously loud breathing because I want to be able to hear if anything is coming. Again, I pull out the map, I am on course at the moment. Once I am through this forest, I have another decent-length slog across open ground that leads to the last forest which is the largest one on the map, then from there the rendezvous is a clump of three buildings on top of high ground.

Almost through the easiest part, I think. I can't tell from the map how far the rendezvous is or how high that ground is that leads to it but by the time I reach it, I know I will be tired. I take one last gulp of water and set back off into the night. I keep a steady run, trying to maintain some speed but also keep some energy in reserve. My mind slowly becomes attuned to my surroundings; darkness has fallen but my eyes have adjusted, everything is easily clear enough to see and with my slowed speed, is taking much less concentration to navigate.

I come to a gully and don't hesitate as I drop to a slide, slowing my descent with my hands dragging behind me. The climb back up the other side has me huffing and puffing but when I reach the top, I can see the forest beginning to open up on the other side and it is a welcome sight. Two forests down, one to go. I can do this. When I reach the edge of the forest, I stare out to the open landscape, keeping completely still and listening for any sound of movement.

The final forest is in my sight and it looks huge, it is going to be so easy to lose my direction in there. I fumble through the pockets on my utility belt and pull out the compass, holding it steady in front of me. The dial spins and I am on a rough north-east heading; if I just keep checking it through the forest, I should be able to hold my direction and stay on course through the last forest.

I hesitate; it makes me uneasy that I haven't seen one sign of Billy and his hunter force, by now he must know I haven't gone the simple route, he must be heading this way. If I could just find a way to slow them down, buy myself some extra time, it would increase my chances of making it to the rendezvous. My brain buzzes at super speed, what have I got to work with? I search my pockets and find the flint and steel, water bottle, knife and then I find a coil of wire. It is thin and strong; I am guessing for setting snares and…

Traps.

In a matter of seconds, I am coiling the wire around the bottoms of trees just inside the treeline; in the dark the wire is practically invisible. I weave in and out from one end of the forest edge, to roughly just over halfway up the length of the forest opening, keeping the wire roughly a foot or so off the floor. It may be a complete waste of time but then again it may not be, anything that could potentially slow them down can't hurt my odds so I tie off the end of the wire around the last tree and then set off at a run towards the next forest.

My feet pound through the long grass, tiredness is really setting in now and the cold is beginning to get to me, my stomach is starting to rumble loudly. I will have to find a place to hide in the last forest and eat some rations. I have no idea how long I have been running, all I know is I must keep running and to do that I need to keep my energy levels up and the distance between me and my pursuers as large as possible. The ground beneath my feet starts to feel more sodden and I can smell the faint odour of rotting eggs.

I am too slow to connect the dots and I sense the danger a little too late as I plough straight into an icy cold and stinking bog. The smell is unholy, the thick, black sludge is icy cold and heavy. I am lucky, I am only knee deep and the safety of hard ground is still close behind me. I throw myself backwards onto my butt and start pulling and wriggling my legs free. The bog's pull is strong, sucking at my legs like a vacuum and very quickly I discover why they are so dangerous. It is a relief when I finally pull myself free; the progress will have to slow now, no use running if I die, drowned in a bog.

Tentatively, I test the ground with my feet before committing all of my weight to the step, it is frustratingly slow, my legs are caked in the slick and stinking slop and it is sapping the warmth from me. After what feels like far too long, I finally find solid ground. I dash towards the treeline and that is when I hear it, a deep yell in the distance. My insides cringe as I realise, they must have found the trip wires and that means they are close… Too close. No sooner do I realise this when I hear the unmistakeable crack of gun fire. A horror-struck swoop of impending doom and dread assaults my gut, paralysing me for a second and then with a jolt, my senses come alive.

I pick up speed I didn't know I had, thundering towards the forest. I chance a peek over my shoulder and I spot them, all clumped together, they are just making their way out of the treeline of the second forest and they are moving fast. My only hope is that the bog slows them down as much as it did me. My feet pound the floor, adrenalin bolstering the speed in my tired legs; I pump my arms back, dig my feet in and power myself along with gritted teeth. I breach the threshold of the forest, skid to a stop, take cover behind a tree and bend to one knee.

My chest heaves and my hands shake as I click the safety off the rifle, I focus them into my sights, take aim at their feet and breathe in a deep breath, hesitating. I am about to fire at real life people for the first time; fear starts to grip me but I shake it away. I exhale and then fire 3 blasts at their feet. They scatter and I turn on my heels and run, I run as hard and as fast as I can, knowing there is no way I can outrun them indefinitely. The distance to the rendezvous must be at least two or three more miles and a lot of it is uphill. No, I don't stand a chance, I need to think, I need time to think but there is no Goddamn time. I run full pelt through the forest and fear is building that in this speed and this darkness, unfocused, I won't see any... hidden dangers...

Oh! That's it! I need to hide!

I skid to a stop and search around me for a tree that looks reasonably simple to climb up. Once I do, I run to it and start to climb. There are thorns scratching at my face from the brush of the tree and my inner thighs scrape painfully against the bark as I monkey climb my way up. I make it up and find a strong, semi-comfortable Y-shaped branch to sit my butt into, about fifteen feet high. It feels a little precarious but I am out of sight just in time to hear footsteps. I cover my mouth with my hand to try silence my erratic breathing and freeze, aware that any slight movement will give away my position. I see a group of six men approach, guns raised moving fast and fluidly in tight formation.

"Slippery one this one, isn't she, Billy boy."

"Yeah, she is doing better than I expected. I want to catch the bitch before she makes the rendezvous, wipe the smug smile off her face," Billy spits.

"I enjoy the hunt; it makes the catch all the sweeter. I can't wait to have my fun with this one," an unknown man leers. My skin crawls.

"That's why I picked you for the job, your perverse enjoyment at inflicting pain is repugnant but it works in my favour today. Come on, let's get moving, she can't have gone far," Billy orders.

A slap to the face, a punch to the gut, the hurt and shock lingers inside me as I hear Billy's voice over and over in my mind. That was... his voice was so hateful. What the hell? My heart slows to a loud, angry thud in my ears. I can't have heard him right. No… I did, I know I did. This dude clearly doesn't like me. What changed? Or has he never liked me? Hurt is quickly making way to anger, they are slowly making their way ahead of me, I need to think this through, I need to plan because one thing is for sure, I have to beat him now.

I take off my helmet and wedge it between my feet, I need air. Anger is flushing my face and I feel rattled. A prickly fear is shivering down my spine at the thought of the mystery man that apparently enjoys inflicting pain. At some point, whether they catch me or not, I am going to have to meet that man in phase two; I can't help but fear what he has in store for me. The familiar tension in my chest begins to tighten as the panic starts to rise.

No… Get your shit together. Worry about phase two, when you are in phase two. Calm your shit! You need a plan, not a freak-out.

I take a deep breath and reach for my water bottle; I lean forward and pour the icy water over the back of my neck and then over my face. The cold is soothing and somehow, I calm myself, bit by bit. I take off my backpack and dig around for the ration packs; sooner or later I will be in that building, I have to eat while I can. My ears are still alert while I explore the contents of the ration packs. I find a silver bag with a white label that says tuna and mayonnaise pasta, the nutritional information is underneath and I cringe as I rip open the top.

I shouldn't have smelt it, that was a stupid idea, my nose crinkles. I love tuna but this doesn't smell like any tuna I have ever had. I steel myself, tip the pack so that the contents slide into my mouth. The texture is slimy, the pasta a little raw but it isn't half as bad as I was expecting. Still, it is bad, it is hard work to eat, I manage half a pack before I give up and eat the much more appealing Yorkie bar.

It isn't till halfway through a massive mouthful of chocolate, my cheeks bulging that my darting eyes stop on the helmet wedged between my feet, the camera pointed directly at me and I smirk, giving the camera a wink. I wonder what Anna and Alfred are thinking, watching me sat in a tree stuffing my face. There is no audio, they can't hear me and I am quite glad for that. Although if they could, they would have heard Billy. I wonder what Anna would have made of that; I guess that isn't my business and it really doesn't help to think about Anna watching me right now. I give the camera a mock salute and put the helmet back on.

I need a plan. What advantages do I have that I can use? It is dark, but that helps both sides. I am one person; it is much easier to move undetected as one person. I take out my map and examine it. My plan was to follow the ridgeline up, it follows up the right side of the hill and it looks almost like a footpath. If I was Billy, I would be keeping my eye on that route.

I could go to the left, circle my way around to the back side of the hill and approach the hill and the buildings above from behind. It is a longer slog and I would have to crawl my way over the left side so I won't be seen but it is a chance at least. I chug some water, my stomach full of nerves and my skin crawling with resentment and hurt. I have to beat them now, I have to. Whatever his problem with me is, it has only made me more stubborn to beat him.

Let's do this.

I slowly creep down the tree, aware of every noise and movement I make and instead of carrying on through the forest and into the open like they are no doubt expecting. I turn to the left. Treading as lightly as I can, I move forward; the forest floor is covered in dead twigs that are loud and crunchy underfoot. My ears are alert to every tiny noise, my senses firing in overdrive.

I make it to the left side treeline and take a knee. I peer through the night vision googles, analysing the field ahead with intense scrutiny for any sign of movement. I see nothing so I make a dash across to the left, keeping low and moving fast; when I get to the very edge of the meadow I dive to the floor. Staying on my front, crawling and dragging myself through the long, wet grass, I start to move forward. I feel the cool rain water penetrate my clothing and it alleviates my hot and sweaty, pissed off skin. It is slow going and tiring but I am confident this is the most cover I am going to get and my best chance.

While I am glad for the energy it is no doubt giving me, I feel sluggish from wolfing down the food. I should be glad that running isn't an option right now, even crawling is giving me a stitch in my side. I feel tense like a coiled-up spring; not knowing where they are and knowing that any wrong move that I make could give away my position, is enough to tighten every muscle and play tricks on my brain.

I come to the foot of the hill and I roll on my back to take a breather. Billy's hurtful words are ringing in my head. That wasn't a part of the game, maybe if he knew I could hear him, yes, but he had no idea I was there. No, that was real. The hurt and betrayal is shocking, I trusted him, I thought we were friends. I feel pathetic that it has cut me this deep which just makes me angry, anger is good. Anger is motivating, hurt slows you down and I need to move.

I roll back onto my front, poke my head up a little and take a look through the night vision goggles. I see one man walking back and forth along the treeline and one halfway up the ridge line, looking through his rifle sight. Where the others are, I have no idea but I am eager to get out of the possible sight of the two I can see. I crawl my way around the hill, impatience making me crawl faster now and once I know it is impossible to be seen by the two men I spotted, I get to my feet and look up at the hill.

This side looks substantially steeper but I can see the buildings on top, I can see my goal and the excitement tingles in my chest. There is a clear impression in the grass, a route made from many walks up this side of the hill so it must be doable. The footpath of sorts moves diagonally up the face; I slide the carbine rifle from my back over my shoulder and into my hands, pulling the butt end tight to my shoulder. I start moving forwards, keeping as low as I can with my rifle raised up and sweeping left and right.

I see it before I feel it, but nowhere near fast enough. I see the muzzle flash brightly; Billy fires his weapon as he stands from a hidden position in the grass. I hear the crack of gun fire echo and my legs are swept from beneath me all before I feel the blinding pain. I cry out, anger seething inside me at my own failure. Billy approaches me with dead eyes; his face, along with faces I don't recognise, loom above me.

"Bag her, gag her," Billy orders coldly.

Pain sears as I feel the impact of the butt of the gun smashing into my forehead, my vision swims and then…

Darkness.

CHAPTER TEN

Hell Hath No Fury

Cold water wakes me abruptly, I inhale sharply at the wrong time out of the shock and I choke on it, spluttering and jolting forward trying to clear my air way to find that, I can't move. My eyes dart around rapidly as I struggle to understand my surroundings. I am sat on a chair in the middle of a large room, it is bland and bare and poorly painted white. The floor is laid with dated black tiles, it is an almost completely featureless room.

A man stands before me, in camo clothes that match my own. I don't recognise him but the pieces are starting to add together in my head, the events are beginning to align. The pain in my thigh is outrageous. I look down at it, a bandage is crudely wrapped around my leg over the top my trousers, the blood already leaching through. I have no boots or socks on, why would they take my boots? Billy shot me and I was captured. So, wherever I am, I lost phase one and phase two has begun. I feel for the smooth nylon of the rope digging into my wrists. I hate being restrained; I gulp on air because my mouth has lost every bit of moisture there was. My head pounds as I look at the three men around the room, they are watching me with stone cold expressions, statue still.

Along the right wall near a closed door a man sits with his head down, his face lit up by a laptop screen and in front of the laptop is a webcam, its lens directed straight at me. My stomach lurches as I realise that Alfred and Anna are watching me and of course, I have been sat in front of a camera while being tortured before. The symmetry and the obvious similarities make my head flicker with flashes of memories. I try to shake them away, I need to stay in the now, whatever it takes. My eyes fall on Billy next, standing as far back in the background as he can get; the resentment bubbles. Closest to me is a man holding a bucket and he is watching me intently with beady eyes, he has a sadistic smirk on his face and my stomach swoops with revulsion. The look in his eyes sends prickles of fear down the back of my neck.

"What is your name and purpose here?" the beady-eyed man asks, his voice surprisingly high pitched.

I need to concentrate; I need to keep control. I close my eyes, straining to think through the fog of pain in my head.

"Let them think they have some control over you but in your mind, you have to stay focused because that is what they are trying to break, your mind, not your body. They will do all they can to manipulate you, so you make sure you play a clever game back."

Alfred's words sing around my mind and the mania of my garbled thoughts calms down. I steel myself, opening my eyes with a cold glare. I lost the first phase; I cannot lose this one.

"I asked you a question and I was polite about it. Are you really going to make me forget my manners?"

I keep my eyes forward, I don't look at him, my eyes fix on the wall behind him. I can do this, I have to do this. I am happy that I feel no fear. My resentment towards Billy surpasses my fear, at least for now it does. I will keep focusing on that, I will live and breathe that if I have to. I am sure it won't last; they are going to do all they can to break me down, the question is, can I outlast them?

"Tell me your name and your purpose here and you can leave. I will make you some food, see to your wounds and you can leave. Don't answer me and this is going to get very unpleasant for you," the beady-eyed man threatens. He has a really big nose, one of those noses where the dark hair pokes through the ends of the nostrils. He is unfortunate looking; he is not blessed with good looks and he has a scar running through his top lip.

Thwack!

He backhands me across the cheek with a swift slap and I feel it but I go straight back to looking forward, trying not to give him the satisfaction of seeing my pain. I am sure I won't be able to hold that up for long, but I am guessing this is the man that Billy said enjoys inflicting pain, I want to go as long as I can without giving him that pleasure.

Thwack!

Again, absorb the pain as best as I can and then resume the eyes forward position. The beady-eyed man leans forward in my face and I look at his ugly nose. If there is anything that I need to remember it is to keep my mind focused and my eyes unreadable; I can smell the stench of bad breath coming off him.

"Oh, I am going to have some fun with you," he drawls. "On your feet," he orders and I ignore him. I am probably provoking him but I don't want to show any obedience just yet. If this is a game, then I need them to think that they have broken me, so I need to wait an acceptable amount of time before I show weakness and start acting like they are succeeding. He drags me to my feet by my collar and then he ties a blindfold over my eyes so tight it stings.

"Right, now you are going to squat," he orders and when I don't comply, he pushes me down by my shoulders; the bullet wound in my thigh screams in protest and my legs give way till I am sat squatting, thighs parallel to the ground, all my weight on the balls of my feet.

"Good, now you are not to move because if you do, I will see you and I will come right back in here and you won't like it when I do."

At first, I don't understand why he is making me do this but after five minutes or so I do. The pressure on my leg muscles is so painful and that doesn't even factor in the gunshot wound. I grit my teeth and try to keep as still as I can but the darkness combined with the whack to the head is making it swim; it feels almost worth the inevitable slap to sit down, I am starting to sweat from the strain and my legs begin to shake.

How am I going to do this? Of all the things they could do to me this is tame and yet it is so painful. I hate the darkness, if you are in it long enough you begin to forget what people look like, it becomes harder and harder to picture a person's face in your mind. I picture Billy's face; I hear his words burning like acid in my brain.

"I want to catch the bitch before she makes the rendezvous, wipe the smug smile off her face."

Fury burns in my gut, molten, liquid, fiery lava… Yes, that helps. I say it over and over in my head, I hear the hate in his tone, I picture his face, his chiselled face of boyish good looks and let the fire fuel me. Burn, burn, burn. Soon though, fatigue and pain start to take over. I wonder what time it is. I left base camp at 9pm, how long was I running in phase one? How long was I unconscious? How long have I been squatting here like a little bitch? Yes… bitch, Billy called me a bitch.

Burn, burn, burn.

I am sat here long enough that my head begins to feel too heavy for my neck to support and it starts to slop up and down. I don't even feel like I have legs anymore, just two slabs of useless, painful hunks of meat. I hear movement and I tense up; footsteps stomp hard towards me and I then feel the impact of a boot hitting me hard in the ribs, knocking me over. It hurts and I yelp at the pain but the relief to be off my feet is incredible. Rough hands pick me up by the armpits and slam me back down on the chair, the blindfold is ripped off and the light is so blinding, I squint my eyes trying to bring them back to focus.

"What is your name and your purpose here?"

The ugly beady-eyed man comes back into my eyeline. He is enjoying himself; I know that look. I have seen that look before, the look of someone enjoying the pain they inflict, it must really wind him up when I don't show him enough pain or fear. I am starting to feel the fear though. Billy isn't in the room; I wonder where he is. The man on the laptop is back. I wonder what he is doing. Probably playing solitaire.

That's right, keep thinking, Mac. Keep your brain moving. Ugly-nosed wanker.

Burn, burn, burn.

"Tell me your name and your purpose here and the pain will stop."

Pain, so much pain as his elbow digs deep into the bullet wound in my thigh; there is no absorbing that. Relentless, white hot, all-consuming pain.

"Argh!" I scream.

"Tell me your name and your purpose here!!"

"Fuck you!" I snarl.

Pain, too much pain… Oh God, please make it stop. I scream and scream; the safe phrase is blaring in my head, no, no, no. Don't! Just hold on, he has to stop eventually. I scream till I run out of breath.

"I can do this all day – tell me your name!" the beady-eyed man bellows.

All day? Does that mean it is daytime? That must mean…

Agony, all-consuming and profound agony, I scream and scream until my head feels like it pops pleasantly and everything goes blissfully black.

***

"I am telling you; pain will not work on this girl." I hear Billy's familiar voice. "We need to get inside her head."

I keep very still; I keep my eyes closed and my ears pricked, listening to every word.

"Maybe not, but it sure is fun." The beady man laughs darkly. "Well, you know the girl, Billy boy. You are more likely to know what will get in her head than I am."

"I have some ideas, but I will let you soften her up some more first. We have plenty of time," Billy says with a hollow voice and my heart drops, I don't think I have plenty of time in me.

"Wakey, wakey."

Another cold-water blast, but this time I am expecting it. No choking but the cold is still a shock to the system. I must be getting tired; the cold is getting to me and my body is shivering to try to keep warm. The beady-eyed man goes over to the table where the webcam is and picks up a bottle of water. He returns with it and kneels down in front of me, shaking it in front of my face. I keep my eyes above his head, staring straight at the wall.

"Are you thirsty? I bet you are. I tell you what, just give me your name and I will give you some."

I keep my eyes forward and then a thought strikes my pain-stricken and exhaustion-riddled brain and for some reason, it is a little too hard to resist.

"Come on, just your name. We can talk about your purpose later."

"I am Groot," I croak.

"Excuse me?"

"I. Am. Groot," I repeat and unfortunately for me, I am unable to control my very brief smile.

The beady man grabs me by the throat, picks me up off the chair and throws me against the wall. I hit the wall hard, then the floor; the impact is shocking, making my spine jar. He repeats this so many times I lose count and I lose my fight. I taste blood, my body throbs like a heartbeat, each beat a new wave of pain. I would give anything for water and sleep. He picks me back up and rips my outer shirt off then cuts the waistband on my trousers and pulls them off too.

For the first time, I feel real fear and humiliation that I am not able to swallow down, as I stand exposed in my girl boxers and t-shirt and my hands tied behind my back. I feel vulnerable in a completely different way and it gets the better of me. The beady-eyed man smiles at me in a hungry and perverse way and I feel the threat in his eyes. I swing my leg back and kick him as hard as I can in his worthless nut sack; the beady eyed man goes down to his knees crying out in a howl and I kick him in the face with a nauseating crunch.

I have about two seconds to enjoy the moment before I bolt to the door with the little bit of energy I have left. I turn my back, my bound hands groping for the handle blindly. Just as I get a grip of it, the door opens and I turn on my heels to see Billy stood in the doorway. He grabs me by the hair and drags me to the centre of the room, he unties my hands from behind my back and then ties them back up in front of me.

"Stand here and keep this held above your head at all times. Arms straight! I don't think I need to tell you what happens if you drop the log," Billy barks in my face and I look at him with disgust. "Seriously, she can't even use her hands! Get up, Jackson."

So, the beady-eyed man's name is Jackson.

They leave the room and I am left holding a large and heavy log above my head. I lock my elbows and dig deep; the blood is draining out of my arms and they begin to burn. Fear rocks me when I realise how quickly I am tiring and Billy clearly said that there is plenty of time. How am I going to endure this? I am already losing the fight, maybe I should give up.

No, stop! Think of something else.

I try to think of Billy but even the anger hasn't got the power to keep me going at this point, I am tired, are they actually going to let me sleep? No, I doubt it. If my hands weren't tied together then I could hold the ends of the log instead of the middle, that would be easier, but they are tied, goof!

Goof... Anna...

A memory flashes in my mind, a happy one. Of us dancing. I smile. Yes... That's good. I close my eyes and picture the sparkle of her laughing eyes as I spin her round and start to sing my voice coming out raspy and strained.

"Big wheels keep on turning,

carry me home to see my kin,

singing songs about the south-land,

I miss 'ole' 'bamy once again and I think it's a sin – Oh crap...

I can't... remember. What is it? Ah, screw it...

Sweet home Alabama,

where the skies are so blue,

sweet home Alabama

Lord, I'm coming home to you. Yeah, see now that's the best bit, as long as you know that you are golden."

I smile, playing the memory of dancing with Anna over and over in my head. The weight of the log is getting the better of me now, the tiredness is weighing just as much as the log and I am starting to feel a bit delirious. I am trying so hard to remember that this is just a game; it doesn't feel like a game, I keep trying to sing but pain is making it hard for me to speak.

"Sweet home… Alabama,

where… the skies… are so… blue,

sweet… home… Alabama,

Lord, I'm… coming… home… to… you.

"Argh!" I growl, raging at my own weakness as my arms begin to shake.

Tears of anger and pain threaten to spill but I don't let them, I don't want them to see that. I drop hard to my knees and then I drop the log. I curl myself up into a ball, shaking from head to toe; I just want it to end. This is supposed to be a game but it doesn't feel like one, the only thing keeping me fighting is the fear of failing. My head feels all messed up, my fractured memories are mixing with my current shit-spitter of a situation. I need to find a way to keep hold of the present.

Come on, Mac… Get the fuck up, before they come back.

I drag myself up off the floor and pick up the log. I have to do this, I can't lose myself, not again, I will never be able to find my way back again.

"Peach… I could eat a peach for hours," I rasp; my voice doesn't sound like mine anymore.

Keep talking… Keep thinking.

"What a cracking film, I would love to watch a film right now, let's play a game, Mac-Attack. Tom Cruise… Um… 'You can be my wingman anytime, bullshit – You can be mine.' …Bruce Willis, oh man, he has so many good lines to choose from, so many but I can't think… 'Yippie-kai-yay mother fucker!' Ha-ha – that was lame, everyone knows that one. Okay next, Leonardo DiCaprio… 'I'm the king of the world!'" I yell and it feels good and I can't help but do it again.

"Ha-ha, I'm the king of the world!!! Ha-ha!"

The door comes flying open and Billy comes powering into the room. "Shut up!" he yells but I can't stop laughing. Call it delirium, call it insanity but I just can't stop.

"What? Not a Titanic fan?" I jeer.

Billy gives me a short sharp jab to the gut and I drop the log, my legs buckle and I fall to my knees and then I topple forwards landing awkwardly on my bound wrists. He uses his foot to roll me over onto my back and then uses it to apply pressure to my windpipe. The laughing stops then; I feel winded, he leaves the room and I roll onto all fours and I gasp, trying to calm myself.

"Get up," I whine.

Pushing myself upright so I am on my knees. I struggle to my feet, picking the log up as I go. A whimper escapes my lips as I heave it about my head, snot bubbles from my nose and my head spins, but I get it there, somehow. Where does Billy keep going? In my mind all I can see is him sat cuddled up with Anna, watching me get the crap kicked out of me; the image is a completely different torture and it is screwing with my head.

No, no, no – stop it.

I feel the exhaustion of trying to keep my focus more and more, my mind wanting to slip into memories and I know if I let it, it will probably be game over. I look at the camera lens, Alfred and Anna are on the other end of there, that is proof this is still a game. I just need to find a way of playing on, I close my eyes and bear down.

It is just a game, get it together.

The pain is becoming too much and I know, I am going to drop the log again. My arms quake with violent shakes and my teeth lock but that doesn't stop the pathetic whine that escapes my lips. My head begins to spin and I feel a sickening hotness flush my skin and I know; I am going to black out seconds before it happens. I don't remember hitting the floor.

***

A warmth spreading over me, strange – it only seems to be my face that is getting warmer, the rest of me is bone cold and juddering on the cold tile floor. The warmth begins to sting and then burn the cuts to my face. I wince, trying to open my eyes then I feel the warm liquid sting my eyes. Through the blur I see Jackson standing over me, limp dick out and pissing over my face. Humiliation slithers up my throat I wail, rolling away from him. I scramble, crawling away desperately and then my mind starts to flash in the memory.

"No, no, no, no…" I mumble.

"Oh, poor dike scared of the big bad penis," he jeers.

"Nothing big and bad about that," I spit.

His hand grabs the back of my neck and his nails dig deep into my skin as he pulls me off the floor. He runs, my toes dragging on the tile floor and slams me against the wall only this time I don't drop to the floor. My face slams against the wall, his grip on my neck tightens as he holds me there, his body pressed against my back, my hands pinned between the wall and my own body.

"How about I show you how big and bad it is," he growls.

The terror is extraordinary, I snarl a strangled noise and I lift and bend my knees, wedging my feet against the wall. I push out hard against it and send us both flying backwards to the floor. I land on top of him and roll off of him scuttling shakily to my feet but he is on me too quickly, his hand clamps around my throat, his face inches from mine.

"Look at you… You really think I want to touch you? You couldn't pay me enough," he scathes, spitting in my face.

He shoves me to ground and I hear his footsteps grow fainter as he walks away. My spirit breaks, on my knees hunched forward, I scream but no sound comes out. The force of the pain, is unfathomable, screaming isn't enough to relieve it, I collapse to the floor in a heap. My eyes wide and unblinking, tears blurring my vision. I can feel it coming, the familiar swim that dizzies my mind and warps my vision, I can't fight it anymore.

The memory swirls.

The boat sloshes from left to right, the waters are rough tonight. The chains that binds my wrists, clink at the rocking movement of the boat. My knees are bruised from the constant pressure of being knelt on them and my arms are numb from being suspended above my head. A man is stood before me, his hair is blond and buzz cut short, his eyes gleaming blue with a taunting smile.

"Please stop, I just want to go home," I beg.

"If I let you go, who will entertain my men?"

Whop-pssh.

Pain slashes across my back with rapid heat as I hear the whip slap across my skin. I cry out but the slaps, they just keep coming.

Whop-pssh. Whop-pssh.

"STOP! Please! I won't tell anyone; I just want to go home. I don't know anything; you know I don't!" I plead.

He smiles at me with disturbing delight and I know my begging will lead me nowhere, there is no use appealing to a humanity that isn't there.

"Kill me… Please, just kill me," I say, my voice hollow.

I just want it to end, I can't take any more, they are never going to let me go, there will be nothing but pain till the day I die. So, why not make that day today?

"You are very important to me – McKenna Scott. I am afraid that the stars have already aligned, our fates are entwined and we were predestined to meet. Yes, I am sure you will die, but not until the need I have of you is no longer necessary."

"Monster!" I spit.

"We are all a bit monstrous sometimes, are we not?" he drools before nodding to someone behind me. He strolls away from me smiling, as my screams fill the air.

The memory dissipates and I find myself on the floor, curled up in a ball. Every time I close my eyes for a minute too long, a bucket of icy-cold water blasts me awake. I lose all sense of time and I am scared that I am losing myself; I know if this doesn't end soon, I will lose hold of the tiny grasp on myself that I have gripped between my fingertips. I flinch as the door opens and a woman walks into the room and it seems so odd, I can't help but wonder if I am imagining it, my mind is treading a fine line between the past and the present, or maybe between sane and insane. The disorientation is profound. Is she real? She looks so clean and shiny.

"I am here to treat your wounds, if you will let me?"

The woman has blonde slinky hair that is as straight as an arrow and her skin is quite tan, she is in her late forties at a guess and wearing a crisp, white nurse's uniform. I am sure I am covered in cuts and bruises but the last thing I need on top of everything else is a stranger touching me and sending me into a meltdown.

"No – just water…" I croak.

I am shocked when the woman brings a bottle of water over to me and starts pouring into my mouth. I guzzle it greedily, extinguishing the scorchy dryness that burns in my throat.

"Can I do anything else for you?" she asks politely.

I shake my head no and she disappears as quickly as she appeared; I guess they can't actually let me die of thirst, that would be difficult to explain. I need to find a way out of this and fast, I don't think escape is the answer, it never was. I think outlasting them is, outlasting and outsmarting. The trouble is I don't know how much longer I can hold out; things are starting to get all bent out of shape and screwy, my smarts are not reliable right now, I am struggling to keep hold of who I am.

How long have I been here? I think it has been around forty-eight hours but there are no windows, no natural light to navigate time with. It could be less; it could be more. Please God, let it be more. Alfred told me the standard time to hold out before the phase stops is 36 hours. Would they really make me do that? Billy is desperate for me to break; I know that much. What is he going to do to try to make that happen? How much has Anna told him about my past? My insides squirm; if she has told him anything, I am in trouble. She wouldn't do that – would she? I don't know anymore, the image of her cuddled up watching me suffer is burning in my brain and aching hurtfully in my chest.

I push myself up off the floor and limp my way over to the chair; my body is weak and shakes violently every time I try to use any muscle. I figure I will be dragged to this chair soon enough anyway, may as well do it myself to save myself being dragged. I am cold, my toes are purple, my hair feels weird, heavy somehow like it's thick with dirt. My arms and legs are varying in different colours of bruising. How long does it take to bruise? Maybe a day or two depending how hard the wallop was that created it. Is that an indication of how long I've been here?

The door opens and Jackson enters. I feel a slight tinge of gratification to see the black bruising forming darkly around his eye. Billy follows closely behind him and revulsion churns acidic in my stomach. I am probably overreacting but it really helps to hate him right now so I am going with it. Billy walks over to me and kneels down in front of me, his expression completely devoid of emotion.

"You have to break, if you don't, I will be forced to do some things, I really don't want do. Do you understand that?" Billy asserts, his voice firm.

"Are you sure they are things that you don't want to do to me, Billy boy?" I keep my voice as even as I can, but there is no mistaking the resentment in my raspy voice.

"Alright, enough of the games. Jackson, cut off her top. A little birdy told me all about how much you hate to be touched. I am ready to test that theory," Billy says lightly.

Anna…

A sting of betrayal lashes at my insides as my teary eyes flick over to the camera lens. Panic grips me, panic and humiliation as my shirt is cut off of me, I wriggle and squirm away but it doesn't get me anywhere. Jackson laughs as my shirt rips from my body, leaving me covered only by underwear.

"You keep your fucking hands off me!" I spit at Jackson hatefully.

"Here now – listen, it is not like I want to touch you, I mean come on, look at the state of you."

Shame and embarrassment sweep over me, my body starts to shake so violently it hurts. My breathing is getting out of control, I have to stop this; I have to stop them. How? Come on! How? What the fuck are you going to do? Call them names? That will only provoke…

Provoke him.

"You can stop this anytime you want, just give me your name and your purpose here and this will all end," Billy says playfully.

His tone revolts me and magnifies the hate boiling inside. I look at him, I can't believe he would sink this low just to break me. What did I ever do to him? Why does he want to hurt me so badly? My mind buzzes perilously to find the way out.

"Why are you doing this Billy?" I ask through shaken breath. I hate that my fear is so obvious, I feel so pathetic.

"I just need you to give me your name and purpose, then this will stop. If you don't then Jackson here will touch you and believe me when I tell you, you don't want that. Once he starts it is very difficult to make him stop," Billy threatens.

"Answer my question, you coward!" I rage, then I lean forward, swing my head back and throw myself forward, headbutting him square on the nose as hard as I can. Pain sears across my forehead but it is overruled by intense satisfaction.

"Argh, you bitch!"

Billy's nose pours with rosy red blood and his eyes water, then his facial expression turns cold as ice. He glares at me with so much hate and I glare right back at him.

"Jackson, do your worst – she isn't going to talk," Billy orders.

Jackson grins sadistically and walks towards me; panic fills my veins making my body shake in protest, the terror so potent I am finding it hard to think. This can't happen, there will be no coming back from this, I have to stop them. It's now or never.

"Hey… Billy boy! If he so much as lays on finger one me then I will talk. I will tell the people on the other end of that camera, what you said when you were in the forest. You see, your dumb ass didn't know I was in the tree above you, I wonder what your little birdy would think, if I told her you…"

Thwack.

Pain explodes across my jaw, knocking me from the chair. It isn't long before I don't feel the blows anymore, I don't feel, I just see Billy's boot come towards me over and over again. I hear the thud of each blow he rains down on me; I see the tearful hate gleaming in his eyes, he is going to kill me and I have nothing left to stop him with.

Then it just stops and what I see doesn't make any sense anymore. I see

Alfred storming into the room, his face a mask of fury like I've never seen before. He launches himself at Billy, ramming him against the wall by the throat. That can't be right, this has to be a trick, it isn't a very nice one, although I do enjoy watching Alfred punch Billy out. Now there is Anna, that definitely can't be right. I am sure it hasn't been long enough yet, but she is stroking my face and that is nice. I will just stay here, in this nice place with Anna.

"Mac, Mac. Please answer me!" Anna cries.

I am not sure I can, although I think I should probably try. She looks upset, why is she so upset? She is lifting me up – oh God, please don't lift me up… Ouch. My head is in her lap, it hurts. It hurts? If it hurts then is this real? Anna takes her jacket off and drapes it over my chest, the sweet scent of her candy-like perfume wafts up my nose and rouses my senses.

"Anna?" I choke.

"Yes, it's me! I am here. It's okay."

"I want… to go home."

"We are going home, I promise. It's over, Mac," Anna chokes through tears.

"That's good. You are beautiful, you know. Please don't cry," I ramble.

"Did you just call me beautiful?"

"Yes, I think so. I'm sorry, I am so tired."

"You can sleep now, Mac."

I feel the salty tears sting my face, I don't want to be alone, I am not sure what is real anymore, I want so much for her to be real. I want so much for it to be over but I am scared that it is not. My mind is dismantled, my thoughts coming out in fractured barks. I just want it to stop, please just let it stop.

"Stay…?"

"I am not going anywhere," Anna vows. She leans forward and kisses my forehead.

Darkness…

***

The room is too bright, it is burning my eyes and blinding me. Hands are on me and everything hurts, the pain unbelievable, the panic is rising. I don't feel safe, I don't like this, it needs to stop right now. Someone is touching me, I must fight them off, there has been enough touching of me, I never want to be touched again.

"Ugh get off, get off!" I groan.

"It's okay, kid, it's just me – you're in the medical wing," Alfred soothes.

My eyes start to focus, my nose burns with the smell of chemicals, I search the room urgently, trying to understand my surroundings. I am here and I am there, on the boat while on dry land. Anna is stood a few feet from the end of my bed, her eyes pained and her jaw tight and as she looks at me, all I feel is betrayal, my eyes well with pain and anger.

"Stop! Just stop. Don't touch me!!" I snap.

Alfred backs away with his hands held up. "Mac, I need to treat your leg so that we can go home," Alfred says softly.

"No…" I shake my head.

"A little birdy told me all about how much you hate to be touched. I am ready to test that theory."

Would she have really done that to me? I don't know who to trust anymore. My head is jumping from memory to present so fast I can't get a grip on what is real. I slide my legs off the bed, wincing, and they buckle when my feet touch the floor. I don't completely fall as I manage to grab the guard rail of the bed but the pain is ridiculous and I cry out. Alfred lunges towards me, trying to stop me falling.

"No! *Stay the hell away from me!*" I rage and he freezes.

"Pa, I need you to leave the room," Anna says firmly, her eyes intent on mine.

"Savannah, I don't think…"

"Pa, please. Just trust me, she isn't going to hurt me, you know that."

Anna keeps her eyes on me and I glare at her as Alfred leaves the room. My chest is heaving with anger, my mind splintering and swimming with revolving sharp imagines of pain.

The boat-Billy-Jackson. The boat-Billy-Jackson. The boat-Billy-Jackson.

"Mac…" she says softly, taking a step forward.

"Stop!" I snap and Anna flinches, freezing to the spot. My legs are shaking under my own weight sending painful judders through my body, my mind splintering from one bloody image to another.

"Mac…"

"He said… you… told…"

"I know what he said but you know me, I would never have told him anything you trusted me with. He asked me, after he cut your eye, why you flinched away from him and all I said was that you don't like to be touched, that is *all* I have ever said. He was using me against you to get in your head," Anna says calmly. She keeps her distance; my mind buzzes with too much horror, I can't make sense of anything.

"It's too loud… I can't make it stop! I don't know what's real or what is a game. What's now and what is before," I struggle through chattery teeth.

"Then let me show you, please."

She takes another step forward with her hands held up.

"Mac, I need you to remember the other night, in the field. I need you to try to only think about that, tell me something you remember."

The memories are not hard to picture, that is not something I can easily forget but what if it was all a game? What if she is manipulating me?

"Your hands… on my face," I croak.

"Yes… Now tell me, why did you let me do that?"

Her eyes are wide and unblinking on mine. I want to believe her but I don't know if this is part of the game. I screw my eyes shut, shaking my head, a whimper escaping my mouth.

"Mac… Please, can I show you what I remember?"

Anna closes the distance, moving very slowly and then she reaches for my hand. My arms are rigid and stiff as she pulls my hand and lays over her heart and holds it there. The memory in my mind flashes, I close my eyes trying to keep hold of it but bad memories keep overwhelming it and I wince. I feel her hand on my face, pulling me gently to her, I don't stop her but I stand tense, distrust barking sharply in my mind.

"I would *never*, ever betray your trust, please believe me. It's over, you asked me to stay with you because somewhere in there, you know you can trust me. Please, come back, Mac. You promised me I wouldn't lose you," Anna whispers and then I feel her warm, soft lips kiss my neck, just once.

A jolt of pleasure flares my chest, shocking me and I gasp embarrassingly loud as the memories flood me. I see it all, every moment, every touch and the horror behind my eyes begins to fade. My muscles loosen and I fall into her, choking on sobs and I hear her breathe a teary sigh of relief. She holds me tight and I feel safety wash over me.

"There she is… It's okay, it's over, I promise," she breathes and I hold onto her, my legs begin to buckle, the pain is becoming too much.

"Mac… I need to get you to that bed, you are hurt and the sooner you let Pa help you, the sooner I can get you home. Okay?"

Anna helps me to the bed, she pulls the guard rail down and then she slides onto the bed and shuffles over, waiting for me as I climb up. The bed isn't flat, the head of it almost upright and as I lay down, she slides her arm under my neck and holds me to her and my head falls on her chest. It is incredible the sudden safety I feel and I can't help but allow myself to succumb to it, to her. Her smell, her touch, her soft gravelly voice as she whispers, "Just stay with me, I'll keep you safe," warming me from the inside out, making me feel like some precious thing. I don't understand it, but I need it, I need her.

"Pa!" Anna calls.

I hear him come back, his loud footfall stomping with a high-pitched tap against the tile floor. He gently moves my leg and I wince as I feel pressure against my thigh.

"Alright, kid, it is a rubber bullet and it hasn't gone in too deep but it has been in there so long the swelling has embedded it. I have to get it out, I will be as quick as I can. On 1, 2, 3…"

I scream, the pain is too much, nausea churns in my stomach and my head spins, I can't take it, I have nothing left.

"Stop, Stop! No-no-no!!" My body shakes, my head spins and I sob. Anna holds me tighter but I pull away, looking at her with frantic eyes.

"I can't, please… I can't take anymore, please make it stop," I beg and bury my face in her shoulder. My body erupts in violent shakes.

"Pa, can't you give her something? She is way past the limit of what anyone can take!" Anna snaps.

"I know, I am on it. The medical stores are locked because there is no one here at this time of night. I will break the damn thing open if I have to, just give me a minute," he grunts as he storms back out of the room and my sobs start to slow.

"It's okay, he will get something. It will be over soon," she soothes.

There isn't one inch of me that doesn't hurt, the shakes are so violent that I am making Anna judder along with me and I am in too much pain to be embarrassed. I feel like a child, broken and scared, clinging onto her for safety. I hear a crash, glass breaking and then soon after Alfred returns.

"Mac, can I have your arm? I just want to give you something to make you sleep," Alfred says gruffly.

Anna helps me roll over onto my back and I wince at the pain in my ribs. I feel something tighten around my bicep and Anna puts her hand on my face, pulling me to her eyeline. Heaviness weighs on my eyelids as I peer into the sadness of her eyes. I lay my hand on top of hers that holds my face softly.

"Thank you..." I slur.

"Don't thank me."

***

Phantoms, that is what they are. Ghosts haunting my mind and poisoning it with their evil presence. Each image permeates my body with venom. I am saturated, too weighed down to move away from the nightmare. The images disturb my mind and ache in my body. Faces, lots of faces, I don't want to see them anymore. Maybe if I tell them to stop, they might listen. I try but I can't find my mouth, that is hardly fair, first you take my mind and then you take my mouth, I can't even scream.

"Mac... Mac..."

I gasp frightfully and my eyes shoot open, the fear squirms in my chest, forcing me to try to sit upright but I am pushed back down.

"Hey, hey, easy. It's just me," Anna croaks.

"Where am I?"

"We are almost home, sorry I had to wake you. You were having a bad dream."

I follow the voice to the source, trying to make sense of where I am. She is above me; I am laying across the back seats of the Land Rover with my head in her lap. Calm returns and loosens the vice on my chest.

"How long have I been out?" I croak.

"About four hours, but you woke up a lot in between."

"You have been sitting here with me asleep on you, for four hours?"

"You asked me to stay with you," Anna says softly.

"I know, I'm sorry but I didn't mean you had to..."

"Whatever it is that you are thinking that is about to make you say that, stop. I didn't have to do anything; I just..."

"You just what?"

"I felt better, knowing that I had hold of you." Anna's voice is hollow and exhausted. Her eyes are tight and she is struggling to look at me. My brain is still too foggy to understand the is pain in her eyes.

"Makes me feel better too."

Darkness.

***

When I finally and fully wake up, I find myself lying in bed in Anna's room. I look down and she is asleep sat in a chair, bent over the bed holding my hand.

God damn it, does she have to be so cute? I start playing with her hair and she stirs.

"I think you are taking this staying with me thing a bit too seriously, girl," I say playfully with a deep croak.

Anna wakes up and doesn't look at me, she lets go of my hand and sits back in the chair and the dreaded blank expression washes over her face.

"Anna, talk to me. Please."

"I don't know what to say," she utters impassively.

"Whatever it is that is hurting you, tell me. Don't shut me out now, not after everything you did to make sure I didn't shut you out."

"Please stop being nice to me, Mac."

"Why would I be anything but nice to you? What exactly have you done?"

"It is my fault, Mac! I knew he had a problem with you. So, please stop being so damn nice to me. I don't deserve it and I don't want it!" Anna rants.

Anna's anger takes me aback a little but I finally understand. I have never seen her this way but I can tell it is not me she is angry with. I sit up, slowly and painfully in bed; my head feels fuzzy and light.

"Mac… Don't. Stay away from me," Anna warns.

"Savannah Mae Slone, this is not your fault. Whatever problem he had with me was his, not yours and I don't remember you throwing any punches."

Anna gets up from her chair and paces, I wish she would stop, the movement is making my head spin. Her hands in her hair and her eyes are wide with anger.

"His problem with you was because of me! Don't you get that? He didn't like how I was with you; he didn't like that you were close to me."

"Then surely that is my fault, not yours. I am the one that got in the way of your relationship. I didn't see that I was causing friction and I am sorry for that but that certainly doesn't make it your fault," I reassure.

"You didn't know there was a problem because I didn't want you to know! I knew if I said anything you would pull away from me and I didn't want that. It was my job to keep the peace and I was doing okay until I had a go at him for organising this for you."

The foggy memory of Anna shouting at Billy and Alfred comes into my mind.

"This is exactly why I didn't want either of you putting her through this, I swear if this messes her up, I will never forgive either of you."

"He seemed okay; I swear he did, Mac. I apologised just like you asked me to and I thought everything was okay but clearly it wasn't. He did this to you because of me, he used me against you and then he beat the crap out of you because of me! So please, stop!" Anna yells, her face flushing ruby red. I meet her gaze calmly; the anger in her eyes is not aimed at me, it is aimed at herself and yet it is still difficult to face.

"Anna… How many times have you needed me to hear you, when it was the last thing I wanted to do? How many times have you had to snap me out of a spiral I was intent on falling down? Now, I am either coming over there or you are coming back over here but either way you are going to hear me out," I say firmly.

With some wincing I swing my legs out of bed and my feet find the floor. My thigh hurts, but I am surprised that it isn't hurting half as much as I thought it would. I grit my teeth and use my hands to brace myself and attempt to push myself up.

"Okay, okay, stop, I am coming, God damn you, Mac," she rambles and I chuckle.

Anna sits back in the chair and bows her head; I bend forward and take her hands in mine. Now I have moved my head is feeling sloshy, my vision a little skewwhiff. I blink and try to keep Anna in focus as my eyes attempt to blur.

"Back in the forest I heard him say things about me, enough to know I wasn't his favourite person and when he was telling Jackson to touch me, I knew I had to do all I could to stop him. I was out of options; I was hurting and exhausted and I knew that was one thing I couldn't come back from. The only thing I could think of doing, was provoking him."

Anna looks up at me; her expression suddenly morphs from blank to concern and she squeezes my hands gently.

"I threatened to tell you what I had heard if Jackson touched me and I did it knowing he would lose it. I can take a kicking much better than the alternative. So, you see this wasn't you. I pushed his buttons because it was the only thing, I thought might end it. This wasn't you, Anna, please hear me, please trust me, this wasn't you," I reassure and I watch the logic play over in her mind and then the pain fills up in her eyes.

"I am so sorry, Mac."

"There is nothing for you to be sorry for. You have done nothing but take care of me and where the hell would I be if you hadn't? I was rather loopy back there; I wasn't even sure if you were real at one point to be honest. I lost all sense of time and perspective, it felt like I was in there for days."

"It was just over three days, if you include the first phase," Anna confirms.

Wow, only three days. It felt like forever but it could have been longer; if it had been, I am not sure how easy it would have been for me to come back from. I am only just starting to feel somewhat sane again. It was so easy to believe it was all real, especially because of Billy. I even forgot most the time that I was being watched.

"How much did you see?" I ask.

"Practically all of it."

I cringe, I wish I hadn't asked but it is not like I am surprised by the answer. I hate that she has seen me that broken, I feel naked and ashamed, my body stiffens and it hurts.

"Mac...?"

"Sorry, I just... I hate that you saw me that messed up. I must have been a pitiful sight. I really wish you hadn't watched; it is hard for me to un-know that," I croak, my voice strained as I try to gulp down the shame.

"I didn't want to watch but it was the only way of knowing you were surviving. Believe me there were times where I had to be stopped from coming to get you. It was unbearable and not just for me but I needed to watch. I needed to know you weren't slipping away, I was scared that you were going to disappear again but then I saw you, doing all you could not to lose yourself and as much as it hurt it also made me smile. You even, somehow... made me laugh," she says, smiling sheepishly.

"What are you talking about?"

Anna giggles shyly, her grin turning coy and she starts to sing:

"Sweet home Alabama,

Where the skies are so blue,

Sweet home Alabama,

Lord, I'm coming home to you."

"Oh man... Yeah. How cringe," I say, wincing, and she laughs.

"Well yes, your singing was awful, even worse than usual but it still made me smile. You were fighting to hold on and I was so proud of you, there is nothing pitiful about the strength you showed. I don't understand how you held on as long as you did and Pa, when you kicked the crap out of Jackson, you should have heard him cheer you on! Gwaan kid! I am surprised you didn't hear him."

We both laugh and I am glad, I needed it and so did she. It helps to get past the embarrassing reality that she was watching me. I never wanted her to come but now I am so grateful that she did, I don't think anyone else could have pulled me back from the mania I was stuck in.

"Okay, I can't deny how good that felt. Where is the old man anyway?"

Anna's smile slips. She pulls back the curtain of the bedroom window to reveal Alfred sat at the fire pit.

"He is blaming himself, obviously. He won't talk to me."

"I think I can fix that but I am going to need your help." I grin and she raises an eyebrow at me. Anna helps me to my feet and I wobble, the world threatening to disappear beneath my feet.

"You haven't even taken a single step yet and you are already falling, how am I going to get you down the stairs?" She steadies me, laughing freely, her smile radiant and I look at her intensely. She stops laughing immediately and stares at me curiously.

"Just what are you looking at, McKenna Scott?" she asks with a coy grin and I smirk at the irony before I pull her into me and hold her close. She melts into me and I breathe her in, then I let go before I act on other instincts that hold bigger consequences.

It turns out, I can walk kind of okay. Although it is a bullet wound, it didn't go too deep but my thigh is black with bruising and still swollen. The problem is I haven't eaten in days so I am weak and I am covered head to toe in cuts and bruises. I got a nasty shock when I saw my haggard reflection in the mirror. My face is blotchy with purple bruising and cuts and my forehead has a nasty gash; I look like a horror movie.

Downstairs I ask Anna to help me make coffee and load a huge plate with custard creams. I take a seat and Anna goes to the fire pit to convince Alfred to come back in. I never thought I would be so happy to be back on the farm. As the time goes on, I feel more and more human and less and less messed up in the head. Alfred comes in and by the looks of it, begrudgingly. He sits opposite me at the dining table with a huff and stares into his coffee cup.

"Alfred, come on man. You can't possibly think this was your fault," I say lightly.

"Yes, I can. It's my job to protect my family. I failed you both. I brought him into your lives and…"

I reach out and I put my hand on top of his and he looks up at me shocked and I smile, blushing a little. I hear Anna chuckle but I keep my eyes on Alfred.

"Alfred, no one could have known. You know a lot of things about a lot of stuff but you are not a mind reader. You do protect us; you have saved my life more than once; I don't think you will ever understand how much you mean to me, bud. Now rub some dirt in it and help me eat some custard creams... You hearing me, soldier?" I wink and he laughs a deep throaty chuckle and I know then, he is going to be okay. We chow down on some biscuits and Alfred fills me in on what happened when they were watching me on webcam.

"I said to Anna, that guy is going to get it if he keeps pushing ya and then boom! Straight to the knackers. I was howling!" Alfred booms.

"It felt good, not as good as headbutting Billy, but still pretty damn good," I admit.

"Ha-ha, kid! You broke his nose, you know that, right?"

"Not so pretty anymore!" Anna pipes up and I lose it, I laugh so hard it hurts but I don't care. I am home, I survived and Billy has a broken nose. That is a lot to be happy for. I got through it with my sanity intact, just. Whatever comes my way – I will be ready.

"No seriously, you done good, kid. I couldn't be prouder, you proved it to yourself, you have much more strength than you thought, both in your body and your mind and do you know what I think you are?"

"What?"

Alfred looks at Anna, winking at her then they both shouted...

"You're the king of the woorrrrld!!!"

CHAPTER ELEVEN

Killing In The Name Of...

"Are you sure you are ready for this? You have only been back for two days. The last time you watched one of them videos…" Anna trails off.

"Yeah, thanks for reminding me." I turn away from her trying to calm myself down.

"Mac, I am sorry. I didn't mean anything by it," she says, putting her hand on my shoulder, turning me round, "just help me understand why it is so urgent. Why it can't wait a little longer."

"Anna, I need my life back. With this hanging over me, my life is on hold. I can't do anything, I can't go anywhere, I can't be… I have had that memory stick for ages and not knowing what Alfred has found, it is like an axe hanging over my head waiting to drop. I need to know; I need this to end…" I stop myself ranting.

"Alright, okay I get it. I'm sorry, Mac. It just… screwed me up a bit, seeing you get hurt over and over again. I hoped it would be longer before I had to see anything like that again but I do get it."

"You don't have to watch it, girl. I am sure we can fill you in afterwards," I say, smiling warmly. "I am sorry for going off, I just want my life back."

"If you had your life back, right now, what would you do?"

"Um… Why?"

"Just curious."

My eyes watch the fire dance in the fire pit and I think about it, there is so much I would do if I could but what I miss most, are the simple things. Even after I returned, I didn't get to enjoy them things because I was too messed up and afraid to leave the house. Now, I feel like if I was given the chance to have my life back, I would take it in both hands and live the shit out of it. Trouble is… I am not free.

"Probably sit in the bar, across from a pretty girl. I would go see my mum; go watch a movie at the cinema. Walk in the park, drive to the beach. I don't know, I just want to be able to have the option, the freedom to make the choice. You know, without someone trying to kill me. It is a bit of a buzz kill" I joke.

"Yeah, I can see how that might ruin dating potential."

"Speaking of… I am sorry, you know, for not realising I was causing a problem with you and Billy. When the situation comes up again, I will be more aware. It is bad enough my situation prevents me from having someone, it shouldn't be stopping you too."

"Mac, I don't want to be with someone who isn't okay with my relationship with you. I don't see why me being with someone should have to change us."

"I get your point, but if it was me and my girl had a Mac, I wouldn't be okay with that closeness. I would be ending that relationship before it had even begun. If Billy had a Mac, would you have been okay with that?"

"Why do I get the feeling, you are trying to push me away?" Anna frowns.

This conversation was not planned. The truth is, Billy may have been a bit psycho but ever since it all went down, it has been nagging at me. I want her to be happy and something tells me that, while she feels obligated to be there for me, she won't be. I am trying to push her away; it isn't like I want to but she will be happier and safer for it.

"Anna, I got in the way of your relationship, I am not doing that again. I would be a wall between you and happiness and I am not okay with that. Whatever obligations you feel to be there for me, you don't need to keep them, I am okay. I am not going anywhere; I am just taking a step back," I say calmly.

"Screw you, Mac."

Anna storms off back to the house and I groan. That went about as well as I expected that it would, I feel like a complete jerk. It's not like I wanted to do this but what I want never really comes into play, I have to protect her from… me. My drain on her happiness, my danger to her life. The truth is, I do want her and this distance is for myself as well as her.

I am still messed up over Alisha. Is it possible to love two people at the same time? Or at least – almost love? I knew while I was with Alisha, I could easily fall for her but then I was taken before that really happened and everything that has happened since then means, I don't know what I feel for her anymore, it is very much a love-hate situation and what good things I do feel for her are felt from the 'before kidnap' Mac. The 'after kidnap' Mac, wants someone else.

I am not convinced Anna feels anything but friendship for me, she is curious maybe but our closeness confuses things. I can't deny that my feelings for her are crystal clear, I do want her, all the time, every day and it is so hard being around that and trying to keep myself from stepping over the line. What choice do I have? I know she is mad at me, but it is better to be mad now than hurt later. I hear the clunky footsteps of a gentle giant approaching and I try to snap myself out of my head space. Alfred takes a seat opposite me at the fire.

"Trouble in paradise?" Alfred asks and I look at him sceptically. "Oh, come on, kid. I am not blind, I have seen the way you look at her. I don't know what you did but she is mad as hell at you."

Oh crap. Crap, crap, crap.

"I… Um. Alfred… Listen…" I struggle, suddenly very nervous.

Oh God, he is going to kill me.

"Relax, kid, I am not mad at you," he chuckles deeply.

"You're not mad?" I ask incredulously.

"She could do worse."

I bow my head. I don't agree with that at all.

"Does she know?" he asks and I just shake my head no.

"I didn't think so. Don't worry, I am not going to say anything but you should realise, the girl isn't stupid, she will figure it out sooner or later."

"Oh, I know. That's why I have been trying to put some distance between us."

"Let me guess, she isn't taking that so well."

"Nope," I answer, looking at my hands.

"Mac, I know you went through a lot back at camp but I don't think you realise what it was like to watch you go through that. She didn't sleep, she wouldn't move from the screen. Twice I had to restrain her from going to you, you weren't the only person being tortured. She was beside herself," Alfred says grimly, rubbing the palm of his hand on his whiskery face.

"I never wanted her to see that, you know that," I say defensively.

"I know, but the way she was, I find it hard to believe she isn't feeling more for you than she is letting on."

"She is just protective; she has done a lot to help me find who I was again.

She didn't want me slipping back."

"Maybe, but you two have this connection that I can't begin to understand. It is not going to be that easy to put distance in and she has no idea why you are doing it so it is going to hurt her."

"I am trying to keep her safe, Alfred. I don't want to hurt her," I explain, my head in my hands.

"Oh, I know that, why do you think I haven't broken your legs?" he teases.

"Ha! There is the silver lining I was looking for," I say, laughing darkly.

He laughs with me and I actually feel some relief that he knows and that he knows I am trying to do right by her. Also, I am pretty sure he could easily break my legs if he wanted to so it is nice to hear that he doesn't.

"Kid, chuck that coffee away. I think this calls for a stronger bevy," Alfred says with a wink as he leaves and heads back to the house.

I have no idea what I am going to say to Anna now. Alfred is right, sooner or later she is going to figure me out and when that happens – what will I do? What will she do? Again, I see the scales in my mind that I am stood precariously on. I feel the strain of the 3 separate people I have become. The before kidnap, during and after versions of myself. If I somehow was able to pull myself into one whole person, would I know for sure how I truly felt?

"Here you go, kid, that will warm the cockles of your heart," Alfred says, handing me a glass and I take a sizable gulp without thinking and I choke.

"Oh, my good God, man! What is that? Rocket fuel?" I splutter as the liquid scorches my throat.

"It's moonshine, made it myself. Will put hairs on your belly."

"It tastes like lighter fluid and I don't want hairs on my belly," I cringe.

"Well go easy. It is strong stuff."

"You do know it is barely two o'clock, fella, I'll be trollied before the day is out."

"Ah well, I am sure it is happy hour somewhere!" Alfred cheers.

It feels good just to spend some time with him. Just some time where it isn't about impending doom, or training or Anna. I just listen to his stories and I even tell him some of mine. I hope one day it can always be like this, that I can visit and hang out, without the looming threat that stalks me. That it can really just be as simple as this again, but I am all too aware that today isn't going to be that day.

"Alfred, I need…"

"To watch the video? I know, kid. I didn't think it would be long before you got round to asking about it. If you feel ready then, I am good to go but you should probably talk to Savannah first."

"I know, I just don't know what to say to her," I admit.

"I think that, you just have to go with your gut, kid."

"My gut has a habit of getting me in trouble," I say and he chuckles.

"Whether you tell her or not, looks like you are already in trouble."

"Good point. I'll meet you in the kitchen in a bit, if I am not back in 30 minutes, call for help."

I walk slowly and by the time I get to the house I have already decided and changed my mind a thousand times about telling her the truth. I hate that I am lying to her, but telling her the truth could just as easily break our friendship. Then again, so could lying to her. I am up shit creek with a lollipop stick and I really don't know what I am going to do.

"Can I come in?"

"It's your funeral," she snipes.

"That might be a bit extreme. Am I really in that much trouble?" I ask lightly.

"Mac, this isn't funny so please stop trying to make a joke out of it. If that is all you have then, leave."

She is standing watching me, pissed off and waiting for me to respond and I still have no idea what to say. There is no joke that is going to make this better, I can't just make light of it when I have hurt her feelings, but I am not good at feelings.

"I am sorry I upset you. I am just trying to do right by you," I say eventually.

"Why exactly do *you* get to decide what is right for me, surely that is my choice?"

"You are right, it is. I can't argue with that. I am just trying to protect you, I would never intentionally hurt you, Anna."

"Well you have," she says coldly.

"I know!" I shout.

First, I hurt her, then I shout at her when she hasn't done anything wrong. Could this be any worse? Could I screw this up any more royally?

"I'm sorry... Anna. I just... I'm sorry."

Anna walks over to me; she doesn't look at me she just stands in front of me, fiddling with the hem of my t-shirt.

"Mac, what is it that you are fighting so hard to protect me from? Because right now, the only thing hurting me, is you," she whispers.

I gasp and take a step back, pulling my t-shirt out of her hands. Her words punch me in the chest with incredible force.

"Mac..."

She is right, I am just hurting her; the longer I stay the more I hurt her. Whatever this is between us I just seem powerless to stop it. We have already moved so far forward that any move I make to distance myself, will only hurt her. If I stay this close and keep pushing her away, then that hurts her too. If I am honest with her about how I feel then I stand to lose her. There is no way for me to still be here and stop hurting her. I feel so much hate for myself; after everything she has done for me, I just keep repaying her with hurt.

What am I doing here?

"Mac... I shouldn't have..."

"No, you are... right... I... You were right. It's okay, there isn't a way that I can stop hurting you... Unless, I leave... I have tried so hard not to, to do the right..." I stammer. My chest tightens with pain and I know I need to leave before I lose my nerve.

"Mac, don't..."

"Please, don't come after me, girl," I croak. There is no way to hide the pain in my voice. I feel my bottom lip quiver.

"Mac, no I'm sorry, please don't..."

I storm out, thundering down the stairs as quickly as my battered legs will allow. I go through the kitchen, picking up the memory stick off of the table and ramming it in my pocket. Crossing the field to my truck, I can hear Alfred calling me but I ignore him, my foot slams on the accelerator and I don't look back in the rear-view mirror because, I know that if I do my heart will shatter into a million pieces. I shouldn't be driving, I know that. I have been drinking and I am falling apart but somehow, I manage to pull up into the warehouse in one piece. As soon as I am inside the pain envelops me and I let it. I sob like a child, ugly and freely.

Wandering around the warehouse aimlessly is only making me feel worse. The photos of Anna and Alfred emblazoned proudly on the wall, the memories of the hours spent here with them. No doubt someone is going to come looking for me eventually, I don't want to be here when they do so I get back in my truck and start driving without any real destination. My phone is vibrating constantly in my pocket and I ignore it.

I drive, and drive and drive.

***

The sun is beaming down on my face as I find myself at Greenland docks, walking along the pier and looking at all the boats. I guess I just wanted to see it, it is one of a couple of places in London that could have moored the boat that I was trapped on for two years. I already walked through the south block and all the boats that are moored there are far too small in comparison to the boat I was held in.

I am not really looking for the boat, I am not entirely sure why I came here. Maybe because it was at this dock, or one very similar to it that my life was stolen from me. The moment I was taken onto the boat, was the moment I became all too easily hidden from the world. The moment that ruined my life. I look out at the boats with resentment; they are supposed to signify freedom, aren't they?

The water is quite murky now I am close enough to really see it. At the Waterside restaurant meet with Alisha, I remember looking out at the Thames and the water looked blue and glittery. It is the same water, but the boats and their movements seem to have disturbed the sediment making the water cloudy and opaque. I wouldn't like to go in there, who knows what is hidden below the surface?

"I'm not a strong swimmer," I mutter.

Why is that damn sentence ingrained in my brain? Probably a random quote from a film I have forgotten. The docks are quite busy, I can see why; it is quite pretty on a nice day like today. There are jolly fellows shaking hands and showing off their boats to each other and gloating about their catch of the day, there are kids being told by their parents not to step too close to the edge of the pier. There are boats coming and going and it is quite fascinating to watch. Since I have returned, I am a bit of a people watcher, I guess that's what happens when you don't see people for so long.

I like to look at people's faces and try to figure out what they are thinking. A woman passes, she is plump with a happy face and she is herding what are probably her grandchildren, away from the water's edge. I bet she is wondering what she is making for dinner tonight, what is going to happen in EastEnders next and what her grandchildren will grow up to be. She looks kind, I bet she makes a banging roast dinner.

Next, I spot a balding man in a blue polo t-shirt, board shorts and deck shoes. He is looking intently at a newspaper. He is probably thinking that the world really has gone down the drain and thank heavens he can escape from it on his boat. I bet he likes a younger lady. He has that Pervy Peter look about him, I bet he holidays in France and enjoys wine tastings.

My eyes fall on another man, he is heavyset with very tan skin and wearing a tan leather jacket. The sight of him revolts me for some reason, he has the type of face that... Oh crap, he caught me watching him, that's awkward. He isn't looking away, now my eyes are locked in some weird battle that I can't look away from, the hairs raise on the back of my neck. I get to my feet slowly, not taking my eyes off of him and mind flickers rapidly like a shrill scream of warning. His face jerks in my mind, making me flinch.

His eyes baring down on me savagely and his face so close to mine I feel the droplets of spit hit my face as he barks...

"Mala suka!"

"No..." I mouth.

Shock rattles me, my heartrate begins to pound unevenly as I see the corners of his mouth pull up into a grin. I turn on my heels and bolt into a run, the ghost of his smile still etched behind my eyes; the panic is tightening my chest, making it hard to breathe. My car is behind him, I have no way to get to it. I look over my shoulder and my stomach plummets with a sickening swoop of dread as I see him chasing me.

Running aimlessly, I dash across a busy road, my head a mess of fear, and run straight into oncoming traffic. Tyres screech against the road and horns sound loudly as a car comes careening towards me. I jump out the way as the car swerves away from me, missing me by inches. I am panicking, my ability to think impaired with suffocating fear. I am running with no plan. What is it Alfred said, that's a good way to get dead?

He is going to kill me, or worse capture me. Fear cripples me and my head swims, skewing my vision and gripping my throat. Tears fill my eyes and pain erupts in my chest as my mind is bombarded with images of the years of pain that he inflicted upon me and I whimper. Defeat fills my heart with a lonely pang and my mind is flooded with faces.

Mum... Anna... Alfred... Alisha...

The panic stops and I breathe a long-dragged breath of relief.

No... I will not lay down, I will not give in. My life is *mine* and I will not relinquish it to him again. Calm washes over me, bringing acceptance. It is time to run smart, not scared, just like Alfred said. He may still catch me; he may still kill me but I will fight and I will fight hard till the bitter end.

I am not his mala suka anymore.

I look over my shoulder and he is roughly 25-30 feet behind me. My feet pound the pavement sending jolts of pain up my bruised legs with every step; my body is weakened and nowhere near recovered from everything Billy and Jackson did to me so I have to think. I will not be able to outrun him, I have to outsmart him. I smile… He is running on my home turf now.

It is time to focus. I tune into my surroundings, just like through the forest I need to use my surroundings to my advantage. I know this area; I have to use that knowledge against him. I am running down a street that has a council estate feel, the houses are blocky, rough looking and all squashed together too closely. I recognise this street, it's close to a park I used to hang out in when I was younger, getting up to no good. If I can get to that park, I may be able to lose him in the thick woodland towards the far end.

With a direction to follow, I focus on trying to keep my legs moving through the pains shooting up them. I grit my teeth as I pump my fists back with every stride, willing myself forward. I weave in and out of obstacles, trying to stay light on my feet. Dead ahead is a large knot of teenagers and I pick up speed, adrenalin propelling me and I skirt around them, obscuring the mala suka man's view of me for just a moment.

Turning the street corner, I burst into the car park of a block of flats and I look over my shoulder. The mala suka man out of sight, so I drop to the ground into a painfully, fast skid against the concrete and drift to a stop underneath a car. Wincing at the pain, I roll onto my stomach and try to calm my breath, my eyes searching as he comes around the corner.

He slows to a walk, his head craning round looking for me and I freeze, my eyes wide as I watch him come closer and closer. I cover my mouth with my hand to silence my breathing, his feet walk past my face as he passes the car, then another. My heart pounds against my ribs as I roll silently out from under the car and I squat behind the wheel.

Please be gone… Please.

Holding on to the wheel of the car I peek over the bonnet and my heart drops. He is stood at the bonnet of a car two cars down, barely 15 feet away. I duck back down and my ears strain for any movement; it is so unnaturally quiet. My breath is held, my body still and every single muscle is tensed painfully. Now

I have stopped the pain is intensifying and so is the fatigue.

Buzz-buzz, buzz-buzz.

My heart plummets with horror as the sound of my phone vibrating in my pocket echoes louder than I ever thought possible. My instincts on full alert, I push off against the car wheel launching myself into a run, looking over my shoulder as I go and he is hot on my heels, 10 feet away at most. Fear finds a new grip on me as I run back in the direction I came and away from the park; my hope is dashed. He is too close and I am having to run flat out to gain any distance from him.

The pain in my legs is becoming too much and I know it is going to slow me down; the fatigue is too heavy and my chest is bursting as my stamina begins to fail me. This isn't going to work; I need to find a place to hide or a place he won't follow me. If I carry on this way, he is going to catch me. Maybe I have to let him, maybe the only play I have left is the choice of where he will catch up to me.

My eyes scour the streets desperately and the only thing I see as a possible out is a primary school. It has to be what, 6pm? There won't be any kids but the fact that there might be, may be enough to deter him from following me and if he does follow me, there will be plenty of places to hide, it's all I have. The gates are closed so I drag myself over the blue-painted security fence; luckily there is no one around because it isn't a graceful climb and the fall to the ground on the other side is even worse.

My energy is bottoming out as I drag myself up off the floor. I stumble my way towards the back of the school building, trying to find a way inside. I come to a door and it is locked. Of course, it is. Following the wall around the corner of the building, I hit the back wall, keeping tight to it and I take a peek behind me.

He is in the school grounds.

My spirit shatters. I can't run anymore; I am so tired of running, what is the point? Even if I could stop him, there are more of them. They will just keep hunting me. The pain of walking away from Anna and Alfred and now running from one of the men who terrorised me for so, so long, breaks something inside me. I will not run anymore. I shrink my back against the wall and wait for him to pass my right shoulder. This is dumb, this is suicide, I know it is. I try to quiet my breathing and keep completely still. Everything slows down, I see him walk past and I run and jump on his back, knees first with my arms around his neck and he hits the floor hard.

I grip his neck with everything I have, my forearms locked across his Adam's apple and pull back, digging my knees in his back and he roars with rage. He starts to push himself up off the ground and that is when I see the knife in his hand. Terror pulses through me as I jump off of his back and run around to his head and kick him in the face hard; his nose explodes with blood. My leg swings back for another kick and he catches my foot in his hands, pushes me backwards and I hit the deck on the flat of my back.

The mala suka man stands above me, wiping his nose on his sleeve. He looms over me and delivers a swift kick to my head; my vision warps with black spots in front of my eyes. I roll over and crawl away, trying to blink away the dizziness. I stumble to my feet facing him and he stares at me with the cold glare that I have come to know so well. I see the knife in his hand and fear radiates inside me, blood is pouring down my head and into my eyes, mixing with my tears.

I am going to die…

…I will die fighting.

"Come on then, you ugly fuck – what are you waiting for!?" I scream.

He explodes into a run at me and I stand frozen, everything moving so slowly. He comes closer… And closer… He is almost on me then I side step, grabbing his wrist and twisting it. My body turning into the knife, I feel the blade meet my flesh and penetrate with a sharp electric-like pain. Then his grip on the knife loosens and he lets go as I twist on his wrist, the point of the blade twists in my ribs. I feel it, but I am separate from it, I feel nothing but cold, rageful, hysteria.

The knife is in my hand and then the blade is in his gut. It is that fast, the instinct to save my own life overriding the repulsion I feel as I drag the blade back out. He drops to his knees, I kneel down, gripping his collar in one fist and hold the tip of the knife against his Adam's apple, my face inches from his.

"Why are you trying to kill me!?" I spit furiously.

"Fuck you!"

Anger and hate bubble inside me, threatening to boil over, fury like I can't explain. I watch the pain illuminate his eyes as I ram the knife deep into his thigh and he screams.

"Why!?" I yell.

"I have orders, kill you and bring your body back," the man struggles, his Polish accent thick.

"What? Why do they want my body? Who gave you these orders?! Answer me!!" I scream and I start twisting the knife still embedded in his thigh.

"Stop! I don't know why, his name Jakub, that is all I know, I swear!"

I look at him and I feel the pain of two years spent being broken at his hand; the hate is so… clean. My hand trembles on the hilt of the knife and he winces.

"Are you going to kill me?" he chokes.

"What would you do?" I ask and his face contorts into a mask of terror. He begins to shake and whimper.

"Please…" he pleads.

"See you in hell, mala suka!" I growl.

I pull the knife out of his thigh and I stab him in a frenzy of rage. I pummel – hard and fast – at his chest as he falls backwards screaming. I stab and stab, willing him to stop screaming, his blood splattering warmly on my face. As I watch the light leave his eyes, I feel the light inside of myself go out and my blood run cold and then I realise… It is my scream that I can hear.

Staggering to my feet, I drop the knife and pain burns in my ribs. I look down, lift up my shirt and see the stab wound. It is probably not life threatening and honestly, I don't care. I don't care about anything anymore; I can't do this. They are going to keep coming for me, they will come for the ones I love; I can't survive that but if I am gone, they have no reason to…

My vision swims as my eyes search the space around me. I spot a bunch of trees halfway down the playing field and decide, that is as good as place as anywhere to pass out. I stumble clumsily towards them and when I reach the trees, I fall into one, my body drags down it till I slump to the floor. I have a vision of the Tom and Jerry cartoon, Tom chasing Jerry towards a tree and Jerry running into a little door-shaped mouse hole at the bottom. Tom can't stop in time and runs splat against the tree and I chuckle. I feel my phone vibrating, only I am not really sure where I feel it. Patting my legs down I search for the source of the buzz. Where is my phone? I only have so many pockets… Oh.

"Hello."

"Mac? Is that you?" Alfred asks.

"Yes, I think so."

"You shouldn't have drove off like that, are you okay? We have been trying to call you for ages."

"I was busy. The mala suka man found me so I ran. I ran, and I ran and splat! Hit a tree, just like Tom. Did you ever watch Tom and Jerry?" I ramble.

"Mac, are you hurt?" Alfred asks urgently.

"It doesn't hurt."

"Kid, why don't you tell me where you are and I will come get you."

"I can't do that; I don't know where I am and I don't think you should find me. It is too dangerous; I am tired of all the running. You know if you just sit still, it feels much better and I will feel much, much better if you don't get dead."

"She is in shock, talk to her. Find out anything you can about where she is and text me anything you can get," Alfred hisses.

"Alfred?"

"Mac, it is Anna."

"Anna, where is Alfred?"

"He is coming to get you, goof," Anna says, her voice uneven.

"No, I told him it's a bad idea, too dangerous. I can't come back; I can't never go back, just like the mala suka man and he *definitely* can't go back," I ramble. My head is getting so heavy.

"What happened to the mala suka man?"

"I killed him, brown bread dead. He followed me to school, not at my school. God, I bet that is far away. This school is nice, nicer than my school. Has nice trees and a nice bus, why would they want an old bus? My school didn't have a bus inside. I didn't think he would chase me in here but I was wrong and now he... I... I am tired, Anna. You know? I want to go to sleep."

"Mac, you can't go to sleep okay? Stay awake, stay on the phone. Talk to me, tell me where you are, please?" Anna pleads.

"I need you to let me go, Anna, please... Don't come for me. Don't come... Or you will die too... And I can't..."

"Mac...?

"Mac? You can't what? Mac!?"

Darkness.

***

My eyes won't open, that is so weird. They are stuck. I am not dead, I don't think. If I was, would I have eyelids? I definitely have eyelids.

"Savannah, I've got her.

"No, she is passed out."

Darkness.

***

"It's just me, kid, Woah, Mac. Calm down!"

I fight, I kick, I punch, I squirm.

"She can't see, she can't open her eyes. Mac, Mac! It's okay."

Someone grabs my wrists and I fight, I don't like this, I can't see, I can't break free of the grip, I don't like the dark.

"Let me go!" I shout.

"Mac! It is Anna, stop fighting me!" she yells and my body slackens.

"Anna?"

The hands loosen on my wrists but don't let go, I slide my hands up the forearms and find hands, small, warm and soft hands, hands I recognise.

"Yes, it is me and Alfred. Blood has dried sticking your eyes together, will you let Alfred wash it off so you can see?" she asks patiently.

"Yes… I'm sorry," I say. My voice is so crackly.

"It's okay, don't be sorry." Her voice calms, her hands gently squeezing mine.

I feel a warm, wet flannel being held over my eyes. Alfred holds it there for a few minutes and then starts to dab and rub the blood away. My eyes open but I keep them down, I don't want to look at them, I don't want to feel anything, I just stare at the floor while Alfred starts to clean the blood off the rest of my face.

"Mac, you have a stab wound to your ribs, it is a flesh wound but it's deep, I am going to have to clean it and stitch it shut," Alfred informs, his voice bleak.

I am laying on the dining room table; I have come back full circle yet again and ended up right where I started, laying bleeding on Alfred's goddamn dining room table. Why do I keep going round in circles?

"Ah damn it, the blood has stuck the material to your skin. I am going to have to…"

I let go of Anna's hands and push myself upright, unbuttoning my shirt and then with a quick swift pull, I rip my shirt off the wound and then I lay back down.

"Wow. That is one way to do it, kid."

I don't want to answer, I don't want to talk and I don't want to be here. I just want to be left alone. I can feel Anna staring at me. Alfred pours something potent smelling onto my ribs, I feel it. I feel the burn, I feel the pain but it is almost like I don't care. I am disconnected from it, from everything, numb. The stitches were worse but my hands gripped the edge of the table till it was over, my eyes stayed unfocused and distant, seeing the light leaving the mala suka man's eyes over and over again.

"Anna has brought you some clean clothes. There is a lot of blood, kid, are you hurt anywhere else?" Alfred asks.

"Not my blood," I say, my voice dead.

"Pa, could you give us a minute? I am going to clean her up."

Alfred leaves the room and Anna walks around the table to stand in front of me. I push myself upright and swing my legs off the table and I watch them they dangle there, as I try to stop my head from spinning.

"You are not cleaning me up."

"Oh, I know. I know you would never let me that close or… you will and then you will push me away again. You haven't looked at us once since you opened your eyes. Why?" she says softly. Has she forgotten why she is meant to be mad at me? This would be so much easier if she would just stay mad at me.

"What do you want from me, Anna?" I ask, my voice monotone.

"I want Mac back."

I take a deep breath and look at her, she looks exhausted with worry.

"Anna I can only say this once so please hear me. I can't do this again, I need to leave and I need you both to let me go, tonight. I need to go and I need to not come back, I need you to forget about me. I need you both to know I am sorry and I need to go. Mac isn't coming back, there is no going back. So please, don't fight me on this."

"Mac, I should never have said what I did." Her voice is so small.

"Yes, you should have!!" I yell and Anna flinches and takes a step back, her eyes wary. That is good, she should be wary, I am a fucking monster.

"Why are you so determined to push me away? After everything we have been through, don't disappear on me now," Anna pleads.

"Because Anna, I will just hurt you again and again and eventually, you will end up dead. Don't you get that?! I have tried so hard not to hurt you and I did. After everything you have done for me and I didn't even mean to! I went for a walk and end up being chased, stabbed and then I tortured and killed a man! Why would you want that around? I am a murderer, I watched him die after I stabbed him over and over! I am a monster and I am going to ruin you. I am nothing but bad for either one of you! Now, I am leaving!"

"No. That's not true! Stop, Mac, don't do this. Please," Anna begs.

"Anna, let me go!"

"No. Don't you dare walk away from me!!" she yells.

"Anna, stop." My head shoots up at the sound of Alfred's voice and I freeze.

"If she wants to leave then let her. There is no place at my table for disloyalty!" Alfred barks, stepping up to me; my insides shrink at his disappointment in me.

"Pa, back off. That is not going to help."

"Alfred I am not being disloyal; it could be either of you next. It will be, it is only a matter of time, unless I leave now."

"We both know that is not the reason that you are running away!" Alfred yells.

"Don't you dare! You don't say a word about that, *ever*!" I warn, pointing my finger in his face.

"What are you both talking about?" Anna asks but Alfred ignores her.

"You are running from the fight! You are running from us and running away from yourself! I thought you were a soldier! I thought we was family! You run away because what? You have made mistakes? Because you killed a man that tried to kill you? You get the hell up and you keep fighting! You never give up, you coward! I never thought it possible, McKenna Scott – a damn coward!" Alfred yelled in my face with fury in his eyes.

"Argh! Fuck!!!" I scream.

I fly at Alfred and punch at his chest uselessly; all the fight has gone out of me. Suddenly the pain hits out of nowhere and all I can do is scream.

"Go on, kid, let it out… Let it out! Hit me, scream at me, shout at me and *let it out*!" Alfred yells. My knees buckle but Alfred catches me, I fall onto his chest and he holds me tight.

"I got you, kid," he soothes and my insides clench and I cringe away from him harshly.

"No! Don't fucking be nice to me! You found me; you must have seen what I did to him. Why the hell would you want me here, around your granddaughter! I am a fucking *monster*!" I bellow. Alfred doesn't even flinch, his eyes stare down my glare unphased. He walks over to me with intent and he grabs my shoulders, his eyes alight with intensity and I recoil.

"That man was trying to kill you! That man tortured you for two years! He broke you, cut you, humiliated you and made you feel so much pain that you wanted to die, just so it would end! It was him, or you! If you hadn't of killed him you would be dead. You snapped! Overkill, yes, but I tell you something, kid. You could kill him the same way a thousand times over and you will never come close to inflicting the agony that he caused you!"

Pain splits me open and I pull out of his grip, turning my back on him. I stand crumpled over, my arms crossed tightly against my tummy – trying to hold myself together and I break. I wail a bloodcurdling howl and sob so hard I can't breathe and then Anna grabs me and I don't fight her, there is nothing left to fight with. I fall into her and then I feel Alfred behind me, his arms around us both.

"You are family. You are not to try to leave us again, okay, that's an order. Now you listen to me and you listen well. I know what you are feeling but it was not your fault. It was you, or him. If you hold on to this, it will destroy you. So, you are going to get up, rub some dirt in it and you are going to tell us what happened. You only have to tell us once and I know it is the last thing you want to do but trust me, it will help and if you want to bring these bastards down, we need to know. Let's make them pay, kid," Alfred growls, his voice breaking.

All I can do is nod.

"Pa, can you give us a minute first?" Anna asks and I feel him let me go and walk away and I am left in her arms.

"I'm so sorry, Anna," I mumble into her shoulder.

"Don't be, you have been through a lot." Anna speaks with a tight voice, trying to swallow down a sob.

"That is no excuse for hurting you. Don't be nice to me because I have had a rough day, let me have it."

Anna pulls back and I force myself to look at her, I see the hurt written all over her face and I brace myself for the incoming tongue lashing that I know I deserve.

"You don't get to do this to me again! You don't get to push me away and decide what is best for me. You just left us and it was so easy for you to do it and I don't even understand why!" Anna scathes harshly, anger burning in her eyes.

"It was not easy for me. I was in pieces."

"Well, I wouldn't know because you left – again! You let me in, you push me away, over and over and it is getting so old, Mac."

"I was protecting you," I say pathetically.

"Seriously, this again? Really. Okay, from what?!" she snaps, laughing darkly.

"From me!!" I yell.

God damn it. I've gone and yelled at her again, I don't know what to say to her anymore, I just feel like I am lying and damaging everything and worst of all, I am hurting her.

"What does that mean, Mac?" Her voice suddenly calm.

I turn my back on her, I go to slam my hand down on the table then I realise it is not my table and my hands end up in my hair, my fingers knotted and I just want to tear it out.

"Fuck!" I growl.

I feel her hands on my back, so careful and gentle and the guilt pangs.

"I'm sorry, that wasn't aimed at you."

"I know, I could tell. Mac, can you look at me please?"

I turn round and I look at her and her face is calm, but her eyes are determined and intense.

"What does Pa know that I don't?"

I look away and tense up; how am I going to get out of this? I knew once he said that I was screwed. I can't tell her; I will lose her. She puts her hand on my cheek, pulling me back to her gaze.

"Whatever he knows, it is why you pushed me away isn't it?" she says softly.

I look at her, pained, and I nod.

"And it is whatever you are trying to protect me from too, isn't it?"

My jaw clenches and I nod again.

"Whatever it is that you are holding on to, it is tearing you up inside and hiding it is tearing us apart. What could be so bad, that you would let that happen?"

It is tearing us apart; it is hurting us both. It feels so inevitable, I can't lie anymore... I could lose her either way. She looks at me, her eyes warm and patient and...

The scales finally tip.

I take a step towards her fast and hold her by the waist, my face inches from hers, catching her off guard and I look into her confused eyes.

"It's not bad... it's beautiful," I whisper.

"I am ready for the answer," she whispers breathlessly.

My hands slide from her waist, up her ribs and lightly onto the side of her neck and she shudders. I move in slowly, my lips hesitating just an inch from hers; my heart pounds as fear grips me, fear that this one action could mean losing her forever. Her breath shakes as I draw in, my lips gently searching hers, unsure if she really is ready for this. Then I feel her surrender to me, her breath shallows and she groans into my mouth, "Oh Mac..." and her excitement releases me from my fears, my chest explodes with tingles that pulsate through me and I kiss her deeper. The feeling of her tongue sliding against mine is pounding pleasure through my chest and landing firmly between my thighs. I step into her, pressing my body firmly against hers and her breathing gains speed in excitement and I respond in kind. I kiss her feverishly, a hungry growing rhythm, a kiss so passionate I never want it to stop. Her lips fit mine perfectly like puzzle pieces, her tongue dances with mine in perfect symphony. I expected her to be timid, I have never been happier to be wrong, she holds her own, her hands firm on my face pulling me closer as she licks into my mouth and nibbles on my bottom lip. I can't suppress the guttural groan that flees my throat, I can't get enough of the smooth plumpness of her lips, of the sweet taste of her, I can't hold her close enough. Explosions of pleasure that there are no words for, radiate from within me in an overwhelming ecstasy. I slow down, my kisses becoming lighter.

"That was worth the wait," Anna whispers through panted breath.

"Yes, it was... Wait, what?" I blurt. I pull back from her, confused and she looks at me, her intensely green eyes bright with desire and glittering with tears.

"How long...?" I ask.

"I was trying not to want you for a long time, I didn't think you were interested in me. It wasn't till the night you let me touch you... God, all you did was kiss my neck, just once and I felt more in that one little kiss than I've ever felt... till now," she adds, smiling. "I could feel you wanting me for the first time and I knew then, there was no going back for me."

"Well, I don't know if you have noticed but I have been struggling ever since that night too, I have never needed to kiss someone so badly. I was trying very hard to persuade myself that you weren't interested because honestly, I was and I am, now more than ever, scared that I am nothing but trouble for you. If anything, ever..."

Anna puts her finger on my lips to quieten me. "I know this is really hard for you to understand but I would rather take that risk, than be with someone who isn't you. I need you to stop pushing me away and accept, that we are in this together and that this is what I want, that is my choice. If you want me too, you can't push me away anymore, Mac."

She is bracing herself; I can tell. Like she is expecting me to say I can't do it and I understand why. How many times have I pushed her away and she has always come back?

"I promise, I will try my hardest not push you away again."

I pull her close, my face buried in her neck. I kiss it lightly and she shudders in my arms. Then my lips find hers again because I can't wait anymore. It is just so easy to get carried away, to get lost in her. I hear a low grumble of pleasure escape her mouth and it drives me crazy, I could kiss her for hours; her kiss makes me feel both weak and strong all at once.

"If… you… don't… stop…" she says breathlessly and I giggle.

"I guess it is time," I say grimly.

"You're not alone in this."

"I know, thank you, beautiful."

Anna calls Alfred back in and he returns with his laptop and he places it on the table. Anna and I take a seat too. I look up at him and I wince.

"I'm so sorry. I never meant to disrespect you, Alfred," I admit, my head hung down in shame. Alfred grabs my chin and lifts it.

"I only said that stuff to snap you out of it, kid. You are shellshocked and that is something a softly-softly approach wasn't going to work with. I am sorry I had to say some harsh things to wake you up, I didn't mean them," Alfred says gruffly, smiling warmly. "Are you ready to tell us what happened?"

I take a deep breath and then I feel Anna take hold of my hand from under the table, her hands are so warm compared to mine.

"I went to Greenwich docks. I know, it was stupid. I went in blind, no plan and I paid the price but I wasn't thinking straight. I was just sat watching the boats and the people and then I saw him, the man from the video I watched. He was even wearing the same leather jacket; he saw me and I ran. He was blocking my way back to the truck so I had no choice, I could only run."

I feel the fear building as the whole thing starts playing like a movie inside my head, the shakes starting to vibrate through me and Anna squeezes my hand.

"I couldn't outrun him; it was hurting to run and I was tiring quickly. I thought maybe, if I could find somewhere to hide, I might have a chance. I found cover in the school but when I looked back, he was inside the grounds and he wasn't going to stop. I guess I didn't want to run anymore, so I attacked him.

"I was losing the fight; as soon as I saw the knife, I was sure I was done for. I used the gun disarming technique Billy taught me. I knew that doing it meant stabbing myself in the ribs but that didn't make it suck any less and if it meant I could get the knife away from him, I had to try. It worked, I got it away from him; as soon as I had it, I… I stabbed him. I didn't even hesitate… I just…"

I see the light leaving the man's eyes, a light that I stole and I flinch.

"Kid, the fact you didn't hesitate, doesn't make you cold or a monster. He was going to kill you. It was your survival instinct kicking in," Alfred reassured.

"Maybe but, I asked him why he was trying to kill me and he wouldn't answer so... I tortured it out of him. I tortured someone, after everything that happened to me, I..."

"You tortured a man to get information because he tortured you for over two years and he was trying to kill you. Kid, you have to let this go. What you are feeling right now, that guilt and pain, that is what makes you different from him, are you picking up what I am putting down?"

I nod, but somehow, I know it won't be that easy.

"He told me he had orders from a man named Jakub to kill me and bring my body back. Why? I watched him die and you know the rest... Oh fuck, what about his body?"

"Don't worry, kid, I have sorted it," Alfred says grimly.

"How...?"

"That is between me and whichever God you may believe in, let's just leave it at that."

A clear warning not to ask questions and I hear him loud and clear; I feel horrific that he had to do that. That I have burdened him in the worst possible way. Where would I be if he wasn't there, strong, always watching over me? I dread to think. I take the memory stick out of my pocket and place it on the table and I turn to Anna.

"You don't need to watch this."

"We are in this together, remember."

Anna leans towards me and kisses me, short but sweet.

"Well it's about time!" Alfred beams and we both laugh, my cheeks flushing pink.

Alfred picks up the memory stick and his smile slips.

"There is nothing happening to you in this, there is no torture but, I have my reasons for waiting till you were ready for this. I hope you will understand, are you ready?"

I look into his wary eyes.

"Play it."

CHAPTER TWELVE

I'm Not A Strong Swimmer

Alfred spins the laptop round to face Anna and I hear a sharp intake of breath coming from her as the image of myself fills the screen. I am in the same place I've seen before, the same room, some kind of cargo hold beneath the ship. Only, this time I am not bound to the ceiling. I am sat with my back against the wood of the curved wall. My knees are up against my chest and my arms curved around them tightly. My wrists and ankles are in shackles that are chained to the floor, I am rocking backwards and forwards slightly, the chains clink with every small movement I make.

Someone seems to have left me alone with the camera still recording. I am covered in dirt, gaunt and bloodied, my eyes are wide and spaced out. It looks like I am muttering to myself, then my eyes peer at the camera and they frown. I watch myself as I slowly crawl towards the camera, the pain evident in every movement I make, the chain drags heavily behind me. I stop and sit closely in front of the camera, making the disturbing view of myself crystal clear.

"It's still switched on… Why…?" my voice on the video says. I watch as the mind of my recorded self thinks, thoughts slow and dragging and then I watch her dead eyes look into the camera, defeated.

"I don't know if anyone will ever see this." My voice rasps and weakly, my head bobs slightly and my eyes droop as I struggle to stay awake. I look out of it and I resemble the girl in The Exorcist. The person on the camera is almost unrecognisable; I never saw my own reflection during this time and it makes my stomach churn to see it now. I have no memory of this.

"I've been here too long. I don't know what day it is, what year it is… I have been in the dark so long, I can't remember people's faces anymore. I would…

give anything to see, just for one second... But I can't remember. I must have been here a long time I think and I know... No one is ever... I am not going to be found."

I hear myself chuckle, a pained and empty chuckle. "I've forgotten so much... But I can't seem to forget the taste of cookie dough ice cream. I am pissed I didn't eat it more... while I had the chance. You should always find... more time for ice cream... I am... getting off track. I... need to..."

My eyes close and my shaky hands rub them, blood is caked on my fingertips and it smears on my face. The camera captures the abrasions on my wrists from the shackles. I rub my wrists absentmindedly, reminding myself that they are gone.

"...These men... They are up to something big. I've seen things, I've heard things, when they think I'm asleep but I never really sleep."

There was a thud and both me in present time and me in the video jump; the fear I see in my own eyes is jarring. I can feel her fear, I watch myself freeze and listen, fists clenched and shaking till it becomes obvious, no one is coming and then I turn back to the camera.

"A man came, a new man. He called me Mac; it has been so long since I heard that name." I see myself smile and tears streak down my dirty face leaving skin-coloured trails.

"He told me he had given me the triangle of truth. He told me, my father sent him and that he was going to try to get me out but... they killed him. They cut his head off, right there."

My head begins to swim as it slides from past to present. I see the pain flicker across my face and then a look of doom and then I feel it as clearly as if it is happening now. I see though her eyes, I feel her grief and exhaustion, I feel the despair of hope lost and the acceptance that it is over, I am going to die. I feel it all, I am there with her now.

The memory swirls.

"Now they are packing everything up, they are probably going to kill me and that's okay. It will be a relief, I am sure." I speak in unison with my recorded self.

I feel Alfred and Anna's eyes draw to me, from somewhere very far away.

"If anyone ever finds this video, you have to find these men. They are some kind of terrorist group. They are..." Loud footsteps echo in the video's speakers and I start to panic.

"They are planning something, horrible, something atrocious! No one is safe! You hear me! No one. They are Polish and I have seen at least five men and they all answer to a man

named Jakub. Find them, before it is too late!"

My eyes look away from the camera, watching the men come at me, my chest heaving rapidly.

"Please tell my mum – I love her," I whisper.

Alfred stops the video. All I can hear is my own breathing. I brace myself on the table as my head swirls with rapid images, the colours morphing as my head begins to slop forward; I feel Anna's grip on my hand tighten.

"Mac…?"

"Ugh… Hold on, something is…" My eyes close.

"I've got you," she replies in the distance.

The memory swirls.

"Mac… Wake up! Mac…" a voice calls urgently and the words come out of my mouth in the present. I feel Anna's hand – her hand is my lifeline; while my mind visits the past, her hand anchors me to the present, a bridge between two worlds.

My eyes open and I panic at the feel of a hand clamped over my mouth. I start to struggle.

"Mac, I am not going to hurt you. Mac!"

Something inside me clicks at the sound of my own name and I stop struggling. The man standing in front of me looks at me with wide eyes but they are not any eyes that I have seen before. They are not angry eyes, they are scared.

"Mac, I am going to take my hand away but you must be quiet, I am not going to hurt you, I am here to get you out. Can I trust you to be quiet?" I narrate in present time.

I nod my head, my arms ache so badly and my hands feel icy cold. The blood long since drained from them being chained above my head. The man takes his hand away from my mouth and he watches me, making sure I am not going to scream.

"Good, that's good, Mac. Now drink this."

The man opens a bottle of water and I moan as he pours it into my mouth; I gulp it greedily. The water is clean and icy cold, sending goosebumps erupting over my skin.

"Who are you?" I whisper weakly.

"My name is Oliver, your father sent me to get you out. Listen, we don't have much time. I have given you the triangle of truth. Remember that, okay, if I don't make it – the triangle of truth, it is important, Mac. Do you understand me?" I narrate, my voice a fast ramble and I feel Anna's hand on my back as clearly as I feel the chains' cold steel against my wrists.

"Not really. My father… I don't have a…"

"There is no time, Mac, I am waiting for the boat to get a bit closer to land and then I will

come back and you and I and going for a swim."

"No... Don't leave... Let's go now. I can make it, please," I sob.

"I can't, Mac. I'm not a strong swimmer, I will come back, just hold on and remember – the triangle of truth."

The vision morphs with a sickening spin. I grip the table, trying to keep my foot in the door of reality and groan. Anna holds my face and my head stops slopping. My eyes adjust the scene of the horror movie being played in the theatre in my mind, the curtains lift, revealing the arena of hell.

Oliver is beaten and bloody, his eyes rabid like a wild caged animal. He is being bent over a wooden cargo box; his hands are bound behind him. I struggle against the chains that hold me, anger and fear rippling through me, a feral growl exploding from my mouth.

The mala suka man stands before him, an axe in his hands. Another man is bent over slightly, looming over him, raging at him.

"Where is Barrett!?"

"Screw you, Jakub!" Oliver spits.

"He sent you! He knows we have her, he knows where she is! Why didn't he come for her himself?" Jakub spits, his Polish accent thick.

"He isn't that stupid. You will never find him. Let the girl go and you might survive this," Oliver threatens.

"I will burn down every city till I do, just as he did mine. The blood he spilled will be repaid... Starting with yours," Jakub scathes and my voice comes out in a cold spit, my body beginning to shake.

The mala suka man lifts the axe, swinging it high and bringing it down in one masterful stroke.

"Noooooo!" I scream.

I gasp for breath as the dining room comes back into view. The disorientation is sickening.

"Oh God... Oliver." I choke on my own sob. "Oh... God... Ugh." I struggle to calm myself, nausea plaguing my stomach at the vision of his decapacitated head rolling onto the floor.

"It is over, you are home. Bring yourself back, it's okay," Anna coos.

"How could... I? Why didn't this memory come back?" I gasp.

"You were sure you were about to die, kid. There is nothing more traumatic than that. I don't think your mind would ever want to remember that moment, it's your head protecting you. You spoke to the camera and you were clearly leaving your epitaph the only way you could. You were trying to save people, even moments before death," Alfred explains calmly.

"But Oliver… He tried to save me, he died trying and I just, forgot he ever existed," I croak, disgusted at myself.

"You watched him being brutally murdered in front of you and in that moment, you probably lost all hope, after fighting to hold it for two long years. Your mind can only take so much. Oliver is probably what motivated you to talk to the camera in the first place," Alfred reassures.

"Hey… You need to stop, you are shaking. Pa, we should stop I think we have—"

"No…" I look at her. "Please, I can't stop… I can't… go through this… twice." My voice trembling with every juddering quake. I look into her eyes begging her to understand.

"Tell me what you need, Mac. Whatever you need," she says.

"Whiskey… a… big… one," I manage and they both laugh.

Alfred moves like a shot and I knock the warming liquid back in one. The woody, caramel alcohol burns the back of my throat pleasantly. Alfred refills the glass, once… twice and by the third the shakes start to subside and are replaced with tiredness.

"They were clearing out because they realised my father knew they had me… My father…"

How is that even possible? It doesn't seem possible.

"Oliver was proof that my father knew I was there, he was also proof my father wasn't going to come himself. They killed him in front of me and I was so sure I was going to be next but instead they let me go. I guess because now they were sure, he was watching me. It wasn't just a wing and a prayer anymore. They knew my father would be watching me, their best hope was to watch me and wait, I don't remember him at all. He was gone before I was a month old. That is a lot of trouble to go to for someone who he turned his back on me so quickly."

"Unless he has always been watching you, your whole life," Alfred offered.

"Barrett… I didn't even know that was my father's name. It still means nothing to me. *'I will burn down every city, just as he did mine.'* What kind of man is that? He may have sent Oliver to rescue me but he sounds just as bad as the people who took me." I tremor, disgust thick in my voice.

"They are not just people, kid; you used the word 'terrorists' and it sounds like you are warning of an attack. You said you felt like something bad was coming, this must be it," Alfred predicts grimly and I nod but it feels like I am missing something, something – more. I always felt like something bad was coming. For some reason, terrorists never entered my mind. It is all starting to fit together and the picture is becoming more horrendous as more pieces are revealed to me. My father… I don't even know how to process that, or what to feel about it.

"Do you remember anything about the triangle of truth?" Anna asks.

"No, but I remember the look on Oliver's face when he told me he had given me it. Whatever it is, it is important."

I rub my temples; I feel like my head is going to explode. There is too much whizzing around in it. Questions and theories all shouting over each other, it is all too loud, too rambled to make any sense of. I need it to settle, so I can think more clearly and that isn't going to happen right now.

"Whoever these people are they need stopping, I have to stop Jakub from hunting me and I have to stop whatever attack he has planned. As for dear old Dad – I am going to need some time to wrap my head around that one. Either way though, we are getting closer and I want to be ready." I turn to Alfred, squinting though my pounding headache. "It is time to get back to training. You with me?"

"Hell, yeah I am," he says a little too enthusiastically.

Alfred disappears excitedly; I am a little troubled by how much he enjoys this stuff. God knows what I am in for, all I know is I could use all the help I can get. Between Jackson, Billy and the mala suka man, my body feels so beaten. I need to get myself strong again and I need to prepare for what lays ahead. Today has been hell, there is no other word for it but then I look down at my hand and see Anna's fingers interlaced with mine and somehow, the hell doesn't seem quite so damning, the pain is just that little bit easier to bear.

"You look so tired," Anna says, her voice a little sad.

"I am a bit. I'm okay."

"Come with me."

Anna leads me by the hand up the stairs and to her room, she lays on her bed on her side and holds her hand out, gesturing me to come and join her. I lay on my side facing her and she starts stroking my face; her touch feels magical and her eyes sparkle beautifully as she watches me. I can't understand how she could ever look at me like that, I can only hope she never stops.

"I can feel it, you know," Anna says softly.

"What's that?"

"I can feel it when the pain starts to overtake you, I have always been able to. I wish I could make it stop."

"Do you remember the first time we met?"

"Of course, our coffee in the sky," she says, smiling.

"That day, I was going to the warehouse for the first time, it was the day that this all started for me. I was broken and scared and I felt completely lost. Then I met you and in seconds, I was laughing. You made me feel alive, you were the first person to treat me like a normal person again. I walked away feeling lighter and stronger and like maybe, I could do this. You have given me that, every single day since. You can't take the pain away, but you give me the strength to fight it. You light up the darkness, you always have," I recount, my voice hoarse and my eyes heavy.

"As much as that just made me melt and all I want to do is kiss you, you need to rest, you look so tired."

"I don't want to sleep, I don't want to move, everything hurts and…" I wince.

Anna strokes my face and she waits, just like she always does but this time, I don't know if I can say the words, my chest is full of pain. The video, the memories, still vivid inside my mind, the tears fall before I even realise that they were coming.

"Talk to me, baby." My stomach does a backflip; even while I cry, I get tingles at the way she calls me baby.

"I killed a man and I can't stop seeing him die. The memories and the video, every time the dots connect a little bit more, we learn more but I also feel what happened more. I remember the pain of trying to accept that I was going to die, I remember the loneliness of not being able picture anyone's faces anymore, I remember the thud noise Oliver's head made when it hit the floor. I even remember wanting cookie dough ice cream, the hunger and the thirst was a constant companion. When I close my eyes, there is nothing but horror."

I watch the tears glisten in her eyes and I stiffen. "I'm sorry, I didn't mean to be so honest," I say, embarrassed.

"Don't you dare be sorry, Mac Scott. I want to know you, not the filtered version of you. I have never heard you be so honest and I feel closer to you because you are letting me see… all of you. Who you are is beautiful, brave and miraculous to me. I am only crying because I hate that this is happening to you and that you are in pain and for the record, it is good that you don't want to move because you are staying right here," she says, wrapping her arms round me and sometime, through the tears I fall asleep inside of them.

***

When I awake the next morning, Anna is gone and there is a note on the bedside table. 'Back soon' is neatly scrawled on it with a love heart underneath and I smile. I slept like the dead; I was all set and braced for nightmares that didn't come. My body feels heavy, like I slept too long; I have no complaints at that. I make my way downstairs and the salty aroma of bacon makes my stomach growl. Alfred making breakfast is the best smell to wake up to. I hesitate in the dining room doorway, suddenly feeling awkward that I slept in his granddaughter's bed last night. We are all adults but, still, it's weird.

"Kid, there a reason you are propping up the doorway?"

"Nothing gets by you, does it bud?" I chuckle nervously.

"I like to think not. Stop hovering and take a seat, you're making me nervous."

Oh, the irony.

I eat quietly, feeling awkward and nervous and not completely sure what to say. This is stupid really, after all we have been through together but still, I have that 'meeting the parents' feeling of doom in the pit of my stomach. I was always terrible at meeting the parents, I am the kind of person that makes an okay third impression, rather than a good first one.

"Mac, for the love of God, spit it out," he mumbles with a mouth full of bacon.

"What?"

"Seriously? Something's on your mind, come out with it, I am getting older here."

"I just want to, you know, make sure we are cool. After... with... Anna," I struggle.

Smooth, Mac, real smooth.

"I am tempted to drag this out because it's really fun watching you squirm." Alfred guffaws. "Look, you two were just a matter of time, anyone paying attention would see that. Like I said to you before, she could do worse."

"I guess that is the problem, I don't really believe that and I can't see how you would either. I am not exactly the safest bet," I admit.

"Falling for someone isn't about safety, it's a leap of faith. The only question I would ever need to ask is, will you do all it takes to keep her safe, and I believe

230

the answer is yes. The rest, kid, is none of my business. So yes, we are cool. Relax." He grins crookedly.

"Thank you, Alfred."

"So, that being said. How are you feeling after yesterday?" Alfred asks.

"Um… It was a bit much, I am not really sure yet. It's still very mixed up. The only thing I know for sure is I want to end it. With your experience, do you have any idea what we are dealing with?"

"That depends greatly on what their capacities are and if this is a single group, or a cell that belongs to a much larger group. I am hoping that whoever Jakub is, that he is the top of the food chain, that would be simpler. You said in the video that you have seen five men, I very much doubt that is the extent of it either way. I have dealt with extremist groups in many countries but never Poland. I have a guy in intelligence running the names Jakub, Barrett and Kaminski and looking for previous attacks linked to Poland, trying to find anything that connects. Don't worry, Mac, we will find them. How about you let me worry about that part, you can worry about figuring out what the triangle of truth is."

I nod absentmindedly. "I feel like I should know what it is, but I am blank so far, it sounds like something from an Indiana Jones movie," I scoff.

"It will come, just like everything else. For now, you need to rest. Your body has been through enough and so has your head. I am ordering down time for you today; no training, no nothing. Before you go to question my orders, you should probably be aware that these orders were first given to me by a fiery redhead, who wanted at least two days, so if I was you, I would take one day as a win."

"Ha, I will take that under advisement. Where is the fiery redhead anyway?"

"I don't know, she said she wanted to pick some things up and that she wouldn't be long."

My eyes gaze blankly into the fire. This week has been — is there even a word to cover this week? It feels like I haven't had the chance to catch my breath, maybe down time isn't a bad thing. I feel like everything from the video and the memory is blowing around my head like a sand storm. If the wind could just stop blowing, the sand could have a chance to settle then maybe, I could figure some of this out.

How much is there that I still don't remember? There has to be quite a lot, there is no way I remember over two years' worth of events. It feels harder every time more returns, the grief becomes heavier. Quite honestly unless it is going to help me stop Jakub, then I am in no hurry to remember.

Barrett...

I am back to repeating his name over and over, trying to feel or think something about him but there is nothing, a big empty void as vacant as his place in my life has been. Mum would never talk about him; she always said if I wanted to know more then she would try to answer any questions I had but I had no interest in learning about a man that abandoned me so easily. Mum seemed so hurt, she would avoid talking about his existence at all costs. Has he been watching me this whole time?

I hear Anna's car pull up and soon I feel her arms wrap around me from behind, her candy-like scented perfume is enticing and is quickly becoming my favourite smell.

"Morning, beautiful," I say and she giggles cutely.

"Hey, you, how are you feeling this morning?"

"Like I slept too much," I say, yawning.

Anna takes a seat on the camping chair next to me. It looks like she has been shopping; my mood improves quickly at her arrival.

"You didn't, you just slept a normal number of hours for a change. You needed it, in fact, you could use more nights like that."

"This wouldn't happen to be anything to do with the strict orders I am under today, would it?" I ask with a coy smile.

"I make no apologies; you have had one hell of a week. You can save the world tomorrow, today, you are spending the day with me."

"You know it is really unfair, using your bossiness against me. I find it really sexy so it is almost impossible for me to argue, you have an unfair advantage," I flirt and she smirks, her eyes daring.

"Oh, you have your own advantages, believe me."

"I do? Name one?" I ask, genuinely curious.

Anna blushes and then she bites her lip and then gets out of her chair, kneels down in front of me, her arms resting on my thighs.

"Okay, just one. Wouldn't want you to know all of the powers that you hold, then you really would be dangerous." She smiles coyly. "Do you know how many times you would be training; you would get all sweaty and dirty and it would drive me crazy. So damn sexy it is unfair, then you would come sit by the fire to warm up and sometimes you would doze off and the temptation to just... kiss you, urgh it was unreal," Anna groans.

My stomach does a pleasurable backflip and I grin through flushed cheeks. To think she saw me that way and I had no idea, makes my insides soar. This girl never stops surprising me and the look in her eyes is immensely tempting.

"Ha! I always thought you looked at me grossed out when I was training."

"That was frustration, not being grossed out," she says, blushing.

"Mm, that is good to know," I say, grinning. "I dread to think what Alfred has in store for me. Whatever it is, I get the feeling I am going to need all the training I can get," I puff in a sigh and I see Anna's smile slip just a little, her eyes turning thoughtful.

"What's on your mind?"

"It is just scary. I mean, you are not just hunting some unknown thing anymore, we are talking about terrorists and for some reason they are trying very hard to kill you. I know you are doing all you can to prepare but there is still a lot more of them than there are of you. You never seem scared of what or who is coming for you, you just seem to want to run head long into it."

This is something that hasn't escaped my notice; I know I am outnumbered and no doubt in way over my head, but this isn't just going to go away, my only option is to fight this. Until now, I never really had to worry about what effect the danger to me would have on anyone else but myself.

"I do get scared, I guess I have just accepted that I might not make it through this because then it is less scary. That doesn't mean I won't be doing all I can to make sure I will, I just can't allow the fear that they will succeed to cripple me or I will be making the fight a lot easier on them."

"I can't just accept that you might die, Mac. How do you do that?" Anna's expression is incredulous, almost angry. I take her hands in mine and her expression softens a little.

"By knowing that there are far worse things that can happen to me than dying. I don't expect you to accept it, I will do all I can to end this, Anna, try to believe in that."

"I do, I'm sorry. I think it is just dawning on me that I have more to lose now, I didn't mean to get all morbid, that is the last thing you need. Sometimes, I just wish I could hold you hostage here with me, where I know you are safe."

"Well for today at least, I was under the impression that I was under your strict orders. I would say it looks like you do have me held hostage. So, what are we doing first, boss?" I say with a wink and that earns an excited smile.

"We are going to the barn, I rented movies for the big screen and..." Anna dips into her shopping bag, "I bought you this."

Anna pulls out a large tub of cookie dough ice cream and I melt at her thoughtfulness. It is quite apt considering where the conversation turned, a reminder to enjoy and appreciate things, while you have them. We go to the barn and put a movie on but we spend most of our time sat on haystacks just talking and learning about each other. We have spent so much time being guarded and trying to keep distance between us that now that wall has come down and we are free to just be, there is so much we both seem to want to ask. Before that wall came down, I always had to think so carefully about everything I said that the liberation to say whatever I want feels awesome.

It feels like everything between us has suddenly been hit with a fast-forward button. Usually, that would scare the crap out of me but I think that we both spent that long wanting each other from afar that it has magnified everything. It feels fast but also natural; our relationship before may have been based on friendship but the circumstances we find ourselves in, the danger and all of its intensity, has forced a closeness on us that most friendships take years to build.

This feels more like a fifth date than a first; she already knows parts of me that I would usually hide, she has seen my darkness and helped to guide me through it. She has comforted me through pain, we have argued, laughed, lusted and cried with each other. Yes, it is fast but it is also slow. It took us a long time, for her to even be able to hold my hand, let alone get to this place.

Now, I am sat watching her with hungry eyes as she laughs at my lame-ass jokes; her smile is so addictive, her intensely green eyes are bright and hypnotic, her rusty red hair hanging in loose curls like fire against her milky white skin. I am captivated by her and it scares the hell out of me, how can someone make you feel so weak and so strong at the same time in equal measure?

Anna sticks her finger in the ice-cream tub and sucks the ice cream off of her finger; the gesture is intended sweetly. Like an impatient child stealing icing off the top of a birthday cake, but the animal inside me doesn't see it that way. The animal inside me wants to take that innocence and corrupt it. As I watch her, I want her more and more, I want to explore her body with mine and it gets harder with each passing second to resist.

Fear is holding me back. I crave her touch, but I also fear it – a new kind of torture. She has broken down some of those barriers but no one has touched me, I mean really touched me since the scars were inflicted on my skin. They make me feel repulsive, the confidence within which I would touch her is the polar opposite to the fearful damaged girl who is scared of being touched in return. I put my finger in the ice cream and dab it on the end of her nose.

"You goof!" she squeals, climbing onto my lap. "That was a waste of ice cream."

"I don't consider it a waste."

I look up to her, my hands holding steady on her hips as she sits on my knees and I pull her to me, her bum sliding down my thighs, her knees either side of them. I wipe the ice cream off with my finger and stick in my mouth, grinning. This wasn't my smartest move; the temptation is painful. Her shirt is unbuttoned low and my face is in the eyeline of her breasts. I keep my eyes on her, trying to keep myself in control.

"You know that the way you are looking at me right now is driving me crazy right? You have the most haunting blue eyes and I have found myself lost in them many times but the way you are looking at me right now..." Anna trails off.

Excitement like electricity pulses through me as I see the desire in her eyes; a low and barely audible growl escapes my lips as I kiss her hungrily. My mouth is insistent upon hers, her lips bending to my will. My kiss is animalistic, sexy and dominant as the lust in my heart explodes from me. My tongue explores her bottom lip and then she bites mine making me moan. My hands slide up the back of her shirt and run smoothly across her soft skin and I feel her tremble. My kiss travels down her neck roughly, my tongue follows the perfect line of her collarbone and I feel her thighs clench as she squirms. Wrapping one arm under her bum, and holding the back of her neck with the other, I stand holding her tightly and her legs wrap around my hips.

I turn around and lay her down on to the hay, climbing on top of her. My hands explore her curves and she pulls on my hips, willing me closer. I start to unbutton her shirt and her hand slides underneath mine. I feel her hand slide up my ribs and then I gasp and recoil. My body tenses up and she feels the change, I squeeze my eyes shut and let out a groan, a mixture of both arousal and fear. My body shakes and shame hits me like a freight train, I make the move to roll off Anna and she holds me there, predicting my instinct to hide.

"Hey... Hey... It's okay," she says breathlessly. "Don't... Stay with me, please."

I feel... emasculated, the shame suffocating me relentlessly. My identity and dominance, a massive part of who I am, of how I express passionately, just shattered into dust.

"I'm... Sorry. I... Fuck," I struggle, trying to catch my breath.

"Mac, I can feel you trying to run away, you promised you wouldn't shut me out."

"Yeah and that promise has never been harder to keep. I am fucking mortified."

Anna lets me roll off her and I roll onto my side and she lays facing me, I direct my burning stare at the floor and she takes my hand and slides it inside her shirt, laying it over her heart.

"Listen to me, feel my heart fly! You have nothing to be sorry for, that was the most insanely sexy and passionate feeling I have ever had and I am still fully clothed." She giggles shyly. "You haven't let anyone touch you, touch your scars since you have had them. What matters is, I could feel how much you wanted me to touch you and how wild you just drove me. If this is how you make me feel, just by kissing me, I will wait as long as it takes for the rest," she reassures softly and I smile a little, but embarrassment still dominating me.

"I feel like there isn't one part of me that isn't ruined by them. Even this, what if I can't get that part of myself back? You would be waiting for nothing," I admit hollowly.

"Oh, believe me that part of you is far from ruined, you are in there and you are not scared of touching me anymore, you knew exactly how to touch me... God." I smile weakly. "I am willing to wait as long as it takes, till my touch doesn't scare you either," Anna says gently, her eyes smouldering with warmth.

"Your touch doesn't scare me. I wanted it. What scares me is the way the scars look and the feel of them to the touch, the ugliness of them. My chest, back and arms got the worst of it and it repulses me."

"I don't know how to say this without it sounding... offensive in some way. So please, try to bear that in mind." Anna speaks warily and I brace myself. "I know they hold a lot of pain for you but from the very brief glimpses I've seen, they are... um... sexy. They give you a dark... sexiness. The night I touched you for the first time, I ran my fingers over the scar across your throat and I don't know what I wanted more – to kiss away the pain, or to bite your neck and cause you more." Anna blushes and I smoulder, the want pooling between my legs only deepening and I chuckle a shaken breath. The combination of her endearing sweetness and daring naughtiness is quite frankly, making me want to devour her.

This girl...

"What part is supposed to offend me?"

"Well essentially, the scars show the pain you have endured and the strength you have shown in the face of that pain… And here is me, finding the evidence of that strength, arousing. It feels a little offensive but I can't deny it's true." Anna's face is a picture of embarrassment and it is very endearing.

"You are not just a princess, are you?"

"I never said I was. God, I used to hate you calling me that."

Before I know it, she is making me laugh again. That is the magic of her, I can hit the lowest of lows and she always finds a way of showing me the light again. It always seems so effortless for her, as easy as breathing, something I can never understand. She radiates light and warmth and again, I fear my darkness will extinguish it all. To ruin the brightness of her, to drain her colours and sap the very energy of her, would be a crime. A crime I am always scared that I am committing.

"Why do you think I kept calling you it?" I taunt and she rolls over on top of me, tickling me.

"Mac Scott you cute little jerk, you will stop calling me princess or so help me I will tickle you till you wet yourself!"

"Okay… Okay… Stop. Ouch… You win!" I laugh and laugh and then wince at the pain in my ribs and Anna freezes.

"Are you okay? What happened?"

"I am fine, I think one of my stitches might have popped open, that's all," I cringe.

"Oh God, I am so sorry. I should have been more careful, I didn't think."

"Hey, it isn't a big deal girl, I am sure it is fine. I am pretty banged up right now, it isn't that easy to avoid my injuries," I say, chuckling, trying to reassure her but she isn't laughing.

"Anna, I am fine."

"Can I check that you're fine? Or at least get Pa to check?"

"It can wait, he said I need the bandage changing later anyway, it can wait till then. I am sure I won't bleed to death," I joke.

"Funny, really funny."

Anna smiles but the smile doesn't reach her eyes, there is sadness there, I can tell that me being flippant is just hurting her and I hate that I am doing that. A knee-jerk reaction and a learned behaviour to keep her at arm's length. I am still pushing her away and it hurts her every time. I take a deep breath and I start to unbutton my shirt.

"What are you doing?" Anna asks anxiously.

"Letting you check it."

Anna grabs my wrists and her eyes soften. "No, Mac, it's okay. Like you said, Pa is changing the bandage later anyway."

"I am asking you to change it."

Anna searches my eyes, probably trying to see if I am being serious. I hold her gaze as best as I can because, I am terrified but I don't want to be. She has seen me with my top off before, but things are different between us now and even so, she has never so much as laid a fingertip on my damaged skin.

"I will get the first aid kit," she says and I nod.

As soon as she leaves the fear starts to bubble up as I lay with my shirt undone but still very much closed, my chest is becoming tight. I can't stand that this is so hard for me, the resentment I feel is so powerful it makes my blood boil. I want so much to be okay with this, I wish I could go inside my brain and delete whatever it is that makes me so scared to be touched. Part of it is that I feel repulsive, but there is another part that feels genuine fear and I don't know where that comes from. Anna returns and comes to sit back in the hay beside me and she looks at me with wary eyes.

"You don't have to do this, don't try to force yourself to be ready. I am not offended," she reassures.

"I promised I would try to stop pushing you away. I may not be able to give you all of myself yet, but I want to try, it is just a step. No, it is not easy for me, but I want it to be. With you, I want it to be," I profess and I see a warmth transform her expression, her eyes glitter beautifully.

"If you need to stop at any time, you tell me, okay? I don't want to push you. This is all you, just like in the field, you can stop me any time. I won't be upset if you do, I will just feel so damn proud you tried."

My breathing starts to escalate, my chest heaving up and down unnaturally fast. I wish it would stop. I open my shirt with shaky hands and I see her eyes fall first on the purple and black bruising up my ribs. One of which is the clear image of a boot print. I see her tighten and her jaw clench.

"Is that from…"

"Billy and Jackson, yeah. Don't worry, looks worse than it is." She nods, taking a deep breath and then she moves on to the bandage.

"You are bleeding through the bandage quite a lot. Do you mind if I take it off?"

"Go for your life, girl," I say through gritted teeth. I know this is going to suck, the bandage is stuck to bruised and swollen skin. I groan when I feel the tug.

"Sorry!" She winces.

"No, you're good," I strain and when it comes away from my skin I exhale, there are black spots in front of my eyes.

"Okay yeah, you are a stitch down. Stitches are all Pa but I can clean it and stick some Steri-strips over it, closing the gap, and then put the new bandage over it, are you okay with that?"

"I am great with that," I say, pained, and she laughs.

I feel the antiseptic being poured over the wound and yelp a little, then Anna goes to work drying, closing and dressing the wound. I watch her the whole time, her jaw clenched and keeping her eyes on the job, trying not to touch me too much; she is trying so hard not to scare me.

"All done," she says, smiling down on me proudly. She picks up the sides of my shirt and pulls them back over me, covering me over. I grab her hand hesitantly and she looks at me smiling but confused. I steel myself, my chest still heaving up and down embarrassingly fast. I open my shirt back up and squeeze my eyes shut.

"Mac…" she gasps.

I lay her hand on my tummy and I hold it there with both hands. She freezes, she doesn't move a muscle. I focus on my breathing, on trying to slow it down. I release the squeeze on my eyes, I keep them shut but not so tightly. I tell each and every one of my muscles to relax with varying degrees of success.

When I manage to slow down my breathing a little, I take one hand away and hold it out for her. She gives me her free hand and I take it blindly and I lay that hand on my tummy too, the only part of my torso that remains relatively unscarred and then I take my hands away. She doesn't move at first, but when she does, she moves very slowly and I open my eyes to watch her. Her fingers trace down both sides of my ribcage, bumping along the ridges of my ribs. My heart wants to burst from pain but there are other feelings too; warmth and excitement tingle in my bones making them feel spongy. She lays her palm flat and runs it across my tummy and smiles.

"So soft…" she whispers.

Her fingertips trace my hip bones that stick out above my trouser waistline and I shudder from the tingles, supressing the squirm between my legs that her touch inspires. So far, she has avoided any scars but then her fingertips trace the curve of the underwire of my bra, then they pause to trace the triangle-shaped branding burned under my right breast and I jerk. A small sob breaks free of my mouth. She freezes. My head screams in revulsion and I try to quieten it by focusing on her face, trying to tell myself if she was disgusted, then I would see it on her honest face.

She doesn't move again till my breathing slows and when it does, she leans forward and kisses the scar that runs around my hip and wraps in an arc over my hip to the bottom of my back. The scar is deep and smooth, like the perfect curve of a blade. It is smoother and more faded than the rest but still, it's there and when I feel her warm lips against it, the lump in my throat threatens to expose my emotions; I struggle to swallow it down. Then she runs her hand over the bumpy circular burns on my chest and I clench my fists, because I know the roughness of it, I know she can feel it. It tips me over the edge and my breathing turns rapid and shallow again. Anna stops and pulls me upright by the hand.

"It's okay to stop, beautiful, I think I have pushed you far enough," she says quietly, kissing my forehead.

I shake my head, no. "Please…" I manage. My voice sounds as small as a child's.

I take my shirt off, completely revealing myself to her, my body starts to shake and she pulls my face to hers, my breath coming out in short sharp bursts.

"You are so beautiful, Mac Scott. Every inch of you, inside and out. You don't have to believe that, but if you trust me the way you always have, then believe that that is how I see you."

My breathing starts to ease, the violent shakes become a tremor. Anna looks at me, her eyes seeking permission and I nod. I watch her run her fingers down the deep gouge-like scar that runs from down my bicep diagonally, it looks like a badly performed skin graft. Her eyes fall on the just-healed bullet wound to my shoulder and she brings her lips to it and I shiver at how good it feels. Anna shuffles so she is sat behind me, she holds my hips lightly and her breath tickles the back of my neck. Not being able to see her face is much harder, not being able to see if she is cringing, makes it too easy to imagine that she is. In my mind, I see the photos on the wall at the warehouse, the photos of my back, a clear image burning into my eyes.

I see the slashes, the obvious whip marks that criss-cross, red and angry against my pale skin. I see the rest of the curve of the smooth blade-like scar that starts on my hip and curves onto my back and ends at my tail bone, just under my trouser line. I see the two deep matching pinkish purple scars, one on either shoulder blade. I see it all too clearly like a meaningless chronicle of living purgatory and the sight is repulsive.

Her hands leave my hips and my breathing quickens, knowing she is going to touch; she touches so gently and I still jump. She holds her hands still on the tops of my shoulders, applying pressure little by little. Then she lets her hands slide smoothly down my back, the pain overwhelms me and the tears start to fall. She starts kissing my back all over and the sobs start to rasp deeply in my throat. Anna wraps her arms around me and holds me while I try to control the sobs and panic writhing in my chest. I feel her lips on the back of my neck and I shiver, both in pleasure and in pain, both danced together in perfect tandem with ever light touch. Soon the sobbing slows and she shuffles round to face me and I can't seem to look at her.

"Mac, don't hide from me now."

And then, her lips are on mine. She kisses me desperately, taking full control of my lips. I feel the intensity bursting from her, raw and fervent. She kisses me bravely and unapologetically and I feel her warmth awaken me. I moan as she breathes life back into me, the cold ice inside my veins melts and begins to sizzle from every emotion that she screams through her kiss and then she pulls back a little leaving me breathless, she looks at me with eyes smouldering of emerald fire.

"I've never wanted you more," she utters softly.

***

We find ourselves laying back in the hay, laying on our sides facing each other. My shirt back on but left open, Anna's fingertips running up and down my stomach. That might just be the hardest thing I have ever had to share with anyone but right now, as I feel her touch my stomach and I feel nothing but pleasure, it was worth every second of pain.

"I know I probably shouldn't be, but I am a bit in love with the triangle, it fits on the curve of your body perfectly," she says, tracing it with her finger tip.

Images flash across my mind at lightning speed, dark and bloody, I jump with a jolt. There one second, gone the next.

"Mac, what's wrong?"

"What did you just say to me?" I ask anxiously.

"I am sorry, I knew I shouldn't—"

"No, Anna, that's not what I mean. The words, exact words – say them again, please," I say urgently and I see the understanding reach her eyes and then the concern.

"I said I know I shouldn't be but I am in love with the triangle, it fits on your body… no, the curve of your body, perfectly."

I am on my feet pacing, my head is in chaos with blasts of violent images. The memory keeps trying to connect and then fails like a loss of signal. Then I feel pain, burning hot pain, my arms cross across my torso and I cry out, falling to my knees.

"Mac!"

Anna runs over to me but my vision flits between the reality of her and the vision of a jumping, shattered memory. Blood, pain, darkness, Anna, repeating in a dizzying cycle.

"Mac, what is it?"

"It hurts, I see it, then it's gone. I see it and it…" I cry out again as my ribs begin to burn white hot. The repugnant smell of burning flesh clouds my head.

"What hurts?! I don't understand," Anna asks desperately.

"I'm sorry, Mac. It will be over soon," Oliver says through gritted teeth.

I grab Anna's hand and place it on my ribs, over the triangle branding.

"Is that where it hurts?" Anna asks and I nod, eyes watering.

"Oh God…" I cry out again.

"I don't know what to do, baby, tell me what to do?!" Anna cries from somewhere very distant. The pain is unbearable and yet I still feel Anna's hand placed at the pain's source, there is pain and yet there is no pain.

"I know I probably shouldn't be, but I am a bit in love with the triangle, it fits on under the curve of your body perfectly."

Body…

"I have orders. Kill you and bring your body back."

Triangle…

"I have given you the triangle of truth. Remember that, okay, if I don't make it — the triangle of truth, it is important, Mac. Do you understand me?"

Truth…

The pain stops and the vision disperses, I feel Anna's arms wrapped tightly around me and my face is buried in her neck but I don't remember having moved here. I pull back from her and I feel her eyes watching me as my hand reaches inside my shirt.

"No…" I groan.

CHAPTER THIRTEEN

The Triangle Of Truth

I feel... violated; my skin crawls with itchy disgust, I have no way of knowing if I am right. No tangible evidence to speak of and yet somehow, I know that I am. The anger and revulsion are building inside, churning in my stomach.

"What happened, Mac? What did you see?" Anna asks.

"I didn't see much, the vision kept going black, I would feel the pain and then everything would go dark like I was passing out and then it would come back as I gained consciousness. It happened over and over so I only saw flickers but... I saw enough."

Anna waits patiently but I can tell she is chomping at the bit, wanting to understand, fear still playing with the shape of her eyes.

"The mala suka man said he had orders to kill me and bring my body back. Why? What use is my dead body to them? And why are the orders now to kill me, instead of watching me?"

"They want your body for something?"

"Exactly and they don't need me alive for it so that means they just want my physical body. When you said about the triangle and it fitting my body it started to click. Anna, I think whatever the triangle of truth is, Jakub wants it. He has found out I have it and he is willing to do anything to get it from me," I explain.

"But you don't have it, you don't even know what it is," Anna says, confused.

"I don't know what it is but I think I know *where* it is," I say grimly and she looks at me puzzled, her eyebrows crumpling slightly.

I pull away my shirt, I look down and I touch the raised skin of the triangle branded into my skin. A wave of sickening enmity poisoning my system making my hand tremor, I look up to Anna and watch the understanding wash over her face, then quickly it's replaced with horror.

"The vision was of Oliver holding me down and cutting into me."

"You think he put it inside you?!" she gasps and I look up at her, swallowing hard on air, my mouth at a loss of all moisture.

"I know he did and it is coming out, I will cut it out myself if I have to," I growl, the anger smouldering. I feel an urge to tear at my flesh and rip out the foreign body.

"Hey… Slow your roll, Mac-Attack – you will do no such thing!" Anna walks over to me, her hands slipping inside my open shirt and resting on my ribs. "We need to talk to Pa and we will find a way but there isn't a chance in hell, I will *ever* allow you cut into that beautiful body of yours," she says, smirking, and I can't help but laugh.

"You are made from magic, Savannah Slone."

"Alakazam!" she whispers before kissing me softly.

***

We spend the next hour explaining everything to Alfred. As always, his face is calm and unreactive. He listens carefully, you can almost see his mind ticking over, unravelling every facet of detail.

"How sure about this are you, kid?"

"Almost certain."

Alfred nods and sighs scratching the bushy hair behind his ear.

"Okay…" Alfred says, after what feels like too long.

"Let's think this through, let's say they put something inside you, it would have to be small. When you were found I am assuming the hospital took x-rays?" I nod to confirm. "Then whatever it is has to be inconspicuous enough to go unnoticed but still I find it hard to understand how they wouldn't have seen something," Alfred speculates, his mind on the go.

"I was a field medic; my job was fast and dirty. Patch up as best as I could, keep people alive long enough to get a med evac to a hospital where the real doctors are. If this Oliver has put something inside you, he must have wanted you to be able to find it again. My guess is it is going to be close to the surface, I mean that is risky, your body could have rejected it but I can't see any other option. He would have had limited resources on the boat you were both on and limited time, given that he clearly infiltrated that boat to try to rescue you," Alfred says grimly.

"He said if anything happens to him, to remember the triangle of truth. Like he was expecting that he wouldn't make it. If Oliver put something inside of me, then that means it was probably on my father's orders. What would he go to such length to hide and why hide it inside of me? Whatever it is, Jakub is willing to kill me for it."

I am not really talking to them anymore, my mind whizzes trying to understand this latest bomb drop. That is what life is now, a series of bombs; every day it seems there is a new wave of bombs to either avoid, defuse, take cover from or recover from the blast of. All I know for sure is that I feel tainted, I can't stand that there is something inside me that doesn't belong, that was put there against my will. There really is only one way to understand the point of all of this.

"I want you to cut it out," I say flatly and Alfred's eyes tighten; his lips press together in a straight line.

"I am not a surgeon, kid; we don't even know if you are right about this and even if you are, I don't have the equipment to knock you out and do this properly and without it, you would be in agony."

"I remember the pain of him putting it inside me, you are not telling me anything I don't already know. If you can't do it, I understand. It is a big ask but it is coming out, even if I have to do it myself," I assert firmly.

"That would not go well, believe me. Would you give me the night to sleep on it? I will see what I can come up with."

"I can do that. Thank you, Alfred."

Anna and I go back to the barn but my mind's elsewhere, things are changing, I can feel that. Sooner or later I am going to have to face Jakub and maybe even my father. My mind is ready for Jakub, I feel a strong hatred and it is fuelling me. Physically though, I am just one person and a pretty beaten up person at that. Am I going to survive this? I hold Anna a little tighter; she is laying on my chest watching the movie. Her arms and legs wrapped around me in a cute knot. Whatever happens, I just need to find a way to keep everyone safe.

Am I ready to face Barrett? I feel cold to him, disconnected. He is a stranger, but there is a tiny nag. The man that abandoned me as a baby, tried to save me. Does that mean he cares or does that mean he had other motivations? Probably the latter. I wish there was a way to ask Mum about him but talking to her over the phone and keeping up the pretence of travelling Europe is hard enough, let alone bringing up a subject she does all she can to avoid.

No, the only way to truly understand any of this, is to confront Barrett. I wonder where he is, if he has been watching me, does he know about the farm? I can't help but worry that he does, he had the resources to find me on a boat in the middle of nowhere when no one else could. Maybe that is just my fear talking. I have taken this giant leap forward with Anna and it is awesome but my fears of her being hurt because of me are still unescapable. My darkness could destroy the magic that makes her.

"I can feel it," Anna says, sitting up.

"Feel what?"

"Whatever it is that is overtaking you right now."

"It's nothing, don't worry," I sigh, smiling automatically.

"Mac…"

"Can we get out of here for a while? Just you and me."

"Let's go."

"You didn't even ask where we are going," I chuckle.

"I don't need to; I was sold at 'just you and me'."

We take my truck, Alfred went down to the docks to retrieve it for me, it is good to have freedom of movement back. It feels good to move, almost like I really am free. We drive around London and we share stories as the drive inspires memories for us both. We stay in the truck; after what happened at the docks, I don't want to take the risk of her being seen with me and after night falls, we stop by the warehouse.

It feels like forever since I have been here, I walk over to the wall that is littered with all of my evidence. It is like a habit now; I am not sure how many hours I have spent staring at it, hoping that something will click. Now, I can't help but feel that the person that started this wall was truly naïve, I had no idea how deep this rabbit hole would go and now I am starting to see that it runs so much deeper than just stopping the people who took me.

"You are somewhere far away," Anna says, joining me at the wall.

"I guess I am. I'm sorry."

"That isn't something you need to be sorry for, why not take me somewhere far away too?" Anna probes.

"I just keep thinking; I don't think this is going to end with Jakub. I set out to find the people responsible for taking me, find them, end the threat and be able to live my life again. Something tells me it doesn't end with him."

"You mean your father?" Anna murmurs and I nod, my eyes still exploring the wall, my mind still ticking over and over in an annoying pointless ramble. "You haven't talked about him."

"I know nothing about him, I didn't even know his name was Barrett."

"You don't have to know him to talk about what you feel about it, what your instinct tells you. It has been on your mind ever since you remembered the triangle of truth, probably even before then. What is it that you are not saying?"

"That this won't end with Jakub and if Barrett was able to find me when everyone assumed that I was dead, then what kind of man am I dealing with? And how long before he finds me at the farm? Finds you…"

"A pretty powerful man, but even if he knows where you are, he hasn't made any move on you. You can't think that way and before you go there, I am well aware of the risk."

"As am I – that is the problem. Sooner or later, I will have to face him and I don't know what is going to happen when I do. If anything happens to you or Alfred, do you really think I can live with that?" I say, my voice hollow.

Anna turns me away from the wall to look at her. Her eyes are determined and locked onto mine; she holds the sides of my neck softly.

"You are going to survive this, Mac, we all will. I need you to believe in that and believe in yourself because I…" Anna struggles, huffing and biting her lip. "Losing you, is no longer an option for me. You have broken me open; I didn't know I could feel like this and now that I do…" Anna trails off and her voice breaks.

In this moment, it isn't just about wanting her anymore, I need her and I can feel how much she needs me. There are no words or clichés that will ever describe it authentically enough. In this moment I couldn't say a single word capable of accurately explaining the way in which I need her. My heart demands it and my body expresses it. I kiss her, unburdening my heart from the desperate ache I feel for her.

Our clothes fall away and with them, every fear and doubt. I lay her down and tremor pleasurably at the sensation that ripples through me when I feel her smooth bare skin against mine. I grind down on her, her hips bucking against mine, her eyelids heavy, her hands buried in my hair, clutching. My hands explore every curve and line of her, admiring. She is so Goddamn beautiful that my usually confident hands are trembling against her heated skin. Anna is so responsive to my touch, like her honest face her body shows everything she feels fearlessly and it is staggering how much I feel because of it, like I am connected in a way I have never been before. Her body quakes beneath mine submissively, her hands pull on my hips, thrusting me against her and I feel her excitement slide down my thigh. My mouth wanders down her body, pausing at the freckles scattered over her tummy and hips. I kiss and nibble at them, her answering whine resonates a jolting thrill powering right through me. My lips travel down her hips as my arms pin her legs over my shoulders. I take my time, appreciating her thighs wrapped around my neck with my tongue and they clench in reaction. I can smell her delicious scent, feel the heat radiating from her and if it wasn't enough to wreck me, the sound of her desperation is, "Mac... Please."

I lean in and taste her and delight at the feeling of her dripping down my chin. Her hands are knotted in my hair as she pulls me deeper into her, my fingers enter her and play in rhythm with my tongue. I build speed in line with the speed of her moans until her thighs shake and tense around my head as her orgasm rushes through her. The sound of her pleasure rip-roaring through my system so hard I grip the bed sheets with clenched fists and I know, I just want to be the cause of that sound, over and over again. Her body turns limp and my lips find hers again. I hold her as her body tremors in the aftershocks of climax. I cradle her face in my hand and I see a tear fall down her flush cheek.

"Hey...?" I begin but she silences me with her kiss, rolling on top of me, her lips exploring every inch of me, her soft hands curiously glide over my skin. She breathes life into every broken part of me, awakening me with rapture. Anna moves slowly, her tongue appreciating my nipples and the throb pulsates through my tummy and rushes between my legs until I drip down my thigh. My head falls back into the pillow, my hand gripping in her hair as I groan in appreciation and the sound seems to embolden her. Anna's hands move firmer, her teeth dragging over my skin, her kiss shamelessly desperate. Her hand discovers my excitement and the breath catches in her throat. We are on our knees, in perfect rhythm with each other, our eyes locked in surrender as we reach ecstasy together. The hot build-up seems to burst from deep inside and radiate over every inch of me, so powerfully I want to scream. My legs buckle and I fall into her, whimpering. My nerve endings singing in triumph, the sensation overwhelms me and I struggle to catch my breath. She holds me tight against her, her fingertips tracing my back, her lips tenderly wandering up my neck, across my cheek and onto my forehead making me feel precious in a way I am certain, no one ever has. My heart aches with the release of sadness and happiness all at once; tears prick my eyes and I choke on a sob, burying my face in her neck to hide the tears.

"Don't hide from me now… Not now… That is not okay," she whispers through rapid breath. I pull back and meet her gaze, her eyes are bright, glassy and full of life and they narrow at the sight of my tears.

"Did I do something—"

"No." I interrupt quickly. "Was just… really intense… After everything…" I manage.

"And you are embarrassed?"

"A little," I laugh awkwardly.

"You saw me cry and I haven't been through what you have," she says, raising an eyebrow.

"Good point," I say, smiling, and I feel better immediately. "Why did you…?"

"I am not sure I want to answer that, not yet anyway," she says illusively.

I kiss her neck and I can taste the salty sweat on my lips and she shudders. She runs her fingertips up and down my back as I hold her.

"That is going to drive me crazy but I will try to be patient."

"Can we stay here tonight?" Anna asks, laying on my chest.

"Of course."

"Good, then you have no reason for clothes!" she cheers, throwing my jeans and shirt over the edge of the platform, down to the lower level floor. She giggles so infectiously, her face lighting up with childlike happiness and I am captivated.

"God, girl, you are every kind of beautiful," I say, smouldering and her eyes grow impossibly brighter before they become thoughtful. Anna places her hands on the sides of my neck, her thumbs stroking my jawline.

"There isn't a single inch of you I don't adore," Anna breathes, not quite able to look me in the eye. "What have you done to me, Mac Scott?" She chuckles but I don't laugh, instead I lean in but pause with my top lip just brushing her bottom lip, relishing in the way her breath shakes.

"I don't know but, I'd like to do it again."

I trace her bottom lip with my tongue and her eyes clamp closed, her breath huffing heavily against my lips before I kiss her again, with intent and I marvel at her reaction once she registers what that intent is. I lose myself in her again, making the most of the time we have. For one blissful night, there is no one in the world except her and I and I never want it to end because with every touch she graces me with, every kiss, every openhearted look, she breathes life into me, her honest, pure heartedness obliterating every barrier I assembled to protect myself and I am powerless to do anything but dive deeper into the warmth of her and allow her to wake all the places inside me that have been asleep for so long. I fall asleep, in the early hours of the morning with Anna curled up on my chest knowing, I am forever altered by her and too happy to be scared of what that could possibly mean.

**

Anna is running, terror on her face like I have never seen before. The expression on her face is enough to haunt me for the rest of my days. Someone is chasing her and she isn't fast enough, I have to get there, I have to save her. My legs won't move, why won't they move? I look down in horror as my hands and feet are back bound in chains.

"No, no, no!" I cry. "This is not happening."

"Run! Anna, run!" I scream.

I jump backwards on the chair, breaking it but I am still chained to the floor. She is running towards me; oh God please make her run faster and then… She stops dead in front of me, I grab out to reach her as blood trickles out of her mouth. Her eyes huge with fear, her legs give up and she falls in my arms.

"Baby – no please, don't go. No. Anna! ANNA! Please. Nooooo!"

Her eyes fix somewhere distant that I can't follow, my heart shatters into dust. She can't be gone, there cannot be a world where she doesn't exist.

"Noooo!"

"Mac…"

"Nooooo!"

"Mac, wake up!"

I jump bolt upright with terror, the ghost of Anna's frozen face, blaring behind my eyes. I ram my palms into my eyes roughly with a groan as the sweat stings them.

"Hey… Was just a bad dream, it's okay," Anna says, her hands on my face. "Oh, wow, you are soaked, that must have been some nightmare."

"Yeah."

"What happened?" she asks, wiping the sweat off my face with the bedsheet.

"It's nothing, like you said. Just a dream," I say, brushing her off. "I am going to make coffee, you want one?"

I busy myself trying to get the images out of my head, I know this is my fear talking but there are very real reasons behind the fear. I am putting her in more and more danger every moment we are together. What is to stop her being taken and used to hurt me or killed? We drink coffee and get ourselves ready to go back to the farm. I feel like I barely slept a wink, my eyes are dry and scratchy and my limbs feel heavy. It is time to get back to reality. We pick up our things and then Anna stops me before we get into the truck. She kisses me lightly and then she pulls back, looking at me with sad eyes.

"Did I do something wrong? You seem distant, after last night it is a bit…"

"No, not at all. I'm sorry, I'm just really tired, I didn't sleep much," I say, pulling her in for a cuddle.

"Well, that makes two of us but for the record I loved every second of you keeping me up half the night. I wish I could hide here with you a little longer," she says softly, eyeing me provocatively.

Then her lips are on mine hungrily, she kisses me passionately and shamelessly, her hands knotting in my hair, she presses herself up against me hard, ramming me against the truck and I groan, tingles spreading through me in warming waves, she pulls back, leaving me overexcited.

"Keep kissing me like that and I will end up making us both more tired," I pant and she giggles, all sadness in her eyes dissolved.

We get into the truck and make our way back towards the farm. As I drive Anna keeps her hand on my thigh; I look down and smile. It is such a small gesture and yet it makes my insides melt. The morning's nightmare is beginning to fade a little behind my eyes, my mind now preoccupied with wondering what Alfred has come up with. If he isn't willing to take whatever Oliver put inside me, out. How am I going to get it out?

The truck wheels judder over the cattle grate and we pull up outside the farmhouse; I spot Alfred sat by the fire drinking his morning coffee. We walk over to him and sit down to join him and await his verdict. His face is grim and he is thoughtful, he doesn't look up from the flames as he speaks.

"I really don't want to do this, kid. Like, I really don't but something tells me if I don't you will only find another way and that way may not be as clean and safe. Am I right?"

"That is about the gist of it, fella," I confirm.

"That's what I thought. So, I would feel a lot better about this if I had some Lidocaine to numb you up but I can't access anything. We could break into a hospital but they keep medications under lock and key. I have bought you some Xylocaine anaesthetic spray, it will numb your skin a little but there is no getting away from it, it is going to suck." He grimaces and my stomach tightens in knots. I am used to pain; I can take it but it's not like I am looking forward to it.

"I am aware of that. When are we doing this?" I ask.

"Whenever you are ready, kid."

I am not sure what has me more nervous, the pain that I know is coming or what I am going to find at the end of it. If I want answers though, I need to man the hell up.

"Let's do it, get it over with," I say, sounding much more confident than I feel.

Alfred heads inside to get everything ready and orders me to drink some whiskey and I don't need telling twice. I stay sat by the fire with Anna, trying to psych myself up; my leg twitches up and down nervously and I hold Anna's hand, maybe a bit too tight.

"Are you sure you want to do this? Surely there has to be another way. One that doesn't involve you being awake while Pa cuts into you."

"I am sure I will just eventually pass out. I don't think you should be in there, girl. I know you want to be but…"

If I am honest, I am not sure I want her to be there. Showing pain and weakness has never been easy for me and she looks a little green and nothing has even happened yet, the look on her face is just making me more nervous.

"Then I will hold your hand till you pass out," she says firmly, giving me the 'don't argue' look and I relent. I haven't got it in me to argue with her and it wouldn't feel right if I did. She is trying to be there for me, any normal person would welcome that, not try to push it away.

I hear Alfred call me and the nerves in my stomach redouble, my legs move shakily and unsure towards the house. When I get inside Alfred has cleared the dining table and placed a clean white sheet over it. On the kitchen side there is a can of Xylocaine, a brand-new scalpel and some other first aid supplies. The sight of it makes my stomach churn. I climb on top of the table and Anna stands between my legs.

"I am really starting to feel a lot of hate for this table," I joke nervously and she smiles at me but the smile doesn't reach her eyes.

"Remember, you don't have to be here. I will be okay," I remind her, but she just kisses me quickly and lifts my shirt over my head. I lay down and my breathing is embarrassingly laboured. She holds my hand and I turn my head to look at her. I don't want to see the scalpel; I don't want to see anything Alfred is doing.

"Can I do anything?" Anna asks, the fear probably obvious in my eyes.

"Tell me something, to distract me. Make it good so I don't leg it off the table."

Anna draws closer to me with a shy but playful grin. "Last night... you made me feel so good, that I wanted to scream. Three times... And I couldn't get enough of you, I can't stop wanting you," Anna whispers and the look in her eyes makes me throb.

"Do you know what you are doing to me right now?" I groan quietly.

"I hope I do."

"Now I want to get off the table for much different reasons," I say, desire in my eyes. She smiles at me coyly, kissing my hand.

"I am ready, willing and waiting..."

"Ugh, now that is just teasing," I whine in a frustrated whisper.

"It's not teasing, if I mean it. Take me now, take me to bed, take me anywhere just take me and never stop."

"Stop... Alfred is going to cut into me while there is a party going on in my pants and there is something really wrong about that," I say quietly, chuckling, all too aware that Alfred isn't far away.

"Now who is teasing!?" she hisses.

"Are you ready Mac?" Alfred asks. I jump a little, looks like she succeeded in distracting me. I smile at Anna nervously then I roll onto my back.

"Nope, but let's do this anyway," I say, taking a deep breath.

"Okay, I am going to spray the Xylocaine on the area first." I cringe as the cold spray hits my chest; it is so cold it kind of feels hot. "It could take up to five minutes to kick in," Alfred informs me.

"Just do it, man, I don't think I can wait that long." My voice shakes, my chest heaving in and out. "Pain is better than the wait for it."

Anna holds my hand and I drape my other arm over my eyes. I focus on my breathing but the waiting is just bringing on the panic; if he doesn't do it soon, I will lose it and I know it.

"We should really wait—"

"Just do it!" I say firmly.

"Alright, kid. You are going to have to try to stay as still as you can, the more you move the harder it is going to be. So, on three."

"One, two…"

My muscles tense involuntarily and I stifle the cry, ramming my forearm over my mouth. I try with all the will I possess not to scream and for what feels like forever, I succeed but forever is probably only a few seconds and then the sharp pain stops in an instant.

"Mac, are you still with me?" Alfred asks.

"Ugh fuck… I think so."

"I think I can see something, but there is only one way to get it out. It is fused to the tissue inside you, I am going to have to get my fingers in and cut it free."

"Oh, Jesus. Do it, just do it."

I feel Anna grip my hand and then the pain becomes so harrowing that I forget where I am. This time, I scream. I feel like I scream for too long, my vision blurs, my body convulses and then my body mercifully allows me to black out but not for long, the pain wakes me up again very quickly.

"Ugh," I manage, opening my eyes to the fuzzy shape of Anna.

"Hey, you," Anna says. I feel her hand on my face and blink my eyes trying to focus.

"Oh, holy mother…"

"Pa has gone to get you some stronger painkillers," Anna informs. Her voice is uneven. My eyes start to adjust and the first thing I see is the worry-stricken look on her face.

"Did he get it out?" I croak.

"Yes, it's out. It was just deeper than he thought."

The pain is ridiculous. My ribs burn from the inside out, but it is out and that relief is palpable.

"That's good," I say, wincing. "Can I see it?"

Anna turns round and reaches behind her. She holds up a rectangular piece of metal. It is brushed steel, about an inch long by half an inch wide and about half a centimetre thick. I frown, confused.

"You see this little join in the metal?"

"Just about," I squint.

Anna sticks her nail in the join and pulls and a tiny tray slides out from inside the metal; as it opened it reveals a SD card sat snugly inside. A jittery apprehension shivers across my skin. Anna puts the steel disk back on the counter and brushes the hair off my face, kissing my sweaty forehead and Alfred returns and he helps me upright to take some painkillers.

"These are for my back pain; they will probably make you a bit spacey, but at least the pain will be gone."

I swallow them down gratefully. "Thank you, Alfred, I know you didn't want to do that."

"It looks like it was worth it. You were right about it being there, Oliver must have had some medical knowledge, it was wrapped in mesh and stitched to tissue under your skin. It kept the disk in place but your body tissue fused to the mesh, I had to cut it free," Alfred cringed apologetically.

"It is out, that is all that matters," I reassure him.

My head is beginning to swim but it is not an unpleasant feeling, more unnatural than anything. I want to see what is on that SD more than anything but I am struggling to think clearly.

"Wow…" I say, giggling, and Alfred laughs.

"Savannah, you may want to get her to bed, the painkillers are hitting."

Anna hooks my arm over her shoulder and leads me to the stairs. A tickly numbness is washing over me, my legs are slow listening to the commands of my brain but eventually I make it to Anna's bedroom. I lay down on the bed and Anna sits on a chair by my head.

"Is the pain gone?" she asks, a smile playing on her lips.

"Yes, gone… Poof!" I say with animation and she laughs.

I feel oddly light and giddy, like I have been holding in a laugh for too long and the feeling has become overwhelming. I turn my head to look at Anna and my vision is dragged and slurry, still clear but it is as if I can see everything moving slowly and exaggerated.

"Will you lay with me for a while?"

Anna lays on the bed facing me and I reach out to touch her face, my fingertips tracing every perfect line and she smiles at me sweetly.

"You look like Christmas morning," I slur.

"You are high as a kite, McKenna Scott." She giggles.

"Yes, but that is beside the point, Savannah Slone. It is still true; I don't think I could lie right now if I wanted to."

"You are lucky that I am such a good girl then, it would be very easy to take advantage of that honesty."

"You are a good girl, too good, it worries me."

My head is getting heavy and my eyelids are beginning to droop, it is getting harder and harder to think, the tiredness weighs so much.

"Why does that worry you?"

"Because I am not good, I am bad for you. You are colours and magic and I am black and white, an old photograph, you know? I don't want to take away your colours."

"You are wrong, you don't take away my colours. You have opened my eyes to a whole new rainbow of colours and you intensify them, making them more vibrant," Anna says softly, kissing me and tears prick my eyes.

"You don't... understand ... I can't... I... won't..."

Darkness.

***

She must have died in my arms dozens of times before my eyes finally open; the drugs held me hostage in a nightmare state, as I failed to save her over and over again. I open my eyes to find myself alone. Tentatively I push myself upright and wait for the dizziness to hit but the hazy mist of drugs has lifted, my head is clear. The pain in my ribs is lingering but bearable, I get to my feet and make my way downstairs. The house is silent, all evidence of my torturous time spent on the table has been cleaned up. I pour myself a glass of water and drink away the burn from my parched throat. When I put the glass into the kitchen sink, I spot Anna sat over by the fire, alone.

Crap... What did I do?

Somehow, I know I have done something wrong. Even if I have no idea what, I take a deep breath and make my way down to the fire pit, braving myself. She doesn't look up when I arrive.

Yep... I am in trouble.

I take a seat next to her; my mind whizzes trying to rewind and figure out what I could have done but the drugged-up fog is making it impossible. I chance a look at her and I see that dreaded blank expression and it fills my guts with lead.

"What did I do?"

"You didn't do anything," she says, her voice hollow.

"Then, what's wrong?"

"You are always fighting not to leave me. Aren't you?" Anna stated.

I don't know how to answer that because the truth is, I am, I don't want to leave her but the longer this goes on, the more scared I am that it will land her hurt.

"That's what I thought," Anna says when I don't answer; she still won't look at me so I kneel down in front of her. I see the pain she wears so obviously on her face and it tears at me, I am causing that pain.

"Anna, you must know that is not what I want."

"What the hell does that matter? That is a shitty consolation, Mac. You are basically saying I don't want to hurt you but I am going to do it anyway. If you are going to do it, get it over with. I am not going to sit here and just wait for you to pull the rug out because every moment I am with you, I am getting deeper into a place I can't come back from," Anna snaps.

Whiplash.

"I can't let you get hurt because of me; you have no idea what you mean to me."

"Really? Well you are failing because even if someone did come for me, it wouldn't hurt as much as you letting me get this close only to cut me off. If this is what it's like to mean something to you, I don't want to mean anything to you!" Anna's words came out as cold as ice.

The truth does in fact hurt.

"I keep seeing you die! Over and over again and I can never save you! I close my eyes and the dreams are so real that I can feel the life leave you in my arms and all I can do is watch!" I yell, getting to my feet and walking away.

"And you think that walking away from me is going to stop that? If it is going to happen, kicking me to the curb won't stop it!"

I feel like tearing my hair out; I am damned whatever I do. Stay or go, they both end in hurt for her. My heart is breaking and I want to scream, I just want to hold her and never let her go, but that could get her killed.

"If they find out how I feel about you, they could use you against me," I say. My voice sounds dead, my back still turned on her.

"How are they going to find out when even I don't know how you feel about me!?"

I am back on top of the scales, wondering which way they will tip. Either way I feel I will lose her; the conflict is torturous. The lump in my throat is painful and I just want to scream. I feel her behind me, her hands wary as she places them on my back. Her loving touch in a moment that I despise myself tips me over the edge and a sob escapes my lips.

"Baby, please don't do this." Her voice breaks and I turn around.

"Please tell me what to do, I don't know what to do. I am not trying to hurt you, please know that. If anything happens to you, I won't survive that. Anna, this is tearing me up and I can't win whatever I do," I sob.

Her lips are on mine desperately and through her kiss I feel every wave of her pain; it overwhelms me. I hold her tight and try to tell her everything in my kiss that I am not able to say. She pulls away, tears streaking down her face.

"Then I will make it easy on you, Mac. We are over, before we even really got started."

Anna walks away, she walks away and she doesn't look back. A coldness sweeps over me and a pain like I have never experienced. She is gone and she took every bit of warmth inside me, with her. I sit on the floor exactly where I stand and lay back in the long grass. I hear a car door slam, an engine coming to life and car tyres screech away and I grow colder. My veins fill with ice, freezing my organs. I get to my feet and walk towards the house, the wind chilling down the damp back of me that the wet grass has left behind. I enter the house and Alfred is waiting for me. I hesitate, for just a second and then I pick up the steel disk off the counter and turn on my heels, not meeting his gaze.

"I know you think you are protecting her, that is the only reason you are still walking but you are wrong, McKenna, and you will regret this." Alfred speaks calmly but I hear the anger he is holding back.

"I already do, but she will survive because of it."

The wheels are turning before I take another breath, it is not until I reach the warehouse and I hear the shutter fully close and screech to a halt that the pain engulfs me. I cry, I scream, I lay silent. I repeat the process over and over again until there is nothing left inside me but cold emptiness.

***

The days that pass, pass painfully slow. I work out over and over; the pain from my injuries screams at me in protest but I revel in the pain, I guess I am punishing myself and it is much easier to focus on that pain instead of the pain inside. The cold hard metal sheath holding the SD card still lays on my desk where I left it four days ago. Somehow, I know I haven't yet got the strength to look at it, it feels like I left that strength at the farm.

She hasn't left my thoughts, of course. The bedsheets still smell like her candy perfume although the sweet scent is fading. What little sleep I get is done on the sofa, trying to hide from the memories that are up there waiting for me. I ache for her; it has taken every ounce of will I possess to stay away, to stop myself from even sending her a text. The only thing that stops me in the end is the knowledge that I will only hurt her more by doing it. I have nothing to offer her but pain.

I wander the warehouse aimlessly in silence. I work out. I shower more than necessary; I force myself to eat to make me strong when my stomach wants nothing less than to be invaded by food. I miss her terribly and that just makes me mad so I punch the punchbag some more. Blood seeps through the bandage that covers the triangle under my breast; I cover it in duct tape and carry on.

I punch and punch as I feel the darkness inside me purr and as I welcome it back into my heart. "Hello, old friend," it says perversely.

Punch, punch, jab. Jab, punch, jab.

I need to find a way to look at the SD card, I know I do. I want to find them all, all the people that ruined my life, that ruined me. Yet I can't seem to find the strength to face it, not yet.

Coward.

Punch... Punch... Punch.

Pain sears and I look down to see blood seeping down from beneath the duct tape. I stop to catch my breath, sweat pouring off me. I feel so much weaker than I was before and it frustrates the hell out of me. Just then, the buzzer of the intercom sounds and I jump. I am not waiting for any parcels. My heart begins to fly and the hope inside its rhythm stings. I turn away from the door and back to the punchbag. I let the high-pitched buzzing continue to ring in my ears and I punch away the pain.

Punch, punch, jab, cross. Punch, punch, jab, cross.

I grunt at the pain; it is nothing but a petty annoyance, just like that incessant buzzing assaulting my eardrums. I don't need anyone and everyone is safer that way, this was my crusade and I hurt people, people that mean everything to me because I was too weak to continue it alone. Not again, I will keep them safe and I will do it alone.

Punch, punch, punch.

"Mac..."

I freeze when I hear her voice coming from feet behind me; my heart leaps so high then plummets to the floor with a heavy, sloppy thud.

"What are you doing here, Anna?" I say, my voice so cold it even surprises me. I don't turn round, I don't want to see her face.

"It is not just Anna," Alfred's voice grunts and I cringe.

"Whatever you are both thinking, I am not in the mood for an intervention so why don't you just leave?"

The anger is bubbling, I can feel the pot is about to boil over. Why did they have to come? Don't they understand that they are just making it harder?

"We are not going anywhere, kid. It is about time you stop running from your problems and face us."

I rip off my boxing gloves, my back still turned from them and hold the top of the punch bag and lean on it; the coolness of the plasticky material is soothing against my forehead.

"I am not running away, I am walking away, there is a difference. This was only ever supposed to be me, that way I cannot risk anyone else. All I have done is walk back to that, so just go, don't make it any harder than it already is, this is the last time I am going to ask." I keep my voice even but I am unable to hide the coldness within it.

"Mac…" Alfred began.

I turn on my heels, keeping my eyes down. "Just go!"

"Let's go, Savannah," Alfred says, his voice furious.

"Meet me at the car, Pa," Anna says firmly.

"Anna, please just get out," I say coldly.

"Savannah, come on," Alfred encourages.

"No! Pa, meet me at the car. Mac, you owe me better than this so you are going to listen to me," Anna scathes.

I turn my back on her; there is nothing I can do to argue with that because I do owe her, there is no way for me to repay her but her being here is so painful. She knows me too well; she knows exactly how to break through and I don't want her to. I hear Alfred's footsteps walk away.

"Mac… At least give me the respect to turn around and look at me."

"I am not doing it to disrespect you. If I look at you, I will break and I can't afford to do that, not anymore. I am well aware of what I owe you and I am paying it back by staying the hell away from you and saving your life. Please, don't make this harder, girl," I choke, not able to hide the pain in my voice.

"You don't owe me anything, Mac, I just said that to get you to talk to me," Anna says, her voice calm.

"I guess we will have to agree to disagree on that."

"I get that it is over, I get that for your own misguided reasons you are trying to protect me. You are wrong, but I accept it, you don't want me, enough said. That doesn't mean you have to disappear from our lives. We can still work together to end this, we want to help you, that hasn't changed."

That got me. The anger re-flares inside me and I turn to look at her. Something in my face makes her shrink at the sight of me.

"How can you possibly say that to me?! Are you being serious right now?!" I snap.

"What did…?"

"Why do you think this is so fucking hard for me, Anna?!"

"Guilt, I know you are scared I will get hurt. I know if anything happened to me you would blame yourself. You were always trying to leave, and now you finally have. What am I supposed to think?"

My stomach falls through to the floor. "You have no clue how I feel about you at all, do you?"

"Why would I? Not like you ever told me, you dropped me like a sack of spuds after you fucked me all night. You have spent most of your time trying to shut me out or leave me and now you have. What do you expect me to think? Somewhere over the past four days, I realised I deserve better than that. I shouldn't have to persuade myself that you want me; I shouldn't have to stop you from leaving me all the time. So, I have let you go and it is probably for the best."

Shame…

"I never… I… Sorry. I can't."

I am dumbstruck by my own idiocy. What have I done? How could I have done this to her? My broken heart shatters. I have lost her; I turn my back on her just before the lump in my throat wins, the tears gush fast and heavy.

"Mac…?"

"Can you go, please? I am so sorry; you are right. I've given you nothing but… Please go." My voice is so strained I sound like a child.

"Mac, I am still your friend, I am still here for you; I always will be," Anna says, walking towards me.

"Don't! Please. I am fine, just go."

"You think I don't know by now when you are not fine," she says softly and then I feel her hand on my back and I flinch back from her, stepping away. "I guess things really have changed," she says, the hurt in her voice cutting.

"What did you think was going to happen? You can't just say all of that and expect me to… I fucked up, okay. I get it. I tried all I could not to hurt you and that is all I ended up doing. Now you finally see me for the darkness I am, for the darkness I was inflicting on you. You finally see how fucked up and bad for you I am and that you always deserved better than me and what? You want me to be your friend? Fine, I will be your friend, but if that is what I am, you can't be that light for me anymore, you can't comfort me, you can't try to pull me out of the darkness because, I live there now. You accept that, then I will be your friend."

I see the hurt that my words inflict and I despise myself and then the hurt trickles away as her eyes harden. "You don't want me to touch you or be there for you in any way. I hear you loud and clear but don't ask me to accept your screwed-up view of yourself. It is not the same as mine."

"I heard very clearly what your view of me is, Anna."

"You hear what you want to hear. Be at the farm in the morning, you have training to do. Although if you keep bleeding like that you won't be any good tomorrow."

She walks out and I feel the iciness build back up in my veins and I welcome it. She has no idea how I feel about her and she is better off for it, I have lost her and she is better off for that too. I walk over to the desk and I pick up the metal disk, remove the SD card and insert it into the reader. The screen loads bringing up one video file. I click it, without hesitation. Things can't really get any worse, can they?

CHAPTER FOURTEEN

The Culling

The video springs to life and I am faced with a man that I recognise, the man whose photo I was shown over and over again. He is sat at a desk, wearing a suit and tie. His dark hair perfectly styled but greying around his ears a little. He is clean shaven, everything about him is clean. His eyes are big, round and piercing blue. Only his head and shoulders are in the pan of shot but it does look like he is sat in an office; the top of a black leather executive chair peeks up over his shoulders.

"McKenna, where do I start? I guess I should introduce myself. My name is Barrett and as you no doubt have realised by now, I am your father. I am sorry that this is the way you must meet me for the first time, it is a necessary precaution I must take and in time, I am sure you will understand why I must be so cautious. I have been watching you your whole life, I had to step away from you because, I have a higher calling, one which I couldn't ignore. That being said, I did all I could to watch you grow up, to keep an eye on you and make sure you that were safe."

Barrett smiles and at first glance he is charming, but his eyes have a coldness about them. I watch and listen to his every word with complete attention. He rubs his face uncomfortably and continues.

"I have made enemies, some of which you have been unfortunate enough to meet. The man who is holding you, Jakub Kaminski, he is after my location. He seeks retribution and he took you to draw me out, but I could not risk myself. You see, what I am doing is a matter of life and death. I started down a path to build a better world, a better life for everyone. After thirty long years my vision is finally becoming a reality and I cannot risk that to save one person, not even for my daughter."

My mind sticks on the word *unfortunate*. What a word to use considering the circumstances. His voice is smooth and his tone is privileged, my skin is crawling.

"I sent Oliver in my place to get you out with orders to play you this video when you were safe and clear. If he couldn't reach his objective in breaking you out, he was to make sure he gave you it in the triangle of truth. We all bear the mark, the triangle is a symbol that can have many meanings, but the one I speak of is the glyph that represents understanding. It is given to true believers of our cause when they show true understanding and fidelity to our mission.

"The world is in jeopardy, this country is *dying*, the very infrastructure on which life is now built on – is collapsing. Generation after generation, we are breeding inferior people who lazily drain the life out of society. Weakness is like a disease, a cancer spreading through the world and it is destroying everything in its path. We have bred a generation of parasites who have become reliant on technology to the extreme. People live through their mobile phones, their social media and spout their opinions from the comfort of their sofas without taking any real action or really seeing that *they*, are the problem.

"Today's children strive for fame; their minds are polluted by greed and entitlement. Is this what our ancestors intended when they fought to give their children's children the life they never had? World War One, World War Two, the Depression – wars, that incurred loss of life of better men in the quest to build a better life in the future. They gave an inch and the following generations took mile after mile, spitting in the face of their sacrifices.

"The government enables the jobless, charities feed the homeless, authorities turn a blind eye and are just as infected by this epidemic as everyone else. How do we free ourselves from the choking grip of this broken bureaucracy? How do we smooth the ripple effect that is amplifying and feeding the wave of this crisis? How do we save the world from hell and damnation? There is only one way that I can see and that is where my mission began.

"I am the founding member of a group of patriots known as 'The Culling'. We are police officers, government officials, doctors, wives, husbands, soldiers, executives, shop and office workers. We are everyone, working from the same agenda to create a better world. We are the hardworking and like-minded united front in the pursuit of annihilating the toxic, and renewing our world to its glory.

"Culling: The rejection and removal of inferior individuals from breeding.

The act of selectively weeding out the weak to make way for the strong. This, is our mission statement, this is our primary objective. We will streamline the human race, obliterate weakness and regenerate humanity to its ultimate potential. Only in sacrifice can we hope to build a strong and peaceful eutopia for ourselves and end this pattern of destruction that threatens our existence, our world.

"I know this may sound a little extreme, I know you may think me an evil dictator but I am fighting a war and wars have casualties. The sacrificed souls of this battle are a regrettable collateral damage but they are a necessary loss to bring us into a new world; the weak will be culled and the strong will prevail and together we will engineer everlasting arcadia. I have been implementing this plan, over the past thirty years. I have worked tirelessly to eliminate the cancers all over the world but I have come to realise, that I am fighting this battle upstream. No matter how much of the cancer I cut out, the stream keeps flowing and more cancer spreads within its fast flow. There is really only one way to stop the flow indefinitely and that is to destroy the stream at its source. A large-scale assault and elimination in one direct hit, a holocaust, a cleansing in the name of truth.

"My plan is coming to fruition and I am getting closer; someday soon you will awake to the new world. I realise that this is a lot to process but I am asking you to join me, McKenna, it is your birthright. Be the voice and representative of your generation and help me lead the new world into a better path. You will be welcomed and you will be safe. You are, of course free to decline my invitation but I cannot guarantee your safety in the coming reckoning, if you do."

My stomach clenches and I stiffen as I watch what little warmth his eyes held, seep away and then saturate with a cold deadness.

"However, if you attempt to thwart my crusade in any way, if I hear that you have made movements to expose me, and I will hear if you do, if you make any attempt to obstruct the trajectory of my mission, you will be culled, make no mistake. I want you to be a part of this but I will eliminate you if my hand is forced, without hesitation. Nothing will stand in the way of this undertaking.

"If by some chance, Oliver fails to release you from Jakub and in future if you wish to contact me, then leave an advert in your local newspaper, make it an 'in search of' advertisement and be sure you sign it: many thanks, Arcadia. I will know that you are reaching out and I will make contact. Think very carefully about the next moves you make; I am sorry for the position that my mission has landed you in. I hope to see you again, safe and well and ready to join my regime. Be well, McKenna."

The screen goes blank, followed by my brain as it attempts to understand the madness of what I just heard. The man is a lunatic, a raving anarchist and he has a plan, a plan to massacre God knows how many people, hijack the world and implement his own screwed up vision for it. I was right, this doesn't end with Jakub, he is nothing in the face of this.

My stomach fills with dread; this mad man is a monster and he has been watching me my entire life and now, I have no choice but to stop him. I *will* stop him but I have no hope of doing this alone. All my hurt feelings and my bruised pride have to be let go, I need Alfred. There is nothing more important than stopping this man. If he isn't stopped, even if I stop Jakub, there may be no goddamn life for me to have the freedom to return to. A cold acceptance washes over me; this is bigger than me, it is bigger than any one person. I will bring him down, or I will die trying. That is all there is now, all I exist for. There has never been a choice for me.

I rip the duct tape off of my ribs and retrieve my first aid kit; my eyes fall upon the needle and thread. I take them and some antiseptic and set to work cleaning and closing my wound. In some ways I am surprised, I wouldn't have thought I would be able to stomach sewing myself back together but it is less painful watching myself press the needle into my flesh and I enjoy the feeling of control it gives me. It is far messier than Alfred's clean stitching but I am happy to see the blood staunched at my own hand.

Blood has spread down my ribs and onto my thigh and has dried tacky against my sweaty skin. I have a shower to clean it all off and then bandage the wound, it is time to stop wallowing in my own self-pity and start working. I need to get strong; I need to shut down the emotions holding me back and I need to end this. Anna is safe, she has let me go because she always deserved better. Now, it is time for me to let her go.

It is amazing how easy it is to shut myself down, the darkness is like an old friend; I envisage the wall being built up around my heart, my heart is nothing more than a muscle anymore. It pumps my icy blood mechanically around my body, keeping me alive enough to exist. Anger is at a constant simmer, bubbling inside me, keeping other feelings at bay. I climb the steps to the second level and I rip the sheets off of my bed, throwing them down to the ground level. I lay on my bed, the cold darkness numbing the pain.

I am ready…

***

The next morning, I arrive at the farm. I walk with purpose to the farmhouse door and nearly let myself in out of habit. I hesitate and then knock it formally; Alfred opens the door and lets me in and when I enter the kitchen, I find Anna sat at the table and Alfred takes a seat back down next to her. They both look up at me and I hold their gazes with cold ease. I clench my jaw as I see the hurt in Anna's eyes, she quickly shakes it off and looks away.

"Wasn't sure you were going to come," Alfred says.

"Neither was I, till I watched this," I grunt and then I take out the metal disk and place it on the table.

"What is it?" Anna asks, her voice emotionless.

"See for yourself."

Anna fetches her laptop and plays the video; I don't sit down with them; I stand leant against the kitchen counter with my arms folded across my chest. I hear Barrett's words all over again and if anything, they sound even more barbaric the second time around. I stare off into space, waiting for the video to end. When it does, I wait for someone to speak and in the end, it is Alfred who breaks the silence.

"Well I'll be damned, I never thought I would see that slimy grin again."

My head shoots in Alfred's direction. "You know him?!"

"Oh, I know him. You will have to excuse my surprise; I was under the impression I had killed him." Alfred frowns.

"You are going to have to explain that one."

Alfred takes a deep breath and stretches in his chair, he scratches his scruffy hair and then he talks; his eyes are glazed over like he is watching a movie inside his mind.

"The Culling is an extremist group responsible for politically driven terror attacks that have spanned across the world over decades. The bloodshed they have caused in the name of their fanatical ideology is… monstrous. They are formidable and for the most part, quite untouchable. What he said about them being doctors, police officers, government officials – is not an exaggeration. They have managed to convert and recruit followers from all walks of life. Over the years they grew more and more powerful as their reach within civilian life stretched, they needed to be stopped and that is where I came in.

"After much searching, questioning, and surveillance we had strong intel on

267

the whereabouts of Barrett. Only back then he was known to me under a different name. Barrett must be his new alias because I knew him as Noah Hyde. I was tasked with a covert mission to take him out, by all means necessary. Bringing him in was pointless, it has been done many times, but he has a hold over all branches of government – people quietly doing his bidding behind closed doors. Every time he was brought in, evidence mysteriously disappeared and he would be released.

"Barrett was hiding in a base he has established. A bunker hidden in the middle of nowhere in Bosnia. We watched the place, sent photo evidence back to Blighty that he was inside and then we blew the place up with enough C4 to leave a crater in the ground. The Culling were a lot quieter for a time, there were still attacks but they were substantially less. We assumed we took the head off of the snake, that was till I just saw him staring back at me on that video. I have no idea how he survived that, he must have known that we were coming for him, tipped off by someone he has placed in the government or even the military. If he says that he has plan to commit a holocaust, be sure to believe it."

"Should we warn someone? Someone in government?" Anna asks.

"And how do we know that the person we warn isn't a member of The Culling?" I point out, without looking at her.

"I can give someone I trust the heads-up but the information will easily be tied to me and to Mac and that would probably get her killed," Alfred says.

"That is not the problem, I am one person versus the lives of a world of people. I think it is obvious that my life doesn't factor here, I would take that if it meant ending this in a heartbeat but would it end it? How far is Barrett's reach?"

"Too far, when I thought I had killed him 17 years ago it was bad enough, now – who knows? I don't have much confidence in being able to safely involve the government," Alfred concludes.

"That is why I intend to stop him, first Jakub, then Barrett. Whatever it takes, I will do it but I am not stupid. I know I stand a better chance of ending this with your help. The question is, can you set aside any feelings you may have about what has happened the past few days to help me?" I look directly at Alfred because it is his help that I need.

"Can you?" he replies.

"I already have," I say coldly and it is true, there is nothing but this for me now. I hold his questioning gaze.

"I will help you but you must know this is suicide, kid," Alfred says, his eyes a little sad and my heart pangs a little as the coldness leaves his tone and warms when he calls me kid.

"You say that like I am not dead either way, it is what it is. If I am going down, Barrett and Jakub are going down with me. Now, are you able to get any information on The Culling discreetly? I want to know as much as I can about them, even if it is old information."

"I can probably get hold of my old file."

"Good, it's a place to start. I will get back on the doom dash and anything else you want to throw at my training is welcome. Thank you, Alfred."

I walk out of the door, pain throbbing in my chest, the anger only getting me so far before the pain of being near her hits me. I dive straight into the doom dash; I am slower than I was and out of practice but I push myself hard, willing myself to run faster, jump higher, react quicker and soon it all starts to come back to me. It is painful and tiring but I keep going, I punish myself for three solid hours before the pain in my ribs forces me to stop. I hold them, bent over trying to catch my breath and find that I am bleeding again.

I walk over to the fire pit, soaked with mud, sweat and blood. I let myself recover as I feel the heat of the flames against my skin. My eyes search over the farm; it has, for a long time now, represented safety for me, warmth and friendship. I came alive here and now the memories are painful and I can't wait to leave. I have treated them both coldly because that is the only way I can be around them, around this place. It is the only thing that is keeping my heart pumping through the loneliness and ache I feel.

I hear the movement behind me and I recognise it, the soft sound of the footfall in the grass. I tense up, I haven't got it in me to deal with this. I get to my feet and turn around and there she is, her eyes cold upon me and I look away.

"I will get out of your way. Tell your pa, I will be back tomorrow."

"Mac… Wait."

I stop in my tracks but I don't turn around.

"Are you sure this is the only way? Barrett said you were free to walk away; the moment he knows you are after him, he will come for you. Pa is right, it is suicide. Maybe there is someone we can tell, maybe you don't have to do this."

"This… is all I have left. I wouldn't give it to someone else to deal with even if I had the option," I say hollowly and I walk away.

***

I spend the days training with Alfred, the nights alone at the warehouse recovering. Things become less hostile between us; we find a formal groove as acquaintances. I spend much of my time avoiding Anna and when I can't, we have reached a level of polite understanding. Sometimes I think I feel her watching me and it aches, what is worse is when I realise, I have imagined it and that pain is extraordinary. I let the rage at Barrett and Jakub consume me, so that I feel less pain and more empty darkness.

Alfred has kicked up his training; he has taught me how to lay C4 charges and set trip wires, we have worked on grenades and improvised explosive devices (IEDs) as well as a lot of practice with the M110 semi-automatic sniper rifle. Something I am not good at. I rarely miss when it comes to handguns and the carbine rifle, the sniper, however, I pretty much always miss. Understanding the effects that the wind direction can have on such a long-range shot really baffles me. Alfred delighted in showing off his skill with the gun and it had me awestruck.

I learn how to safely move around and clear buildings while using a rifle and handgun. The silent fluid motions you use, how the gun becomes a part of your arm, your body turns with it, searching every corner systematically for threats. We run drills over and over where Alfred hides and I try to find him using these movements, before he is able to sneak up and ambush me. I am getting better and better at it; Alfred is surprisingly light on his feet and can move fast but I am learning quickly.

We work on silent subduing of hostiles; I feel the weight of the silencer fixed to my Glock and carbine and how it plays with the sights. I learn how to silently subdue a man from behind, both with a choke hold and a knife to the throat. I learn flanking positions, battle strategies, survival and fieldcraft skills. We go deeper into close-quarters combat and this time, Alfred is the one kicking my butt. We fight with sharp-edged melee weapons such as knives and bayonets wearing stab-proof vests but still, it has given me much more practice stitching myself back together again.

Alfred has taken on a whole new level of arsehole; he roars at me, now by my surname as if to depersonalise the role he has taken. He barks orders at me and I follow them without question or complaint. He says this is a part of altering and preparing my mind, the humiliation and aggression under stress will build my resilience to the demands of whatever battle may come my way. I say I think he is enjoying this a little too much. I could be dozing off on the grass and if he catches me, he yells in my face, showering me in spit and has me running drills again.

"Come on, Scott! Show me your war face! Kill the fuckers before they take your scrawny arse! Go! Move, move, move!"

I take it all, all the pain, the humiliation, the knowledge, I take it all. I live and breathe it like it is all I have, because... it is.

The nights are the hardest; I return to the warehouse time and time again, beaten and bloodied and exhausted but unable to sleep. My thoughts are instantly invaded the moment the shutters close on me, thoughts of Anna, of my mum, thoughts of Barrett and Jakub. The loneliness is at times, unbearable. The tiredness makes it harder to keep the bad thoughts at bay; I start wishing I had energy left to continue being shouted at by Alfred if only just to not face the cold, hard truth when I return home. It is this dread that has me sat by the fire, taking far too long to stitch up the small but deep gash across my thigh, I am stalling the inevitable.

"You are getting good at that," Anna says, joining me at the fire. I don't look up when she arrives, my coping mechanism whenever she is around. I can talk to her easier this way; I know if I spend too long looking at her, then I will break. This means that at least we are able to talk now.

"Practice makes perfect, I guess," I say, wincing as I ram the needle in the bloody flap of skin.

"You look like hell," she jabs coldly and I wince.

"Thanks for pointing that out."

I feel the latest sting of her jabbing comments, I take it on the chin because we are at least talking, her snapping is better than us avoiding each other completely as we were but I can't deny it is hard to keep taking.

"Sorry, I didn't intend that to come out quite so harshly."

"It's fine, I am used to it and in any event, I probably deserve that and worse."

I finish the stitches and pour a second helping of antiseptic over the closed wound then grab the first aid kid and look for a clean bandage, I am going through so many bandages.

"You shouldn't have to be used to it. I have punished you because you hurt me, but you didn't deserve it and I am going to do my best to stop. I am sorry," Anna says calmly, her voice still cold but she sounds much more like the girl I knew and somehow that hurts more than the coldness she has given me. My eyes close as the wave of pain washes over me.

"Mac…" I flinch and open my eyes, shoving the emotions back down.

"Don't be, like I said I deserved it. It is easier for me, you being cold. So, as much as I appreciate the effort, please don't be offended if I remain cold. It is the only way I can…" I trail off, the pain burning in my chest.

"The only way you can what?"

"Be… here. It is too…" I struggle, I am losing control. "I have to go."

I get up and walk away, I hear her call my name and I just keep walking. The pain in my chest is unbelievable; tears prick my eyes and blur my view out the windscreen as I drive away. I blink them away and get control of myself, I can't afford to break. I screech to a halt inside the warehouse and slam the truck door hard in anger. The sound echoes and booms, vibrating off the walls of the empty space. I put on the boxing gloves, I punch and kick over and over again. Ramming the emotion down with every hit. I pummel the bag; I pummel the pain.

Bag, pain, bag, pain, bag, pain.

Till my limbs burn so much I can barely lift my arms. I collapse on the floor, emptiness taking over and it is a relief, I let the dark destructive thoughts penetrate my mind.

She doesn't want you; she has seen who you are. You are marked for death, you – the destruction of anyone who comes near. You are darkness, she is the light. She deserves more than you can ever give her.

I hear her words. *"I realised I deserved more, so I am letting you go."* They cut me and I focus on them. *"We are over, before we even really got started."*

Calm sweeps over me and I fall asleep right where I fall.

***

The next morning, I awake too early, my body stiff from sleeping on the cold hard floor, my hands numb from the boxing gloves still attached to my wrists. I slept in my own dirt and I am frozen to the bone, so at the ungodly hour of 4am, I have a steaming hot shower. I am in for a hard day's training today, Alfred intends to take me away from the farm for the day, I have no idea what is in store but he told me to wear the combat boots and camo trousers he gave me when we were at Sennybridge Training Camp. I put them on and make my way to the farm, arriving when it is still dark.

I take advantage of the chance to sit alone by the fire; this is something I don't get to do much anymore because one of two things will always happen. Either Alfred will come bark more orders at me for sitting down on the job, or

Anna will come over and then it is too painful for me to stay. I don't think she realises how much it hurts for me to be around her. She mustn't, she genuinely has no idea how I feel about her, she may never know. Like she said, it is probably for the best.

The trouble is, I know. I know that she holds my heart in the palms of her delicate little hands, I fear she always will. If I survive this, if I end the threats that Jakub and Barrett pose, I would love to think that maybe, there would be a chance for us. The truth is even without all of that, I am damaged and I will always be a drain on her and I have hurt her so deeply, I don't think there is any coming back from that. Every day that passes, I learn to accept that just a little bit more and realise that if I survive this, I will have to simply disappear.

I have been studying the files Alfred has given me on Barrett and it doesn't take much reading to see that this man is a monster, it reads like a dossier of his deplorable achievements, a catalogue of death and destruction. One crime against humanity after another, I am slowly coming to realise that there is only one way to stop a man like that and that is to end his life. This thought doesn't make me feel good; he is a monster, yes, but the fact that I will probably have to execute my own father, weighs heavily on me.

First, I must find Jakub, take the pressure off of myself. With his threat gone then I will have more freedom of movement to track down and face Barrett who so far, shouldn't have any idea of my plans. If I can't find him then I will no doubt be forced to take out the advert in the paper and let him come to me. The problem is that then gives him the upper hand, I won't know when he is coming for me, or where I will be when he does. The advert has to be the last resort.

I am lucky enough to watch the sun slowly begin to rise, the sky glowing purple and red. What is it my mum says? Red sky at night, shepherd's delight. Red sky in the morning, mother's warning. I am going to try not to see that as an omen, I watch the sky get ever brighter and my eyelids get heavier. The heat of the fire, the crackle of the wood, the peace of silence, the stillness of the farm. My eyes get heavier until I eventually doze off. It feels like seconds before I hear Anna's voice rousing me awake.

"Mac…"

My eyes shoot open and I jump, Anna puts a cup of coffee on the floor in front of me and takes a seat opposite me. I notice that at some point she has already been out to me and covered me in a blanket, I keep my eyes low and thank her for the coffee.

"Military greens still suit you," she says and my eyes close as the memory licks flames of pain inside me.

"Sorry, probably shouldn't have said that. It has just been a long time since I have seen you asleep in that chair, I guess the memories got to me. To be honest, you look like you haven't slept in weeks, I didn't really want to wake you," Anna says; her voice almost sounds normal again.

"That is a polite way of saying you look like crap," I say with my eyes down but I smile a little so she knows I am joking.

"Are you ever going to look at me again, Mac? Do you hate me that much?"

"You think I hate you?"

"Maybe not hate, but God, Mac, it has been weeks. Do you have any idea how much it hurts? You are like a ghost, you are here but the person I knew, the person who meant so much to me is gone, you are so cold, I don't recognise you anymore. I know things have changed but I didn't know I would lose all of you."

Her voice breaks and the sound cuts, I feel the tears fill my eyes and I take a deep breath, trying to swallow it down. I look over to Anna and she is bent forward, her head in her hands. I get to my feet and go to her. I bend down to my knees in front of her, she flinches when she feels my hand lightly on her shoulder and then she looks up at me. I meet her glaze, my jaw tight.

"I don't hate you, girl. I could never hate you; I am sorry I have made you question everything to the point you could ever believe that. I don't look at you because it hurts too much. Losing..." I stop myself before I say too much. "Whatever you may think of me, there is a lot I can't say and it is probably easier that way. All I can tell you is no matter what happens, you mean more to me than you know and that, will never change."

Anna breaks, the tears come fast and heavy, she rests her head on my shoulder and folds her arms across her stomach like she is trying to hold herself together, I recognise that pain all too well. I hesitate, I have never seen her break like this, the pain in my chest is horrific and I need to walk away but then, how many times has she held me when I needed her, even though it probably wasn't easy for her? I gently unwrap her arms and then I pull her to me. For a fraction of a second, she freezes, shocked by the sudden closeness, then she melts into my chest and wraps her arms around my waist, holding me closer. I feel the sobs rumble through her and I hold her through them. Slowly she begins to calm down.

"Was any of it real? For you?" she chokes.

"It really hurts that you have to ask me that."

"I'm sorry, it just happened so fast, it is so easy to persuade myself it was all in my head. You were kissing me one second and then gone the next, I don't know what to believe."

"Please hear me, Anna, because I can't hold it together much longer. Every single second was real. From the Shard all the way to now. You know me, better than anyone. Now you look at me and tell me, do you believe it was real?"

I look at her and I let the pain sink in, I let the desire I have for her burn in my heart. I let the need I have to reach out and touch her, envelop me for just a moment. I let it all play out in my eyes, and she gasps.

"Oh God… I have missed you," she whispers as her eyes fire up with desire. My heart pounds and shivers run up and down my spine, the pain in my chest becomes unbearable, she pulls me to her.

"Thank you, thank you for giving me that," she whispers in my ear and I start to break. I pull away, standing up and turning my back on her.

"Mac…"

"Just need a minute, I am fine," I say a bit too sharply. I swallow the pain down and I get control back and I turn round and walk back to my chair and sit back down.

"I'm sorry…" Anna says, her voice strained.

"What for?"

"Not believing you."

"I didn't really give you much to believe in," I admit.

"You did. It was just easier to…"

"It is okay, Anna. I get it."

We sit in silence for a while, the whole time, my heart aching to touch her, to kiss her. The pain of knowing I never will be able to is astronomical. Worse than missing the way she used to look at me and touch me, is missing the girl who somehow made me feel brave and so… me. I feel a gaping hole where she used to be and nothing I do, to try to fill it, seems to work.

"Do you think, when this is all over, you will find your way back to me?" Anna asks, her voice tiny, her eyes down.

"I can't undo what I did to you. It is like you said, you deserve better. I think, when this is over, I will probably have to disappear for a long time. It is best for everyone."

"There you go again, deciding what is best for me. You know how much I hate that," she says and I laugh darkly.

"Oh, I remember that very well."

"I deserved better than guessing how you felt about me, than being scared of you leaving me all the time but those things were a symptom of the situation you are in, not how you treated me, Mac. You kept quiet to keep a distance from me, to protect me, you left me to protect me. If the threat was never there and you didn't feel you had to protect me, would you have done those things?"

I hold her gaze; I don't want to answer but I know my lack of answer would also be an answer. Damn it. This conversation has gone too far and now she has me in a corner.

"I think you know I wouldn't have," I admit.

"Then why would you choose to disappear from my life after all this is over? Even if you don't want me anymore, why do I have to lose you altogether?"

"Because Anna, I will always be broken. The threats can disappear but who I am, will still very much be here. I am a drain on you. If I somehow survive all of this, what will be left of me? How many people will I have to kill to end this? Jakub? The Culling? My own father? I can barely hold on to who I am now. How much more of myself am I going to lose along the way? You deserve someone whole and one of these days you will find them and... I..."

I have said too much, how did this happen? This conversation needs to end, I have already let on too much. The truth is I know that she will find someone else, someone who she deserves and I will be happy for her happiness, that is all I want for her. That doesn't mean it won't be agony for me to see, I won't be sticking around for that.

"You are so wrong about yourself, Mac. I never felt that way about you, I have seen the darkness inside of you but it's nothing in comparison to the light you hold. Shutting yourself away, turning your back on people that care about you, that is what feeds the darkness and you want to disappear?"

"I need to stop, girl. I can't take..."

The lump in my throat is rising and I look away from her. I jam my knuckles in my eyes, rubbing them. I can't make her understand, not without saying too much. This is hurting too much; I hear her move towards me and I tense up. She kneels down in front of me and my hands begin to shake. I feel her hands slide on top of mine, pulling them away from my face. I keep my eyes down, the pain of having her so close is ripping me in two. Anna puts her hands on the sides of my face like she has so many times and the memories swirl, breaking me, a sob escapes my mouth. Why is she doing this to me?

"Stop… Please… It hurts."

"I will stop, but first I need you to hear me so please look at me." Anna lifts my face and I start to fall apart, my breath coming out in loud drags. I meet her eyes with my jaw clenched, trying to get control of myself.

"One day… you will see that the only person who thinks that you are broken, is you. You will see that my life is better, because of you. That I am more myself with you, than I have ever been without you. I intend to be there for that day. I know you need to let me go and I will let you but if you think for one second that means I am giving up on you, you don't know me as well as I thought you did."

Anna leans forward, kisses my forehead and returns to her chair as if nothing happened and I am left to put the pieces of myself back together again. I calm myself down and stare dazed into the fire; she doesn't understand how bad I am for her and this has only made it harder, I know it is only a matter of time before she does.

Eventually we make small talk and act as if nothing has happened. I try every so often to make sure I make eye contact with her, so she knows that I am trying. I knew things had to end between us, but I never wanted her to think I hated her. I think in my own screwed up way I have been punishing her too and I can't do that to her anymore. Thankfully it isn't long before Alfred comes over, the distraction has never been so needed. I put on my game face as he begins running through the training we will be doing today.

"So, basically we are going to enter a whole new world of suck today. That sound, about right?" I say and Anna laughs, I smile at her. We seem to have come to an uncomfortable impasse.

"Well no, you will enter the suck, not me, I just get to enjoy watching you suffer it," Alfred jokes.

"I think you enjoy—"

My phone rings in my pocket and I frown; it is odd because no one ever calls me and the phone is untraceable. There are very few people who have the number. I take it out and see the name emblazoned on the screen.

"Alisha," I say, confused, and I feel Anna's eyes on me.

"Hello?"

"Mac, I am so sorry. They found me; I don't know how…"

I hear a scream and my blood runs cold.

"Alisha! Where are you!?" I hiss urgently.

"Hello, McKenna."

My stomach bottoms out, fear strangles me at the sound of that leery voice. My eyes find Alfred and I grab his arm to steady myself, somehow find strength in him.

"Jakub," I growl.

"Ah, good, you remember me, excellent," Jakub mocks, his voice playful.

Alfred mouths at me silently, telling me to put the phone on loud speaker and I hit the button. My hand is shaking with rage and fear as I hold it up for Anna and Alfred to listen.

"Let her go, Jakub, this has nothing to do with her."

"No, I quite agree it doesn't. I tell you what, you come to me and hand yourself over and I will let the girl go. How does that sound, McKenna?"

"How do I know you won't kill her before I even get there?"

"We both know that you have something I want, it is in my best interest to keep my word. Besides, the girl means nothing to me. My only interest is with you," Jakub drawls, his voice smarmy. My skin is crawling like an angry rash. Anna shakes her head, her eyes giving me a firm no. I look away, there is no choice here.

"When and where?"

"Meet me at the abandoned brewery on Eastfield's Avenue in one hour and come alone. I see that you have brought one person with you, first I kill this one and then I come for your pretty little redhead."

My eyes flick to Anna. I watch her eyes widen fearfully and the anger flares inside of me like molten lava.

"I will kill you, Jakub! You go anywhere…"

"I wouldn't make threats to me right now, McKenna. You are the one I want; you make it easy then I have no reason to kill either of them. Do we understand each other?"

"First let me talk to her," I growl and Alfred nods encouragingly.

"You get thirty seconds," Jakub agrees.

"Mac…"

The sound of her voice so terrified wipes away my fear and turns it into hardened resolve. I failed her, twice. I won't fail her again.

"Alisha, are you hurt?"

"No…"

"Don't worry, I am coming for you. How many are there?"

"Too many, at least twenty, you can't come, they will kill you!"

"Alisha… I am coming, just hold on. Keep your head down, do everything they say and hold on, you hear me? Alisha?"

"I think that is quite enough. Now, I will ask you again. Do we understand each other?" Jakub jeers.

"We do," I say coldly.

"Good. You have one hour."

"No Jakub, I need more—"

The phone goes dead. Shock paralyses me; all this time I have been scared he would take Anna. I never thought for one second, he would take Alisha. The reality, the weight of my mistake is harrowing.

I have to save her.

I look at Alfred and he looks back at me in a way he hasn't in what seems so long; I wrap my arms around him and he gives me a big bear hug. When he lets go, he smiles at me.

"I will grab you my gear. You have got this, kid. You are ready," he grumbles and then he runs off towards the farmhouse. I turn to look at Anna, bracing myself.

"No! You can't. No! Mac, you can't do this! You want me to admit that you were right? Fine, I admit it, okay?! He could have come for me anytime but you can't go. I know you want to save Alisha, but you can't go, he will kill you!" Anna yells at me furiously, fear tugging at her eyes and I walk over to her, taking her face in my hands and the anger immediately melts from her eyes.

"I never wanted to be right!" I assert passionately and her eyes close forcing the tears to escape. I catch them with my thumbs and her eyes open as I speak again. "I am not just saving Alisha. I am saving you; I am saving myself. It was always going to come down to this, you know that. I am okay with this; if I have to go out saving you and Alisha, there are worse ways to go but I am not just going to give up. I will fight, I am not the person he took before," I say calmly, then my eyes pause on her lips and I have to let her go, dropping my hands and taking a step back but she advances, not allowing me to look away, her anger reignited.

"No. You might be okay with dying but I am not okay with it. This is not okay; don't do this! You heard her, there are at least twenty of them, you walk in there it is suicide!"

"Anna, I have to do this. I will not leave Alisha behind; you have to have a little bit of faith. Don't make me walk away from you mad at me, please. I am always stronger knowing you are behind me."

Anna's eyes burn at me with anger and then they melt as there is no point to this argument. She closes the gap between us and she wraps her arms around me tightly.

"I will always be behind you," Anna whispers. Her lips roam away from my ear and down to my throat and then I feel them warm against my throat, just once and my breath shakes. "Don't you dare die on me, Mac Scott. I will never forgive you if you do."

Anna pulls away and I look at the floor, taking longer than I would like to calm the storm that her lips have rained down on me in just a single kiss. When I finally do look up, I manage to deliver a steady smile.

"No pressure then, huh," I chuckle.

"You goof," she says, playfully jabbing me. "Are you scared?"

"Yes, but not of Jakub."

"Then what?"

I hear Alfred's footsteps approach and I am relieved at his interruption. He puts my bulletproof vest on me and wraps the utility belt around me.

"This is my knife; it did three tours with me and many missions, I consider it lucky. You have two grenades on either side of the back side of the belt. Right for boom, left for smoke. I have put the silencer on the carbine and you should lead with that. Hide the Glock inside your trouser leg for backup; they may find it, but it is worth a shot. I have packed this rucksack full of goodies, you should have everything you need inside."

Alfred hands me the rucksack and then an earpiece. "We can't be with you but we can listen in from a few streets away so you know you are not alone in this. Kid, you have the upper hand here. He has no idea the person you have become and I for one, couldn't be prouder if you were my own. Now – you *end* them, no hesitation. You end them and you don't get dead, you hear me?!"

"I hear you. Thank you, buddy." I give him one last hug, put the earpiece in and turn to Anna. Alfred walks away and that just makes the temptation to kiss her, to tell her how I feel even harder to resist but it would only serve to hurt us both in the end. Instead I just hold her.

"Kill them, Mac, kill them all and find your way back to the farm. I believe in you, you don't get to die on me, that is not how your life ends, after all of this, it can't be." She pulls back from me and looks at me with fire in her eyes. "Make. Them. Pay."

I feel the strength, the strength she has always given me that has been missing from inside me for weeks, warm my chest and I smile.

"Magic," I whisper and she smiles back at me; suddenly all our troubles seem trivial.

I turn away and walk towards the truck. I feel her eyes on me the whole time, I see Alfred standing at the door of the farmhouse.

"You hear me, kid?" I hear Alfred's voice inside my ear.

"Loud and clear, fella."

I get in the truck, turn the key in the ignition and the truck moves off. My legs have never felt so heavy, driving away from them has never been so hard.

"We are with you, all the way. Now go teach them all about the suck!" Alfred booms in my ear and I laugh.

"Sir, yes sir!"

"And Mac... remember..." the voice of Anna calls. "*You are the king of the world!*"

I laugh and cry and I hear their laughs in my ear until I hear the crackle as I drive out of range of their earpieces. Inside me I am both full of light and darkness and I am stronger for it. My friends are with me, until the very end, I grip the steering wheel tighter.

"Jakub... I am coming for you."

CHAPTER FIFTEEN

I Will Raise Hell

My body is rigid as I drive too fast; the streets are not yet full with the London morning rush. This is luck; I weave through the streets with ease. One hour isn't much time for me to prepare but in a way that is good, less time to overthink. I know the brewery that Jakub has chosen, I have never been inside but the building is old and huge, there are so many places he could hide and it is impossible to know how many people are inside. The street is always dead because it is lined with abandoned derelict buildings and broken-down warehouses. His choice makes sense, he can take over as much of the street as he wants without fear of onlookers and I imagine that is exactly what he has done.

Alisha said there at least twenty of them, does that mean twenty inside the brewery and more outside? Does that mean twenty in total? Either way I am severely outnumbered. I am ready to face Jakub, but will I survive long enough to get to him? I have to find a way, freeing Alisha and ending Jakub is the only way to ensure that anyone tied to me will be safe but it doesn't escape my notice that, my chances are not good.

My mind falls to my mum, my loving, overbearing and eccentric mum. She has already been through losing me once and now, she stands a good chance of losing me forever and never really understanding why. Tears fill my eyes but I stop them, what I wouldn't give to hug her one last time, I can't remember the last time I did. I have barely spoken to her, it is selfish but it was easier for me to deal with all of this that way. Now, I am haunted with regret knowing all I have left her with are some fake emails and a lot of pain.

I keep waiting for the fear to hit but I feel nothing but rage. The hate is building up; like icy cold fingers inside me, dark and crawling tendrils are threatening to drag me back down into the darkness. I will succumb to it; the darkness will fuel my will but not yet, I am not ready to let go yet. Anna asked me if I am scared and I didn't want to answer her because the truth is I am scared, not of dying but that I will die without her ever knowing how I feel about her. Stupid really, I had the chance to tell her and I didn't. Even if I survive this, I will still be the broken version of myself that is a drain on her. Telling her how I feel would only hurt us both but still, to know I will never have the chance makes this all feel so final.

I fear the darkness inside me, I fear that once I tap into it, there will be no coming back for me. How much pain and darkness can a soul withstand before there is nothing human left? There is no doubt that I need that side of me to do this. I have killed before in self-defence, I still see the light leave the eyes of the mala suka man, the image is engraved behind my eyes. Anna and Alfred managed to pull me back from the darkness then, just as they did when I first came to the farm but this is different. I am driving towards an unknown number of men with only one intention, to execute them all. Do I even deserve to come back from that? Probably not. My soul is an acceptable loss, if it means I can keep everyone safe.

Alisha…

How could I have missed this? This is the second time I have underestimated the danger she is in. Suddenly all of the contempt I held towards her seems petty; my anger made it too easy for me to put her in a blind spot and now, she could die because I couldn't just get over myself. I can't bear it if anything happens to her, no matter what has happened I would never want anyone to hurt her. My fist clenches the steering wheel tighter, my foot presses the accelerator harder, the tendrils of darkness creep a little higher. I will save Alisha and I will kill Jakub and in doing so, I will make Anna safe again. No matter what it takes, whatever the price – I will pay it.

This ends today.

The truck comes to a stop, I have pulled up in a street behind Eastfield's Street, everything is eerily quiet. I am thankful – dressed up like a freakin' commando, carrying a rifle is bound to attract unwanted attention. A shiver runs down my spine as I look out of the windscreen; on the other side of these buildings is a force of unknown size that is hell-bent on killing me. I must be just metres away from Jakub's men. I shake my head and try to push the nerves away.

Upon unzipping the rucksack that Alfred gave me I find a small arsenal. C4 charges and remote detonators, extra grenades, extra ammo and an extra handgun. It looks like the old Browning pistol that Alfred first trained me with and I smile at the memories. I slip it inside my boot and put my new Glock in the back of my trouser waist band and cover it with my shirt. I fill the pockets of my cargo trousers with magazines for the carbine rifle.

The gravity of what is happening is finally starting to eat away at the rage that was fuelling me, revealing my fear underneath. I step out of the truck and my stomach is knotted and my hands start to shake but when I hear Alfred's gruff voice sing in my ear, I snap out of my panic.

"Mac, you copy?"

"Yeah, I'm here. Parked a street away from Eastfield's, just setting up," I confirm.

"Oh, I know. I can see you."

"What are you talking about?"

"Check your six, highest building, west corner," Alfred requests.

I whip around, my eyes searching the building and there, another street behind me are the very small outlines of Anna and Alfred. Anna is stood looking through binoculars and Alfred is laid on his stomach, I can just about make out his head behind the barrel of the sniper rifle.

"You didn't think I was going to let you have all the fun now, did you?" Alfred says, chuckling.

"What the hell are you thinking?! This puts Anna at risk! How could you do this, Alfred?!" I spit furiously.

"I told you she wouldn't take it well," Anna interjects.

"Not funny!" I snap.

"Oh, don't get your tighty whities in a twist. They already know about Anna, which means they know about the farm. At least with us here she is not somewhere they expect. She is *my* granddaughter – you are not the only person that has a stake in protecting her! Now put up and shut up. You are good, kid, but no one is that good, you are massively outnumbered. There at least thirty hostiles on the street and that is just what I can see. I will be your eyes, I will back you up, I will help get you inside the brewery alive but once you get inside it is all down to you. Are you picking up what I am putting down, soldier?!"

"Stubborn, lovable, arsehole! Fine, for the record they are not tighty whities, they are lady-boy pants," I rant and he chuckles.

"Good, I am glad we understand each other." Alfred beams smugly at his victory.

I check my watch and I have just over thirty minutes before I am due inside the brewery. I pick up my rifle and click off the safety. I take a few steadying breaths.

"Okay boss, I am going to make my way up the street and then find some cover in a position to give me eyes on down Eastfield's Street."

"Copy."

I move fast, my feet light on the ground. My senses beginning to awaken to the danger I am about to face, my body hunched low and pausing to check for movement in the gaps between buildings. Once I am clear I set off running again; twice I have had to wait because I have seen men roaming, both times the fear trickles inside me as I see the men armed and looking ready for a fight. My stomach is knotted, I could do with a nervous pee but I keep moving, weaving in and out of stationary cars, trees and wheelie bins to try to keep myself hidden. This looks like a nice street where nice people live, shame they are about to get a rude awakening.

"Right kid, I think you are far away enough; you should be able to find some cover now but keep your eyes open," Alfred instructs.

I stop running and pause outside a warehouse. I lean my back against it, my breath heavy and fast. I pivot round the corner and see no one, so I slide around to the side of the warehouse and follow the wall towards the open street of Eastfield's. At the corner of the building I pause and kneel, taking a peek around the corner to the street. My eyes register the movement and scan quickly and then I take cover behind the wall again. My legs weaken and I slide down on to my butt and panic starts to grip my throat.

"Alfred…" I gulp.

"Yeah, I copy."

"I found cover, I can see down the street, all the way to the brewery and I saw at least 5 different groups of 4 or 5 men huddled together, spread all the way down the street. There are two on the roof of the brewery and at least 10 more single hostiles roaming. They are carrying handguns mostly but I saw some semi-automatic rifles. Jakub brought a fucking army," I ramble, fear in my voice embarrassingly obvious.

It is becoming hard to breathe. How the hell am I ever going to reach Alisha alive? There is no surviving this.

"Kid, take a breath. Try not to look at the mass of them. It is a game of chess; plan your first three moves and while you are making them, plan your next three. Move methodically and without hesitation. Take them down one at a time, remember how to use corners and cover to your advantage. Move efficiently, use your surroundings to work for you. You have got this and don't forget, I am here – your eye in the sky. I have your back."

My head is spinning, my eyes are beginning to blur, the panic is gripping me tighter with every passing second, strangling the breath out of me.

"Mac…" Alfred calls.

"Mac… Do you copy?"

"Alfred will you… do something for me?" I ask through panted breath.

"Name it, kid."

"We both know the odds… If I don't… Find my mum, make sure she is safe, tell her everything. Tell her I didn't die alone, tell her I died loved, lie to her. Say whatever the hell you think she needs to hear to give her peace, tell her, promise me." I struggle.

"Mac, you can tell—"

"*Alfred…*" I growl.

"Okay kid, I hear you loud and clear but you will get through—"

"Mac…" Anna interrupts, her voice broken. "Listen to me, no one is going to be lying to your mother, we love… the person you are. Right now, I need you to remember everything this man ever did to you! Everything he stole from you. Every pain he ever inflicted on you! I need you to go to that dark place, use it, punish him with it! I need you to make him *pay*! Kill him, Mac, kill every last one of them. End all of this. Do you understand me?!" Anna growls fiercely and I close my eyes; I can see her expression so clearly as she speaks.

"I might not be able to come back from that," I admit.

"You will because you are wrong, Mac. We all have darkness inside us but you are not bad inside, there is nothing but good inside of you. I know, I've seen it, I have touched it. I know you don't see it so, if you can't trust yourself, then trust me. You will come back, because you own the darkness, it doesn't own you. The good in you will always win, I promise you."

I feel calmness begin to sweep over me. My breathing slows, my hands steady and the tightness in my chest begins to ease. How does she do that?

"Thank you, Anna," I breathe gratefully.

"You can thank me by staying alive. Do whatever it takes, promise me?"

"I promise, I will do whatever it takes to make you safe again," I vow passionately.

"That is not the same thing," Anna points out.

"I know."

My eyes close and I let the memories swirl. Every moment of pain, every moment of humiliation, the loneliness, the isolation, the fear, I let it all engulf me. My mind fills with the images of horror, faces of the men that broke me whizz around my head like a sadistic sketch show. The hairs rise on the back of my neck, I feel cold tendrils of darkness creep over me perversely as I let myself fall into the darkness. I feel the ice build up in my veins and my blood runs cold. I open my eyes.

"Eye in the sky, on my signal – take out the two on the roof top… I'm going to raise hell," I growl.

"Oh, now that's what I'm talkin' about. Copy that, Mac-Attack, copy that!" Alfred cheers and I smile; he has never called me that before. I hear the clicks in my ear as he loads the sniper rifle.

I peek around the corner, keeping low. There are two small groups; the one closest on my left is about 15 feet away. The next is inset further right about 20 feet away; they are huddled inside an alcove of a doorway of an old abandoned bike shop. There are also two men roaming. I grab three grenades, one smoke and two explosives. I zip the rucksack back up and strap it on my back.

"I am in position, eyes on the target, awaiting your go," Alfred confirms.

"Copy that, go on my boom."

I grit my teeth, take a long steadying breath and pick up the two explosive grenades. My finger hooks inside the metal hoop attached to the firing pin of the grenade, then I pull the pin on the first and throw it into the closest group, closely followed by the second group on the right. I pick up the smoke grenade and I launch it as far down the street as I can; hopefully it will obscure me from hostiles further down the street.

I hear a commotion of urgent buzzing voices and I am on my feet as the grenades explode with deafening booms in quick succession. I pivot back around the corner and see the two roaming men scrambling round to find the source of the threat. I take aim, my mouth suddenly dry and fire a clean head shot at the first and he goes down.

Don't think… Just move…

I run to the other side of the street skidding to a stop and turning, landing my back hard against the wall. I take aim just as the second roaming man spots me; he lifts his gun but I pull the trigger just in time, blood exploding from his chest and my bullets rain down on him.

"Rooftop clear, Mac there are two hostiles coming up the alley on your left side, I repeat, your left side. Ten feet, take them out."

I kneel down and take aim; I fire as soon as I see movement but only one man comes out.

Damn it!

I check over my right shoulder to see if I am clear and then I run back over to the other side of the street to the alleyway. My back against the wall, I wait for the second man to emerge. I see the tip of the gun outstretched, I grab it and twist it, kicking the guy hard on the kneecap with a crunch. His knees buckle and he drops, crying out in pain. I keep a grip of his gun, turning it on him, his eyes wide and pleading; I shoot twice and turn away. I check up the alleyway to find it clear so I kneel down in the small opening to plan my next move.

"The alley is clear," I announce and then a storm of bullet blasts fly in my direction; the bullets ricochet off of the wall of the alleyway kicking up dust. I freeze, panic holding me in place.

"Take cover!" Alfred yells.

I dive to the floor, down the alleyway and roll onto my back, gun raised in time to see five men trying to scramble through the narrow entrance of the alleyway. I shoot aimlessly in their direction and the two leaders of the pack go down, while I am stumbling back to my feet. I mow them down using far too many bullets in a panic. I drop the empty magazine and reload with a new one while on the move. I need out of this alleyway, it is pinning me down.

I spot the smoking alcove where the second grenade blew and decide to make a run for it; my jaw is set as I blast into a run, gunfire is biting at my heels. I launch myself into the air and land on a pile of charred and smoking bodies. The smell of burnt flesh assaults my nostrils with nauseating force and I gag. I get to my feet then I feel pressure on the back of my neck as my head is rammed towards the concrete pillar with a stunning and painful crack.

I reach for Alfred's knife and turn to face the threat; the man grips my throat and my stomach revolts. Half of his face is melted away and is blackened and bloody; his eyes are furious. I grab the collar of his shirt in one hand and I ram the knife deep into his throat. His eyes widen in shock; warm blood spurts from his throat across my face.

"Mac, 9 o'clock!" Alfred yells.

The burnt man is still in my grasp. I turn just in time and use him as a shield as bullets fly into his back; I feel the force of them pound into his lifeless body. I swing the rifle fast over my shoulder and fire rapidly, taking three more down.

"Oh damn, that was sexy…" Anna says and I laugh in spite of myself.

I throw the man down to the ground; blood starts pouring down my face and into my eye so I take cover behind the pillar again, grabbing some brick dust from the floor and ram it into the wound to staunch some of the bleeding.

"I can't believe it; she actually rubbed some dirt in it," Alfred says, chuckling.

I retrieve Alfred's knife, wipe the blood off and put it back in the sheath on my belt. Peeking around the pillar I see another large knot of men off to the left around thirty feet down the street, too far for me to throw a grenade accurately. My eyes scan; there is a small wall jutting out around ten feet away, that would be close enough. Just then I spot two roamers running in my direction guns outstretched. I turn, but not quick enough. Pain explodes across my chest, winding me and I go down.

"Urgh!" I grunt.

"Mac!" Anna screams.

"It's okay, it hit her vest; she is just winded! Mac, get up!" Alfred booms.

I struggle to my feet, in time to see the first man ploughing straight towards me and the second man going down by Alfred's hand. He barges into me, sending me pounding into the pillar; the impact forces oxygen back into my winded lungs. He has a knife pressed to my throat, the tip drawing a tiny trail of blood.

"Gaaahh fuck…" I growl.

"He's going to kill her! Shoot him, Pa!" Anna yells.

"I can't, he's too close – I could hit Mac! Come on, kid! Come on!" Alfred yells.

A roar escapes my mouth as I fight to keep the knife away from my throat. The man's breath hot, heavy and stinking on my face. He is too strong, if I don't do something I am going to die. I scream, cock my leg back and bring my knee up hard between his legs and he cries out. I grab the blade of the knife and it slices into my palm as I twist it out of his grip. He drops it and I ram the knife hard into his chest and then I twist it mercilessly. His shocked eyes are inches from mine; I see the monster of myself reflected in them and I fall backwards against the pillar. My breath catching in my throat as I hyperventilate, a strangled whining escaping out of my mouth.

"Oh… God!" I whimper.

Monster.

"Mac… Take a breath, it's alright, kid, it was him or you," Alfred reassures.

"Him or me, him or me, him or me," I garble in a panicked ramble.

The smell of burnt corpses, the blood and gore, pleading eyes begging for their lives, explosions and gunfire rattling my teeth. I am drowning in the bloodshed of the massacre I am unleashing.

"Scott!! …Snap the fuck out of it! You have a job to do! You can fall apart when it is done and not a moment before! Now dig in… Get the fuck up… Get up! That's an order!" Alfred commands and somehow my limbs start to move and I drag myself off the floor.

"That's it, Scott. Take a deep breath… Remember why you are here. What's his name, Scott?" Alfred goaded.

"Jakub…" I growl and the anger flares, calming my nerves.

"Say it again!"

"*Jakub!*" I yell.

"Good… Now, remember why you are here! Alisha, Anna, think of them and bring on the pain!" Alfred bellows.

Icy coolness spreads over me like a blanket of snow, goosebumps spread over my skin, I must get to Jakub. I peek round at the little wall jutting out ten feet away.

Can I make it?

I unclip a grenade from my belt, pull the pin and hold the firing clip. I jump out from behind the pillar and thunder into a run toward the big clump of men; everything slows down, I see them slowly raise their guns and my arm shoots back. I growl at the exertion as I throw the grenade towards them. I hear the gunfire and drop to the ground, full speed skidding along the floor and into the cover of the wall, which I hit hard, feet first, sending a jolt up my spine. I feel the boom of the explosion, the shockwave pounding in my chest and I feel a rush of adrenalin as brick dust and grit shower over me.

"Woo! Direct hit! Now you are just showing off," Alfred booms.

I know that he is trying to pump me up, trying to keep my head in the game and it is working, his voice is my guiding light. I swing the carbine round, ram the butt hard into my shoulder and peek over the wall to see a mess of bodies running everywhere. My finger squeezes the cold metal trigger as I open fire, the butt of the gun kicking back into my shoulder over and over again. My ears are ringing, my teeth are rattling, I watch them go down one after another after another, till I hear the click of the magazine emptying.

"Reloading! Cover me!" I yell.

"Hell yeah!" Alfred booms and I hear the unmistakable whizz of the bullets flying down with intense accuracy. I fumble for a magazine, ram it in and I take another look over the wall. A field of bodies laminate the ground. I take aim and fire three shots and then duck for cover.

Shoot, duck, cover. Shoot, duck, cover.

Over and over again until the field clears. I see another clump of men running towards my position and I know I have to move. My eyes bulge as they search desperately for somewhere to take cover and I spot an old abandoned bakery; the sign above the door is weathered and peeling. Vaulting over the wall, I launch into a run towards it; bullets start flying towards me forcing me to kick my speed up another gear, adrenalin fuelling my exhausted body. I shoot the glass to weaken it and then jump, diving through. I hit it with dizzying force, pain burns in my thigh and I cry out.

Terror twists in my gut. I roll on my back, gun raised and wait for gunfire that doesn't come. I peer around fearfully, my breath rasping and shallow. I drag myself behind the shop counter, my eyes fall on the jagged shard of glass sticking out of my thigh, my head spins at the nauseating sight.

"Oh, mother fucker," I groan.

"Mac, are you hit?!" Alfred asks.

"Nah, just glass sticking out... My... argh... thigh. Ugh, that sucks," I say, pulling out the glass. The blood flows fast; I take my jacket off, rip off the sleeve and wrap it round my thigh tightly.

"How bad?"

"How far to the brewery?" I ask, ignoring the question. Does it really matter how bad it is? It's not like I can ask for a time out.

"Four buildings down from your position, you have one more clump, two buildings down, it's a big one on the left side. They are moving towards your position, then you are clear to the building but there are a few men on the entrance and probably around the back too."

"I can make it. How long do I have?" I say, getting to my feet. I am not sure who I am trying to persuade, him or me. I reload my rifle and handgun from inside my waistband and put it back.

"They will be on you in 60 seconds."

I take off my rucksack and clip two more grenades to my belt and keep one in my hand. I hug the wall of the bakery, making my way to the front of the shop. Staying low, I peer round through the broken glass. I see the clump of men moving fast towards my position and the men are starting to spread out. I pull the firing pin on the grenade, dash to the entrance and throw it towards the clump. The throw is slightly off, I feel it before the explosion hits. It goes slightly wide but still takes out a good quarter of them. I open fire, willing the pack to thin out.

I am so close, so very close but I am weakening. My body is battered and my mind rattled from the stress. I fire, watching them go down, my heart sickening with every broken body that drops. There are so many of them, I am both fearful that I can't kill them all, and hopeful that I won't. The devastation of my actions is finally beginning to sink in and it is a lonely feeling. Then, I see bodies going down not by my hand and realise I am not fighting the hoard alone. I smile, new strength inside me, Alfred has my back.

"Mac, watch your six!" Alfred booms.

I turn on my heels, gun outstretched but they are too close and there are too many; the carbine jolts against my shoulder and I take down three but then the two men behind them launch themselves at me. Fear grips me; I dive out the way of one gunman only to have the other knock me down. I feel a boot raining down on me, pain exploding in my ribs.

"Grab her, let's get her to Jakub."

"Mac, if I stop shooting the hoard, they will be on you. Get up, kid! Move!"

The words rouse me, waking me from the pain, forcing me to roll over and avoiding the boot careering towards my face, scrambling to my feet. My rifle is on the floor and out of my reach. I pull the Glock from tucked in my waistband and take them both down. I stagger towards my rifle and take cover in the doorway of the bakery, opening fire.

Anger at myself for almost being caught turns me into a machine; I fire fast and efficiently, with zero mercy. I watch the bodies fall like puppets with their strings cut, blood spraying like pink mist. Angry tears filling my eyes as I witness the carnage I inflict; the hoard thins out and I watch in relief as the last man goes down. I spit blood, I feel woozy but I have to keep moving.

"Nice shooting, eye in the sky," I grunt.

I reload the rifle and raise it, leaving the shop entrance and moving slowly and fluidly. My ears pricked to high alert and my rifle sweeping left and right with every twist of my hips. I move in angles making sure my back is always covered, using the walls and the trees. My senses are attuned and alive with pin-dropping vigilance. I stop one building away from the brewery and my heart leaps, I am almost there. I peek round and see three men at the front entrance.

"Boss, I am going round the back of the building. On my mark, take out the three at the front entrance," I order.

"Copy, in my sights and awaiting your go."

Moving down the side of the building I peek around the back towards the brewery, spotting two men guarding the back entrance. Laying on my front, my heart pounding hard against the floor as I take aim. They both go down, their bodies thudding to the ground and I freeze, waiting for movement but nothing happens. Hitting the wall, I move along the back of the building, keeping low and I peek down the side and there is one man pacing.

"Boss, you are a go," I whisper.

Three consecutive whizzes fizz through the air followed by three thuds as the bodies hit the ground. The man pacing is distracted by the sound, raises his gun and starts to walk towards the front entrance. I take out the knife, running up to him and I jump up onto his back, one hand muffling his scream as I push the knife blade into his throat. He struggles and then his legs give way. I lower him to the ground. Moving to the back entrance of the brewery, keeping low I peer down the left side of the building and it is clear.

I make my way to the front entrance and sweep the street to check the coast is clear. Bending to one knee I remove a block of C4 from my rucksack. The block is rectangular, about 2 inches by 11 inches long and wrapped in green film. I wedge the block securely between the two door handles and then I insert the detonating clips into the mouldable clay-like block. The clips are attached to detonating cables which I run around the side of the brewery to the back entrance.

My back drags down the wall as I sit on the floor with the remote detonating trigger in my shaky hand. I check my watch and I have ten minutes till my hour is up; how did this only take twenty minutes? Time seems to have slowed down, my body aches and the wound to my thigh seems to be draining my energy away.

"The outside of the brewery is clear. I have laid a charge at the front entrance. I am going to blow it, then go for a soft entry around the back," I confirm, my voice a little uneven.

"Good work, kid, solid distraction. Listen, not to add to the pressure but I have heard over the scanner, the police are preparing to move in on your position," Alfred informs.

"It's alright, I was expecting it. Surprised it took them this long."

"Explosions and heavy gunfire are not something they regularly deal with smack bang in the middle of London. They will have had to call in the cavalry and will no doubt be working on clearing the area before they go in. They don't know what they are dealing with, so that buys you a little time but not much," Alfred says grimly.

"You two need to bug out, I don't want you tied to any of this. However this plays out, you need to be long gone," I order.

"We are going to change position; I need to stow my rifle but we are staying close by. You will still be able to reach us on comms. There is no time to argue, just get in, end this and stay alive, kid."

"Copy that. I wouldn't have got this far without either of you. I hope you both know what you mean to me," I say, somehow keeping my voice even.

"No goodbyes, kid, you are going to come home again. I will have a large whiskey waiting for your victory dance," Alfred says proudly.

Tears prick my eyes but I shake them away; it feels like goodbye. There are a thousand things I want to say but I know that saying any of them will only make me lose control. I am scared and I can't see a way through this alive; hope is all I have now and it is in short supply.

"Mac…" Anna's voice sings in my ear and it sounds strained.

"Yes, princess."

"I… Don't…" I hear her struggle and it hurts so I interrupt her.

"It's okay, Anna. You don't need to say anything, just get yourself somewhere safe. I will feel better knowing you are away from here."

"No, please listen to me, Mac. Don't do anything stupid… I know how much you want to save everyone and I know you are prepared to die to do it but we would run from these people for a lifetime if it meant you came out of that building alive. Losing you is not an acceptable loss to us so, don't let it be acceptable to you. You want to save me? Then come out of this alive because that is the *only* way you will save me."

Pain and longing hit my chest like a battering ram. The force with which I need her closer awakens the purpose inside of me, crushing the cold and lonely fear. All I feel is warmth, she relights the strength inside me, determination courses through me like electricity. Warmth and the fear that I will never see her again.

"If there is a way through this alive, I will find it, Anna – I promise you," I say fiercely.

"That is what I wanted to hear, now go – show him the unstoppable force and tenacity that is, Mac Scott. *Destroy* him and then get the hell out of there!" Anna fires.

I breathe, slowing down the rapid breath drying out my throat; the salty taste of blood is the only moisture in my gritty mouth. My thumb presses down on the trigger of the detonator and I brace myself. The explosion is incredible, my ears ring and I feel the building quake against my back. I am on my feet smoothly and I open the door and slide inside, my gun sweeping in fluid motions as I move. My eyes register the scene with lightning speed; the brewery opens up into a vast space. Running through the centre of the space are huge copper tanks with pipes tapping off of them that maze up and along the ceiling; it is a haunting and intimidating place.

To my left and right are metal steps that lead to a balcony that skirts all around the main fermenting room of the brewery and leads down to the floor on the other side of the tanks. I side step right moving up the stairs, keeping my sights sweeping for any movement and my back against the wall. On top of the balcony I keep moving this way, my gun flitting up and down from the lower level floor to the balcony walkway ahead of me.

I hear movement from beyond the tanks to the left of me and I crouch low; my breath is heavy, my body jittery with adrenalin as I pause and look for the source of the sound. Beyond the tanks the space opens up to a second adjoining space. It is dead opposite the centre of the balcony making the space a large T shape and I see the tops of some heads bobbing around behind the tanks.

Creeping along the balcony I move to the centre and the view into the adjoining space opens up, revealing more men waiting there. I crouch on one knee, the muzzle of the rifle poking through the grate of the balcony guard. I take aim and open fire, taking them by surprise. I take two down before they scatter, hiding behind the tanks. I move along the balcony, feeling the blood pounding in my ears, my senses wide awake.

As I move further along the balcony towards the steps that lead down to the ground level, sparks fly as bullets barrage on my position, hitting the metal grate;

the noise is deafening, making my ears ring. I fire back blindly as I run for the stairs, forcing them to take cover. I hit the wall and then take aim, taking down two more men but in my panic, I don't sense movement on the stairs till it is too late.

I feel the power of a bullet hitting the vest at point-blank range and the force knocks me back against the wall. Pain erupts in my abdomen and I cry out at the shock. I can barely lift my gun and I see him lift his to take a second shot. I react, shooting out of blind fear. The bullets take out his kneecaps and my ears fill with the sound of his blood-curdling scream as he rolls backwards down the stairs. I buckle against the wall trying to break through the pain, my legs shake and I whimper at the pain.

"Mac... Sit rep, sit rep?" Alfred booms.

"What... the fuck is... sit rep?" I wince, still winded.

"Situation report."

"Well... I report... that the situation well and truly fucking sucks! But I'm not dead yet, thanks for checking!" I growl and he chuckles.

I push myself off of the wall and will myself to lift my gun and keep my boots walking but there is no getting away from it, I am running on empty. Pain is exhausting me and I am feeling lightheaded and woozy; the makeshift bandage on my thigh has bled through and I am weakening.

The smell of smoke is burning my nostrils so I guess that I am coming closer to the entrance that I blew up. I shuffle down the stairs sliding and leaning on the wall and stop before reaching the bottom to step over the man who shot me on the stairs. He is crumpled on the bottom step; his left hand lays over his chest and my eyes spot the wedding band on his finger and I recoil, sadness rocking me unexpectedly. My eyes prick and guilt twists in my gut. I force myself to look away but the image of ring on his finger is burning behind my eyes. The opening ahead of me is now quiet, the bodies of the men laying in unnatural positions on the floor. I take a deep steadying breath and peer around the wall that I am leant on.

There is a wide corridor with wooden kegs stacked up neatly on either side of the walls and at the end of the corridor is a door with a small window. Anxiety fills my stomach with dread as I stumble down, keeping myself out of view from the window. I approach it from an angle and carefully peek through. My heartrate escalates and I crouch out of view.

I made it.

"I have eyes on Alisha and Jakub, he has a gun on her and there is another man standing the other side of her. They are at the end of what looks like a control room about twenty feet down. I see two men pacing in front of the door, there could be more but I can't see anyone," I report in a hushed tone.

"Home stretch, kid, well done. I know you are hurting and you are exhausted but you got to keep your head in the game a bit longer. That man in there is your primary objective, but facing him isn't going to be easy for you. He will no doubt try to get in your head, you must stay focused, just like with Billy and Jackson – you've got to play smart. Do not let him manipulate you," Alfred warns.

"Thank you, Alfred. Are you both safe?" I whisper.

"We are clear, don't worry about us. Now, *finish* this," Alfred orders.

I kneel in front of the door and unclip my last grenade; I feel its smooth cold metal against the palm of my hand. I lay my rifle down on the floor beside and just behind me and breathe. Adrenalin swells in my heart, flooding my system with energy and elevating my senses once more. I picture the smarmy grin on Jakub's face and I fantasise about wiping it off; everything becomes slow and calm, it is almost peaceful. I pull the pin on the grenade and hold on tight to the firing pin.

Silently, I turn the handle and open the door just enough to fit my fist inside the gap. I drop the grenade into a gentle roll and shut the door. I roll backwards fast, picking up the rifle mid-spin. On my feet I take aim at the door just as I hear and feel the explosion. The door smokes and groans and I launch myself at it; my boot pounds into the wood, kicking it through easily. I run into a cloud of thick, black, choking smoke; my vision obscured for just a moment. My ears ringing so loud I feel off balance, the two men closest to the door are down. The man flanking Alisha's left side raises his gun and he is too late, I feel the rifle kick in my hands as I gun him down without hesitation. From behind Jakub I see two men running towards me with guns raised as another runs at me from the left side.

Too many…

I take down the closest gunman with one with a clean shot as the man from the side throws himself towards me. I let him knock me down to the floor and out of the gun-sights of the second gunman. I keep aim and fire as I go down to the floor and I watch the second gunman go down. I hit the floor with painful force as the man who knocked me down lands on top of me. I am on the flat of my back, his weight is overpowering and he is too close for me to use my gun. I struggle against his strength but he is too strong, too heavy for me to move; panic starts to take hold of me. I am so goddamn close, this can't happen, not now. Please... not now. Punches bluntly pummel my face, making my vision blur.

"Mac!!!" I hear Alisha screech.

I grab for the man's throat and squeeze with every bit of strength I have left but it isn't enough, the man laughs in my face. His eyes alight with perverse pleasure, my wide eyes fall upon a scar on his cheek, a half crescent jagged impression and my mind flickers.

"Did you miss me, mala suka?" he spits.

He holds me down, his knee ramming hard between my legs and I cry out in rage but it is muffled by his forearm pressing hard against my throat. I look into his eyes, alight with excitement and my skin crawls, then I gasp.

The memory swirls...

Pressure... Undeniable, relentless pressure.

He is on top of me, I fight the pointless fight.

I struggle, I squirm, I flail.

Chains restrain me, his weight suffocates me.

Forcing me open, breaking me in two.

I scream, I push, I bear down.

"No use fighting me, mala suka," he drawls.

He enters me with force.

Pain radiates, despair penetrates.

"Mm, nice and tight..."

Rage erupts and I lunge for him,

I taste the blood as my teeth sink into the whiskery skin of his jaw.

He wails in pain and blows rain down on me.

The wind is knocked out of my lungs, I have nothing left to fight with.

He takes my body and destroys my spirit with every sickening thrust.

"Maaaaaac!!" Alisha shrieks and her fearful cry snaps me back to reality. At least, I think it is reality.

Oh God... Oh God, please let me forget. Please.

My feet have left the ground, a vice-like grip around my throat is holding me suspended in the air. I stare into the depraved eyes that I know so well and I feel tears prick my eyes. I feel for the hilt of my knife, my hand closes around it tightly.

"Ahh, she remembers me," he leers.

"You are going to... wish... I didn't," I choke.

I slide the knife out and ram it into his ribs. His grip slackens and I drop to the floor, landing on my feet. He drops to his knees, pain written all over his face. I slide out the knife slowly as I draw close to his face and watch the pain as the cold metal drags out of him.

"Should I violate you with this knife, the way you violated me?" I growl.

"No please..." he begs.

"But you didn't listen when I said no... Did you? *Did you*!?"

"No... No. I'm sorry," he whimpers, tears running down his face.

"Oh God... Mac..." Anna whispers.

"You are so very lucky, I am not quite as big of a monster, as you!"

I snarl as I stab him three times in a quick and but controlled frenzy, right in the heart. I scramble for my rifle and raise it, spinning on my heels, till finally... I freeze, my sights focused and trained in between the gleeful eyes of Jakub.

CHAPTER SIXTEEN

Hello Darkness My Old Friend

I blink the tears away as my eyes scrutinise Jakub; his olive skin glows with a sheen of sweat, his blond hair buzz cut short, his blue eyes gleaming with delight as he looks back at me. He stands by Alisha's side with his gun pointed at her head. Alisha is tied to a chair, her body shakes violently, tears streak down her beautiful face.

"Well that was dramatic, wasn't it?" Jakub speaks lightly with a playful tone, grinning. "McKenna, I have to admit, I am impressed."

My jaw clenches so hard it hurts. I am statue still, my rifle steady as a rock. I want so badly to pull the trigger.

"Mac, I am so sorry… I…"

Jakub slaps Alisha with the butt of his gun and she cries out and anger rocks me.

"Don't you fucking touch her!" I snarl, my teeth bared.

"I'm sorry, I just can't help but find her interruptions so very irritating; she would do better to keep her pretty little mouth shut," Jakub drawls. His leery voice makes my skin crawl almost as much as his sadistic Cheshire cat grin.

"Let her go, Jakub!" I spit.

"All in good time, you have something I need."

My mind races so fast it is dizzying; he wants the triangle of truth but does he even know what it is? The resentment and hate I feel is overwhelming.

"And you will get it, as soon as you let her go."

"It has been a long time now, hasn't it?" Jakub muses.

He wants to chat; he is enjoying this. Fine, I will chat.

"Not long enough."

"You are much different to the snivelling little girl, I once knew. Tell me, how did you manage to destroy all of my men? Not alone, I suspect."

Anxiety erupts in my stomach – he knows. If he knows then why hasn't he killed Alisha? Fear trickles in my chest; the only reason to keep her alive is so he can force me to watch her die. That, and she is the only thing stopping me from pulling the trigger.

"You see anyone else with me?" I bluff.

"No, but I would be willing to place a significant bet, that you had help. Tell me, can they hear me right now? Anna and… Alfred, is it?"

"He is trying to rattle you," Alfred informs me from inside my ear.

"That Anna… She looks… quite delicious," Jakub sneers.

"*I will rip you, limb from limb you vile piece of shit!!*" I roar.

He laughs jeeringly, his eyes bright with satisfaction. My hand shakes on the gun and it vibrates just a little; fury is bubbling inside me. My muscles so tight that everything hurts, my face flushes hotly and I glare at him hatefully.

"Now that really would be impressive," Jakub beams.

"Sweet home Alabama,

where the skies are so blue.

Sweet home Alabama, Lord I'm coming home to you…"

I hear Anna's voice sing in my ear and I smile. Warmth spreads through me, my body releases some of the tension and I start to calm down a little.

God, that girl…

Jakub cocks his head to the side with a perplexed frown. "Well that is interesting, what has you smiling?" Jakub asks.

"Something you would *never* understand."

"Why is that?

"Because it requires a heart," I say coldly.

"You think me evil?" Jakub asks.

"You stole over two years of my life, you had me tortured. I watched as you had a man beheaded because he tried to save me, you assembled an army to kill me, you are threatening the lives of people I care about and you think, what? You are one of the good guys?" I say incredulously.

"That is exactly what I think. I needed the location of your father; my army was for him, not you. He unleashed hell on my village, extinguished hundreds of innocent lives. Nothing is more important than finding him," Jakub spits.

"It didn't take you two years to realise I had never even met the man! I was innocent!" I scorn.

Jakub's expression turns vengeful and I know I am getting to him, I am goading him, I have no idea what I am doing but I have to keep him talking, I don't know how to get out of this and I need more time.

"My wife and two daughters were innocent and they were among the dead. They died slowly and painfully. Your father took my daughters, so I took his. I confess, I kept you much longer than I intended but hearing your screams, quietened the screams of my daughters. I still hear them; you see. Plus, my men did so enjoy you, why not let them have their fun with you while I waited? I knew sooner or later Barrett would send someone for you. I had hoped he would come himself but he proved himself a coward, once again," Jakub muses playfully. His eyes are taunting me but I am in control now, I will not let him bait me again.

"You are no better than the monster you hunt," I sneer.

"I am no terrorist! I only seek to kill anyone associated with The Culling. I will end their reign of tyranny; I will do whatever it takes to find Barrett," Jakub rants and he rubs the barrel of his pistol down the side of Alisha's face and she whimpers. Rage bubbles in my belly and my hands grip the rifle.

"Stop it! This is about you and me, let her go! I am here, you got what you wanted! Let her go!" I yell.

My eyes make contact with Alisha's for the first time. I have never seen so much terror and it galvanises the fear inside of me. What if I can't get her out of this? My head spins trying to find the way out that doesn't kill her. My eyes back on Jakub, the revulsion burns but I hold the gun steady, the sights trained on his forehead. My body hurts so bad and inside the panic is building. I don't know how to get Alisha out of this alive. All I need is one second and I can put a bullet between his eyes, but I can only do that if his gun isn't pointed at her. The rifle is heavy in my arms, I am scared to even blink. I keep my eyes on him, my mind whizzing. Sweat stings in my eyes. I have to end this, whatever it takes.

"You have a gun pointed at my head, the only reason you haven't pulled the trigger is because I have a gun pointed at hers, so why would I let her go?"

My brain stops whizzing… Clarity hits. This is the only way to save her; my instincts scream in protest but there is no other way. My eyes flick down to Alisha and she sees the defeat in my eyes and I let my gun twitch down a little.

"Mac, don't do it; he will kill you!" Alisha begs.

"I am already dead, girl," I say, laying it on as thick as I can. I give Jakub my best sad eyes.

"Fine, I drop my weapon then you let her walk. Do we have a deal?" I say through a strained voice.

"Mac, no!!!!" Anna shrieks.

"Savannah, you have to trust her, she knows what she is doing," Alfred reassures.

"Certainly," Jakub grins.

"Give me your word!" I spit.

"You have my word, McKenna," Jakub promises.

I start lowering the weapon to the floor, my eyes never leaving Jakub. My limbs are shaking, which right now, I am grateful for. It is helping me portray fear. I watch the satisfied smugness of his expression grow as my rifle shakes in my hand, inching closer to the ground.

That's right, wanker – I'm a beaten, defenceless, loser.

"Oh God, Mac… Please don't do this, baby, please," Anna sobs.

My chest pangs but I ignore her, I cannot lose focus now. My mind is screaming at me, my mouth feels like sand, my heart pounds in my ears. The rifle makes contact with the floor; I am totally exposed.

"My weapon is down, untie her and let her go – now, Jakub!"

"Get on your knees, hands on your head. Then, she walks," he orders.

My jaw is set as I follow his instruction; my legs shake as I lower myself to the ground. The rough concrete digs into my knees and I feel weak, I don't know how much longer I can keep this up. I let the pain show. I want him to think I am weak, I want him to see the pained defeat in my eyes. Jakub unties Alisha but keeps the gun to her head.

"You walk… Slowly," Jakub orders Alisha and she starts to walk slowly away, stumbling over her own feet and Jakub keeps his gun sights trained on her. Somehow, I need to get his gun off Alisha, I just need one second.

"Mac…" she whimpers.

"It's okay, girl, just go, alright." I reassure her but my eyes stay on Jakub.

Alisha moves behind me and out of my sight but Jakub keeps his gun trained on her. I think about Billy and Jackson and I play the only card I have got left.

One last push… Come on, Mac.

"You know what I find really funny, Jakub?" I say, laughing. "You are so busy trying to find my father, that your stupid, ugly ass missed one very important thing," I goad him.

Jakub turns and points his gun at my chest and my stomach flips in triumph; his eyes bear down on me coldly and his smile is gone.

"Oh yeah, and what's that, mala suka?"

"I am the one you should be afraid of!" I growl.

I spring to life; my hand slips down from my head and behind my back as I jump to my feet. I charge towards him as I draw the Glock from the back of my trousers, a rageful roar escaping my mouth. I feel a sharp impact hit my arm as the barrel of his gun flashes before my eyes, blinding me. I scream in fury as I plough into him. Jakub falls backwards and I fall with him, my gun aimed at his chest and I pull the trigger over and over and over. By the time I hit the floor, I hear the click as the magazine empties of bullets.

On my knees, straddled on top of him I am paralysed. My finger still pulling the trigger pointlessly. Unable to tear my eyes away from the shocked expression that is frozen across his face.

Click, click, click.

"Mac...!?"

"Mac? Answer me please!?" Anna begs.

"Mac, do you copy? Come on, kid!" Alfred calls.

"Jakub is... dead... It's over," I choke.

"Oh God... Mac! I thought you were dead! Oh God! You did it! Are you okay? Are you hurt?" Anna says urgently.

Then the pain hits, as if her question brings it to reality. Every inch of me hurts. I crawl off of Jakub and roll onto the floor, my head spinning in nauseating circles.

"Ugh... I wish people would stop shooting me," I whine and Anna laughs.

"Mac! You are alive!" I feel Alisha's hands grab at me and pain shoots up my arm.

"Ahhhh," I wince.

"You are bleeding!" Alisha cries.

"Thank you, Captain Obvious," I joke and I laugh at myself, giddy with adrenalin.

I can't believe it; he is dead and I am not. How am I not dead? Alisha is safe, Anna is safe, It's over!

"You jerk!" Alisha says laughing, playfully slapping my chest.

"Mac..." I hear Anna's voice and she sounds little broken.

"I hear you, princess."

"You have to get out of there now, I hear sirens coming your way fast," she warns.

"I know, I heard them," I confirm weakly.

"Who are you talking to?" Alisha asks.

"Then why aren't you running?!" Anna asks nervously.

"Because, girl, you are safe now and... I can't run anymore."

My head spins and I feel cold; my vision begins to blur. Funny, nothing really seems to hurt anymore, that can't be a good sign.

"Mac, you need to stay awake, you have lost a lot of blood," Alisha says anxiously. I feel her hands on my face.

"Mac, please get up! We will come for you but you have to get up!" Anna cries.

I hear a pounding of dozens of boots stomping across the floor and hands roughly grabbing me. I cry out in pain as I am flipped on my front and I feel the cold metal of handcuffs enclose around my wrists.

"I'm sorry, girl... It is too late."

I want more than anything to pass out, but something inside me is telling me if I let my eyes close, I will die. Still, it is tempting. My vision is blurry but I keep my eyes open. I feel strong arms hook under my armpits and drag me towards an ambulance. I am lifted inside and roughly shoved onto the end of a gurney. The brightness hurts my eyes as I try to focus them.

"You can't handcuff her like that, she has a GSW to her upper arm. How do you expect me to treat her?" the woman in green asks pointedly.

I feel my arms release from behind my back and the pain eases a little, my gunshot-free arm is tugged and cuffed to the gurney. I look down at it, my chest panging with sadness.

"I am going with her! Let me in!" a familiar voice asserts firmly.

"This woman is under arrest; I cannot allow—"

"You don't understand what has happened here! She is not the bad guy; she just went through hell to save me and if you think I am leaving her side..."

"Officer, she has a nasty head laceration, she needs stitches so you may as well step aside and let her through," the paramedic suggests. The police officer steps aside and Alisha climbs up and comes over and sits by my side, holding my hand.

"Right, can you tell me your name?" the paramedic asks. She has a kind face and she smiles freely at me. She is a shapely black woman and her name tag reads Naomi.

"Mac Scott," I croak and I frown at how raspy my voice is.

"Hi Mac, here – drink this, try not to gulp it." Naomi hands me a plastic cup with icy cold water inside and I take it gratefully.

"I am going to take a look at you, okay?" Naomi says softly. She puts her hand on my arm and I flinch, panic flutters in my chest, I grip Alisha's hand reactively as I stiffen.

"She is not so great at being touched," Alisha warns.

Embarrassment floods me and I feel my eyes prick with tears. Naomi's eyes fall on the jagged scar across my throat and then to my eyes; I hold her stare and I don't have the energy to hide my fear.

"Officer, I think this would go a lot easier if you were to follow us in your squad car, this young lady doesn't need an audience," Naomi says firmly.

"She is under arrest and she is dangerous, she requires an escort," the police officer argues.

"She is handcuffed to the bed, in shock and she has lost a lot of blood. She isn't going anywhere, if you don't leave then I can't stabilise her for transport to the hospital and she will die. So, if you want her alive to prosecute then please *leave*." Her eyes don't leave me as she speaks and I manage a small smile; this woman is awesome, I like her.

The police officer leaves reluctantly, slamming the back doors to the ambulance as he leaves and I do feel a little relief.

"Mac, I understand it might be difficult but I am not going to hurt you, I only want to help. I am not here to judge; you are hurt and I am here to try to fix that and that is all I want to do. Can you let me help you?"

"I think so," I agree.

"Thank you, Mac. Okay, so first, I am a little worried about the wound on your leg and the gunshot wound to your arm, both are hard for me to get to because of your clothes so either you need to let me take them off and put a gown on you, or I can just cut enough clothing off to get to them but, I have to warn you that they will put you in a gown at the hospital anyway. It is up to you."

I think about that. I don't want anyone taking my clothes off but I am cuffed to a bed, I don't have many choices before me. I know Alisha is trying to be here for me but I don't want her taking my clothes off either. I feel so trapped and pathetic. Alisha squeezes my hand.

"Just… take them off," I relent.

"Okay, I will be as quick as I can, I promise."

Naomi grabs scissors and begins cutting up the centre of my t-shirt. My body begins to shake the more exposed my torso becomes. The vibrations send shockwaves of pain through my body; I try to shut myself down but all I can manage is to not completely have a meltdown.

"Mac, you have some blunt force trauma to your chest and abdomen, can you tell me what caused them?" Naomi asks.

"Bullets."

"Okay, I will put that in my notes, they will have to check you for internal injuries. I have put a compression bandage on your arm to slow the blood flow, they will treat that at the hospital. I am going to put the gown on now, then we are going to lay you down so I can see to your leg."

I zone out, my mind far away. Exhaustion is hitting me hard. Naomi lays me back on the gurney and fits a nasal cannula and gives me oxygen. I feel Alisha's hand stroking my hair and my eyes become heavy.

"I can't believe you came for me," Alisha whispers in my ear.

"I was in the neighbourhood," I croak and she laughs her musical laugh.

"Can I go to sleep now?" I slur as I feel cold painkillers invade my veins, making me shiver.

"Yes, you can sleep. I will be here," Alisha soothes and the last thing I feel is her lips on my forehead before I let the weighty sleep take me.

***

"There are no internal injuries, but she lost a lot of blood. I have advised the police that she cannot be moved till late tomorrow or preferably the next day but they are pushing. Apparently, they are in a hurry to transfer her to holding." A smooth low voice speaks clearly but I don't recognise it.

"Thanks, Doc, appreciate everything you've done for her." A gruff voice speaks and this voice I recognise.

My body feels unnaturally heavy; the room is too bright and the light is shining through my closed eyelids making them glow orangey red. The smell of chemicals burns in my nose and my mouth tastes like plastic. I try to open my eyes and it hurts, actually everything hurts.

"Ugh…" I groan.

"Mac…" Anna exhales; the relief in her voice is massive. I try to focus my eyes; everything is fuzzy but getting clearer by the second. My eyes find Anna sat at my bedside, her hands holding mine.

"Hey…" I manage.

"Hey, you," she says. Her voice sounds sad and I frown.

"What's wrong?"

"It's nothing. I am fine." She smiles weakly.

"Why are you lying to me right now?" I probe, trying to sit up and I wince, then I hear the clank and realise, I am cuffed to the bed.

"Let me help."

Anna helps me sit up and then shuffles me back a bit, putting a pillow behind my back. She sits back down and takes hold of my hand again; she looks at it and doesn't meet my gaze.

"How are you feeling?" she asks.

"Like I was hit by a truck. Why won't you look at me?" I ask, a little hurt.

"You nearly died. The wound to your leg, was really deep. You lost a lot of blood and they nearly lost you on the table." Anna speaks so quietly, I can only just hear her.

"But I didn't, I am here and you know that so why won't you look at me?"

Anna looks up and meets my gaze; her eyes look pained, I squeeze her hand and wait.

"We were behind the ambulance, we followed you here. The earpiece was still in your ear, we could hear everything over the coms."

"Okay, and?"

"Alisha, after you went to sleep. She said she loved you, she has barely left your side; she only isn't here now because the police are questioning her," Anna rambles, her voice deadened.

"I was asleep. I don't understand, maybe my head is foggy. Can you just tell me what I am missing here, please?" I ask, a little frustrated.

"I guess because of the history you had, her betraying you. I always saw her as the villain but… seeing the way she has been. She is totally in love with you. I never thought about it because, I don't think I wanted to but… You two have a history together. I find it hard to believe that those feelings are not still there for you; even though she hurt you and seeing it has forced me to face the reality that… I can't compete with her. I don't want to try, I can only see that I will lose in the end, I will end up hurt and I can't let that happen."

Pain hits me so hard in the chest I feel winded; it takes all I have to keep my emotion off of my face.

"So, what are you saying?"

"I think you did the right thing, letting me go and now, I have to let you go too. I don't want to lose you. You are important to me, but I think I have to… move on."

My heart shatters. I let go of her hand and look away.

"Mac…"

"I understand. Look, I could do with some rest if that's okay, I would like to be left on my own for a while," I say evenly, not looking at her.

"Mac… Please." Anna's voice breaks.

"Please what? What do you want me to say? Does it even matter what I say?"

"Of course, it matters."

"Obviously not. Look, I'm sorry, I just woke up from hell and I wasn't expecting… I get it, okay. I always said, you deserved much more than… It's fine. I just want to be left alone."

I don't watch her leave, but I feel it the moment she does; the cold hard reality that I have lost her sweeps over me. I hear voices arguing in muffles in the corridor. Then Alfred comes in, he walks over and sits in the chair that Anna was in.

"Hey, kid."

"Don't pretend you don't know what just happened, fella," I croak and Alfred takes my hand in his giant bear claw of a hand and holds it gently. The lump in my throat begins to rise at his touch.

"You are in love with Anna, aren't you?" he states directly and I look away. "She has no idea; you know that, right?"

"It doesn't really matter anymore. She always deserved better than me. I set out to make her safe, I have done that. She made this decision while I slept, she didn't ask me how I felt. She decided that she was done and my eyes were barely open 20 seconds before she did it. Besides, it looks like I am going to prison so, she probably made a good call," I joke darkly.

"She is scared and heartbroken. She loves you; I know she does but she thinks you love Alisha so she is running away. She wouldn't have done that if she knew how you felt, you have done a good job in persuading her that you don't want her."

"You don't know that for sure, she was pretty clear. I always knew she would see the light eventually. You can't honestly tell me that she wouldn't be better off with someone else. She is better off and you are not going to ever tell her any different. I am guessing I am on the hook for some serious charges. I told her when this was over, I intended on disappearing. In truth it is because I can't bear to be around her, it hurts and I knew she would move on. I only want happiness for her but I didn't plan on sticking around to watch. I guess now, I will still be disappearing, just not in the way I expected. For what it's worth, I am going to miss you, brother."

Alfred sniffs and wipes his nose on his sleeve.

"I am so proud of you, kid, and I am grateful, you protected Anna and you are my friend, my family. Don't shut me out, okay. Wherever you end up, don't just cut me off."

Alfred puts his arm around me, pulls me into his chest and I break, I sob into his chest and it feels like I will never stop. He sits there with me for hours, just holding me tight while waves of pain hit me, I don't even have the energy to be embarrassed.

***

I fell asleep curled up on him, I must have done. Hushed voices wake me. I keep my eyes closed, my ribs hurting from being curled up in a ball on his lap.

"Pa, you should come home."

"She has only just fell asleep, she fell apart and she has been in pieces for hours and quite honestly Anna, I don't even want to look at you right now," Alfred scathes.

"Pa…" Anna begins but Alfred cuts her off.

"How could you do that? She only just opened her eyes for God sakes. She just went through hell and the first thing she gets when she opens her eyes is that?!" Alfred hisses and I keep my eyes closed; as touched as I am, she hasn't done anything wrong. I brought this on myself.

"I didn't want to do that; you know I didn't. Especially then, but she knows me too well so she knew I was holding something back," Anna whispers, pained.

"Did you even bother to ask her what she wanted?"

"I didn't need to; she has made it pretty clear," Anna snaps.

"I hope you can live with that. I am going to stay; she is going to be taken by the police tomorrow and she shouldn't be alone in this. I am going to spend time with her while I can," Alfred says in a firm whisper.

"Maybe I should come back tomorrow," Anna suggests.

"No, she said she doesn't want to see anyone else and she sent Alisha away too. I had to persuade her to let me stay. She is stubborn as hell, but she is scared so she is letting me. Don't expect me home, I will stay with her till the end."

I feel Alfred move me off his chest, lie me gently on the bed and cover me with a blanket. My body aches and no matter how gentle he is with me, trying not to wince at the pain is taking all of my will.

"I am going to get some coffee, you should head home, get some rest," Alfred instructs.

"I will, I am just going to sit with her a while," Anna whispers.

I groan internally. I really don't want to have to lay here fake sleeping, but I want to face her even less. It hurts her even being here, I just want her to go but she sits in Alfred's seat and I feel her fingertips lightly slide down my cheek. How I don't jump I do not know; I hear her sob and the pain in my chest doubles.

"I'm so sorry, I hate myself for hurting you. I only ever wanted to protect you, from the moment you barrelled down our driveway with a bullet in your shoulder, I just wanted to protect you because it seemed like everyone was trying to hurt you and I think, I might have hurt you in the worst possible way. You trusted me, you let me in and it was you who protected me in the end. You were right all along; I was in danger and today you nearly died protecting me from that. I repaid that by walking away from you because, I know you will never feel for me, the way I wish that you would. It hurts so bad to be around you knowing that, I pushed you away, before you could hurt me by walking away first. I already regret it, I just hope one day, you can forgive me."

I feel her hand lightly on mine and then she kisses my forehead and then she walks out of the room. I hear her sobs grow further and further away and when I can't hear them anymore, I open my eyes.

For fuck sakes, I can't even be mad at her now.

When Alfred returns, he brings me coffee. It is nasty hospital coffee but it the first thing I have tasted that isn't water in what feels like forever.

"Try not to be too hard on her, I brought this on myself. It's not her fault," I advise.

"How much did you hear?"

"Enough, I am not mad at her. She is hurting and I can't be there for that. She needs you and I will be okay. So, let her off the hook, will you?"

"You are a better person than you give yourself credit for, kid. You both make me want to bang your heads together. Knock some sense into you," Alfred says, chuckling.

"I think I have had enough knocks to the head to last me a lifetime and they don't seem to have made any difference."

"True that, you did good out there. You held your own against ridiculous odds but I know that look in your eyes. You have to find a way to let the guilt go or it will tear you up. Those men you killed, would have killed you if you hadn't acted first. That was their objective, try to remember that," Alfred reassures and I look away, my jaw tight.

I guess he understands the feeling well. I know it makes no sense; he is right. They were all trying to kill me and yet I feel guilt. I see the man, broken at the bottom of the stairs and his wedding band glowing in my eyes. Maybe this is why going to prison doesn't seem as hard of a pill to swallow as I thought it would be, it would relieve some of the guilt that is already beginning to gnaw at me.

"Could you do something for me?" I ask Alfred.

"Sure, kid, what do you need?"

"I need to see my mum, before... While I still can. I need to somehow explain all of this before my mugshot is plastered all over the newspapers. Will you call her in the morning, ask her to come down?"

"Of course," Alfred says, smiling. "Don't envy you there, it is a lot to explain," Alfred jokes and I laugh.

"Yeah, can't say I am enthusiastic about it but she deserves to hear it from me. Now you, look knackered, my friend. Go home and get some shut-eye, that's an order."

Alfred claps me on the shoulder. "Be back tomorrow." And then he leaves and I am finally left alone. I lay back on the hospital bed, the blankets scratchy against my skin. The beeps and ticks of the monitors around me are the only sound except the slow rhythm of my breath. The pain I feel physically is nothing compared to the torture of the memories. The crescent-shaped scar, the fear in the eyes of men as I snuffed out their lives, Alisha's terror, Anna...

I just want to shut down, I want to allow the cold darkness to take me over because everything hurts less when I do. I can't do that yet. First, I need to see my mum, I need to tell her everything and somehow break the news that her daughter is going to be locked up. I can't be cold when that happens, not to her. I am nervous; what is she going to think of all this? Her Milky Bar Kid – the mass murderer.

I am a little bit scared of going to prison, I can't deny that. I think more than anything, I am just scared that I will never get to leave again. What kind of existence am I going to have, locked away forever? Not a very bright one but, I have accepted my fate. I look at my wrist, cuffed to the guard rail of the bed. I reach over with my other hand to rub beneath the cool metal that is beginning to irritate the skin and the bangle on my other wrist twinkles reflectively in the light. My heart pangs, as the memory swirls. It hasn't left my wrist since my birthday; I am pretty sure that I can't wear that in prison.

I always knew I would lose her in the end, but that knowledge didn't make it any easier when I finally did. It is impossible to be mad at her, I want to be because that would be easier but I can't. I have hurt her so badly; she is just reacting to that hurt; she will never know the love I hold for her and now she has walked away, I am glad for that. Alfred says she loves me too, but there is a difference between loving someone and being in love with someone.

Anna said that Alisha told me she loved me while I was asleep, I am not sure what to make of that. Emotions were high, she was kidnapped and could have been killed at any moment. I came for her and it would be easy for something like that to slip out in the heat of the moment. I realise I am just trying to persuade myself that she doesn't love me because I don't know what to do with that. I don't feel the anger I once used to; thinking she was going to die and fearing I wouldn't be able to save her, cured me of that.

The before kidnap, during kidnap and after kidnap versions of myself still feel like three separate people, although the dots between the three are lessening as more memories return. Things are becoming clearer, my feelings are becoming less and less confused but now, it doesn't matter at all how I feel or who I feel it for. It is a choice, I will never have to make.

I guess I won't have to face Barrett now after all. I admit that I am as relieved about that as I am frustrated. He is a danger to the world. Who knows what he has planned and who is going to stop him? I wanted to stop him; however, my mind is splintered, I already feel haunted by the lives I have taken. My body feels broken, the cold tendrils of darkness are getting harder and harder to resist and my attempt to bring him down would have again, put everyone I care for in jeopardy. I can't even tell the police because who knows if there are Culling moles inside?

Alfred has been a relentless bouncer, warding off the police every time they try to question me. He can be an intimidating man; he has managed to keep them away so far, insisting I am too weak for questioning and that it can wait until I am stronger. I appreciate it but at this point I just want to get it over with, there is no game plan, all I can do is tell them the truth or tell them nothing at all and I am still undecided which way I will go.

The door to my room swings open and a nurse strides in. The plus side to being a dangerous criminal, you get your own private room. The nurse comes over; she is curvy with tight blonde curly hair, she is very chirpy and checks on me often. She is very smiley and it makes me feel like I have to smile back or I seem rude.

"How are we doing, McKenna?"

"Can't complain, I guess."

"How is your pain level?"

"It is bearable."

"Well, you are due your next dose of morphine but I would really feel better if you ate something before I give it to you. You haven't eaten since your surgery; can I persuade you to have some food?"

My stomach churns uncomfortably.

"I don't really have much of an appetite," I admit.

"That is understandable but your body is hungry even if you aren't and trust me, you will feel better for it. What about something light, like a sandwich?"

"Is there cheese?" I enquire and she laughs brightly.

I have such a weakness for cheese. Screw the bread, just give me a healthy chunk of cheese and I will be laughing.

"I am sure I can arrange that."

The nurse turns out to be right. Eating felt like hard work, like the food was alien in my mouth but once I ate it, I felt a bit more human. The nurse injects cool liquid into the IV bag and I feel an unnatural tiredness weigh on me. It is not a bad feeling; I quite enjoy it. I try to fight sleep because I want to stay in this peaceful and floaty place but it is no use. The canopy drops and I drift into a heavy and drug-induced sleep.

***

When I open my eyes again, I find my mum sat at my bedside and tears immediately fill my eyes. Her loving eyes are worry stricken, her round face blotchy with tears. She still looks beautiful, her face plump and her dark wavy hair that matches my own, is tied elegantly with a decorative clip. I see Alfred leave the room discreetly and then it hits me.

"How much did he tell you?" I ask.

"Everything," she chokes.

Tears roll down her face and I take hold of her hand in a tight grip. Her hands feel so warm around my cold icy fingers.

"I am so sorry, Mum," I say as my own tears start to fall.

As I see the pain on her face, I am nothing but grateful to Alfred. Now she is here I know; I would never have had the strength to explain of all this to her. Guilt burns inside me and I feel ashamed.

"Don't be, it took a while for me to understand. I was angry at first but by the time Alfred explained everything, I realised you were just trying to keep me safe. He seems like a nice man, a little scary but nice. I am grateful he didn't leave you alone in this."

"He is a nice man; I wouldn't have survived without him or Anna." I wince, as her name comes out of my mouth.

"You have been so brave; it feels so unjust that they are going to take you away. I can't believe I finally have you back and they are going to lock you away from me. You don't deserve this, it's wrong and I am going to help you fight…" Mum chokes through her tears as anger starts to leak through.

"Mum, I killed people. No matter what my reasons were, I still did it and I will take whatever punishment they throw at me because, I have to pay the price for what I did. I am ready to face the consequences. I need you to be ready too."

She breaks and my heart breaks with her. I slide my legs off the side of the bed and I hold her. The relief that she isn't mad at me, she isn't disgusted with me, is immense. I hold her against my chest and my eyes spot Alfred outside in the corridor. I mouth, "Thank you," and he smiles, giving me a nod and he walks away.

"It is going to be okay, Mum." I reassure her and she gasps.

"McKenna… You are hugging me…" She cries and I laugh.

It isn't till she says that, that I register the change. I haven't been able to hug my mum since before I was taken; I hold her tighter, making the most of the moment. Soon she calms down and we drink coffee and I hold on to as much time with her as I can. She has questions, of course. I try to fill her in as much as I can but most are hard for me to answer.

"I can't believe your father, after all this time."

"Believe me, I am still trying to wrap my head around it. He is a monster, Mum; I can see why you never spoke about him."

"He was always a cold man. His beliefs scared me but I never would have imagined he could do this. The extent of his depravity, it is shocking to me. I knew he was capable of many things but, mass murder? Terrorist attacks? It is incomprehensible and the fact that he has been watching you, it makes my skin crawl. I am a little relieved that you can't go after him now," she admits sheepishly.

"I can understand that."

Saying goodbye to her was excruciating for us both; she didn't want to leave but she also understood that I couldn't handle her watching me being taken away. I want to walk away strong and I just can't do that watching her falling apart as I leave. It is time I mentally prepare for the next battle I am about to face; my mum isn't the only goodbye I need to face.

"Thank you for telling her everything, Alfred. Once she was here, I realised that there is no way I could have done that."

"I thought you were going to be mad at me to be honest." He smirks crookedly.

"Okay, maybe I was for about three seconds," I say, laughing with him. I take a deep breath and sigh, steeling myself. "Look, I know they are going to come for me soon. I don't want you to be here when they do. Before you protest..." I say when I see that he is about to interrupt and he smiles. "You watching me being taken away, is going to be no easier for me than Mum. You are my family. Saying goodbye to you, is going to tear me up and I need to prepare for what I am about to face. I want you to know, getting shot in the shoulder that night gave me so much to be grateful for. I am privileged to have had that time with you both, I treasure every single stolen second of it. You both showed me love when I felt my most unlovable. You put me back together again and again, every single time I broke. You both saved me. There is no way I can thank you for that."

My throat screams from the lump inside of it, strangling my voice.

"So, I need you to take this, because I can't take it with me. Look after it for me and look after her for me. Let her know, she is off the hook. Tell her I am not mad and that I understand. That she has nothing to feel bad about. She more than anyone, owes me absolutely nothing. She can move on in peace, I want that for her," I manage and I hand Alfred the bangle and he takes it; he busies himself fiddling with it, keeping his head down.

"She is desperate to come see you, you know," Alfred mumbles.

"We both know, that won't help anything. Just help her move on, I don't have the strength to say goodbye to her and that is what it would be. I don't want her visiting me in prison. She wants to let me go and that is half of the battle; I don't want her holding on out of obligation. I will be okay, as long as you make sure she is."

Alfred nods and clears his throat. "I can do that, but don't you cut me off, kid. You need anything, you just call me. I will be visiting, when you are ready. Do we have a deal?"

"We do."

"Stay safe, kid, I got your back. Always."

I watch him walk away and I feel the cold sweep over me the moment he has gone. I feel the loneliness leach through my system with alarming speed; there is no one left for me to say goodbye to. I have dotted the I's and crossed the T's. There is no reason to hold back the icy fingers of darkness. Instead I meet it halfway, shake hands with it and welcome it into my heart.

***

My eyes daze dreamily; I am numb, I almost don't notice them arrive. I watch, a bystander, a witness to a fucked-up movie without the Hollywood happy ending. I stand, barely aware of the handcuffs that are being secured to me. I walk steadily and surely, flanked by police officers and I am blind to the gawking faces of the hospital staff and patients that ogle me with curious eyes as I leave the hospital. I am detached from the feeling of the officer's hand that bows my head as I enter the back of the police car.

I sit in a nondescript room, where I am sure they are trying to sweat me out, intimidate me, the stench of strong coffee and body odour strong in the air. They don't understand that there is nothing left inside to intimidate. I hold their glares with ease, I take their snipes on the chin and I keep my mouth shut. I hear their charges against me and I am emotionless to them.

I grit my teeth and shut myself down as my clothes and my identity are taken from me. I walk smoothly to face my fate, the flip-flops I have been issued slapping with every calculated step. Everything is painted white with flashes of turquoise blue; my legs are heavy as I follow the guard up the steps to a second level. The wound in my thigh still painful, we reach the top and I see turquoise-painted doors uniformly placed, one after another.

As we walk past each door, I hear the bangs and taunts of prisoners as they leer at me through the narrow slither of a window in the centre of each door. We stop outside a door and the guard opens it, I step inside the cell; it is neat, cramped and it smells of urine. Exactly what I expected, but somehow, worse. I turn around and face the guard and hold up my wrists, she unlocks the handcuffs and I step back.

"Welcome, to HM Bronzeford," she says coolly.

The door shuts in my face, the locks turn.

My name was Mac Scott, but now I am prisoner 6642. I am 32 years old and I reside here, at HM Bronzeford Prison. I used to be a photographer, but that feels so very long ago now. I set out to find and destroy the people who took me and I did that. I was lost, but in the pain, I found myself again, for a while. I am *alive* and you are dead, but I had to become a monster myself, to defeat you. Now I am right where I belong, just like you. Victory is bittersweet, but it is victory – nonetheless.

CHAPTER SEVENTEEN

Five Weeks Later

"6642, it is time for work detail. Let's go," the guard barks.

I stop mid press-up and get to my feet, my arms are heavy and stiff. I follow the guard obediently out of my cell and down to the kitchen and mess hall. There I clean the kitchen, the tables and mop the floors. I do this every day, three times a day, once after every meal. Routine – the foundation on which 'rehabilitation' is built. I don't mind, it breaks up the day and helps me keep track of what time it is.

Time, so much time, all I have is time. The days merge into one long day very quickly here, it is slow, dragging and repetitive until something happens to break up the grey monotony of it all and makes you wish the incessant dullness would return. Usually a fight amongst other inmates or a guard wrestling an inmate for a shiv. I just keep my head down, for the most part people don't seem to mess with me. For the most part.

"Hey 6642, you got a burner?" a voice yells from across the dining hall. I ignore them and keep my head down, swirling the mop from side to side, lost in the rhythm, the bleachy fumes tickling my nose.

"She ain't gonna listen to yo, she hasn't spoken a word since she rocked up. Think she is retarded or sumut," a voice jeers.

I grit my teeth and keep on mopping and I don't stop even when I see the two of them walk up to me. One girl is big and black, her hair a mess of braids, the other painfully skinny, with long blonde greasy hair, her skin white and transparent looking. The black girl squares up to me, bumping her chest against mine.

"She asked yo a question, yo don't answer and we are gonna have beef," she fronts, kissing her teeth.

I look up from the floor and meet her gaze with a cold hard glare and I see her shrink a little.

"Oh, so it's like dat is it? Who yo think yo are!? Getting up in ma face."

Her hands pound on my chest and she pushes hard against it, I step back absorbing the force with my back foot and then step back up to her again, my chest bumping hers. She grabs me by the throat and I smile, then I bring my head back and headbutt her nose; the crack is loud and nauseating, she drops back and the skinny woman picks up a tray from one of the tables and swings it. It makes connection with my face, splitting my eyebrow.

I whip the mop round and hit her with the butt end three times in quick concession. Cheek, gut, back of the knee and she cries out as she falls on her arse. I flip the mop back around and continue mopping. I feel the blood drip down the side of my face and I wipe it on my sleeve. You don't get anything here without asking, not even tissue so my sleeve will have to do.

The adrenalin tingles; I suppose I should be bothered, or at least feel bad but those two have been giving me crap ever since I arrived. Usually I just shrug them off, they are not the smartest fighters and I am able to stop the fight without really having to fight, it means I get hurt but it also means I stay out of trouble. I guess I met my limit. Once I am done, I am called over by the guard.

"6642, the governor has requested to see you. Follow me."

The governor, his name escapes me now, I met him when I first arrived, he seemed nice enough. Sweatiest bloke I ever did see though, like a fat Lee Evans in a grey suit without the laughs. I am handcuffed, taken to his door and the guard knocks.

"Come in," a booming voice calls.

The guard leads me inside and I am directed to a chair opposite the governor's desk which is messy and disorganised; the smell of stale McDonalds makes my stomach growl.

"Leave us," he directs and the guard obeys.

"McKenna Scott, prisoner 6642. You seem to be bleeding. I was advised of the… situation, in the mess hall. Don't worry, you are not in trouble. I have reviewed the CCTV footage, I should be advising you not to fight but when two convicts threaten you that way, unprovoked, I don't see the point. You had every right to protect yourself and given the crimes that you have committed, that was a very… *controlled* response. Your record is clean thus far so I am willing to look the other way on that."

I maintain eye contact, respectfully, and I nod my head in thanks. The sweat is building up on his top lip. He should grow a moustache, soak up some of the moisture there.

"You have been here over a month and you haven't made one phone call, received one visitor or even spent a penny in the commissary. You don't speak to anyone, you eat alone, you have no personal effects in your cell – you are segregating yourself. That isn't a smart plan, you are still on remand pending sentencing but you are looking at consecutive life sentences, there is no getting out for you. If you continue this way, you will end up in the psych ward."

I glare at him.

"I am not threatening you, Scott. I am merely just concerned for your wellbeing." I bow my head and nod, apologising for misreading his intent.

"You have had no visitors which isn't unusual, lots of convicts never have visitors because their families abandon them. What is strange here is the flurry of visitor order requests I've had, along with a number of phone calls, which means people want to see you and you are refusing access. I am sure you are aware of these requests as they get passed down to you. Why on earth would you ignore these people?"

My throat is tight. I don't want to see anyone, I know I made promises but that was before I came in here and discovered how hard it was going to be to keep myself sane. I have had visiting orders from my mum, Alfred, Anna and Alisha. They are all reminders of a life I have had to leave behind. To see any of them, to even speak to any of them on the phone would break my resolve and I can't face that. I keep my head down and remain silent and I hear him sigh.

"Well, the last thing I need is another suicide risk so tomorrow at 5pm you will be going to the visitors' lounge to meet with one – Mr Alfred Slone. This is non-negotiable, after many phone calls from him, he has concerns and I mirror them."

My head shoots up and I shake it no, glaring at him.

"Usually I wouldn't be taking the word of a civilian but like myself he is a military man; and he speaks very highly of you. I am inclined to trust his judgement, you would do well to heed my warning; if you do not attend this visit, I will consider you a risk and you will be forcing my hand and I will have no choice but to transfer you to the psych ward. Do we understand each other?"

I stare at him coldly, considering my options. I know with certainty I don't want to end up in the psych ward to spend my days drugged up and attempting to lick my own elbows. I am livid; why can't they just leave me the hell alone? I nod, reluctantly. What choice do I have?

"Good, then you are dismissed. Guard, take her to med bay, get her eye seen to."

I leave the office and I fume; how can Alfred do this? I think my lack of response is hint enough, I told him I would see him *when* I was ready. That is not right now, that may not be ever. I don't want to be reminded of the life I have lost. I deserve to be here, there is no question of that but I have to live it, I have to survive it and this is the only way I know how to right now.

I arrive back at my cell with my eyebrow throbbing from three new stiches and the door is locked behind me, I am okay with this. I am classed as a category A – high-risk inmate. Mostly I only come out of my cell to eat, shower and work. I get two showers a week and an hour in the yard, three times a week. I have the option at meal times to use the phones, but I never have. I spend my time alone in my cell, passing the time by working out and reading any books I can get my hands on. I find myself awake a lot, it is hard to sleep when your body is essentially inactive most of the day, it just isn't tired enough to allow for sleep.

When I do sleep my dreams are haunted by the fearful eyes and contorted faces of each and every man that I killed. My dreams run red in the sea of slaughter I inflicted and they never leave me, there is no peace. Their screams penetrate my ears whether I am awake or asleep, bringing on visions and memories I can't escape. The screams of my fellow inmates (of which there are many) activate the visions, triggering them like a bullet from a gun. My mind is a prison just as bleak and inescapable as this shit hole I am trapped in.

Consequence… My actions were deliberate, I weighed the options, measured the risks, foresaw the outcome and I did it anyway. I made the choices that led to this place and the truth is, I would do it all over again. My life is forfeited, there is no chance of retribution for me, I could live fifty lifetimes and still never repent for the lives I have taken. All I can do is keep breathing, survive as long as I can to pay the price and live with the penalty because there is no way to change the fact that I am a monster deserving of this purgatory. The wraiths that haunt my every living moment, with their screams and horror-stricken faces are justified and they have earnt their place of residence in my mind.

The cell is six by eight foot, the walls are plain and painted white, although previous prisoners have scratched the paint and scribbled angry phrases on the wall. They are painted over to try to cover them but some are still legible. On the wall above the mirror scrawled in angry script reads the words 'special addiction'. It makes you wonder who was in this cell before me. Are they still alive? Still addicted? Or did they turn their life around? If they did, it wasn't this place that helped them – that is for sure.

I have a steel sink with a toilet attached and a small plastic set of shelves that are fixed to the wall. The plastic is smooth and the corners and edges are rounded for safety. They wouldn't want you to get hurt in prison now, would they? Along the far wall is a bed, well… they call it a bed; I call it a cot. It is just a flat surface with a three-inch foam mat covering it. The cot is dead opposite the door so that guards can shine their torches through the small window at night, to make sure you aren't hanging yourself with your bed sheets.

I stand up and take a look in the mirror; it isn't something I do much of anymore. What is the need? I tie my hair back and put on my prison-issue clothes, I repeat the same laborious day, every twenty-four hours. Who cares what I look like? Something has me staring at my own reflection, maybe the fact that I have no choice but to see someone I know tomorrow, I wish I hadn't looked.

I have lost weight; my eyes are dark and have a rabid look about them, my skin is thin looking and my lips are dry and chapped. The angry slit across my eyebrow glows red and black. I don't recognise myself anymore and that would be fine, it has been fine – till now. My stomach is in knots, emotions are starting to take me over and I am doing all I can to stop them. I haven't even seen him yet and I already feel pain. This is why I wanted them all to stay away, I can't stay cold and emotionless if they are going to come and stir everything up inside of me.

Since being here I have received letters from my mum and Anna. It took me a long time to get the nerve to open them because I knew the barrage of emotion that would come from seeing their words, from feeling that broken connection to them. My mum's letter was very… Mum-like. Full of badly concealed disappointment at my lack of contact, while swearing to fight this injustice and simultaneously talking as if this is a completely normal situation. She spoke of her shopping trips, work life and her new-found love of vegan recipes. I know I should write back; it is the very least I could do but, then there will be more letters and I just want the world to forget I exist. The sooner she lets me go, the better off she will be.

The cot bed thuds as I throw myself onto it and I pull up the edge of the foam mat, finding the letters hidden beneath. It is madness, the magnitude with which a piece of paper can twist in your heart. I haven't read either of them since and I swore I would throw them away and yet, here they are in my shaky hands for the millionth time and here I am fighting the urge to read them. It is sick really; I know they can bring me nothing but pain but the fight still remains. Do I read them? Throw them away? Put them back? Round and round and round.

So far, my cowardice has meant I just keep stowing them under the bed, hiding from the pain of reading them or throwing them away but now, the pain is prominent with the impending visit from Alfred and I find my hands pulling Anna's letter from the envelope and seeing her bold and slightly slanted writing. There are deep dots of ink where she has held the nib too hard against the paper, probably in pause to think of what to write. It is easy to imagine her vividly green eyes tighten and her nose crinkle as she writes.

Mac,

Please read me, don't rip me up, goof! No! I mean it! Don't even think about not reading me, I am important. In fact, I dare you to read me, we both know Mac Scott never backs down from a dare ;)

I know you don't want to hear from me, you have made that clear and I don't blame you but I need you to hear me out. Please, just give me a chance. I am so sorry, I should never have said the things I did. I got scared and stupid and I hurt you badly, I know I did. I am so sorry; I regret it more than you can imagine.

Whatever has happened, wherever you may be, I need you in my life, Mac. I hate that you are in there, you don't deserve this and it still doesn't seem real. I keep walking over to the fire pit and expecting you to be sat in your chair, asleep. God, I miss that. You were always so scared of ruining me, you are blind to the amazing effect you have on people's lives, the only thing ruining me is the thought that I have lost you forever.

It's hard to think about what you are going through in there and I know there's nothing I can do. I know hearing from me is probably just going to make it harder but I can't let the last words I ever said to you, be what I said to you in hospital. You saved me and Alisha, you sacrificed everything and now you are paying the harshest price, I have never known anything so unfair.

I have made many mistakes, but you are not one of them and you can be damned if you think I am just going to disappear on you now. Please, don't shut us out, we only want to be there for you. I know, I told you I was letting you go but I was scared, I don't want to lose you, Mac-attack. Please, write to me, let me visit you, call me – Anything, just don't disappear.

Whatever you are going through, don't give up, keep fighting, keep breathing and keep hold of Mac Scott. She is the bravest, most incredible person and she is thought of every single day. Also, would it kill you eat something? I am staring at your photo on the front page of the newspaper, Jesus – do you ever eat? Pa was all for tossing bacon sandwiches over the wall, he says if he throws over enough, one is bound to get to you eventually.

We are not going to give up on you, with love and stubbornness,

Anna

Tears prick my eyes and I already regret reading it but I needed to; in this place it is easy to let the loneliness screw with you, I am sure everyone under this godforsaken roof has their own way of surviving this hell, mine is to accept that Mac is gone, all that remains is prisoner 6642 and I need to find a way to make them accept that too. While I understand the guilt she may feel, that doesn't mean she made the wrong choice and there is nothing I can do to relieve that for her. Eventually, after long enough with no reply, I am sure I will just fade into the background of her mind, it is only a matter of time.

***

The doors to the cells all unlock simultaneously with a clunk, which can only mean that it is lunch time. It is a tiered system; all the inmates eat in an order in accordance with what floor their cell is on. All food breaks are an hour long, then I am ushered back to my cell until all the floors have eaten, only to return to the chow hole, to clean up after everyone. I can't think of anything I want to do less than eat right now but I get to my feet, step out and walk in single file with the other inmates while flanked by about 15 guards along the line. There are between 30 and 60 inmates on each floor, mine has 32, less than most because we are the high-risk level.

My eyes are peeled and darting as I walk tensely to the chow hall, my mind on constant alert. It doesn't matter how many guards there are along the line, you are never safe. My floor houses the worst of the worst; most like me, are lifers and that means they really haven't got anything left to lose. If any one of them feels the need to blow off, segregation is the only real deterrent they face and in a lot of the cases of the psychos that surround me, it's a small price to pay.

The only other consequence is being shipped out to another prison but it doesn't seem to happen much and it is hardly a deterrent to someone serving life. I have only seen it happen once and that was a move to separate two inmates that were clearly a couple and had grown close and that kind of intimacy is strictly prohibited inside. Lots of girls seem to be just 'gay for the stay', clinging on to any affection to starve off the loneliness but some connections are real and those are quickly broken by the powers that be.

My white-socked feet slop inside the flip-flops, slapping against the metal grate floors, the taunts and jeers boom and screech around me as inmates both greet and threaten each other, guards bark out orders to be quiet and I just keep moving, following like an obedient Labrador while keeping my game face secure.

When we reach the ground level, we move through the recreation room which is basically just a large area with pods of seating areas that are welded to the floor. There are some offices along the far wall with an observation room in the middle. Behind thickened glass are guards' faces lit up by the TV monitors they sit behind as they scan through cameras for any trouble kicking off.

To the left are the kitchens and food serving area where you line up with your tray for slop that doesn't actually resemble food, let alone taste like it. I have found that porridge is my survival food in this place, it is the only thing that is served that halfway tastes like it is supposed to, although it does leave a metallic aftertaste. Inmates serve the food through the hatch and you just have to hope that they haven't spat in it, or worse. The commissary is also there, you can buy drinks, sweet foods and toiletries or you could, if your money wasn't still on hold like mine is.

To the right along the wall is the payphone bank; the dark blue retro-looking payphones are mounted inside the turquoise blue, thick painted stripe that seems to line every wall. From what I have seen, the phones are not used as much as I expected them to be, maybe I am not the only person who finds that contact impossible or maybe some people just have no people to call. Right next to the phone bank, inset behind the wall of phones is the toilet block that I do my best to avoid unless it is for a scheduled shower. Too many times I have seen inmates walk in there and then either stagger out or have had to be carried out after a beat down.

There are no cameras inside the bathroom, only one above the door that shows who enters and exits, inside is a complete blind spot that is easy and convenient for inmates to exploit for everything from drug deals to beat downs. If six inmates were to enter and one gets beaten, it is impossible to tell who the culprit is and snitching is a good way to get dead in prison, so no one ever reports it and no one ever pays for it. The toilets are vile, as are the showers and I leave feeling no cleaner after I have showered beneath the, usually cold, water. Other than that, it is best to avoid the rec toilets at all costs.

All of our phone calls are recorded and only preapproved numbers are allowed to be called. When I first arrived, I put my mum and Alfred on the call list. It didn't take long for me to realise, calling anyone would only make it harder for me to adjust to prison life and that is why I have never done it. I haven't heard a familiar voice in five weeks now, not even my own. Of course, I long to hear any one of their voices, I miss them all but the cost of it is too high and it would serve no one in the end.

It feels a little petty that I never put Anna or Alisha on the call list, but I didn't know Alisha's number off by heart to add it. The last time I spoke to Anna she made it clear that she wanted to move on, I never really trusted myself not to lose my resolve and call her at the beginning and that is why I did it. It has been easier to resist than I expected.

Not so easy right now.

My appetite is non-existent so I take a seat alone in the closest pod, purposely making sure no one can sit behind me, my eyes darting around but I can't seem to stop them flicking towards the phones. If I called Alfred and told him not to come, would he listen? Would I still be thrown in the psych ward if he just didn't turn up? It is tempting; if I could stop him, the pain of the phone call would be a lot less than a visit. The idea of seeing him tomorrow causes as much pain as it does anger, I just want to be left alone.

My stomach tingles in anticipation as I weigh up the pros and cons. Trays of food clatter on tables around me, the loud tension-filled buzzing of the people around me eating and talking seems to melt away as I torment myself with the aggravating… 'Do I? Don't I?' inner monologue. My feet are moving heavily, I know he probably won't listen to me and yet my hand is on the phone, my fingers punching the numbers and my heart is in my throat as the dial tone rings in my ear. I know this is a mistake but I can't seem to stop myself, if I can get him not to come it will be worth it; my chest tightens as I await to see his gruff grumbly voice.

"Hello?" Anna's voice greets in her smooth gravel tone. "Hello? Anyone there?"

My breath catches sharply inside my throat, it didn't even enter my mind that

Anna would answer. I called Alfred's mobile phone, why… Pain sears inside my chest and I suck in a sharp breath in the shock of it.

"Mac…?" she chokes. "Is that you?"

I freeze as I hear my name, the memories invade my vision with extraordinary power as the lump begins to rise in my throat. God, I have missed her voice.

"It is you; I know it is, please talk to me. Just tell me you are okay, tell me you are not, tell me anything, please. Just show me it is you, please Mac," Anna pleads, her voice breaking.

My eyes are blurring with tears as I fight the battle with myself to keep my mouth shut and attempt to force myself to hang up.

"If you can't talk to me then listen, I know you don't want to hear from us but we are worried sick and… We miss you. Please just—"

I slam the phone down and quickly rub the wetness from my eyes, my breath ragged as I try to shove it all back down before anyone sees. Oh man, it hurts. What the hell was I thinking? I probably wouldn't have been able to stop him anyway and I know that. This is just weakness because I know he is coming, this is the very reason it has to stop and tomorrow, I have to make sure he never comes back again.

It takes a minute but I collect myself as best I can and turn around to face the pods. I am relieved when no one seems to be looking my way; the pain still thick in my chest, the ache for her threatening to break me, I take a step forward. My insides cringe and I jump at the sound of a commotion, my eyes scan for the source of the noise rapidly to find four inmates stood on tables kicking people's food trays onto the floor. Guards scramble to get control of the situation, my attention is diverted and I am too slow to see the threat.

I stumble forward under the force of the hands pushing me towards the toilets and just have time to hold my hands up so I don't hit the door face first. The door swings open and I am shoved inside so hard I trip over my own feet and hit the wet, pissy-smelling, tiled floor. I scramble to my feet as quick as I fall, turning on my heels to find five inmates closing in on me. I run full pelt at the centre of the knot of them, knocking one flying and headbutting another.

Hands seize me, pinning my arms behind my back; the hold is too strong to be just one person. Fear and anger rattles in my chest, I shoot my head back but it connects with nothing. The two girls that I hit are back on their feet thundering towards me and a third stands back from them, watching with a keen smile on her face, while filling a sock with bars of soap. I kick out; the woman I head butted sprays blood from her nose as my foot plants in her gut.

"Fucking do her already, the screws will be sniffing before I get a taste, useless mala sukas!" the woman with the sock commands.

My insides recoil and I freeze, my fight evaporates as my vision fractures, I see the light leave the eyes of the mala suka man, feel his warm blood spray on my face as I sink the knife in, over and over. My momentary freeze ensures they overpower me, fists pound my gut and I am dragged against the wall, four sets of hands pinning me as the girl with the soap-filled sock approaches. She would be attractive if it wasn't for the predatory look on her face; she is athletically built with long blonde hair and a long face and high cheekbones.

"I have waited a long time for this," she goads, her accent thick.

I am not fighting anymore, there is no point with four of them holding me. I need to find the right opportunity, a way through and if I don't fight, they might get complacent so I can catch them off guard, unlikely but still worth a try. The smile slides off the girl's face, the sock dangles from her clenched fist.

"So quiet, that won't save you. You think we don't know who you are? Every Polish inmate doing their bid here knows your name, all of them wanting a piece of you. I just happened to get there first."

My blood runs cold, all fear washing away. What's the point? I know what is coming, I could fight but I will no doubt lose, the odds are not exactly in my favour and really… I don't care anymore. The tendrils of darkness claw their way up inside me and I welcome the icy numbness that it brings. A rag is rammed into my mouth so hard I gag and then I see the sock swing. Her eyes are alight with hateful excitement that brightens with every blow; pain spreads across my rib cage, the air sucks out of my lungs and I start to choke and gag on the rag when it is pulled out of my mouth. Her hand grips my throat and she draws in close, spitting in my face with her furious words.

"I don't think you have much time left in this world, mala suka," she drawls, her face bright and smug. I hold her gaze and then, I spit in her face.

Smart, Mac, real smart. At least it felt good.

She wipes the spit off of her face, turns away and then pummels her elbow backwards sharply in my face. I taste blood and then I am dropped to the floor, landing on my hands and knees. I listen to the sounds of their laughs fade away along with my pride and then I drag myself to my feet and hobble to the sinks. My hands shake as I cup them under the tap's flow, rinsing my mouth and spitting crimson water. My jaw is stiff and it hurts to stand up straight but when I manage it, I see my reflection in the mirror, the split in my bottom lip pouring with blood and already bruising.

Could have been worse.

I turn away, trying to stand and walk taller than I feel, as I walk back to the rec room. My feet carry me towards my seat as I try to act inconspicuous but I am stopped by a guard.

"6642, do you have an incident to report?"

The guard eyes me with contempt, most of them do. Maybe it is in the job description to be an emotionless hunk of useless with keys. I keep eye contact, say nothing and she huffs.

"Very well, let's take you to the sick bay."

Oh, for the love of God, twice in one day. Great, just great.

I am handcuffed and led back to the medical wing; it isn't very large. There are three beds, cupboards fixed to the wall – like everything in the room they are bright white, all the cupboards have locks, there is even a fridge that has a lock on. It is the cleanest place inside the prison; it has that horrible chemically hospital smell. There are always two guards in the room that never seem to speak or move.

The nurse is nice enough, she is quite an intimidating woman with a strong presence but a soft smile. Her hair is dark and wavy, she wears it in a loose knot and her facial features are sharp, giving her a severe look until she smiles. She has a Marilyn Monroe mole on her lip; I can't make my mind up if she really has a mole, or if she has drawn it there. I am sure that was a thing once. She eyes me with concern and I realise I am staring at her mole and I look at the floor.

"Ms Davis, prisoner 6642 appears to have had an accident." The guard confirms the obvious and Ms Davis frowns at me.

"Back again so soon?" she asks and then she huffs when I don't reply.

"Alright, let's take a look at that lip. Take a seat on the bed, please."

My stomach clenches as I hesitate but the guard nudges me and my feet start moving. I wince as I attempt to climb on the bed, the handcuffs restricting the use of my hands to help me up and my ribs flaring with sharp aches. The guard unlocks my handcuffs, keeping one wrist shackled and secures me to the rail of the bed and walks away.

"Are you hurt somewhere else?" she asks and I shake my head no and her eyes narrow suspiciously. She turns to her computer and taps away at her keyboard and then she turns back to me, her hands on her hips.

"6642, McKenna Scott. My name is Shannon, I thought I would tell you. If you are going to be here this frequently, we may as well be on a first-name basis. Now, I noticed you were struggling to get up on that bed so, I am quite sure that you have other injuries. Is there a reason you are hiding them?" she says sarcastically but with a warm smile.

The panic starts to rise instantly, there is no way out of this without me either telling her I don't want to be touched or her checking my ribs and touching and seeing the scars. I feel my insides tremble as my brain searches desperately for the way out. She stitched my eye earlier but that was easier than this. There is blood pouring down my neck, over my scar, how am I going to get out of this? I shake my head, wide eyed and she frowns, taking a step towards me. Fear causes me to overreact, adrenalin still pumping from the fight. I cringe back and wince, my free hand cradling my ribs.

"Okay, easy McKenna... I can't force you to accept medical treatment but I encourage it. You have clearly hurt your ribs, took a good beating by the looks of it. This is a safe place, however long your stay here is, how long will it be before you incur more injuries? Eventually you are going to have to let someone help you, so why not me?" Shannon asks, her face warm.

That point isn't lost on me. I don't need help, the injuries are nothing to write home about but that doesn't mean they won't be next time. I have no idea what I will do when next time becomes this time, I can only deal with what is happening right now and I am not even dealing with that very well.

"I..." I croak and then I shake my head and look at the floor.

Shannon takes a measured step closer and my head shoots up, her hands held up and her face calm. I hold my hand up and shake my head, warning her to stop and she freezes. Her eyes grow determined and thoughtful, like she is thinking something through. I just want her to stop thinking, just give me some tissue for my lip and send me back to my damn cell.

"Are you wearing a vest under the jump suit?" she asks and I nod, confused.

"Well, how about you undo the jump suit and I check your ribs through your vest? I mean, if the injury is bad enough, *maybe* I will have to keep you in med bay for a few hours to ice it. You would miss your work detail and that really would be a shame, wouldn't it?" Shannon says with a smirk.

I can't help but smile a little; I consider my options while I survey her face. Missing work detail right now is a temptation I can't pass up. The idea of trying to clean the kitchen and mess hall in this state is not appealing; while I am sure I could do it, I am not sure what state I would be in at the end of it. It seems people are out for my blood, any time in safety to recover a little is the only chance I have of getting my strength back up. I grit my teeth and unzip the jumpsuit to my waist, struggling to shrug my arms out of the sleeves. My breathing escalates painfully as I lay down on the bed.

"Thank you, McKenna. I am just going to apply a little pressure to check your ribs, okay?"

I grit my teeth, close my eyes and think of England; it isn't so difficult, there is no skin contact but still, I am fighting the urge to panic. There is no hesitation, I feel pressured fingers on both sides of my ribcage moving down my ribs. The pain sucks but I have had worse and I know they don't hurt enough to be broken but that doesn't stop me gasping when she finds the middle of my ribcage.

"Okay, so I don't think there are any breaks, but there is swelling to the right fifth true rib and your left eighth false rib. So, I suggest we ice you up and load you with some painkillers and anti-inflammatories and keep you off work detail till morning. I would feel better keeping you off tomorrow too but there is no way that will swing. After all, I am just the nurse, what do I know?" she says with a wink and I manage a silent chuckle.

Ice packs are loaded onto my ribcage and although it makes me shiver, it also feels good against the heat radiating from my torso; she also gives me one for my face which according to Shannon is turning a gorgeous lilac colour around my chin and bottom lip.

"So, McKenna, is there a reason you don't speak? I am certain that life inside these walls would be easier if you did, you would be able to make friends and pass the time quicker and maybe your enemies wouldn't find it quite so easy to catch you unawares if you weren't always alone," Shannon probes.

I keep my mouth shut but I hold her gaze and she lets out a long sigh, her face patient and her eyes a little sad.

"I get the hint, if you change your mind, I am around if you want to talk. Rest up, you won't be leaving till after dinner this evening," Shannon huffs and she walks away.

She is clearly one of very few decent people in this place, she reminds me a little of the paramedic that treated me after the battle with Jakub. I lay, watched by two guards as Shannon informs the guard that escorted me that I will be missing work detail and the guard leaves. My body begins to relax a little as I listen to the beeps and ticks of hospital monitors and the rustle of paperwork being shuffled and my mind wanders.

I guess I shouldn't be surprised, I lost focus making that phone call and now I am paying the price for it, I won't make that mistake again, lesson learned. Although it sounds like it was only a matter of time; no amount of keeping to myself would have prevented it in the end because their grudge with me started before I even entered this place. I can try not to make waves but my actions on the outside have already painted a target on my back. I wonder how many people there are just waiting for the same opportunity.

As much as it is good to have a change of scenery, I long for the solitude of my cell. The guards eye me with suspicion while Shannon looks at me with pity and I just want people to stop looking at me altogether. Time drags; the quiet and lack of distraction ensures there is nothing to keep me torturing myself over the broken sound of Anna's voice playing over and over in my head.

It was almost impossible not to answer her, the same as it was with her letter. I miss everyone and everything including her but, her loss is the hardest to bear because I don't just miss her, I miss the light she brought to my darkness. She has always made me feel safe to break, she broke through every defence I had, her touch is the only touch I allowed and I crave it. In my weakest moments, I long for the safety she inspires and severing that connection, is a daily fight. She isn't here, this is how it is now, how it will always be.

Man-the-hell-up.

A food tray is delivered to me, this is a welcome indication of the time. I am not hungry in the slightest but I know I need to eat if I want to keep myself strong. I think, the chunk of brown sludge is meant to be cottage pie but it tastes like feet. I notice a smirk playing on Shannon's lips as she watches me attempt to swallow the mush down with a crinkled nose. I scowl playfully at her and she chuckles.

"You must have the constitution of an ox, is it as bad as it smells?" she asks and I raise an eyebrow. I use my hand to gesture towards the tray, indicating she should try it for herself and she snorts.

"Oh, so kind! I will take a polite pass thank you, McKenna."

I chuckle silently and go back to trying to shovel the unknown into my mouth. It isn't actually too bad after a few mouthfuls, as long as you don't chew, I don't manage much of it but it is better than nothing. I push the tray to the end of the bed and Shannon comes over to take it away, then she hands me a

Mars bar and my mouth waters. I hesitate and look up at her.

"It probably has better nutritional value. Take it, hide it in your pocket and eat it in your cell, I am not supposed to give inmates treats," she whispers in a hiss.

I take it and do as I am told, offering her a smile, hoping she knows that I appreciate it. Her kindness seems so alien in this place, it is jarring.

"They are going to take you back to your cell in a minute. Keep your chin up, McKenna Scott," she says, returning my smile and then turns away. I tap her elbow hesitantly; she turns back to me, her expression curious.

"It's... Mac," I rasp, my voice barely audible through its squeak and she grins warmly with a sigh.

"Mac, I like that. Stay safe out there, Mac." Shannon winks.

I never thought I would be relieved to be back in my cell. I groan like an old man as I lay out on my cot. Another day is ending, another mark on the tally of time. Today marks the fifth week that I have been here and already it seems like so much longer. I walked into this place convinced I could handle this; after spending two years in captivity on a boat, I admit I expected this to be a piece of cake in comparison and in some respects it is. I do at least have a toilet, access to water and food, a door to shut on the psychos, a cot to sleep on, cleanish underwear, all luxuries I wasn't afforded on the boat.

The hardest battle inside this place happens in your mind, constant endurance in fighting your own weaknesses. The moment your focus slips and you allow loneliness to seep in, you slide down a slippery slope and it is hard not to let that slide spiral out of control, it is even harder to dig your heels in and force yourself to stop the tumble mid spin. I slipped today and I am still trying to dig my heels in; now more than ever I wish there was a way I could stop Alfred coming tomorrow.

***

No sleep is had, my mind a constant whirl of sharp images, memories of the past invading my present, my fears of facing Alfred and the pain seeing him will inflict has me jumpy, rattled and angry. I splash cold water on my face and wait for the guard to take me down to work detail for the second time today. My head swims with exhaustion and pain from yesterday's beating. I grab for the Mars bar that Shannon sneaked me, hidden inside my pillow case.

The taste is so intoxicating that I moan; the sugary sweetness is almost too much after tasting nothing but bland nothingness for the past five weeks. The hairs on my neck rise and I shudder as if I have never before tasted chocolate. The moment passes too soon even though I try to savour it but I do feel less weak and wobbly for eating it. I have always had a weakness for the three Cs. Chocolate, coffee and cheese.

The buzz of the sugar doesn't hold out long, the arduous task of leaning over tables to wipe them clean is testing on my ribs. My hands shake in the vile washing up water as I cringe when bits of food float and touch my hands beneath the surface. The work is long and tiresome and time seems to be moving unnaturally fast. My best guess is that I don't have much time till Alfred comes, maybe an hour or two and as time goes on, the painful ache in my chest gets heavier.

It is when I am filling the mop bucket with water and bleach that I hear the shouting; there are only a few people it could be because there are six people working kitchen detail including myself. I hesitate, wondering if I should go investigate. The shouts are coming from the rec room, someone is getting a beat down.

None of my business.

The bucket full, I start to work mopping the kitchen floor when I hear a long drawn-out cry of pain and I tense up, the sound jolts and agitates my mind, triggering images so vivid I have to brace myself on the sink as my head begins to swim. My teeth bare, an angry growl rumbles in my chest, adrenalin fizzing through my limbs. The mania of the memories conflicting with my present vision is fuelling the raging frenzy inside me. My feet pound against the floor, the mop handle gripped in my fists, I burst out of the kitchen into the rec room.

The same two girls that attacked me yesterday, one big and black, the other painfully skinny with almost transparent skin are beating down a girl that I have never seen before which means she is probably a newbie. The skinny girl has a shiv held up against the girl's throat, terror is wide in her eyes as they fall on me. I don't break my stride; my feet power towards them, mop held out horizontally, my face a mask of fury. The bigger girl cowers back a little and I swipe the mop around, lashing the skinny girl holding the shiv around the face.

She lets go of the newbie and lunges for me with the shiv. I side step out of her reach and swing the mop over my head as I turn, meeting her shoulder to shoulder, arching the swing and using the momentum and power of the turn, I drive the mop into the backs of her knees. Her legs sweep beneath her, she lands on the flat of her back and I hold the mop head against her throat and I kick her hand, the shiv flies across the floor.

"Simone! You gonna help me blood?!" she chokes, the mop head against her throat making her voice sound garbled.

I feel movement behind me that has me turning on my heels; my arm thrusts out without hesitation and my fingers tighten around the bigger girl's throat. Her eyes fill with fear as I stare hatefully into them, my grip tightening. Revulsion fills my stomach and it snaps me out of the rage, my hand drops and I gasp. They both high tail and run and I feel disgust tingle over my skin, tears fill my eyes, shame and fear burning in my chest.

What the hell is happening to me?

"Thank you," a tiny voice cowers, but I am already walking away.

The floor has never been so clean, I am sure of it. I drive the mop hard into the floor, my ribs screaming at me but the pain is calming the fury burning inside me, clearing the blur of the angry tears welling in my eyes.

Swish-swish. Swish-swish.

I swirl the mop left and right in aggressive figure of eight motions and I resent the moment that I run out of floor to mop. Sweat is glowing off of my skin as I am taken back to my cell, my heart pounding hard inside my heaving chest. The door bolts locked and the pain engulfs me, I fight the sobs, swallowing the lump in my throat, growling at my own weakness.

"Get it together!" I roar.

The time is ticking down, I know I don't have long. In my mind's eye, I can see him rumbling along in his Land Rover and the image inspires surges of hurt in my chest. Out of everyone, if I had to choose – I would have chosen Alfred, the kind and unjudgmental Alfred but his connection to Anna, is going to cause me pain. I do all I can not to think of her, I hope that she is happy, I always hope for that but I don't want to even hear her name, let alone see Alfred who will no doubt have things to say about her. I can't do this, that is the repetitive thought and feeling but like everything in prison, I don't have any choice.

I pace my cell, muttering silently to myself. I know the time is ticking down but I don't have any idea what the time is. Being inside this cell has never messed with my head so much. Well… not since the first week. I can't deal with this; I feel about ready to tear my hair out when the guard opens the door.

"Visitation, 6642," she informs and my stomach drops.

As always, I am handcuffed and then I follow her obediently. My arms and legs are tremoring from both anger and fear and it jolts painfully in my ribs. I know how much this is going to hurt me and it terrifies me. He should know that; he must know that.

I follow the guard to a part of the prison I have never been to before, but it all looks the same to me. Plain white walls with a thick turquoise stripe that runs through the centre, very minimal furniture, dark wooden doors that I assume are offices and turquoise metal doors of cells and secure areas. The air is thick, but that is the same everywhere here. I think it comes from the lack of open doors and windows, plus the amount of people locked up inside. I have gotten used to it, but right now my lungs crave clean air more than ever. I am stopped at a set of double doors.

"Visits last one hour, you will be cuffed to the table and your visitor is allowed to touch your hands *only*. You will not cause a scene or your visit will end and you will earn a week in segregation. If you think you are going to cause a scene, you ask a guard to return you to your cell before that happens. Are we clear, inmate?" the guard warns and I nod.

Almost seems worth kicking off but not quite, once in segregation was quite enough for me. I earnt that because I was strip searched on the way in. Needless to say, I lost it and tried to run away. A pointless overreaction that landed me a week of darkness and complete isolation. I lost it, it felt like I was breaking from reality. I screamed and screamed; I have no idea why I thought that would help. Eventually I stopped screaming and I have kept my mouth shut ever since. I have been asked why, the truth is I don't know, I just know I don't want to talk and I have nothing to say.

The guard opens the door and introduces a large white room with the same turquoise stripe, the floor is littered with hexagonal tables and benches that are bolted to the floor. It is very bright, the sunlight is shining in from the windows, it is so odd to see big windows and there are no bars, I have the urge to launch myself towards them to check the world is still outside. There are vending machines and a coffee machine lining the left wall by the entrance doors, guards flanking every wall in watch.

I am led to a table where I sit down and my handcuffs are bolted to a small steel loop that protrudes from the centre of the table. I look around and there are eight other inmates going through the same motions on other tables. The position forces me to sit forwards slightly, the table digging into my ribs.

I look at my arms, stretched out in front of me uncomfortably. Something about this is humiliating, I can't quite pinpoint why it irks me. It isn't like I haven't been confined before; it isn't like I am not used to being handcuffed, the marks on my wrists glowing purple against my white skin say that I am. I just feel exposed in a way I don't like. I watch my arms tremble, my eyes following the lines of the bluish-purple veins inside my inner elbow. My chest tightens and I cringe against the handcuffs.

That's what it is, I want to cross my arms. I want to cover my face and pretend I am not here. I want to hide but I can't because my wrists are chained down out in front of me, my arms are two thin, white, trembling lines and my hands are frozen in place, palms up. A position of forced openness, of vulnerability, the very last things I want to feel especially in prison.

The double doors open and families of people start to walk in; panic starts to rise when I realise that more than one family member is allowed in at once and fear that Alfred might have brought Anna starts to cripple me. Then I spot him and I am relieved to see him alone, that is the extent of my relief, he takes a seat in front of me and I glare at him.

"Hey, kid."

CHAPTER EIGHTEEN

Subterfuge

The sight of his worn and weathered, red and yellow plaid shirt, the familiar smell of hay and engine oil, the gruff farmer tang in his deep voice is already ripping at my insides. The trembles down my noodle-like arms are making the handcuffs rattle against the metal loop on the table. I look down at my hands. I don't want to look at him, I don't want to hear him and I don't want to talk to him.

"Yeah, I figured you would be pissed," he says, his expression calm.

My chest is heaving with the effort of trying to keep control of myself. I don't know what I want more, to hug him or sock him one in the jaw.

"Ah, the no talking thing. I have heard you haven't spoken since you got here. Why not talk to me? Have a go at me if you want."

I keep my eyes down, dazed and unfocused. Hopefully if I ignore him long enough, he will accept that I am not going to talk and leave. I don't hold out much hope, if the fact that he is here proves anything, it is that he is as stubborn as they come.

"Come on, kid, please talk to me. You made me a promise, don't shut me out," Alfred pleads and I feel his hand touch mine.

"Don't," I snarl throatily and Alfred takes his hand away.

"Sorry," he mutters and the guilt pangs in my chest.

Damn it.

"I'm… sorry," I croak, not looking up, my voice gravelled and barely audible.

"It's alright, kid. I shouldn't have done that; I have to be honest, I wasn't prepared for how bad you would look. Now, I am more worried than ever."

"I am fine. I just… don't want to see anyone, I can't. It is the only way I am surviving this," I say robotically.

"Mac, you don't look like you are surviving at all. You don't even look like you, you look ill and like someone knocked ten bells out of you," Alfred says in a strained voice.

"What do you want from me? What did you expect?! This is prison! This is forever! Did you think I was going to be all rainbows and fucking sunshine?!" I scold.

"Prisoner 6642, keep the volume down," the guard barks at me.

I flinch, then I nod at the guard. As much as I want to leave, segregation is the last place I want the destination to be. I pull in a breath to calm myself, my fists ball into tight knots and I lean my forehead on the table. I need to keep control, whatever it takes.

"They call you by a number?!" Alfred asks, disgusted and I look up and laugh, the sound is unnatural and bleak.

"Why are you laughing?"

"Of all the things to prompt that disgusted look on your face, my number tips you over the edge. I quite like it, it is strong, direct – imagine if they had called me 1234, the humiliation!" I mock darkly with a joking shocked face, my tone cold and cutting.

"It really isn't funny, kid," he says, smiling a little, but his eyes are sad and I feel the pang of guilt pull heavier in my chest. I know this is hurting him, but it is the only chance I have got of getting him to see sense.

"You called last night, didn't you?" he asks and I nod, looking back at my fists.

"Why?"

"To tell you not to come," I grunt coldly.

"Mac, you are our family, we just want to be there for you, why won't you let us?"

I finally look at him properly, I see the pain in his kind eyes, the gentle giant is still trying to have my back, as always. I wish he would just give up. I have nothing left to give him except the truth.

"Look… I'm sorry. You just, you shouldn't have come. I know I promised you, but it isn't a promise I can keep. There is no Mac anymore and any reminder of the life I lost, is just agony. I need you to let me go because this is it for me. I am in here for life, all I have left is the fight to keep breathing. Trying not to think of the people I have lost, it's the only way I know how to do that. It is the only thing that has gotten me through the past five weeks. You have to let me go; you all do."

My chest feels fit to burst; my throat burns from speaking for the first time in weeks. I sound like a hormonal teenage boy whose voice is breaking.

"You haven't asked about her."

"Why the hell would I?" I spit.

"She is desperate to visit you, she has a lot of regret, I am worried about her and that was before you put the phone down on her last night. She is a mess and I can't get through to her. I was hoping I could persuade you to write back to her letter or call her or something, she is hurting and I think you are the only person that can release her from that."

Pain sears inside my chest and the anger bubbles.

"Just tell her how it is, receiving a letter from me will only make it worse. I am not getting out of here; she will soon move on but only if she feels she has no obligation to me. Tell her there is nothing to regret, she made the right choice. I may have not liked her reasons but it was the right choice. I am not seeing or speaking to anyone, the only reason I am seeing you is because the governor is threatening to throw me in the psych ward if I didn't see you because you wouldn't drop this!" I hiss.

I am starting to lose control, the pain in my chest is becoming too much. I need him to leave almost as much as I want him to stay. The conflict is torture and it is only leading to more hell for me.

"I am trying to help you, Mac," Alfred grumbles sadly.

"So, what… you think a pep talk is going to fix me up quick smart? You don't get it, do you? You think I want to be this way? I don't have a choice; I can't even talk to my mother because I still have to go back to my cell and try to survive the pain that talking to her would bring. The memories, the loneliness, the pain of missing her, the knowledge that I will never be out there with her again! It destroys me! You want to help me? Stop reminding me of what I have lost, leave me the fuck alone and *never* come back!"

A sob escapes me and I grit my teeth and will myself to stop. The last thing I need is to be seen by other inmates crying. My chest heaves and I lean forward, roughly wiping my eyes on my bicep.

"Mac…" Alfred's voice breaks.

"No! Now listen to me, I treasure every moment I got with you both. I have no regrets; I would make the same choices if I had to do it all over again. I deserve to be here and it is time you both see that. I am sorry she is hurting; you know how I feel about her, I don't want that but if you are honest with yourself, you know, she is much better off away from me and this place. She owes me nothing, she made her choice in the hospital that day and it was the right one. It is your job to make her see that. If you care about me, about what I need, let me go, Alfred. Open your eyes, fella, I am already gone," I profess. I hold his gaze just long enough to see his eyes well and then I turn away.

"Guard!" I call.

The guard comes over and I request to be taken back to my cell. The guard checks my hands to see if there is anything inside of them, then unbolts me from the table. I pull my arms back stiffly and push myself up from the table. The guard holds my elbow and starts to pull me away.

"Take care of yourself, brother," I utter with a pained smile and then I walk away.

***

I don't know how I got through that first night, or the second or the third, I only know that I am colder than I ever have been. The cost of seeing Alfred, was high. The reality, that they are all out there and I am not forgotten is somehow harder. The depths of darkness I have sunk to, the coldness and anger I feel has meant that the following week, I managed to land myself in a whole world of trouble. My temper is short and I ended up in a fight that put me in a cold, dark segregation cell. I am unsure how long I have been here, two days, maybe three.

This place breaks you down, it is hard to be angry in here. It strips back your layers one by one and anger is one of the first things that gets peeled away, I imagine that is why they do it. Rage becomes despair, despair becomes fear, fear becomes defeat, defeat becomes emptiness. Once you get to that stage, there isn't anything left. You can't see anymore, you can't try to entertain your mind because you have been in the dark so long that the images in your mind become blank sheets of paper. I am at that stage right now, blank.

It isn't always so bad, it feels like if there is a line between sanity and bat shit crazy; I am dancing precariously on it but I am blank and empty and I don't care about the danger that crossing that line can bring. The silence is deafening – I never really understood that phrase till now. When I was on the boat for all that time, it was very rarely silent. There were always the waves crashing rhythmically, there was shouting, arguing and deep laughter of the men above deck, there was always noise.

The only noise here is the sound of my lungs, continuing to inhale and exhale. Occasionally there is movement outside my door, keys jingling and a light being shined on me, then darkness again. Every so often a tray of food is passed through the door and then taken away again sometime later. I tried to count the trays, the meals, to keep some track of time. Three meals a day, the last I remember was tray number eleven, huh. It must be longer than three days. Maybe five, that is good, I think they let me out in seven days or maybe that was just last time.

I only tried to run away last time, this time I beat up another inmate. I lost control; they provoked me but I could have easily walked away without losing it like that. The truth is it felt good to lose it, just for a moment. It happened during lunch, in front of everyone – maybe people won't mess with me so much now, they all think I am a lunatic; maybe I am, I feel a little loony. It wasn't too bad, it isn't like I hurt her badly but what is scary is that for a second, I wanted to. This place doesn't tame monsters, it feeds them. One thing is now certain, I am right where I belong.

My back still hurts; the fight in the rec room started because the Polish girl who beat me with a soap sock was shouting that I am murdering scum, amongst other things. I threw the first punch and once I started, I realised, it felt good to hit her and I didn't want to stop. The fight turned into a brawl, other inmates jumping in for the hell of it. Then I was hit with a few blasts of taser guns to my back, that sucked.

The electric coursed through my body; the familiar sensation of my body convulsing, of my muscles tightening and my joints locking, spurred on a memory with the mala suka man. My head began to swim, the rec room warped and disappeared from my vision, I stopped fighting, and I felt the fists pound into me as my mind slipped from the now, to the then.

The memory swirled.

The boat is sloshing from side to side violently, the sea is rough and the waves loud as they crash into the boat. The sensation gives me constant nausea but I am long since empty, my body trembles as goosebumps bump along my naked skin in the cold air. My arms have been chained above my head for so long they are numb and they no longer feel attached.

"Please God, just let the boat sink, drowning isn't the worst way to go and if it means they all die with me, I can be at peace with that. Please, let us all drown," I whimper.

Footsteps pound down the stairs and terror surges through me once again; will I ever stop feeling this fear? Is it possible that my heart will just one day give in from the strain of the quickened, erratic beats? Maybe I should pray for that instead.

The mala suka man steps towards me and I look up at him, it is hard work keeping my head up but he likes to see my face when I scream and he will only pull my head up by my hair if I don't do it. I glare at him with all the hatred my heart holds and his savage eyes flash with cold satisfaction. He holds the cattle prod to my tummy and my chest heaves with terror.

"Are you going to beg me not to do it?" he drawls.

"Fuck you."

The electricity courses through me and I taste blood, my jaw clenched so tightly that my back tooth breaks in my mouth, my vision begins to darken and then the pain stops. I spit blood and gritty pieces of tooth as I choke.

"Now, I know you want to beg me to stop, mala suka," he jeers.

"Fuck you!!" I scream.

The electricity pulsates through every cell, boiling my blood and scorching my nerves. My scream rattles with every convulsion, the pain is too much to bear.

I can't stop the screaming; I scream and scream and scream and...

The vision cleared and I found myself on the rec room floor, the scream still exploding shrilly from my mouth, gawped faces staring down at me, both inmates and guards alike. Now, I am certain they all think I belong in a booby hatch, five cans short of a six pack, mad as a freaking hatter. This could be a good thing, they might think twice before messing with me but then, what the hell does that matter if I end up thrown in the psych ward?

That is a very real fear, I mean, sure – I will get to spend my days high as a kite, making jewellery boxes out of dried pasta shells and ash trays out of papier mâché but I will lose what tiny bit of life I have to left to live; the only thing left of Mac Scott is my mind. If I end up in the quack shack, that really will be the end of me. I am trying not to think about that; if they were going to do that, surely, they would have done it by now. I have been here long enough. How long has it been? Three days? Five? Six hundred?

I don't know how much longer I can stand it inside this place, the thoughts are too loud, the visions too real and there is too much nothingness. In here the angry numbness I survive on doesn't exist, the darkness has abandoned me. I thought I could do this; I have survived worse but my mind is an arsenal of horror stories to be used against me and it is beating me down. The sobs jerk in my chest before I can stop them. I can't do this for the rest of forever, I can't, I won't.

Is this really it? Is this really all my life will now be? A series of fights, fights with inmates to stay alive, fights with my mind to stay sane, fights with my emotions to stay fighting. I don't want to fight anymore, what is the point? There is no life to fight for anymore, no love or happiness to strive for.

In the darkness, I flinch and cringe as my mind is invaded by the only thing I can really seem to see clearly, the memories on the boat and the memories of the battle on Eastfield's Street. A sequence of eyes, boring into my psyche. Jakub, jeering with delight. The man with a melting face, wide with pain and vengeance. The mala suka man, cold and satisfied with the sound of my screams. The man with the crescent scar left by my teeth, predatory and perverse.

"Ugh stop…" I whimper.

I have nothing left inside to fight them with, I seethe at my own weakness. I feel the loss of everyone and everything but as I lay here shaking on the cold dank floor, I long for only one person and the magic that her touch brings, the strength and warmth it inspires and I hate myself for needing her. She let me go and I have nothing but understanding for that, I always knew she would see the light eventually. As time goes by, minute by minute, I am letting her go, just like I have everyone else but when it is dark and quiet it is always harder to shut out the ache that I have for her and here in isolation, that is all there is.

"Anna…" I choke.

The door to the cell opens and the light burns like fire in my eyes. I squint through my tears; the disorientation is incredible.

"6642, on your feet – you are being shipped out."

My body is stiff as I climb to my feet. I really didn't think the fight was that bad. Why would they transfer me over that? Plenty of people fight and don't get transferred, I was only just starting to get used to this place. Why do this to me now? I guess it doesn't really matter where they put me but I hate not knowing what is being done with me, the unknown has always scared me a little, the unknown and change.

At least it isn't the psych ward.

Handcuffs are put back on my wrists, along with ankle shackles. I am walked through the prison and then to the processing area. This area has a completely different feel to the rest of the prison. Soon-to-be inmates are sat lined up, handcuffed to white plastic chairs with faces of doom. There is a large reception area in the middle and on the other side of the room is the 'Processing out' area, the faces waiting on that side of the room are giddy at the prospect of getting released. Somewhere I will never sit, the thought hurts.

The fact that the people sit facing each other, both sides staring down the barrel of very different fates, seems almost cruel somehow. I remember sitting in processing, watching prisoners being released and it is the worst kind of jealousy you can imagine, it is almost like it is another form of punishment, making you sit there and watch as people's handcuffs are taken and they walk freely out of the doors.

We walk past the main reception and towards the doors that lead out of the prison, I am the complete opposite of free and yet my heart is in my mouth as the doors draw nearer. When they open them, the cold air hits my face and it brings tears to my eyes. I want to stand still, breathe in the clean air and take it in but my elbows are tugged and I am hurried along. We cross a short path and I see a big white transport van, the windows obscured with wire mesh and I start to panic.

"Are you going to tell me where I am going?" I utter throatily.

"Oh, she speaks. That is above my pay grade, 6642. In you go."

I stumble up the two steps into the van, the shackles on my ankles making it nearly impossible to walk properly let alone negotiate steps. I am taken to a seat at the back of the van and secured to it. The guard walks away without another word, she jumps into the front passenger seat of the van and I am left alone. The engine roars and I feel the rumble as the van starts to move. I didn't even get to pee; I have no idea how far away the prison is that I am being transferred to.

I try to shut my worries down but I feel rattled from being in segregation and now shell shocked from the sudden change. I try to look out the window; it is difficult because of the security mesh over them but if I squint just right, I can see some things. My mouth waters when we drive past a Starbucks, what I wouldn't give for a caramel latte. As with everything lately, I have no idea how long we have been driving but it feels like a long time. There is no one for me to ask, my palms are sweating and my throat is so dry it is hard to swallow. It is too hot in the van and I haven't eaten in a few days, or drank since yesterday… I think. The combination is making me feel woozy and nauseous, I guess it is good that I have an empty stomach.

I wonder what the next prison will be like; it isn't like I am particularly sad to see the back of Bronzeford, the food is vile, the inmates are out to get me, the guards are useless and there is never any coffee, but there is nothing to say the next prison will be any different. It could end up being worse. Ugh, that isn't helpful, I need to try to keep my mind occupied, all this overthinking is just freaking me out.

I start to see things I recognise; places are becoming familiar and I realise with a jolt that we are back in London. Everything and everyone I know and love is here and that hurts and I decide, I don't want to look out the window anymore. It isn't long though, before the van stops and the side door slides open. I am led outside and it is a relief to be in open air, the aroma of chicken hits me and my stomach growls, that is a good smell after prison slop. I don't even really like chicken.

I walk forward towards a large, grey and very square-looking building; it looks like it was once painted white but the paint has weathered and become dirty over the years, it looks familiar, I am sure I have been here before. Something doesn't feel right and I am feeling jittery and jumpy, that is probably due to being down in segregation, it took me a good day or two to feel semi-human after I left it the first time. Yes, I am just wigging out, it isn't like there is much left that could happen to make life any worse right now.

My eyes warily search my surroundings; there is a KFC next door, that explains the smell. We walk towards the entrance of the big blocky building and above the large double doors is a crest that has an English shield in the centre and it is surrounded by three prideful dragons. Below the crest reads – Bishopsgate Police Station. Confusion, I have been shipped out… to a police station?

Clink-clink. Clink-clink. Clink-clink.

I walk through the double doors, my feet shuffling with the restriction of the shackles that clink loudly with every step. We come to the reception desk, people are staring at me and I would quite like for the ground to swallow me up. I look down, my eyes falling on my turquoise and white prison jump suit; there is still blood on it from the fight. I haven't showered in at least five days; I must look as rancid as I feel. My eyes fall on the chains running between my wrists and ankles and I suddenly feel angry. Why the hell am I here? I have already been remanded, so why am I in a police station being stared at?

"Prisoner 6642, McKenna Scott, transfer from Bronzeford. Here is the paperwork," the guard informs.

So, she does know my damn name then.

"Yes, she is expected in consultation room one. If you will follow me," a nasal voice instructs.

I keep my head down as I shuffle along until I am out the main reception and away from ogling eyes. We walk through a corridor with thin grey carpet and creamy coloured walls, there are wooden shields and certificates mounted, a wall of photos dedicated to fallen police officers, their portraits beaming with pride and their uniforms handsome. The doorways and skirting look like old dark wood, there are lots of offices and people busy on phones or shuffling paperwork, we walk past a cold-water dispenser and my throat burns.

God, I want a drink.

We stop at a door and the nasal-sounding woman opens it and I am led inside a small windowless room, the walls lined with blue cushioned panels, not like a padded cell cushioning at all but it is clear that this is to deter from injuries during questioning. There is a desk in the middle of the room, with two chairs either side of it, I am led to the closest chair and instructed to sit down. On top of the desk is a black box with cassettes on top; when I see the voice recorder, clarity hits my sluggish brain.

I have been here before; this is where I was questioned before being formally arrested. Is that why I am here? I have already been charged, what more can they ask me at this point? This doesn't feel... right. The guard said I am being transferred. Are they going to ask me questions and then transfer me? I feel the guard hovering behind my right shoulder and I am tempted to ask her what is going on but the guards are never very forthcoming with information.

I spent hours in this room after I was taken from the hospital, many of those hours I spent in here alone while they left me to sweat; they couldn't see that at that point I was that broken down, that their attempts to break me down were pointless. I was numb and their constant badgering was never going to penetrate. I could have told them the truth, part of me wanted to but I didn't want to relive it, my fate was already sealed, what was the point?

"Some of the victims were executed with sniper rifle rounds, from long range. We know where the bird's nest was, if you tell us who you were working with we might tell the judge you were cooperative."

There was no way I was giving Alfred up and after three days of questioning I think they got the message. I was then formally charged and carted off to Bronzeford to await trial. My trial date is still yet to be determined, but it doesn't really matter, it is an open-shut case, I was found at the scene of the crime, bearing the wounds of battle and carrying weapons and explosives. The trial is just a formality that I am looking forward to being over with.

The door behind me swings open and I flinch a little; two people pass me and then sit at the desk opposite me. A man and a woman, both dressed in suits. The woman is young and attractive, her face has soft features and her hair is tied back in a plain and professional-looking way. The man is balding and slender, his face is stubbly and he has intense eyes that blink a lot. The woman speaks first and I look up to meet her gaze but she isn't looking at me.

"Officer, you can remove the restraints and leave, we will be taking over care of Mac Scott now," she orders and the she then looks at my shocked expression and smiles.

"You do prefer Mac, to inmate 6642, I am guessing?"

"Yes," I manage but I am so thirsty the words get caught in my throat and the woman looks at me frowning.

"Officer, when was the last time Mac had a drink?" she asks, her tone accusatory.

"I am not the prisoner's keeper; she has been in solitary confinement for five days so, I don't know."

The guard unlocks the last lock and I suddenly feel very light, almost naked; I rub my wrists. The male officer gets to his feet and leaves the room and the guard follows him out. The disorientation is mind boggling.

"Mac, my name is Lexi Holt, my partner is just going to get you a drink. Is there anything else you need?" she asks softly.

I feel uneasy, not knowing what is going on is making my already tired brain, overthink. I don't know if I am being paranoid or if this really is weird. I don't know anything except this doesn't feel right.

"An explanation," I croak and she looks at me with sympathetic eyes.

"That is coming, I promise."

She has a sincere face, I think, but I don't know if I trust her. She is being nice to me, and I don't understand why. The least people should be is nice, but she seems concerned for me and she has no reason to be, it all feels a bit off.

"Am I going back to Bronzeford?"

"I should hope not and definitely not today."

Is she being vague on purpose? Because it is really annoying. I don't want to get snappy with the pretty woman being nice to me but still, I am tired in all the ways it is possible be tired, my patience is wearing rather thin. The man returns with a bottle of icy cold water and a can of Coke. My heart skips a beat, it feels like forever since I drank something that wasn't water or tea.

"Thank you," I croak. I gulp the water down but try not to look like an animal in the process. The relief to my throat is amazing.

"You are welcome. This is my associate, Agent Derrek Lawson," Lexi introduces.

"Agent?" I rasp.

"Yes. Agents of the security service, more commonly known as MI5."

Holy crap.

I want to laugh because that sounds ridiculous but the look on Lexi's face tells me that this is no joke. Now I am intrigued; they are being too nice to me, it doesn't feel like I am in trouble and really, what more trouble could I possibly be in? I really hope I haven't just jinxed myself.

"Okay, I will bite. What interest could MI5 possibly have in me?"

"A lot, actually. You are facing some serious charges but I am more interested in what brought you to Eastfield's Street that day and how you were able to take down 43 men, alone – as a civilian."

I flinch at the number, 43 lives taken by my hand, well. less if you include however many Alfred took down but still, I am definitely nervous now, a stillness creeps over me.

"Are you telling me that you don't know? I am sure there are police reports and if you already know the number, you have read them," I say evasively.

"Mac, we are not trying to trick you. You have a lot of reasons to distrust people, I understand that but we are not here to add charges to you." Lexi has quite a soothing voice, the kind of voice that makes you feel comfortable and free to talk, but I am not that trusting.

"Then why are you here? Why am I here?" I ask and Lexi holds my questioning stare; I want to look away but I also don't want her to think I am that easy to push around. So, I hold it and then I watch her hand reach inside her blazer.

"Because of this."

Lexi puts something on the desk in front of me, the small rectangular disk made of steel glares at me as she slides it towards me with her index finger. I feel a horrible swoop in my stomach and my heart skips a bit.

The triangle of truth.

My fingers warily reach out and touch it because it doesn't seem possible and then my face is in my hands. This is about Barrett, are people ever going to stop trying to get his location out of me? I rub my eyes and flinch as I accidently press too hard into the bruising left from the fight.

"Mac, are you alright?"

I uncover my face and stare wide eyed at the metal disk; the memories of the day Alfred took it out of me, the memories of Anna are like a punch to the gut, my eyes close trying to shake the images away and then it hits me.

"How did you get this?" I ask, a little snappy.

"Retired SAS officer Alfred Slone, brought it to my attention. He reported its national security threat to us. He hoped that if he came to us, then the information wouldn't fall into the hands of any potential Culling members that have infiltrated other government agencies. That is when I started asking questions about you, the daughter of the founding member of The Culling. Mr Slone filled in a lot of the blanks that your police records don't cover."

Suddenly my head is pounding and I feel dizzy; lack of food is getting to me. That and the whiplash of this weird-ass situation.

"If you did your homework, then you know I have never met the man and I don't know where he is," I groan.

"We know that. Like I said, Alfred filled in the blanks."

She is annoying me now with this elusive crap, I am out of patience.

"Listen, Lexi. I don't know what you do or don't know so I am just going to be frank with you. I can't remember the last time I showered, ate or slept, I have been carted in a van for hours without knowing where the hell I was going, after spending 5 days locked in the dark. So, respectfully – can you just tell me what the hell you want? You obviously want something because you are being nice to me." I speak firmly, being careful to keep my temper in check. I wait for Lexi to get annoyed at me but she just smiles at me, her eyes looking at me with pity and it pisses me off further.

"Do you like KFC?"

"I like anything that is food right about now," I grunt.

"Right, Derrek is going to get us all some dinner and while he is gone, I will explain everything."

I wonder if Derrek likes being bossed around like that; I like bossy. Bossy is sexy but I wouldn't appreciate being the food and drink delivery girl. Derrek scrambles out of the room without hesitation. Funny, to look at them both, I would have thought he would have been the one to do the talking. Is she good cop and he bad? Is that a real thing?

"Firstly Mac, I don't have any reason not to be nice to you. You don't trust me, I understand that. So, I am going to be as blunt with you as I can and then hopefully, that will earn me some trust. I know some of your history, I know you were kidnapped and for over two years you were held, tortured and questioned. I know that you spent time training, in hiding to try to track and bring down the people that took you. I know that those people tried to kill you more than once and they kidnapped someone you cared for to lure you to them, I know that you nearly died to bring them all down but these are just headlines.

"What is really important is, this situation – *your* situation, isn't black and white. You are not simply a murderer. Your back was against the wall, you acted to protect yourself and others from harm and with skill, I might add. How you survived all of this, I will never know. I can't imagine, the stress of doing this alone."

"I wasn't alone," I interrupt.

"I know that too," she says, smiling, "but it was you fighting the battle, with memory loss, trauma and men hunting you. It was you who took down Jakub Kaminski in the end, saving Alisha Cole and probably many others."

Has she rehearsed this? How does she remember all of the names?

"It didn't land me anywhere good though, did it?" I brood.

"No, it didn't and for what it is worth, I find it hard to believe you deserve the hand you have been dealt. As I understand it, you were planning on tracking down Barrett after you dealt with Jakub. Can I ask you why?"

"Because he has a plan to kill a lot of innocent people and he has already killed countless people. From what I know, he is a hard man to find and he has people working in many government agencies so, I couldn't just report him and hope for the best. Also, if it wasn't for him, I wouldn't have been taken. Why wouldn't I want to stop him?" I explain, and she laughs and it aggravates me.

"Why are you laughing at me?" I frown, my tone a little cutting.

"I am not really, not *at* you as such. Just at the fact that you say that like anyone would do that. Track down a terrorist and try to stop his cell before they attack our country. Most people would run away from the danger, not towards it," Lexi explains with a chuckle and then her face grows serious.

"What does it matter?"

"It matters because you are brave and you are clearly hard to kill. It matters because I have nothing but respect for who you are and what you have done. If you were a soldier, you would have a medal pinned on your chest, not be thrown in prison but to me – the only difference is a job title. I think, you have far too much potential to rot away in prison."

"But, I am in prison."

Lexi leans forward and she puts her hand on my wrist and I flinch.

"What if I told you, you didn't have to be?"

My heart drops into my stomach and my mouth dries up. Why the hell would she screw with me this way? Anger flares in my gut and I rip my wrist out of her hand.

"I would say that is a cruel and unwise joke to play. Stop messing with me."

Lexi gets up off of her chair and steps around the desk, she kneels down in front of me, her eyes intense and determined. She takes my hand and squeezes it, completely ignoring my flinching and tensing up.

"Mac, I am not messing with you," she says, squeezing my hand.

I stare at her wide eyed, I feel totally disorientated. She is messing with me; she has to be. Why would anyone do this to me? I start to panic and my hands shake and she feels it. She takes my hand in both of hers and the contact shocks me. I stare at her hand trying to understand and the shakes jolt me even harder.

"Mac... Look at me, hey! It's alright, just look at me." Lexi raises her voice and I jump, my eyes holding her gaze. "I am *not* messing with you. I can get you out but it isn't a get out of jail free card. We have been trying to bring down The Culling for decades; you are the first real opportunity we have had to do that, for a very long time. The deal is, you will work with me covertly, you make contact with Barrett and you will gain his trust. You become the member of The Culling that he wants, then you help me bring The Culling down from the inside. It will be dangerous and it won't be easy. We need the name of every member so we can not only dismantle it for good, but cut out any dirty cops and corrupt government officials there are too. If you succeed then not only will you remain free, but your record will be exonerated."

I choke on air; it is loud and embarrassing. Tears well in my eyes and I grip the arm of the chair for stability.

"Is this real? Like, I'm sorry but I can't... I want to believe you, but... you can understand why... Please, don't mess with me, I can't take it," I struggle fearfully.

"I promise you, Mac. I would never mess with you. This is real. So real, that if you accept this offer, you will sign a contract with us and be released... tonight."

Something inside me clicks. The fiery look in her eyes, the determination and the conviction melts my suspicion and I supress a sob; tears fall down my face as I try to control the mania of emotion that is fluctuating inside.

"Oh, God…" I mutter and Lexi laughs. "Can I stand up, please? I need a minute."

"Why are you asking permission?" Lexi frowns.

I get to my feet and walk to the other side of the room. I lay my head against the spongy cushioning of the wall and I let the tears fall, silently. I can't believe this is happening, this can't be real. I am feeling so many things all at once. Good things and bad. Mostly, I am still scared this woman is fucking with me. Lexi walks over to me silently.

"Are you alright, Mac?" she asks and I wipe my tears away and face her.

"Sorry… I uh… just find this all so hard to believe, I felt like I got what I deserved."

"Don't be, you have been through a lot. I would be worried if you weren't a little overwhelmed right now. Listen, between you and me, the powers that be only agreed to this because you are in a unique position of power that benefits them. For me personally though, I never thought you deserved to be locked away, you are not some thrill killer, you did what you needed to do to survive and acted with honour and bravery. I am happy I got to be the one to tell you that – not everyone thinks you got a fair shake."

"I don't know what to say." I stare at her, stunned.

"Say, you are going to help me bring the bastards down," she says intensely.

I search her face, waiting for the punchline to the joke but it never comes. Her eyes are determined and her expression steady and sure.

"Lexi, I will help you bring the bastards down; I will do whatever it takes," I say, matching her intensity.

"I know you will. Now will you please sit down before you fall down! You look dead on your feet. Derrek should be back any minute with food and while we all eat, I will go through everything with you."

***

Surreal. That is what this is; a couple of hours ago I was laying on the cold damp floor of segregation. Now, I am sat across from two secret agents of MI5, sharing KFC. Oh man, this is the best food I have ever tasted. The hairs on the back of my neck rise in satisfaction as I take my first bite. I listen to everything Lexi says carefully, as if my life depends on it – because it literally does.

Lexi will be my contact within MI5 but this mission is secret, even from a lot of the people within MI5 because if it goes tits up then they will act with plausible deniability. I will work for her, but I won't be coming in and out of the headquarters. Barrett will be watching me and any sign I am working against him, my cover gets blown and I screw the mission, either Barrett will kill me or I will end up back in prison. She will support and provide anything I need, discreetly.

The plan is for me to use the personal advert in the paper that he advised me to, in order to make contact with him; he will hopefully reach out to me and I have to somehow persuade him that I believe in his cause. There are rumours that he holds a 'wet list'. A black book of sorts and it contains the list of names of all his contacts. I have to gain his trust, get my hands on this wet list and get close enough to find out what attack he has planned and stop it.

I am warned over and over of the danger I will be putting myself in and I am acutely aware of it but to go back to prison, for me is a fate worse than death. Plus, I really do want to be the person to stop him. My intentions are not all together honourable, yes – I want to destroy the terrorist group that threatens innocent lives, but this is also personal. If it were not for Barrett, I would never have been kidnapped by Jakub.

"Barrett probably knows I have been arrested; how do I explain my sudden release from prison?" I ask.

"We plan on leaking a fake story to the media, it will hit the news tomorrow. Convictions overturned due to lack of evidence, a biased trial, that kind of thing – it really isn't that difficult for us to fluff it. The media is a good tool in situations like this. It will be your job to sell it. You will have to act like everything is normal, that means spending time with friends and family and continuing with routines that were normal to you before you were incarcerated."

The food is making me feel heavy and sleepy. That feeling you get when you eat too much Christmas dinner and you want to nap; I am fighting a food coma. I haven't eaten this much since I before I was in prison, before I fought Jakub even. What I wouldn't give for a power nap right about now.

"I didn't really have routine because I was in hiding from Jakub. My life was being trained by Alfred and trying to track Jakub. I cut ties with almost everyone but them, so I didn't endanger anyone else," I explain.

"Well I will be bringing Mr Slone in on this. Purely because, I need a go-between to help feed information back and forth. Your face is too well-known and would send alarm bells to Barrett and Mr Slone has decades of experience working in covert operations. He will be the perfect support for you, just as he always has been and he will also be able to work with me discreetly."

My stomach tightens and I groan, rubbing my eyes.

"What's wrong?" Lexi asks.

"I was hoping to leave him out of it," I say and by him, I mean Anna, of course. "How do you know he will agree to be involved?"

"Well from the way he was fighting in your corner and the way he spoke of you, he clearly thinks very highly of you. Plus, I already asked him," she explains and my heart begins to pound uncomfortably slow but forcefully.

Of course, she has.

"He was a part of the deal, Mac. I need you supported if this mission is going to succeed and it *must* succeed. Whatever it is nagging at you right now, you must let it go. Nothing is more important than this. I will do my best to support you from a distance but because of the covert nature of this, if it goes wrong, I cannot be tied to you in any way. That would have serious consequences for both myself and more importantly – MI5. I will be giving you instructors to mentor you, but you are going to need Alfred."

A nervous tingle of dread is swirling in my stomach; this is not what I wanted to hear but she is right, nothing is more important than stopping The Culling. Lives are at stake and so is my own future.

"I read you loud and clear, Lexi. Don't worry – I am committed to this. I will do whatever it takes, I understand the magnitude of the situation. I guess, it is all just a bit of a shock to the system, I still feel like a prisoner. Alfred visited me just over a week ago and I was horrible to him. Cutting ties with everyone, was my only way of surviving in there and he wasn't accepting it. I had to be cruel to be kind, I am a bit surprised he agreed to this."

"Mac, I spoke to him this morning. That man is nothing but relieved that you are getting out, in fact he shared some colourful language in his jubilant reaction. He was more than willing to step up. He seems to have some unfinished business with Barrett and I guess, once a soldier – always a solder," Lexi explains and I chuckle, tears pricking my eyes.

"That sounds like him," I say, smiling in spite of myself. He never stops having my back. No matter what I have done, his loyalty knows no bounds.

"So, for now, that is it. I think you need a couple of days' rest before we get to work. No offense but you look terrible, you have seventy-two hours to rest up and get your strength back. We have an apartment for you, you should be comfortable there. Unfortunately, your warehouse has been raided by the police and shut down so you can't return there but I did manage to retrieve some of your personal effects and they are at your apartment waiting for you."

Lexi places a set of keys and a mobile phone on the desk and I stare at them with wide, incomprehensible eyes.

"Are you ready?" Lexi asks, snapping me out of my trance.

"I am."

"Then I will call Alfred, he has requested to pick you up and take you home."

Home… I'm going home…

CHAPTER NINETEEN

Reunions

My stomach is quivering with butterflies as I await Alfred's arrival. Lexi is right, there is a lot at stake and I have to let go of things that could disrupt the job I now have to do but there is no getting away from it, I am nervous to see him. My leg jumps up and down, bouncing on the ball of my foot. Nervous energy tingles in my limbs, apprehension thick inside my chest. I sit at the desk, my head in my hands as it pounds painfully with exhaustion and I wait, trying to imagine what I am going to say when I see him.

Much worse than that, how long is it going to be before I have to face the second and much fairer Slone? If Alfred knows I am out, you can bet that Anna does too. I am not sure whether I want to get it over with or if I am too mentally spent to even consider it. Probably the latter. I want to see her as desperately as I don't want to. I jump out of my skin as the door knocks.

"Miss Holt, we have a Mr Slone at the front desk," the nasal-voiced woman informs.

"Send him in," Lexi requests and I take a deep breath, as deep a breath as my tight chest will allow anyway.

"Are you okay, Mac?"

"Yeah, just tired," I lie.

The door opens and I gasp a little, I hear a heavy footfall and then the door shutting. I get to my feet and slowly turn to face him. His face is unreadable and I feel a pang of guilty fear. I have no idea what to say to him and I have no idea what he is going to say. All I can do is hold his gaze, and brace myself. Then I see a smile start to play on his lips and I exhale.

"Come on, kid. Let's get you home," he says gruffly and I turn to Lexi, unsure. I still feel like I need permission to move and she smiles at me in understanding.

"Go get some rest, Mac. I will talk to you in three days," Lexi says and I nod at her, returning her smile and then I follow Alfred out of the room.

I feel like I am floating along, dazed. My legs move freely and every step feels too light. I am aware I am walking but I move on auto pilot. My mind feels overwhelmed with pressure, a little like I am underwater. Everything is slow, my hearing muffled and my eyes straining to stay open.

We reach the entrance to the front door and Alfred holds it open for me. I walk through, the bitter night air hitting my face and making me shudder but it is such a good feeling. I follow Alfred down the street, unable to speak as my senses are overloaded with the outside world. The cars zipping past, my lungs filling with clean, crisp air. The sight of the odd person walking their dog or queuing inside KFC. The feel of my arms swaying at my sides as I walk, free from the restrain of handcuffs is completely bizarre. I am overwhelmed and terrified the rug will be pulled any moment.

I spot the Land Rover and I freeze, my feet fixed to the spot. Pain rips across my chest as I see Anna, leant against it, her eyes widening as she sees me. I look down at the floor, as if that is somehow going to relieve the pain.

"You didn't really think I was going to be able to stop her coming, did you? Come on, kid, it's alright," Alfred encourages.

My heart rate quickens, I don't know if I am ready for this. I wish he had warned me but would it have really helped if he had? I manage to get my feet walking again; the closer I get to her the harder it is to breathe. When I reach the Land Rover, Alfred gets straight in the driver's side and shuts the door and I am left standing in front of Anna. I look up from the floor and meet her gaze with a tight jaw and clenched shaky fists. She takes a step towards me and I tense up and she looks at me warily, her eyes pained.

"Sorry... I am not used to... I am still in prison mode," I admit and it is true, but not the whole truth. Our last conversation in the hospital is playing over in my mind.

"Are you sure that is the only reason?" Anna askes, her expression pained. She looks away. I hate seeing that pain on her face. She turns to get inside the car, her hand on the handle.

"Wait..."

She stops, turns round and I keep my eyes on the floor.

"Come back," I croak and she strides towards me, her arms wrap tightly around me and she sobs into my neck.

"Oh, thank God. Thank God, you are okay; I was so scared, Mac," she sobs.

The conflict between wanting her close and wanting to push her away, rages on painfully but I breathe her in anyway. God, how I have missed her touch, her smell, her voice... Her. I stand rigid, unable to let myself completely let go but the coldness inside me is melting away and the reality of the last two long and lonely months start to hit me. It is as if her touch gives me the permission and safety to finally break. To be touched, after so much time alone is the best and worst feeling. My chest vibrates violently as the sobs begin.

"It's okay, it's over – I've got you," she soothes in my ear, kissing my cheek and I freeze. Pain rips in my chest, I pull away abruptly and back away from her, wiping my eyes.

"Mac..."

I can't let her be this person for me again. It is a road that only lands me in hurt. I may be out but she let me go, I can't keep needing someone who isn't mine to need.

"I can't... You can't." I struggle, trying to get control of myself.

"I made a mistake, I should never..." she begins but I don't want to hear it.

"No, you didn't... And you can't just... I can't talk about this, okay. Please."

I don't wait for her answer, I walk around the Land Rover and get into the back seat. I put my seat belt on and my arms cross against my chest, leaning my forehead against the cool glass of the window. Anna gets in the front seat and the engine rumbles. As the car moves the images outside the window become a colourful blur and I focus on that. It is quite dizzying; I remember doing it when I was a kid.

I honestly can't wait to get out, I can feel Anna's hurt from the back of the car. I can feel Alfred's eyes on me in the rear-view mirror. I just want some peace. We drive deeper into the centre of London and pull up the street where my new apartment is; I was expecting an apartment complex but it is a lone building. I recognise it from when I was looking for a flat when I first returned but the prices were insane. The area alone, I know is pricey.

"This is you, kid."

"Thank you." I fumble for my keys and pull the car door handle with a clunk.

"I will pick you up tomorrow around 10am, we need to talk things through," Alfred advises.

"Okay, tomorrow then," I croak.

I get out of the car and close the door behind me and my eyes pop as I take in the huge white building. It reminds me of Alisha's place, like a flat pack home from Ikea. Modern and contemporary, all the edges sharp with white panelling and sheet glass. It has two levels; the top has a glass guarded balcony that has outdoor seating. This apartment looks more like a house and there is more glass than there are walls.

Fish bowl.

I walk up the drive and come to the white front door; the handle is about half the length of the door. I slot the key in and pull, the door is heavy and I smell paint the moment the door opens. I am stunned, everything is so clean and bright. All the walls are white or glass but there are accents cleverly placed, flashes of bright colour that enrich the place. The lower level is open plan, straight ahead of me is the living room area, the sofas arranged in a squared C shape. The opening facing an open fireplace built into an exposed brick wall and above it, a huge flat-screen TV.

My eyes sweep right and my legs move towards the kitchen; the surfaces are cold and smooth black and white marble. The cupboards shining gloss black. I go to the fridge, reach for the handle and hesitate, I almost feel like I am about to do something wrong. I haven't opened a fridge in a long time. I shake the ridiculous thought away and open it. It is stocked with food and I find a bottle of Jack Daniels inside with a note attached and I smile.

Welcome home, Mac.

L x

I wonder how she knew this was my favourite, I guess she is a spy. I pour myself a generous glass, as soon as I am able to find a cupboard with glasses in and turn to the left side of the room. There is a spiral staircase which again, has more glass that spirals around it beneath the hand rail. It looks like the stairs are floating. I climb them and come to a very elegant bedroom, more glass, white with flashes of deep purple.

The bed is the most inviting sight I have seen in a long time, it is gloss white and a four poster, it is screaming out for me to jump on its cloud-like bounciness, but I resist because it is huge and white and clean looking and I must be disgusting. This room is grand and actually rather sexy, then my eyes spot something I think I recognise over at an ornate mirrored dresser. I walk over to it and feel a pang deep in my chest. I pick it up, feeling almost like it can't be real. It still has the same effect on me when I see it, as it did the day I first saw and took pictures of its full-size version in Alfred's yard. I run my fingers across the lettering 'Blessed mess'.

I put the statue back and start looking through the drawers of the dresser and my heart leaps when I find my own clothes neatly stacked inside. It has me excitedly searching other drawers and the built-in wardrobe and I almost squeal when I find my beloved combat boots. I move across the hardwood floor and open the doors to the balcony and it makes me wobble a little when I see that the floor of it is made from toughened glass. I tread unnecessarily carefully as I walk the balcony, it runs around the entire apartment in a big square; out front is a seating area with nicer chairs than I had inside my old flat.

Finally, I make my way back inside and discover the bathroom. I could cry, my eyes widen at the sight of the massive walk-in shower, gleaming with clean shine. I throw the prison-issue uniform off and giggle in pure excitement. I walk into the shower and feel the powerful water beat down on me and I moan, I am going to have the longest hot shower, with no one watching over my shoulder and I won't even have to wear flip-flops. This is amazing. My body tingles with pleasure. I stay in there long after I have washed myself, not once but twice because it feels so damn good.

By the time I get out of the shower, I am lobster red and my fingertips are wrinkled like prunes. The time has finally come, I get to lay in an actual real-life bed. I pull back the heavy duvet and slide in and it feels even better than I could have ever possibly dreamed. I am not a person that usually spends time naked, not since my body was so scarred up but the sensation of the silky sheets gliding over my skin is wonderful. This place is pure luxury, everything feels amplified because in prison I had nothing, no pleasure, no freedom and everything was cold and grim. I would have been happy with any place that didn't mean I had to sleep three feet from my toilet, but this place is a palace.

I lay in bed, the whiskey warming my insides and my muscles finally starting to relax after what seems like forever. How is it possible that so much has changed in just one day? This all feels so unreal, although seeing Anna and Alfred brought it home a little, the pain was a wake-up call. A swift kick in the butt by reality but I still feel like this is some elaborate dream that I will wake up from any moment.

I know I hurt her, but I can't have that closeness with her anymore. She is a part of my life and I want that but she wanted to let me go, and move on. I have accepted that as best as I can but if I am going to be around her, then I need that distance or I am just going to keep getting hurt and I can't bear that. Nothing can get in the way of what I have to do now, I have to be able to work with Alfred, which means I have to find a place of peace with Anna.

All I have to do now is track down an evil villain, hell-bent on bringing on hell and damnation to the world and bring down his killer empire, sounds simple enough. I wonder what tomorrow will bring. I am not looking forward to going back to the farm, to face a whole barrage of memories but I guess I can't really avoid it. Tomorrow, the media will announce my release and I am sure everything will be very… different.

Mum is going to flip her lid, that is for sure. I will have to make sure I see her as soon as I can, she is going to be mad that I cut her off while I was gone. Hopefully my return will soften the lecture I am in for. Barrett will know I am free; I wonder how long it will take him to track me down. Whatever happens, I will take him down or die trying. I am never going back to prison again.

***

The next morning, I awake feeling stiff like I have slept too long and looking at the time, I see that I have. Alfred is due in 30 minutes and I haven't even left the bouncy heaven of my bed yet. I whip round, trying to find clothes in a home I don't yet know. I pick up the prison-issue clothes and throw them unceremoniously into the bin and it feels good. I'm finally about to have a latte, brewed from the very fancy coffee machine in the kitchen when the doorbell sings. I dash to the door to let Alfred in and am faced with Anna, standing on the doorstep and I cringe.

"Can I come in?" she asks.

"Um… Sure."

"Wow," she says with awe, her eyes widening at the sight of the apartment.

"Yeah, I know. Subtle, isn't it?" I reply awkwardly. "Uh… Can I get you a drink or anything?" I ask, feeling more uneasy by the second.

"No, I am fine, thank you. I really just came to pick you up but I wanted to talk to you first. Now I am here, I don't know if I can."

Anna wanders over to the sofas, her eyes curiously wandering over the apartment. She takes a seat on the sofa and I sit opposite her. She is looking at the coffee table with too much interest and I feel more nervous the longer I wait for her to spit out whatever she has to say.

"What did you want to talk to me about?" I ask warily and her eyes leave the table and look at me.

"You look better... Not quite like you yet, but better. I think it is going to take you fifty of Pa's bacon rolls and a lot more sleep before you look like you again," she says as her eyes survey me, making me feel embarrassed of how rough I look.

"It's prison, princess, not summer camp – it has an effect but it looks worse than it is, I'm fine. That was a valiant effort though, on your part... Trying to avoid the subject. Not quite good enough though," I say playfully and she smirks but it falls from her face quickly.

"Pa told me that you didn't say a word the whole time you were in there."

"I didn't have anything to say. He was the first person I spoke to and that was only because it was that or the psych ward. If that is what this about, I didn't speak to anyone, the only way I could survive was letting everyone go, including myself. Your letter wasn't the only letter I didn't reply to."

Anna leans forward, crossing her arms and leaning them on her knees. I can see she is struggling with what to say, trying to be careful not to say the wrong thing.

"No, it's not that. After the hospital, I wouldn't have expected you to want to see or speak to me ever again," Anna says, her voice quiet and childlike.

I feel myself stiffen; so that is what this is about. The one thing I really don't want to talk about, I don't want to drag this back up but I need to get to a place with her where we can be around each other. I have to work with Alfred, and they are a package deal.

"I wasn't mad at you, I told Alfred to tell you that, to tell you that you did the right thing. You did what was best for you, I didn't take it well because I was a mess and I didn't agree with your reasons, but I had been telling you for a long time that you would be better off far away from me, how could I be mad at you for finally seeing sense?"

"Ugh!" Anna growls in frustration, covering her face. "I knew it."

"You knew what?"

"From the moment the words came out my mouth, I knew I was making a massive mistake. You spent so long trying to persuade me that you were bad. The way I turned my back on you, the way I said it, the timing – I knew that I was solidifying that inaccurate thought for you. Telling you it was true, when I

364

never felt that way about you. You are not bad, Mac, and after spending so long trying persuade you of that, I went and made you believe it even more!" Anna snaps, her voice coming out in a fast ramble.

"Anna, you have got to let yourself off the hook. I really don't want to talk about this, it is done, you got what you asked for so I don't see why it matters."

"It matters because now you are back and you are pushing me away again, only this time you are doing it because I told you to. I told you, I wanted to let you go, so you did and now you are always going to keep me at arm's length. I can see it in the way you look at me, you are back but you don't want me anywhere near you, you don't even want to look at me," Anna rants.

"What was I supposed to do?! That is what you wanted! Me coming back doesn't change anything. You said it, you were letting me go and moving on, knowing I was going to prison for life! As far as you knew, you would never see me again and yet you still had to make damn sure I was clear you were done with me, before they took me away! So, it obviously meant a lot to you! Why has that suddenly changed just because I am back now!?" I snap, anger feverishly burning at my face.

She can't just go back, she can't un-ring a bell. Anna holds my gaze; her eyes turn from hurt to fearful so quickly. I wish I could understand what is going on in her head.

"I never should have said what I did, I… can't blame you for feeling the way you do. Whatever has happened between us, you deserved better than that. I wish… I…" Anna struggles, her voice breaking. "I should go."

Tears well in her eyes and she gets to her feet, walking away without another word. Guilt pangs in my chest and I get to my feet. I don't want to get hurt anymore but that doesn't mean I want to hurt her.

"Anna, stop," I blurt and she freezes but she doesn't turn round. I take a few steps closer but I keep my distance.

"I don't want you to hold on to this, I am not mad at you, I am sorry. While I was in there… I…" I struggle, huffing at myself and she turns around taking a step closer, her eyes warm and concerned.

"Tell me… Please."

My chest tightens, I want so badly to tell her how much I wanted her, how she never left my thoughts but, no matter what she regrets she let me go for a reason, I can't just shake that.

"It hurt, so much to even… *think* about the people I had lost. I let you go because you asked me to, yes. But even if you hadn't – I would have done it anyway, because while I missed everyone, the loneliness, the pain of needing…" I look at the floor, knowing I can't finish that sentence and I see Anna take another step forward, making me tense.

"It was enough to destroy me. So, you can let yourself off the hook, I had to let you go, you just did it first. I had to do things to survive… that have left their mark, I have learnt who I really am and I am not a person you should want to be close to. I am not just distant because I am hurt, something inside me broke, I don't trust myself anymore and I don't know if I will ever…" I falter, the pain in my chest is too much, I just want to hold her and I know that I need to find a way to stop wanting that.

"Mac…" Anna chokes and I flinch as she closes the gap between us and her hands find mine, my eyes are on the floor and I can feel her eyes on me.

"You are not a monster; I don't know what happened to you in there but it isn't hard to guess at least some of it." Anna hesitantly brings her hand up to my face and gently traces the bruising to my eye and temple, the new scar from the stitches to my eyebrow and I flinch, but I don't pull away; my mind says I should but my heart won't allow me to.

"You are bruised, you are exhausted, you are thin and you are shell shocked. Whatever did happen, you obviously had to fight to survive it and if you hadn't, you wouldn't be here. Whatever you think has broken inside of you, it will heal again. You are not lost; you are home and so many people are glad for that. I am so glad for that, I just… I wish that you being home meant that you were going to let me in, but I can already feel you shutting me out. I understand, it is my own fault, I just hope you know that is not what I want."

I look up at her, wishing I could understand. She doesn't make any sense to me anymore; the difference between the Anna now, and the Anna at the hospital is so conflicting, I don't know what to believe anymore.

"What do you want?" I ask.

"Lots of things, most of which I know I will never get. Right now, I just want…"

I watch her struggle, wondering if she is ever going to finish her sentence; she doesn't look at me, she just looks at her hand holding mine. It reminds me of when I attempted to hug her for the first time at the warehouse and suddenly, it isn't the only similarity.

Anna pulls me by the wrist drawing me closer and lays my hand on the small of her back. My body tenses up, only unlike the time at the warehouse it isn't fear making me freeze up, it is pain. The pain of needing her as much as I want to push her away. The instinct to protect myself from more hurt is as powerful as the want I have to be near her. She steps into me, her eyes still not meeting mine, her arms wrapping around me hesitantly. She nuzzles her face finding the crook of my neck and I can't seem to move, I can't hold her close, nor can I pull away. Her hands slide up my back, pulling me a little closer, her lips move up to my ear.

"Right now, I just want this. From the moment they took you away, it is all I have wanted. I know you might not ever let me in again, but that doesn't mean I will ever stop trying to show you that you can. I won't let you down again, I promise. I am so sorry this happened to you, you are not a monster, you never deserved this and I will never be able to thank you, for the way you protected me – I just wish I could have done the same for you," Anna says softly.

She keeps holding me and I am losing the fight not to hold her back; the smell of her candy like perfume is both enticing and warming, her breath tickling my neck as I tremble slightly from the fight that rages on. I lay my other hand awkwardly around her back.

"You don't need to thank me, Anna. No matter the cost I would have still made the same choices, you don't owe me anything and I still respect the choices you made, you don't need to feel guilt for them or obligation to me, there is none. I can't pretend to completely understand, it feels like you are only telling me half of the truth but, I do understand why you did what you did and it is okay."

For what must be mere seconds, I let go of the tense freeze in my arms and I pull her close, my hand sliding up her back onto the back of her neck and she shivers. I kiss the top of her head and then let her go, taking a step back. For a moment I see pain in her eyes, then she rights herself so quickly, I wonder if I imagined it.

"The irony of you saying that to me," Anna says with a smirk. "I can't tell you the whole truth, I would lose you and I am not willing to do that again."

"You don't know that, girl," I argue softly.

"I do. Listen, I have something for you. I don't know if you still want to wear it but, it is yours. I have been wearing it the whole time you have been gone." Anna puts the bangle in my hand; the memories swirl vividly.

"I guess, I just want you to know, no matter what, you still have a home there with us. I have screwed up a lot and now I am paying for it but I can't lose you again, Mac. I can't tell you how hard it was, it drove me crazy knowing you were suffering in there every day and I couldn't do anything and... I missed you."

Oh God, she is so hard to resist when she looks at me like that; the tingles erupt inside of me and it is so hard to stop myself from kissing her. I hold my wrist out and hand her the bangle.

"Thank you, for looking after it for me but... I would love to have it back," I say and her face lights up. She pulls the sleeve up and gasps a little at the sight of my wrists. The bruises and indentation marks from the handcuffs are still very present.

"It doesn't hurt, don't worry," I assure her. Anna clenches her jaw and puts the bangle on my wrist and she looks up at me, smiling the bright smile that I have missed.

"Back where it belongs," I say, smiling back at her. "Anna, you shouldn't have to pay for anything. We all screw up, I have dropped some uber-sized fuck-ups, I am sure you remember. I missed you too, you know. Things may have changed but you still mean more to me than you know."

"That is nice to hear. We should probably get going, leave your mansion," she teases.

"Hey, don't act like you aren't dying to watch a movie by my open fireplace!"

"Show off! Okay... Yes, that was the first thing I saw, I will be honest," she admits and I turn to her, my face more serious.

"I hope one day you can tell me the truth, be honest about more than just fireplace envy."

Anna catches me off guard, she moves in close keeping eye contact and the desire in my chest purrs intensely, then she moves to my ear at the last second.

"Be careful what you wish for, Mac," she whispers and then she walks out the front door and I am momentarily paralysed.

***

We jump into Anna's car and she revs up the engine. Everything is still feeling a little surreal. I half expected to wake in prison this morning to find that that yesterday was all a dream. I stare out of the window, and see that the world is still there, feeling overwhelmed by all of its colour and movement.

"You want to go anywhere before we head to the farm?" Anna asks.

"What do you mean?"

"Mac, you just got out of prison and before you did that, you defeated a small army led by Jakub. He is gone, you are free, you don't have to hide anymore."

Oh my God… How did I not even think of that? My jaw drops.

"Wow…" I say, stunned.

Anna loses it, she is howling with laughter and then I am laughing too. God, it feels good to laugh, to be outside again and yes, I admit, it feels good be with her.

"Oh man, I didn't even think. To be honest everything still feels a bit unreal, like the fact that I was able to open a fridge last night. Never mind that there was food in it – I was excited that I could open a fridge door, that the toilet isn't three feet from my head and I didn't have to ask for toilet paper. Oh, and man you should see my bed, it is amazing…"

I pause because I catch sight of her raising her eyebrow and then she laughs at me.

"That didn't come out quite right, did it?" I say, cringing, but laughing too.

"I can't answer that for you," she says, blushing.

Yeah, this keeping my distance thing, going fucking brilliant.

"So, tell me Mac-Attack… While you were locked away or even before that, what were some of the things you wanted to do?"

I think about that. I missed the world so much. It feels like I have been in prison for a long time. First the boat, then losing my memory and being scared to go anywhere, then having to go into hiding from Jakub, then prison. That is a lot of time to fantasise over what I couldn't have.

"Honestly, I could tell you a list for an hour, girl – I still wouldn't run out. I missed people, like smiling people, strangers. Opportunities, exploring… *Possibility*. I missed the cinema – although you probably gave me the best cinema experience ever. Just even… walking around outside, there was none of that in the boat and 3 hours per week in the prison yard felt like nothing. Clean clothes, showering, hearing music or going to a bar and watching a gig. The freedom to go into a shop and buy a new pair of Converse. Oh, food, I always missed food… God," I ramble and I look at Anna and smile, a little embarrassed.

"You lost a lot."

"Yeah well. I gained a lot too," I say, smiling, realising I have made her sad.

"I don't know how you got through prison. I don't think I would have done."

"Sure, you would have done. You would have had a prison wife named Pam. A burly woman with curly hair and facial tattoos, she would protect you as long as you gave her pudding, and by pudding, I mean…" I wink at her suggestively, "cos there's no actual pudding in prison, at least there wasn't in mine."

"Oh gross! You are so mean! Great, you have ruined pudding for me now, I will never again be able to think about pudding, without thinking about sex. What do you have to say for yourself?" she pouts.

I howl, I can't remember the last time I laughed so much. My face actually aches from smiling. I feel like all the tension between us is finally starting to lift. It is still hard; it is still complicated but we can still have this and despite the pain, it feels good.

"Is it bad that I kind of want some chocolate cake now?" I ask.

"Are you serious?"

"Yeah, I totally am. Alfred loves cake, I need to butter him up a bit. I was pretty harsh to him when he came to visit. Cake can't hurt my case," I explain.

"He wasn't mad at you, you know. He was shell shocked when he came back. It was hard for him to see you like that and from what he told me of how you were, I don't blame him but he was upset, not mad," Anna reassures.

Ugh, great, that is worse somehow, I definitely need cake.

***

We stop at Cutter and Squidge, a quirky little cake shop with artificial grass features on the walls. I can't fathom why this is a thing, it looks ridiculous. They have a hugely tempting array of different pastries, cakes and biscuits. I really am like a kid in a candy shop, excited to be out in the world. How strange it is to be able to do this again and not even feel the need to hide or look over my shoulder. I spend too much money and I definitely buy too much cake but I don't care. I am enjoying myself.

We get back in the car and set back off to the farm and I am feeling more human than I have for a long time. I feel kind of giddy but there is this gnawing in my stomach. It is quiet, but it's there. I feel like this isn't my life, like I am borrowing someone else's and any minute they are going to say, "I think that's about enough, don't you?"

"Mac, are you okay?"

"Yeah, just trying to adjust. This still doesn't feel real, I keep waiting for the rug to be pulled. I was convinced I was going to wake up to the guard yelling, *'6642, on your feet, it's time for work detail.'* I am sure it will stop eventually but it hasn't yet. It is a bit of a head fuck."

"6642?" she asks, with an almost identical disgusted expression that Alfred had when he heard the guard call me it.

"Not you as well. Seriously? There are much worse things in prison than being called a number. Alfred didn't like it either, it never really bothered me. Made it easier, if anything. I had to let go of Mac, not being called by my name made it feel easier to accept that."

"What was the worst thing?" she asks softly.

"You don't want to know, girl."

"You don't have to tell me, but I wouldn't ask, if I didn't want to know," Anna replies. I can hear the sadness she is trying to hide. I know me shutting her out is hurting her, I don't want that, but I also don't want to let her too close either. How do I find that balance with her?

"Okay... The segregation cell, you get put there if you misbehave in some way. I was put in there twice. It is completely dark, no windows, no sound and nothing but a sink, toilet and a foam mat and it smells like vomit. The first time I was in there for seven days and I thought I was completely losing it; it screws with your mind. The second time I was there, on the fifth day I was pulled out and told I was being shipped out. That's when I ended up at the police station with MI5. That was the worst thing about prison for me because once you are there, it feels never ending and you only have your thoughts for company and mine, were pretty dark."

"That sounds... like absolute hell, Mac," she says with tight eyes.

"Sorry, you did ask."

"I did and I am a little shocked that you answered me. You always censor yourself and I get why but even when it is hard to hear, I like hearing what is real, what is you. You shouldn't feel the need to hide, don't feel like you have to on my account."

I look down at my hands and nod; I get the feeling she is trying to show that she is there for me and I appreciate that she is, I just don't think I can let her be. Needing her in prison was the worst pain I have ever endured, the idea of letting her even halfway close enough for me to get hurt that way again, is terrifying and not something I am looking to repeat.

***

We pull up to the farm and I am hit with so many memories, it is like an overload of emotion. Both good and bad, I lost and gained so much here.

Coming back, hurts just as much as I feared it would but it also feels good and I wasn't expecting that. Seeing the place, feels a lot like coming home. I guess this place was more my home than anywhere else for quite a long time. It is comforting to see that some things haven't changed.

I step out of the car, and the aroma of the smoky fire makes me smile. I have missed that fire even if there are memories attached that sting. We walk up the drive and into the farm house and I see the dreaded dining table that became my makeshift operating table, too many times. The sound of Anna shouting for Alfred snaps me out of it. I hear movement coming down the stairs and my stomach twists nervously. I stand, feeling awkward while Anna and Alfred sit at the table.

"Sit down, kid. You are making the place look untidy," Alfred mutters gruffly and I do as I am told, but it just makes me feel more awkward because he is just staring at me with sad eyes and I don't know what to say, then Anna giggles.

"God, it is so awkward. Seriously guys, someone has to say something. We are all getting older here." I smile, thankful she broke the ice.

"I am sorry I was such a jerk to you, Alfred. I know you were only trying to help but I wasn't in a place where you could, where anyone could."

"I get it, kid. I pushed when I shouldn't have. It just wasn't easy for me to leave a man behind. Didn't sit well, I just wanted to get you out of there but I couldn't."

"Actually, you did."

"What are you talking about?" he asks, frowning.

"Lexi told me that you gave her the flash drive, she told me you fought my corner, told her everything. Whatever you said to her made her take a closer look at me. If you hadn't done that, she wouldn't have had me released. You did get me out, brother. I am only here because of you."

I watch as I see his wise eyes well up and he smiles and I flood with relief.

"Well I can't take all the credit. You fought your ass off on Eastfield's Street. It may not have ended how we all wanted but you sure got Lexi's attention. That sure was something to watch!" Alfred booms excitedly.

We all laugh, the tension of the past starting to lift. We all have been hurt by this in one way or another but somehow, we have all found ourselves back together again, laughing and joking about it, healing. We eat cake and swap war stories; it is strange but fun to hear it from their perspectives.

"Have you seen this?" Alfred asks.

He hands me the morning newspaper and I cringe. There on the front page is my face, although it barely looks like me. The photograph is the mug shot that was taken after I was taken from the hospital. My eyes are cold and distant. I remember vaguely when they took that, it was right before the strip search that sent me off the rails. I brace myself, my eyes falling on the headline shouting from the page and I read.

MCKENNA SCOTT ACQUITTED – ANOTHER LUCKY ESCAPE.
Femme fatale or fallen angel?

McKenna Scott, 32, was today released from Bronzeford Prison after the London high court ruled there was insufficient evidence to convict her. Scott, a photographer that resides in Central London, was facing life without parole for the massacre that was carried out on Eastfield's Street. Her charges stacked up to include multiple counts of murder, crimes against humanity, possession of deadly weapons and destruction of public property.

The judge was heard to say in his closing statement, "There were stunning flaws in this case that were impossible to ignore – Miss Scott is innocent till proven guilty and the prosecution failed to persuade the court of her guilt, beyond a reasonable doubt. We reserve the right to re-try Miss Scott if new evidence comes to light, but as it stands – she is a free woman."

Michael Abbott, Scott's defence attorney, made this statement after Scott's release. "The spotlight on this case has resulted in a rushed investigation, as means of satisfying media thirst for a rapid conviction. The effort to search for substantial truth was thin at best and has, as a result, seen my client serve time in prison for a crime she didn't commit. I am satisfied that I managed to correct this miscarriage of justice."

Big questions still remain about a case so shrouded in mystery. Is Scott misunderstood? Was she just in the wrong place at the wrong time? Or is she – as we all feared, damaged from her time in captivity and now as dangerous as the people who took her? Only time will tell but one thing is for sure, this won't be the last we hear of Miss McKenna Scott.

"Your boss didn't pull any punches, did she?" Alfred speaks, warily.

"Wow. Did she have to be so harsh?!" Anna interjects.

"She couldn't have made it believable if she hadn't of been harsh. I am actually quite impressed. She knows exactly what she is doing," I commend.

"You are okay with this?" Anna asks and I shrug.

"Not really bothered, it isn't like I didn't commit the crimes. The only thing that worries me is the fact that this is how my mum has found out that I am back. I will have to go see her in a bit. Problem is, I don't have a car… Again," I pout.

"I will drop you off, kid, I need to head into town anyway."

"That would be great, thanks fella."

We seem to have broken the ice. We haven't really spoken about what is to come, but we all know that inevitable conversation is soon to come. Today I found some kind of peace with them both, a place to move forward from.

"Do you want me to pick you up tomorrow? I can take you out car shopping?" Anna asks.

"That would be great, thank you. What time?"

"Same time as this morning? We could get breakfast, seeing as you still haven't been anywhere much and then I can drop you off at the car lot," Anna suggests.

"Oo, nice. I like how you're thinking, girl. See you in the morning then."

I jump into the Land Rover with Alfred and we set off to my mum's. I honestly can't wait to see her but I am nervous as hell too. She has been hurt enough, I am not sure what I am going to say to her or how honest I should be. There is only so much I am allowed to tell her.

"You and Savannah seem to be getting on okay," Alfred insinuates.

"We are trying to; we have no choice but to try to move on from what has happened. We have to be able to work together."

"Kid, you really think it is going to be that simple? You forget, I know how you feel about her."

"It doesn't matter how I feel, we have a job to do. I can't afford to complicate that and anyway, things haven't changed that much. She's still the girl who told me she wanted to let me go and move on. You saw how that broke me. So, I let her go. That is the end of it, so let's just leave it at that, okay, brother?"

"If you say so, kid."

***

Things go about as well as I expected with Mum. She opened the door and burst into tears, then got mad at me, then more tears, then mad at me again. I take it on the chin because, I hate that I have put her through so much.

"You could have called me, even once just to let me know you were okay. You went to prison and you just disappeared, like that wasn't hard enough for me the first time, McKenna."

"I know and I am sorry, Mum, I just couldn't face it. It was hard to adjust to that place. I did miss you, every day. I am sorry I have put you through so much," I grovel.

"You have, you are making me prematurely grey, it is unforgivable," she jokes, smiling slightly. "None of it was intentional, I don't blame you. I am so relieved you are okay; I am just worried. They let you out to lead you like a lamb for slaughter. Who are these people? Your father is a mad man, how can they expect—"

"Mum, I can't tell you everything, I am not allowed, but I am not alone in it. It won't be that dangerous and if it means I don't go back to prison... I would do just about anything."

The worry on her face is horrible to see but I can see that I am finally getting through to her. I hope one day, I won't have to bring that worry to her face anymore. She needs a holiday from the hell that it must be, being my mother.

"Will you promise me that this time, you are going to keep talking to me? I understand why you are doing this; I don't have to like it but I don't like you in prison either, so I understand. It would be a whole lot easier to take, if you wouldn't keep shutting me out."

"I promise, Mum. I am back and I will keep you in the loop this time."

"Thank you. Now... let me make you some food, you are far too skinny, McKenna, do you even eat anymore?" I laugh and I feel a weight lift off of my chest. Now that sounds more like my mum.

It was so good to spend time with her. I enjoyed toasted cheese sandwiches; no one makes them like my mum. The oozy cheese and crispy toast were enough to make me feel like a kid again. She told me about her new promotion at work and surprisingly she has even started seeing someone; her excitement makes me glow inside and it is nice to know she isn't alone.

"He sounds like a good man; he better be or he is going to have one pissed daughter to deal with," I say, winking.

I give her a big hug at the door. There really is nothing like a mum hug and I promise to see her again soon. I leave feeling lighter and ready for the walk back to my apartment. I walk along Mum's curved pathway that weaves in and out of her flower beds, smiling freely and with a spring in my step.

"It has been a long time since I have seen that smile."

I look up, already knowing who it is, I would know that voice anywhere. Alisha stands leant against her car parked just opposite Mum's house. I walk over to her and return the easy smile that she is giving me.

"How did you find me?" I ask.

"Well, I called your mum when I saw the paper. She said you were popping round and when. I figured if I waited out here long enough, I would catch you."

"You figured right."

"Do you think, you could come for a drive with me? I have some things I would like to say," Alisha asks.

What is it with the women in my life all needing to talk? Must there be so much talk? Ugh. I can't deny it is good to see her but I am exhausted from all of the talking. I knew that I would eventually see her, I wanted to know that she was okay but I wasn't expecting it to be so soon.

"Sure, let's go."

I get in her car; it has that new car smell. The leather is smooth, the engine so quiet compared to what I am used to, it hardly feels like we are moving at all.

"Where are we going?" I ask.

"Where do you want to go?"

"I don't mind, as long as it isn't too far to walk back to my apartment. I don't have a car at the moment."

"We could just go to my place; it isn't far from here and I have Dr Pepper."

"How do you know I like Dr Pepper?"

"At the hotel you asked me; if I could only drink one drink for the rest of my life what would it be? I told you and then I asked you, you told me Dr Pepper, hands down. I think you used the words 'sex in my mouth' describing it. You also told me you like it as mixer with Jack Daniels," she explains and I chuckle.

"That sounds like me. I guess there are still some things I don't remember. What was your answer?" I ask her, trying but failing to remember.

"Strawberry…"

"Daiquiri, that's it! – I remember now." I look over to her; she is smiling with her eyes on the road. I remember thinking when I kissed her, she tasted like strawberries. The memory gives me unhelpful tingles and I shake them away.

We pull up outside her house and she parks the car on a gravel driveway; she actually doesn't live far from my mum's place at all, or my new apartment. The house is modest and much different to the appearance of the old place that she had, where her office was. This house looks much more suburban and traditional. The brick is exposed and smooth, the garden well-kept and minimalist, it even has a white picket fence.

I get out of the car and follow her to the front door which is a rich mahogany colour that matches all the window frames. Alisha leads me inside, through a small hallway and into a kitchen. It is large and very country style. The cupboards warm oak wood, it reminds me of Alfred's kitchen, only bigger.

"This doesn't look anything like the sort of home I would picture you in," I report.

"Well, it is just a rental. This is the first place I have been since I didn't have to run anymore. It is just temporary, until I figure out what I want to do next but after a lot of cold hotel rooms, I like the warmth of this place. You are right though; it is not my style at all."

Alisha hands me a glass of cold Dr Pepper, I take a large gulp; the caramelly fizz makes my insides smile and I grin.

"Oh, holy hell, that is good," I breathe and she giggles.

"You are a little too excited about that."

"Hey, I just got out of prison, you don't know how much I have missed this, I am just getting reacquainted. Give me a minute, will you?" I joke.

"Would you like me to give you a moment alone?" she teases, smirking at me and we both laugh.

I put the drink down and lean against the kitchen counter, with my back turned to her. I can feel her watching me and it is making me nervous. I don't know what she is going to say to me and right now I am exhausted by all of the words. I am exhausted by everything. It is good to see her, but I feel on edge. Seeing her brings up so many memories about the battle of Eastfield's Street. I feel... breakable.

"Are you okay, Mac the knife?" she asks. I turn and look at her, my heart heavy.

"I don't know anymore."

"I didn't think so," Alisha replied.

"What do you mean?"

"You talk a good game, you joke, you smile, it is easy to think you are okay but your eyes give you away, they always have and right now, they have a sadness in them that I have never seen before and I was your therapist," she explains softly, smiling at me warmly but I feel defensive, I don't like the idea that I am that easy to read.

"Why should I be sad? I am out, free, alive."

Alisha walks a few steps closer and leans against the counter opposite me. Her expression plain, her poker face still going strong and right now, I appreciate that.

"But what did it cost to get you here, Mac?"

The question hits me right where it hurts and I look at the floor, my hands grip the counter, white knuckled. My mind flashes with hellish images; pleading eyes of fear, a wedding band on a dead man's hand, a melting face, a crescent-shaped scar on a whiskery cheek, my reflection in my prison cell mirror, my face on the front page of the newspaper, Anna's hurt eyes as she said she was letting me go.

"Everything," I choke.

Alisha steps forward, she moves slowly and carefully and stands just in front of me, hesitating. I can feel her watching me, waiting for me to react. When I don't, she steps into me, she wraps one arm around my waist and the other on the back of my neck, pulling my face into her neck and I let her. My arms respond, pulling her to me and her breath shakes.

She doesn't say anything for a while, she just holds me there and I am in no hurry to move because while she has hold of me, I feel much less like the monster that I know I have become. Because she knew me before the darkness overcame me, before I snuffed out all of those lives, before I enjoyed the feeling of killing the man that forced himself on me, before I wanted to hurt that girl in prison. Holding her means that the cost of my soul, at least meant something.

"I will never forget the moment you walked into that building. You were bloody, beaten and determined to save me and I thought, if she dies trying to save me – then the world will never make sense to me again. Mac Scott who is pure of heart, who is righteous and loving, cannot possibly die for someone like me. I don't think anything has ever scared me as much as that thought did."

"There is nothing pure about my heart anymore, I killed a lot of people getting to you, you can't just wash that off. They are all with me, wherever I go," I state, my voice as hollow as I feel and Alisha leans back a little, forcing me to look at her.

"If that was the case then you wouldn't be in this much pain. Remorse, regret, pain over killing people that were trying to kill you – that shows your humanity, it shows that you have a soul. Evil people, they don't feel what you are feeling right now," she soothes.

I look into her eyes, wanting so much to believe her words. I wish it was that easy, but inside I feel the cold reality of what I have done and it is a lonely place. I am back, I am with the people I have missed so much and yet I have never felt so alone.

"I am so sorry, Mac. If I hadn't…"

"You have nothing to be sorry for. Regardless of what I feel I would still have made the same choices. It was the only way to keep everyone safe, myself included. It isn't on you."

"It isn't on you either," Alisha says, her eyes full of tears.

"What's wrong?"

"It's nothing."

"Alisha…?"

She sighs and keeps her eyes on me and it is hard to look back at her because I see the pain inside of them, but it is not the only thing I see.

"Do you have any idea, how much I wish, that you would kiss me?" she says softly.

"Do you have any idea, how much I wish, that I didn't want to?"

CHAPTER TWENTY

A New Beginning

There are no thoughts, I act with need, the need to feel nothing but my hand on her face, pulling her in. My lips meet hers urgently and they remember hers perfectly. I kiss her fiercely and she gasps in excitement; the sound sends turbulent pleasure up into my chest, quelling the lonely ache that lives there. Her body quivers as my hands wander roughly and her wild, ardent reaction compels me, feeding me with animalistic lust. I walk her backwards, her back hits the kitchen counter behind her and I lift her petite frame onto it with ease. Her legs wrap around my hips, pulling me closer. My lips travel down her neck boisterously, I rip open her shirt and my lips travel down her chest.

"Mac… Take me to bed," she groans.

The bedroom door flies open as she slams me through it, her lips never leaving mine. She pushes me onto the bed and I watch her as she reveals herself to me, fearlessly. Her clothes falling away, her eyes seductive, her smile daring. She straddles and I kiss her as she hovers above me, my hand impatiently slipping between her thighs.

"Oh… God…"

She moans at my first touch, my fingers dipping inside her heat and she thrusts her hips in perfect rhythm with my hand. Her moans quickly begin to escalate, I lift her up and lay her down, pinning her arms above her head with one hand while the other responds to her excitement. I feel the walls of her tense around my fingers as she begins to climax, her mouth falls open in a silent scream. I watch her eyes widen only for her eyes to be replaced by his perverse eyes, flashing sadistically across my vision. As her body trembles with pleasure, mine does so with pain and I bury my face into her neck, the sound of her pleasure groaning loudly in my ear, drowning out my whimpering fear.

"God, I have missed you so much," she whispers.

She pulls my face back into her eyeline, holding my cheeks lightly in her hands. I smile at her weakly, as the pain in my chest smoulders.

"You are not going to let me touch you, are you?" she asks.

My eyes close, ashamed as a single tear slips between my eyelids without my permission and I feel the anger at myself flicker. I have tried so hard not to let the hurt spill out. I wipe it away roughly with my wrist, the anger overriding the tears.

"Baby… I understand," Alisha comforts softly and I frown; there is no way she can possibly understand. I wince as the crescent-shaped scar flashes in my mind and I tense, the tremble in my limbs redoubling their assault.

"It's okay…"

She kisses me lightly and pushes me, rolling me onto my back. She lays her head on my chest, wrapping herself around me. I will myself to calm down, the lonely pain returning to my chest with icy vigour, his depraved eyes still violating my mind. I lay, my body tense and my teeth clenched for what feels like too long before calm begins to return.

"You never did tell me what you wanted to say," I say, remembering that is why she asked me to come.

"There was a lot I wanted to say, but now isn't the time for most of it. I can tell you one thing though," she says and she pulls back and props herself on her elbow; her hazel brown eyes are bright and thoughtful. "I didn't think you would come for me that day and I didn't want you to. I didn't realise at the time, what a sexy badass you had become," she says playfully and I chuckle. "I was scared he would kill you and I thought I was already dead, it seemed inevitable. It sounded like a war was going on outside. The explosions, the gunfire and the screams – I was sure there was no way anyone could survive that but, the explosions kept getting closer and closer." She grips the collar of my shirt in her fist, her eyes somewhere distant, seeing something I can't see.

"Then when I saw you… God, so much power in you, I never knew that rage could look so… beautiful. You looked fearless, I couldn't believe it, I still can't. You came for me, you saved me and there is no way for me to thank you for that. I just hope you can understand, how much I wish there was, how much it means to me." I hear her voice break just a little and I hold her a little tighter.

"Believe me, I wasn't fearless. I was terrified I wouldn't be able to save you and if it wasn't for Alfred, I wouldn't have gotten as far as I did. By the time I got to you, I was spent, I was sure I would keel over long before I got you out of there. Why did you think I wouldn't come?"

"Because, I thought you hated me. The last time I saw you, I saw in your eyes how much I had hurt you. Like I said before, your eyes always betray you and you looked at me like…"

"I don't hate you; I never did. I tried to – I can't deny that. I just – there is so much conflict. There is the part of me that remembers how I felt about you at the hotel, the part that hoped I would see you again while I was stuck on that boat, that part is still here. Then there is the part that didn't remember you, that grew to trust you with my pain over many hours of therapy, the part that got broken when I found out you were working for them, that is still here too.

"Then the part of me that is here now, unsure how to bring all the pieces of myself back together again, wrestling with the separated parts of myself. This part of me wonders if I will ever really be a whole person again because only then, will the conflict stop. That conflict isn't just with you, it is with everything and everyone, all at once. Like I think and feel three different perspectives."

I feel her body shake and I know my honesty has hurt her. I see the tears drip down her flush cheeks and I hold her tight. I can't take the words back because lying to her would be much crueller but that doesn't make it any easier.

"I am so sorry I hurt you," she chokes.

"Alisha… We are long past the stage where you need to be sorry. I forgave that a long time ago. Thinking you were going to die, kind of changed my perspective a lot and I haven't forgotten that you saved me, too. Remember?" I reassure.

"Maybe, but I am not blind, Mac. I know where your conflict truly lies."

"What are you talking about?" I ask. I look down at her, frowning.

"I saw it, in the hospital, through her eyes as we both waited for you to wake up. She was frozen like a statue, holding your hand and her eyes never left you. She would kiss your hand when she thought I wasn't watching, stroke your cheek. That was real fear that I recognised because, I felt it too."

"She said something very similar about you," I admit. My insides seize up; I really feel like a prized arsehole.

"Therein lies the conflict," she whispers, her voice tiny. Her quiet words hit me like a right hook from the fist of Mike Tyson.

"Why on earth did you say you wanted me to kiss you, knowing that?"

"I have my reasons… Stick around this time, you might be lucky enough to find out," she says playfully but her eyes are serious.

"Don't worry, girl. I think the chances of me getting kidnapped again are pretty low. Although, saying that – with my luck…" I joke and she laughs her musical laugh, her face lighting up.

"Thank you, for letting me freak out, for being there for me," I say gratefully.

"I always will be, if you will just let me be. I think that might have been the first time you ever really have. You have always been so stubborn!"

"My therapist once said, I have a problem showing weakness," I say, winking.

"She sounds very smart."

"Oh, she is… Extremely bossy though," I joked.

"Jerk, don't pretend bossiness doesn't turn you on." She smirks flirtatiously.

"Ah… Damn, yeah… Guilty."

Alisha insists on driving me home but I decline; it feels like forever since I really walked anywhere. I say goodbye to her on the doorstep and I walk away, relieved to have some closure with her but also feeling horrible for hurting her. I was honest with her, about my feelings for Anna, about everything in my own way and I was sure that would mean she would want to back off but – it doesn't look like she plans on going anywhere.

It was good to see her; after everything that has happened, that jokey, flirty, ease between us is somehow still there, so is the lust. The truth is though, those things are still true with Anna too. I kind of wish they weren't because, she made her feelings clear and, in all honesty, she broke my damn heart, how I feel for her is crystal clear. If we didn't get on so well, it wouldn't hurt as much to be around her. It would be easier to keep my distance but it is so easy to slip into old ways with her.

Conflict.

I guess none of it really matters, the longer I spend out of prison the more I feel this fear creeping over me. Fear that I don't deserve to be out because I'm a monster. Fear that they will chuck me back inside and throw away the key. Those fears are getting louder and louder in my head and there is nothing I can do but try to keep my head above the water. All I really want to do is talk to Anna about it and that annoys the crap out of me. She has this way of making me see through it all but I know that I have to keep her at a distance. She can't be the light for me anymore, when she is that close it hurts all the more. I am doing all I can to let her go, just like she asked.

***

The sandman has abandoned me, barely any sleep has been had as my mind is invaded once again by the images of horror from the battle of Eastfield's Street. By the time the morning arrives, I feel hungover from lack of sleep, my eyes are inside out and I am weary. I am hugging my umpteenth cup of coffee when the doorbell goes. I open the door and smile, inviting Anna in, I am relieved for the distraction and I would be lying if I said seeing her doesn't improve my mood almost immediately.

"You ready to go?" she beams chirpily.

"Definitely."

We jump in her car and set off. I am happy to be moving and looking forward to breakfast and car shopping. I do feel a little stranded without a car, I don't like the feeling. Maybe it is a learned behaviour from being in hiding but without a car, I feel vulnerable. Plus, I hate that need to scrounge rides from Alfred and Anna.

We pull up to that 60s diner that the three of us went to last time I went car shopping. Its retro décor still as brash on the eyes as can be, but I kind of like it. All we need is waitresses on roller skates and it would be like a scene straight out of the Grease movie. We take a seat in one of the booths; the shiny red plasticky seating areas are squashy and plump. Unlike last time when we sat in the corner trying to hide my existence, this time we sit in the middle of the diner by the window.

My eyes curiously scan the room, people watching. People in deep conversation, kids laughing with ice cream over their faces, a man frowning at the newspaper while sipping his coffee, a group of women chatting excitedly – their laughs boom and I feel myself smile.

"What are you smiling at?" Anna asks, smirking, and I snap out of my trance.

"Just watching people. You know… Just doing their thing. Got a bit lost in it… Sorry."

"Don't be, it is very… endearing. I forget how weird this must be for you. Being out, around people. When was the last time you were able to do this, freely?"

I try to think about that but I can't pinpoint the last time, where it was or who it was with, unless you count the hotel with Alisha and I don't really want to bring that up.

"I don't know, before I was taken so… three years ago nearly."

The waitress comes over, she has a jolly face. Her cheeks are rosy and her hair big and bouncy. She has one of those accents where her tone peaks in pitch at the end of every sentence. Her name tag reads Bella; she has scrawled a smiley face just after her name.

"What can I get you both, lovelies?" she asks and Anna nods at me to go first.

"Um… Can I get some pancakes, with syrup and ice cream? Oo, do you have waffles? Can I have a waffle too? And a Dr Pepper?"

"Waffles *and* pancakes… together? Uh… sure, would you like some strawberries and chocolate sauce to go with it?"

"Does a bear poop in the woods, Bella?" I ask, winking.

"Um, yes… Okay – strawberries and chocolate it is." Bella frowns, flustered as she looks down at her notepad, scribbling down my order. "No problem, and for you, miss?"

"I will have waffles, just with ice cream and syrup and a coffee please."

The lady leaves and Anna giggles.

"What?"

"I think you broke the waitress – her face!" She laughs.

"What? I am hungry." I scowl but I can't help but laugh too.

The food arrives and my jaw drops at the mass of sugary treats piled on the plate. I feel giddy before the sugar even enters my system.

"Okay, I might have been a little overambitious," I admit with a snort.

"Yeah, I would say so. How did things go with your mum?"

Just then there is a loud clatter, the sound is so familiar and jarring it sends terror pulsing through me. I jump out of my skin and launch myself backwards, sliding to the edge of the of the curved seat and pressing my back against the window. My eyes search rapidly for the threat, my chest heaving and my eyes wide; images of inmates stood on tables kicking trays to the floor flood my mind, the loud clatters piercing my ears, the thick dank air of the prison filling my nose as my breathing escalates.

"Mac… Hey…" Anna coos, reaching out for my hand and I flinch, pulling away, my vision flickering from the rec room to the diner, the disorientation is intense as I jump between the then and the now. I feel Anna's hand take mine, she is closer now.

"Mac, it's okay, it is just me, look at me," she says more firmly this time, her hand pulling my face into her eyeline.

My vision begins to clear and over Anna's shoulder I see a waitress picking up the tray of food that she dropped, understanding hits and I start to calm down. I look back at Anna and her hand is on my face, her eyes concerned and looking at me with pity. I pull away abruptly and I see hurt wash over her face.

This keeping a distance thing is going really well.

"I'm fine, sorry," I grunt.

"You are not fine, what happened?"

"Anna, it's nothing, just a bit jumpy that's all. Um… What were you asking before?"

Anna's jaw clenches, she takes a deep breath and returns to her seat. I can tell she is hurt; she is trying to be there for me, I know that, but after everything that has happened, I am not sure how to let her be. Once she sits down, I manage a rigid smile.

"Sorry, I am just not…" I begin.

"It's okay, I get it, Mac. I don't expect you to… I can wait. Umm… I asked you how things went with your mum."

Wait? Wait for what? Ugh. Why doesn't she understand that I need her to back off? That needing her and not being able to have her was the very worst thing about prison.

Because you haven't told her – douchebag.

I rub my temples, the adrenalin beginning to fizzle out and I work hard to right my expression. I pull myself back to the middle of the seat and take a deep breath before I look up to her, my expression calm and nonchalant.

"Umm… About as well as you would expect. I am glad it is over, let's put it that way. It was good to see her but I had to be really vague, I can't really tell her about how I got out. Only that I was taken out to bring down Barrett and she is just thrilled about that," I groan.

"I can't say I blame her there," Anna says, stealing a strawberry off my plate playfully. "What else did you get up to yesterday?"

Urgh, crap. She has asked me outright, I can't not tell her now, I can't lie to her.

"Well… Alisha tracked me down at Mum's. So, I caught up with her and then I went home." I try to say it casually, watching her reaction carefully but she doesn't give anything anyway. I guess she isn't bothered, I shouldn't be surprised by that but now I kind of wish she was. How messed up is that?

"How was that?"

"Um… It was good to put away some of the baggage. A lot has happened so it was nice to move forward from that. It feels like I spent all day yesterday apologising to people, trying to mend all of the things I broke."

I get off track, I don't want to talk about Alisha, in fact this conversation is starting to make me not want to talk at all. I rub my temples again, massaging the pound that is starting to hurt. This is not the easy-going breakfast I had hoped for.

"I don't see what you need to apologise for, Mac. Not everything that goes wrong in the world is your fault. No wonder you look tired, carrying all that unnecessary blame must weigh a bit." Her voice is playful, I am surprised.

"Funny." I smirk, relieved at the lack of drama.

We leave the diner and I have definitely eaten too much; we talk and laugh easily and it is a relief. Anna helps me pick another car and I can't help but feel a little awkward when the sales person turns out to be none other than Sadie, the flirtatious saleswoman that sold me the last truck. She is all up in my personal space and I respectfully remain polite, with Anna's eyes burning into the back of my head. Truthfully, I take a little pleasure in it, just a little. I make plans with Anna to meet her at the farm and start to enjoy driving the new truck; it does feel good, I hope that I can keep hold of this one a little longer. The drive is smooth and I am feeling good when something makes me pull over suddenly. The truck lunges to a stop and I get out and see Anna's car fly past me.

I know immediately, I probably shouldn't have stopped, but it didn't feel like a conscious choice, it felt like I had to. My feet move uncertainly, my legs wobble like jelly, the soles of my shoes dragging across the pavement lazily. I duck under the yellow police caution tape and the destruction of Eastfield's Street opens up in front of me. The road and pathways are covered in rubble. The entire front of the brewery is destroyed, completely caved in and a mess of brick and metal. My chest tightens at the sight of the warzone I created.

I tear my eyes away and keep moving; what I am moving towards I don't know. I see the bakery, the window I took a dive through is still smashed, I walk a little closer and see bullet holes punched into the wooden window frames. The ground is covered in dust, rubble and glass that crunches under my feet. I walk back to the middle of the road and just stand there, taking in the destruction like an onlooker visiting an exhibit of hell.

I see the bike shop, it is blackened and scorched from the grenade I launched over there. That's where the melting-faced man nearly pierced my throat with the tip of his knife, he very nearly got me. I can still see the hate in his eyes, I can still remember the stench of burnt flesh. The rage that overtook me when I took his life, is that the moment when the monster inside me woke up?

"Mac…?"

I guess I should have known she would follow me here. When I don't answer she walks over to me and stands next to me, her eyes forward, surveying the wreckage just like mine.

"What is going on in that head of yours?"

"I am just… in it. I just want to stay in it for a while longer," I murmur, dazed.

"Can I stay in it with you?" she asks and I nod.

I feel her take my hand and this time I don't pull away. Somehow, being here has finally started to make it all feel more real. This is happening, I am out of prison and the reason it doesn't feel real is because I am scared that I will end up back there again. That fear makes it very hard to accept that I am really free, because I am not, not unless I end The Culling.

"Anna… I am scared."

"I know, I can always feel it when something is taking you over. Tell me, please?"

"I can't ever go back there. I am not going to stay free unless I end The Culling and if I fail, they are going to lock me back up and I know, I won't survive it again. I thought I would, I have survived worse but…"

Anna squeezes my hand. "But what?"

"It got in my head, so quickly. I don't know why. The police took me away and I really thought, I could get through it but – I couldn't have been more wrong … I can't do it again and I can't stop being scared I will fail and end up right back there," I whisper.

"You are not going to fail," she reassures.

"You don't know that."

"Actually, I do. You are an unstoppable force, Mac Scott, and you are always at your strongest when you are threatened. You have this fierce force inside you, it only comes out when things are really bad. You call it the darkness but I have always seen it as a light, a strength. You used it to survive the boat, Billy, Jackson, the mala suka man, Jakub, to save Alisha, me… And I know that no matter how hard this fight gets, it will help you destroy The Culling too," she declares warmly, her thumb rubbing the back of my hand lightly, soothing.

"You are not alone in this, you have us — just like you always have and you are working with MI5 too — which, I hate by the way. First you go all sexy commando on me and now you go full on spy girl. Are you trying to kill me?" she teases with a scowl and I laugh. "They broke you out of prison because they believe you can do this; we believe you can do this. There's a reason people believe in you, Mac," she concludes and I finally stop looking at the destruction and look at her instead.

"I don't know how you do it. Even when I try very hard to stop you, you somehow break through. You always make me feel like I can get back up, no matter how hard I fall. I wouldn't have been able to do any of that, without you. Even after everything that has happened, you are still there, being all fucking magic," I groan, playfully frustrated but she doesn't laugh.

"You do the same for me, you know. You think you are this bad and dark drain on me but you make me feel alive and brave and free and you managed to make me feel like that, during a time that you were going through hellish battles, against people who wanted you dead. I can only imagine what you would be capable of if you weren't in danger all the time."

She looks at me in that paralysing way, like she is searching my face for something and it hurts. I bite my tongue; it isn't really fair for her to look at me that way but I don't want to bring it up, it never leads anywhere good. I close my eyes and turn away from her, letting go of her hand.

"We should go," I say, walking away, probably a little too harshly.

We arrive at the farm and I walk towards Alfred down by the fire while Anna disappears off into the house, probably a reaction to my bluntness but I am relieved to have a little space. I appreciate her, the way she is always there for me but she doesn't always make it very easy. Approaching the fire pit, I feel a little touched to see that my camping chair is still there waiting for me, familiar and welcoming and also covered with ashes from the fire. I sit, letting myself get lost in the flames as I so easily do. It is still my happy place, regardless of the memories that are attached.

"So, how are you enjoying your freedom?" Alfred asks.

"Um, it's still a little weird to be honest."

"You are bored out of your mind, aren't you?" he says, chuckling, and I laugh back.

"Yeah, you could say that. I don't know why, but I don't know what to do with myself now no one is trying to kill me. I was up most of the night wandering the apartment. Talk about itchy feet," I grumble.

"Some people are more comfortable in chaos – I should know, I am one of them. Well, I would try to enjoy it while you can. Looks like Lexi is coming to gate-crash the party. She is coming to the farm tomorrow night to debrief you."

My stomach clenches and I gulp. Suddenly I want to go back to being bored. I am nervous about seeing her again, not because she is intimidating to me, but because I feel like I need to persuade her I am ready for this.

"Party?"

"Well, it is Savannah's birthday tomorrow, as you know. Nothing big, just some drinks around the fire, just the three of us but Lexi will be dropping in," Alfred informs.

"I knew it was coming up, I got her something ages ago but it was at the warehouse and it doesn't really seem like an appropriate gift now anyway. I will have to find something else tomorrow."

I cringe. What the hell am I going to get her now? I bought her a gift, during the very short time we were together. It wasn't going to be a birthday present, I just wanted to give her something because she is always so thoughtful, I wanted to show her that she was never far from my thoughts. We ended before I could give it to her, so it stayed in my bedside drawer at the warehouse. I haven't been back there; from what Alfred told me the police ransacked the place and I am in no hurry to return to all those memories.

"You could just give her this," Alfred says.

I look in his direction and there in his hand is the small wooden box that was in my bedside drawer. I take it out of his hands and look at him with a raised eyebrow.

"I snatched it when I went back to get your clothes. It didn't take me long to figure out who it was intended for," Alfred says with a knowing smile.

"I can't give her this, fella."

"Why? Afraid she might actually think you give a crap? I can see why that would be terrible," he jibes sarcastically.

"We are in a very different place to when I had this made, I am not afraid of her thinking I give a crap; she has moved on and I have to respect that," I say, hiding the box inside my jacket, the dull ache in my heart beginning to brighten.

"Oh, don't give me that bull, Mac. We both know she hasn't; this isn't about you respecting her feelings – it is about protecting yours. She busted your heart, I get it – I was there but you busted hers first, if you remember. She deserves to know that you thought about her, you should at least give her that. Let her know what she had was real because believe me, she doesn't think it was," Alfred argues and I scowl at him, whining dramatically.

"Alright, I am butting out. At least think about it, kid."

"I will think about it. You meddle like an old woman, you know that, right? Meddler!" I rant at him jokily.

"But I am so good at it." He grins, winking. "Oh, can you pick up a cake for her?"

I like that he can ask me now because, I couldn't even do simple things like that before, through fear of being seen. I plan on some serious retail therapy tomorrow anyway. If I am seeing Lexi, I want to look fresh – I want her to see that I am ready.

"Sure, anything in particular?" I ask.

"You know what she likes."

I return home to the apartment, the wooden box weighing heavily inside my jacket. I take it out and place it on the kitchen counter and I stare at it, the memories swirling. I remember sitting at my laptop as she slept, the night she stayed with me at the warehouse. The night she broke through every barrier that separated us. I watched her sleep, beautiful and peaceful. The flush from hours of enjoying each other, still pink in her cheeks.

I found myself wanting to do something for her, she is the kind of girl you want to do things for. I had something made for her, agonising over every detail, wanting it to be perfect. When it was finally done, I felt giddy with excitement, I couldn't wait to give it to her. I didn't realise that, hours later we would fall apart. It arrived a few days later and it tore me open to see it. I haven't opened that box since and I can't even face opening it now.

Alfred has a good point. I broke her heart first and maybe she does deserve to have it, to see that it was real for me. I just don't want to overcomplicate things that are already complicated enough. I would be lying if I said I didn't want to; the part of me that aches for her, wants to give it to her, to see her face light up the way I know it would. Then there is the part that is still heartbroken over the way she pushed me away, that part doesn't want to show how much I was into her. I wonder which will win.

I spend the rest of the evening working out, just like I used to in my prison cell. I fill the apartment with the glorious sound of classic rock music and it quietens my mind. Now is not the time to get unfit so I push myself hard, working myself into exhaustion. Determined to work away the nerves eating away at my stomach. Lexi coming tomorrow only brings it home that things are about to start moving and although I am scared to fail, I am also anxious to get started, it is time to stop talking and start doing.

Lack of sleep, a killer workout and a hot shower ensure I sleep like the dead, a long overdue, dreamless sleep. When my eyes open, I feel much better, much stronger. Both in body and in mind. The past two days have not been restful, they have been full of the tension and drama of returning and building bridges but that is all done now. Today, will be a good day. I jump out of bed with pep in my step, get myself ready and set out for a day of shopping and much needed 'me time'. My mood is buzzed as I pull off in the new truck and make my way into the city centre. It is a warm day; I soak up the sun and breathe in the fresh air as I walk the streets, my eyes curious and my wallet ready.

I buy a ridiculous amount of new clothes, aftershaves and some new accessories, ties and jewellery mostly… Everything I used to buy to make myself feel good. I stop by a hairdressing salon and decide, it is time for a new look. My hair is lank and unhealthy looking, I can't actually remember the last time I had anything done to it. My time in hiding and then in prison, weight loss and stress has meant that it looks tired and boring. I opt to have my hair coloured darker with flashes of red; the style is choppy and messy, just about long enough to put up in a ponytail if needed, but it now looks good down too, edgy. The hairdresser smiles at me through the reflection of the mirror as she sees my face light up with happiness at the sight of myself.

"That is hot. Would you like your eyebrows done too?"

This has me wondering what is wrong with my eyebrows. I figure, why the hell not and I let her go ahead but that feeling quickly dissipates as she applies warm wax to them. The end result is just about worth the sting.

I stop by the Whiskey Exchange in Covent Carden and my eyes pop in wonder at all of the beautifully bottled whiskeys, all lined up and sparkling under lighting. Shelf upon shelf of them uniformly stacked like a whiskey library. I pick up a bottle of Angel's Nectar for Alfred, apparently it is smoky with a rich tone of toffee apples and dark chocolate, sounds right up his street. I drag myself away from the store before the temptation becomes too much to buy more.

I find myself in a florist and decide impulsively to send my mum some flowers. The shop makes my nose itch with sneezes, but I am happy with the thought that tomorrow I will give her something to smile about. Once I have overspent on myself adequately, I wander the stores in search of an alternative gift for Anna's birthday. I look at perfumes and chocolates and jumpers and jewellery and everything feels wrong and impersonal. I groan as time ticks on, and I am still coming up blank. I start to notice people staring at me, I shouldn't be surprised after my face was plastered over the front page of the newspaper yesterday. I make a beeline for the cake shop and decide enough is enough for one day.

The chocolate fudge cake perched on my passenger seat, looks decadent and tempting. I am excited to get home and be spoilt for choice of what to wear tonight.

I have another killer workout, my muscles still aching from last night but I am determined to keep myself strong. I shower, using all new products and splash myself with new aftershave. The smell is strong and masculine and I love it. I am feeling more myself every moment and I am glad I had this time to myself today, I needed it. I even had time to send a little package off to Bronzeford Prison; it is addressed to one Ms Davis, inside is a huge box of Mars bars. The note simply reads, 'Thank you, Shannon - 6642'.

I let the music pound too loudly and I dance around trying clothes on; in the end I opt for a black shirt and dark red skinny tie that matches the red flashes that now highlight my hair randomly. After, I hide my tiredness with some make-up and mess my hair up a little with some wax. I feel much better about the thought of facing Lexi. The smell of leather fills me with happiness as I put on my new jacket; I have wanted a new one ever since my old one got ruined with a bullet wound to the shoulder. With one last look in the mirror, one last spray of aftershave, I bounce towards the front door and then stop in my tracks as Anna's present still sat on the kitchen counter catches my eye.

***

"Mac, you didn't!!" Alfred beams, his face lighting up in awe at the sight of the bottle of whiskey I bought him.

"I did, you know," I say, smiling. His excitement makes my insides glow.

"Thanks, kid. I am touched."

"Well, you're welcome, now crack that bad boy open, we have some drinking to do. I am just going to take the cake in and then I will be right back. Where is Anna?"

"Could you bring some glasses out? She is still getting ready; you know what girls are like," Alfred informs.

"Dude, I'm a girl," I say, raising an eyebrow.

"Well… Yeah… But you're like… a boyish girl… No, that's not what I…" I watch him panic and I laugh.

"I'm just playing with you, bro," I say, winking.

"Ugh, you little git. Go get us some glasses!"

Walking off, I am still laughing because that was too easy. I make my way to the kitchen and search for somewhere to hide the cake. I hear movement upstairs and quickly ram it into the fridge with just seconds to spare before Anna comes down the stairs. I am reaching for glasses from the cupboard when I hear her behind me.

"Hey, birthday girl," I call, as I finally manage to grab the last glass.

"Hey, would you do me up?"

I turn round to see Anna, looking painfully gorgeous. She is holding her dress to her, it is understated, floral but figure hugging. Her hair freshly curled, her eyelids sparkling with gold bringing out the intense green of her eyes. She has the 'country girl next door' look down.

"Sure… Why not?" I say, trying to sound casual.

I walk over to her and she turns round, the back of the dress open, revealing the dip of her back all the way down to her tail bone and I bite my lip.

Seriously?

I zip the dress up and she turns to me, smiling.

"Happy birthday, you look gorgeous – obviously," I say smoothly.

"I was about to say the same to you, that hair is working for you," she says, twiddling the end of my hair between her fingers. She doesn't look up at me, if anything her eyes are a little sad.

We all sit around the fire and it is the most natural things have felt in a long time. Although that might be the whiskey, which is unbelievably strong but complex in flavour and very moreish. There is a lot of laughing and chatter but I can't really escape the fact that Anna looks troubled. Alfred leans over to me and asks me to get the cake discreetly and we have a good billowy verse of Happy Birthday. Alfred cuts the cake and he is very jolly from the whiskey.

"Who wants pudding!?" he yells and my eyes immediately shoot to Anna and we both howl with laughter.

"Yeah, Anna – you like pudding, right?!"

"Shut up… I will kill you, Mac-Attack." She cackles.

The night starts to darken a little, that in between place that falls between dark and light, when the sky is dark purple and blue but it is still light. The stars are just about starting to peek out behind the canopy and it gives the sky a glittered, shimmery effect. The sound of the fire, of Alfred's loud and rather tipsy chuntering, Anna's radiant and infectious laugh have me sitting back in my chair feeling content and taking them both in. Anna goes inside to get some more drinks and I watch her walk away, feeling conflicted.

"So, what did you decide, kid? You going to give it to her or what?" Alfred probes from across the fire. I smile at him sheepishly and pull out the wooden box from inside my jacket.

"Yes!! …Gwarn, kid, what are you waiting for? I will just prop up the fire and drink up me whiskey. Don't mind me," he chunters jollily.

"You are still a meddler, but I love you, old man."

I pat him on the shoulder and then I set off towards the house, the box in my hands and my heart in my throat. When I get in the kitchen Anna has her face in her mobile phone and hasn't noticed I am there.

"So, did you get everything you wanted for your birthday?" I ask.

Her head pops up and she smiles at me, putting her phone down. Her eyes fall to the box in my hand and my nerves double, my mouth suddenly dry.

"I think that would be asking too much," she says shyly, walking over to me.

"Ah, I don't know, girl. You don't ask, you don't get."

She looks at me curiously and I am struggling, wishing I hadn't made this choice. I can feel her waiting and watching me as I fidget. My mind buzzes furiously as I try to figure out what to say and I see a playful smile tugging at the corners of her full, pink lips.

"What is this? Is Mac Scott… Nervous?"

"Ahem – um… Yes, I am actually. You see, this isn't a birthday present," I manage, looking at the box with a furrowed brow.

"Oh, you got me an empty box?"

"No, I bought this… before, when we were… together… And by the time it was made, well… we weren't… anymore. It stayed in my bedside drawer at the warehouse ever since. I assumed it would be lost after the police raided it."

I chance a look at her and she is watching me unblinking, so I try to keep eye contact with her and I take some tentative steps forward on jelly-like legs.

"When Alfred went to get my clothes, he found it and yesterday he gave it back to me and insisted that I gave it to you. I wasn't going to, I didn't think it was appropriate but no matter what has happened, it is yours, I want you to have it – appropriate or not. I guess I don't feel it is right to keep it from you but that doesn't mean, that you have to keep it."

I gulp and I open the box and my eyes fall upon the bangle; it is much more feminine and delicate than the one she got me and it is gold instead of silver, because I think it suits her. I hear her gasp and I take the bangle out, showing her the inscription inside the bangle.

My sweet home Savannah,

Girl, I'll be coming home to you.

The play on words to our song, which I can no longer listen to, followed by a small symbol. I look at her nervously, tears welling up in her eyes.

"What is… that symbol?" she whispers in a crackly voice.

"It is a moon glyph; it signifies light."

She looks up at me, smiling through tears and I flood with relief, my chest tingling at the sight of her happiness, happiness that for once, I have inspired.

"Mac… It's so perfect. I can't believe you did this. I…"

The way she is looking at me, hurts but, I take it anyway because I always wanted to see that look on her face when she saw it. This is not how I imagined it, but I will take it. She holds her wrist out and gives me the bangle and my insides soar.

"You want to wear it?" I ask, shocked. "You don't have to…"

"Mac… Of course, I want to wear it, it is beautiful."

I am certain my face lights up like Christmas, because she laughs at me. I put it on her wrist, and I feel my chest burn with a painful pleasure when I see it there.

"Gutted, I am going to have to tell him he was right. He is going to love that," I joke.

"Thank you, you made this day – almost perfect. I love it and I am glad Pa pushed you. To know you did this, means everything to me," she says, her eyes troubled again. She wraps her arms round me and I hold her, feeling glad I didn't wimp out.

"What would make it perfect?"

"It doesn't matter, I am lucky to get almost perfect," she mumbles into my chest.

"I am just curious," I probe, wondering if I can use it for Christmas, trying to find something for her to replace that today felt impossible. Anna pulls back from me a little but her hands stay on my hips, her eyes intent on mine, it is becoming too painful being this close.

"If you had given me this when you intended to, what do you think I would have done?" she asks, her voice soft.

I frown at her, confused. She would have kissed me for sure, that bracelet is serious girlfriend points.

"Because that, is what would have made the day… perfect," she says, her eyes burning with intensity and she isn't looking away. It is like gravity, the pull she has on my heart. I feel the tug and I act upon it; consequences be damned.

My hand slides up the side of her neck and her breath shakes, my heart pounds so hard I fear she will hear it. I move in so slow, the pain in my chest in competition with the desire but I already know which is going to win, because I need her, I have always needed her. My heart needs her, my mind, my body and when my lips finally meet hers, everything I feel bursts through my kiss. The sensation is, indescribably powerful. I kiss her deeply in a way that I know I never have before, with my heart bared, with honesty, and with love.

I hold her tight as she melts into me; I have missed her touch so much. Her hands are on my face, then in my hair, pulling me close like she can't stand to let me go and then suddenly, everything becomes incontrovertibly clear. Tears fill my eyes and I let them fall proudly. My moans become her moans; they are desperate, like pleasurable cries of the relentless need we have for each other. She kisses me so deeply that everything else disappears… That is, until she pulls back from me. Her eyes pained but full of exhilaration, her hands still on my face, she wipes my tears away with her thumbs and I know, there is no way for me to hide how I feel anymore.

"Anna… I…"

"Mac… Oh God… I am so, so, sorry. I need to tell…" she chokes.

"Anna… Oh, sorry…" Alfred says as he realises, he has interrupted and Anna steps away from me. "There is someone here to see you, she said her name is Danni."

"Okay Pa, I will be there in a minute," she says and he leaves the room very fast. I look at her and the pain on her face blatant, it doesn't take me long to figure out the troubled look in her eyes was her trying to tell me, about whoever Danni is.

"Mac… I am so sorry; I was trying to tell you but then you gave—"

"Please, don't. It is fine, really. You told me you wanted to move on and now you have. I am… happy for you. I just wish you hadn't…" I falter, the lump in my throat is choking me, making my voice strained, I can't seem to look up from the floor.

"Mac…" Anna cried.

"Anna, can you go? Please," I choke.

"No, please let me explain…"

"There is nothing left to say!" I snap. Anger forces me to look at her, tears pouring rapidly down my face and she breaks down.

"Anna… I have never asked you for anything, I am asking you now. Go out there and be happy. I will be fine, don't worry, okay. Just go, please," I say calmly.

Anna wipes her face and steadies herself; she looks at me with pained eyes, glittering with tears and then she walks away. The moment the door closes I break – the agony I feel is torturous. All I want to do is run, far away but I can't because I still have to wait for Lexi. I feel my heart break and I promise myself; I will never allow her to break it again. The door opens, I look up at Alfred and smile through the tears.

"I am so sorry, kid, I didn't know. I wouldn't have pushed you to give her it if I did." His eyes are so sad, I can barely look at him. I wipe my eyes on the sleeve of my shirt and sigh a long shaky breath. Well at least I know now, I just wish she had found a better way to tell me.

"It's not your fault. I shouldn't have let myself… Urgh fuck…" I trail off. "Do you know when Lexi is due?"

"Any time now."

"Okay, I need some air, will you send her to the back fence? I will meet her there and I will ask her if she wouldn't mind dropping me off. I will fill you in tomorrow with whatever she says, if that is okay?"

"Of course, kid," he mumbles, eyeing me with sympathy and I turn on my heels and walk out the door but I only get about three paces before I hear him.

"Hey, kid."

I stop in my tracks and I wish I hadn't because I can see Anna watching me out of the corner of my eye and I just want to get away. He walks towards me and pulls me in for a big bear hug.

"I love you too, you know, you are like the son I never had. I hope you understand me meaning. I am here for you, I've got your back, whatever happens. We will end this together – I promise. Do you understand? You and me," Alfred says, his voice gruff but powerful and I give him a squeeze.

"I get you. Thank you, for saying that. Means everything to me," I croak.

I let him go and stride away. I make sure I don't walk too fast. I can almost feel Anna's eyes on me although I am probably imagining it, I think it's clear where her attention now lies. I let the chill of the night's air sting my face and I breathe it in, trying to shut down the pain. Trying to smother the sobs that are trying so hard to escape me. I feel the familiar icy fingers, like tendrils of darkness, dragging me down and it is a relief. The overgrown grass makes a swooshing sound with every step I take; it is wet and the legs of my trousers begin to stick to me. When I reach the fence, I lean my crossed forearms against it, keeping my back to the farm. I look out into the peaceful night and I allow the darkness to take me over – once again. Something tells me, it is here to stay this time.

The low purr of an engine rumbles in my ear and I see a car approach the farm from behind me. The headlights are making the darkness of my view glow eerily as the bright beams cast creepy shadows on the farm. The tires crunch on the gravel and I wait calmly, I hear the engine cut and a car door open and close. I feel the familiar cold calm fill my veins with ice and I breathe in relief. Lexi approaches me, almost silently, stands by me and I turn to face her with a slight smile.

"Agent Holt," I greet her politely.

"Mac, you look… Wow, better. This," she looks me up and down, "is much better than prison-issue uniform," she says, smiling.

"I don't think that is very difficult, turquoise isn't many people's colour."

"True," she says, shuffling a paper folder from under her arm. "Right, down to business. Here I have a file of everything on Barrett that we have, you need to familiarise yourself with every detail. If you're going to infiltrate The Culling, then you cannot be shocked or disgusted by the things they have done or intend to do, you have to sell that you want to be one of them, that you are committed to their cause and that you would be an asset to them.

"The advert Barrett requested you put into the paper if you wished to make contact with him, will go to print tomorrow. That means, any time from then, he could approach you. We have come across some intel suggesting that he is currently in Bosnia, but it still wouldn't take him long to get to you.

"Let me be perfectly clear, once you make contact, you will be on your own. We can watch you and guide you, we will even train you and support you; but we can't protect you. I have given Mr Slone what you need to enable us to stay in contact. You must gain Barrett's trust because if he suspects you, he will kill you. Do not underestimate him, your blood ties will not save you; he only cares about his cause.

"Once you get on his side, you may have to do things to persuade him of your loyalty. Bad things, things that you won't want to do but you must obey. Gain his trust and find out what his primary target is and how he intends to execute his attack. Find his wet list; we need names, Mac. Even if we take the head of the snake, we can't have his loyalists within our governments holding positions of power. We must expose the whole hive, not just the queen bee.

"I have placed you in a work cover, should be nice and easy for you – you are returning to Pic Studios as a freelance photographer. The work is flexible, barely any hours, you just need to be seen working for them sometimes, you need to seem like you are returning from prison back to a normal life. See family and friends, go to work, be here training with Mr Slone. Appear normal but don't lose focus for a single second because he could be watching you, any time, any place.

"Your training with Alfred must continue but I will also be sending other instructors here to mentor and train you, you will meet them tomorrow. I know you are weapons proficient and extremely capable but we," she smiles deviously, "have some toys and tactical training that you will not be familiar with. I will keep in contact with you, I will always come to you and you should only contact me if absolutely necessary.

"If you are arrested you will not be released again, you will not mention MI5 or my name or your life will be ended, swiftly. If you die while in the line of duty, a proper funeral will be provided but no mention of your sacrifice will ever be said. It will appear as if you died in a tragic accident. If you succeed, no one will ever know, there is no glory, no fanfare – the only thing you will receive is your freedom, a clean slate, the pride and gratitude of MI5 and of course, the pride in yourself, knowing you protected your country from the greatest threat it has ever faced.

"So, tell me, Mac – how do you feel about that?" she asks and I hold her gaze intensely, determined and I speak firmly.

"I needed these three days, to put my affairs in order. I feel at peace with everything and that has made the path forward a lot clearer. There is nothing more important to me than this now. I won't rest till I bring Barrett down; I will earn my freedom; I will bring them all down or I will die in the attempt. I am committed and I will do *whatever* it takes, Lexi. *I am ready.*"

"Welcome aboard, Agent Scott," Lexi grins, her eyes beaming with pride. She holds her hand out to me and I grasp it firmly.

"Thank you, Agent Holt."

That is going to take some getting used to.

"For what it is worth, Mac. Please try not to die. I have high hopes that once this is over, you will finally get to live in peace, I would like to see that happen. Now, before I leave is there anything else you would like to ask me?"

"Actually, I do have a few requests that I hope you can help me with."

"Go ahead, Agent."

"In the event of my death, could you please make sure that my mum is safe and taken care of and that my assets will be split equally between my mother, Anna and Alfred Slone?"

"Consider it done. Anything else?"

"Yes... could you drop me off home?" I ask sheepishly and she cackles.

"Come on, you, let's go."

My name is Agent Mac Scott, no longer prisoner 6642. I was in prison, but now I am free and I intend to keep it that way. I was a photographer but have been many things, thanks to you. I thought I killed my enemies but now I realise, the real enemy has been out there watching me, all along. You are the danger that lurks in the shadows, you are the monster under the bed. It takes a monster, to catch a monster so, live or die... *I am coming for you.*

THE END

The story continues in
RETROSPECT
The Salvation of Mac Scott
Coming soon!

ABOUT THE AUTHOR

A.J. Hutchinson-Forton is a newly emerging author who seeks to shock and thrill readers with brutal and honest action, shamelessly scorching intimacy, and unforgettable goosebump-inspiring moments. As a member of the LGBTQ+ community, she aims to bring strong queer characters boldly into the limelight with realism and authenticity. Parallel to this mission, she hopes to break the stereotype that many people on the Autistic spectrum have no imagination.

So, if you're looking for action, suspense, and compelling characters you can't help but fall in love with, you came to the right place.

AJ is studying for her BA in English Literature and Creative Writing. However, her most notable qualification as a writer is the lifelong obsession with creating other worlds. She enjoys cake, a dash of whiskey, and consuming unhealthy volumes of cheese, as should all right-thinking people. She's a terrible cook, an enthusiast in all things good and geeky, and enjoys spending time with her wonderful wife and insanely fluffy Akita, Pepper, at home in the UK.

My website: https://www.inthewordsofhutchinsonforton.com/
My Author Facebook page: https://www.facebook.com/inthewordsofaj/
My Author Instagram
page: https://www.instagram.com/ajhutchinsonfortonauthor/
My Author Twitter page: AJ Hutchinson-Forton (@AjForton) / Twitter

Made in the USA
Columbia, SC
16 July 2022

62999173R10226